Breakfast in the ...
and Other Stories

The Michael Moorcock Collection

The Michael Moorcock Collection is the definitive library of acclaimed author Michael Moorcock's SF & fantasy, including the entirety of his Eternal Champion work. It is prepared and edited by John Davey, the author's long-time bibliographer and editor, and will be published, over the course of two years, in the following print omnibus editions by Gollancz, and as individual eBooks by the SF Gateway (see http://www.sfgateway.com/authors/m/moorcock-michael/ for a complete list of available eBooks).

A Cornelius Calendar
comprising –
*The Adventures of Una Persson
and Catherine Cornelius in
the Twentieth Century*
The Entropy Tango
The Great Rock 'n' Roll Swindle
The Alchemist's Question
*Firing the Cathedral/Modem
Times 2.0*

Von Bek
comprising –
*The War Hound and the World's
Pain*
The City in the Autumn Stars

The Eternal Champion
comprising –
The Eternal Champion
Phoenix in Obsidian
The Dragon in the Sword

The Dancers at the
End of Time
comprising –
An Alien Heat
The Hollow Lands
The End of all Songs

Kane of Old Mars
comprising –
Warriors of Mars
Blades of Mars
Barbarians of Mars

Moorcock's Multiverse
comprising –
The Sundered Worlds
The Winds of Limbo
The Shores of Death

The Nomad of Time
comprising –
The Warlord of the Air
The Land Leviathan
The Steel Tsar

Travelling to Utopia
comprising –
The Wrecks of Time
The Ice Schooner
The Black Corridor

The War Amongst the Angels
comprising –
Blood: A Southern Fantasy
Fabulous Harbours
The War Amongst the Angels

Tales from the End of Time
comprising –
Legends from the End of Time
Constant Fire
Elric at the End of Time

Behold the Man

Gloriana; or, The Unfulfill'd Queen

SHORT FICTION
My Experiences in the Third World
War and Other Stories: The Best
Short Fiction of Michael Moorcock
Volume 1

The Brothel in Rosenstrasse and
Other Stories: The Best Short Fiction
of Michael Moorcock Volume 2

Breakfast in the Ruins and Other
Stories: The Best Short Fiction of
Michael Moorcock Volume 3

Breakfast in the Ruins and Other Stories

The Best Short Fiction of Michael Moorcock

Volume 3

MICHAEL MOORCOCK

Edited by John Davey

This edition published in Great Britain in 2014 by
Gollancz
An imprint of the Orion Publishing Group
Orion House, 5 Upper St Martin's Lane,
London WC2H 9EA
An Hachette UK Company

3 5 7 9 10 8 6 4 2

A CIP catalogue record for this book is
available from the British Library

ISBN 978 0 575 11553 8

Printed in Great Britain by CPI Group (UK) Ltd, Croydon, CRO 4YY

The Orion Publishing Group's policy is to use papers
that are natural, renewable and recyclable products and
made from wood grown in sustainable forests. The logging
and manufacturing processes are expected to conform to
the environmental regulations of the country of origin.

www.multiverse.org
www.sfgateway.com
www.gollancz.co.uk
www.orionbooks.co.uk

Introduction to
The Michael Moorcock Collection
John Clute

H E IS NOW over 70, enough time for most careers to start and end in, enough time to fit in an occasional half-decade or so of silence to mark off the big years. Silence happens. I don't think I know an author who doesn't fear silence like the plague; most of us, if we live long enough, can remember a bad blank year or so, or more. Not Michael Moorcock. Except for some worrying surgery on his toes in recent years, he seems not to have taken time off to breathe the air of peace and panic. There has been no time to spare. The nearly 60 years of his active career seems to have been too short to fit everything in: the teenage comics; the editing jobs; the pulp fiction; the reinvented heroic fantasies; the Eternal Champion; the deep Jerry Cornelius riffs; NEW WORLDS; the 1970s/1980s flow of stories and novels, dozens upon dozens of them in every category of modern fantastika; the tales of the dying Earth and the possessing of Jesus; the exercises in postmodernism that turned the world inside out before most of us had begun to guess we were living on the wrong side of things; the invention (more or less) of steampunk; the alternate histories; the *Mitteleuropean* tales of sexual terror; the deep-city London riffs: the turns and changes and returns and reconfigurations to which he has subjected his oeuvre over the years (he expects this new Collected Edition will fix these transformations in place for good); the late tales where he has been remodelling the intersecting worlds he created in the 1960s in terms of twenty-first-century physics: for starters. If you can't take the heat, I guess, stay out of the multiverse.

His life has been full and complicated, a life he has exposed and hidden (like many other prolific authors) throughout his work. In *Mother London* (1988), though, a non-fantastic novel published at what is now something like the midpoint of his career, it may be possible to find the key to all the other selves who made the 100 books. There are three protagonists in the tale, which is set from about 1940 to about 1988 in the suburbs and inner runnels of the vast metropolis of Charles Dickens and Robert Louis Stevenson. The oldest of these protagonists is Joseph Kiss, a flamboyant self-advertising fin-de-siècle figure of substantial girth and a fantasticating relationship to the world: he is Michael Moorcock, seen with genial bite as a kind of G.K. Chesterton without the wearying punch-line paradoxes. The youngest of the three is David Mummery, a haunted introspective half-insane denizen of a secret London of trials and runes and codes and magic: he too is Michael Moorcock, seen through a glass, darkly. And there is Mary Gasalee, a kind of holy-innocent and survivor, blessed with a luminous clarity of insight, so that in all her apparent ignorance of the onrushing secular world she is more deeply wise than other folk: she is also Michael Moorcock, Moorcock when young as viewed from the wry middle years of 1988. When we read the book, we are reading a book of instructions for the assembly of a London writer. The Moorcock we put together from this choice of portraits is amused and bemused at the vision of himself; he is a phenomenon of flamboyance and introspection, a poseur and a solitary, a dreamer and a doer, a multitude and a singleton. But only the three Moorcocks in this book, working together, could have written all the other books.

It all began – as it does for David Mummery in *Mother London* – in South London, in a subtopian stretch of villas called Mitcham, in 1939. In early childhood, he experienced the Blitz, and never forgot the extraordinariness of being a participant – however minute – in the great drama; all around him, as though the world were being dismantled nightly, darkness and blackout would descend, bombs fall, buildings and streets disappear; and in the morning, as though a new universe had taken over from the old one and the world had become portals, the sun would rise on glinting rubble, abandoned tricycles, men and women going about their daily tasks as though nothing had happened, strange shards of ruin poking into altered air. From a very early age, Michael Moorcock's security reposed in a sense that everything might change, in the blinking of an eye, and be *rejourneyed* the next day (or the next book). Though as a writer he has certainly elucidated the fears and alarums of life in Aftermath Britain, it does seem that his very early years were marked by the epiphanies of war, rather than the inflictions of despair and beclouding amnesia most adults necessarily experienced. After the war ended, his parents separated, and the young Moorcock began to attend a pretty wide variety of schools, several of which he seems to have been expelled from, and as soon as he could legally do so he began to work full time, up north in London's heart, which he only left when he moved to Texas (with intervals in Paris) in the early 1990s, from where (to jump briefly up the decades) he continues to cast a Martian eye: as with most exiles, Moorcock's intensest anatomies of his homeland date from after his cunning departure.

But back again to the beginning (just as though we were rimming a multiverse). Starting in the 1950s there was the comics and pulp work for Fleetway Publications; there was the first book (*Caribbean Crisis*, 1962) as by Desmond Reid, co-written with his early friend the artist James Cawthorn (1929–2008); there was marriage, with the writer Hilary Bailey (they divorced in 1978), three children, a heated existence in the Ladbroke Grove / Notting Hill Gate region of London he was later to populate with Jerry Cornelius and his vast family; there was the editing of NEW WORLDS, which began in 1964 and became the heartbeat of the British New Wave two years later as writers like Brian W. Aldiss and J.G. Ballard, reaching their early prime, made it into a tympanum, as young American writers like Thomas M. Disch, John T. Sladek, Norman Spinrad and Pamela Zoline found a home in London for material they could not publish in America, and new British writers like M. John Harrison and Charles Platt began their careers in its pages; but before that there was Elric. With *The Stealer of Souls* (1963) and

Stormbringer (1965), the multiverse began to flicker into view, and the Eternal Champion (whom Elric parodied and embodied) began properly to ransack the worlds in his fight against a greater Chaos than the great dance could sustain. There was also the first SF novel, *The Sundered Worlds* (1965), but in the 1960s SF was a difficult nut to demolish for Moorcock: he would bide his time.

We come to the heart of the matter. Jerry Cornelius, who first appears in *The Final Programme* (1968) – which assembles and co-ordinates material first published a few years earlier in NEW WORLDS – is a deliberate solarisation of the albino Elric, who was himself a mocking solarisation of Robert E. Howard's Conan, or rather of the mighty-thew-headed Conan created for profit by Howard epigones: Moorcock rarely mocks the true quill. Cornelius, who reaches his first and most telling apotheosis in the four novels comprising *The Cornelius Quartet*, remains his most distinctive and perhaps most original single creation: a wide boy, an agent, a *flaneur*, a bad musician, a shopper, a shapechanger, a trans, a spy in the house of London: a toxic palimpsest on whom and through whom the *zeitgeist* inscribes surreal conjugations of 'message'. Jerry Cornelius gives head to Elric.

The life continued apace. By 1970, with NEW WORLDS on its last legs, multiverse fantasies and experimental novels poured forth; Moorcock and Hilary Bailey began to live separately, though he moved, in fact, only around the corner, where he set up house with Jill Riches, who would become his second wife; there was a second home in Yorkshire, but London remained his central base. *The Condition of Muzak* (1977), which is the fourth Cornelius novel, and *Gloriana; or, The Unfulfill'd Queen* (1978), which transfigures the first Elizabeth into a kinked Astraea, marked perhaps the high point of his career as a writer of fiction whose font lay in genre or its mutations – marked perhaps the furthest bournes he could transgress while remaining within the perimeters of fantasy (though *within* those bournes vast stretches of territory remained and would, continually, be explored). During these years he sometimes wore a leather jacket constructed out of numerous patches of varicoloured material, and it sometimes seemed perfectly fitting that he bore the semblance, as his jacket flickered and fuzzed from across a room or road, of an illustrated man, a map, a thing of shreds and patches, a student fleshed from dreams. Like the stories he told, he seemed to be more than one thing. To use a term frequently applied (by me at least) to twenty-first-century fiction, he seemed equipoisal: which is to say that, through all his genre-hopping and genre-mixing and genre-transcending and genre-loyal returnings to old pitches, *he was never still*, because 'equipoise' is all about *making stories move*. As with his stories, he cannot be pinned down, because he is not in one place. In person and in his work, it has always been sink or swim: like a shark, or a dancer, or an equilibrist...

The marriage with Jill Riches came to an end. He married Linda Steele in 1983; they remain married. The Colonel Pyat books, *Byzantium Endures* (1981), *The Laughter of Carthage* (1984), *Jerusalem Commands* (1992) and *The Vengeance of Rome* (2006), dominated these years, along with *Mother London*. As these books, which are non-fantastic, are not included in the current *Michael Moorcock Collection*, it might be worth noting here that, in their insistence on the irreducible difficulty of gaining anything like true sight, they represent Moorcock's mature modernist take on what one might call the rag-and-bone shop of the world itself; and that the huge ornate postmodern edifice of his multiverse *loosens* us from that world, gives us room to breathe, to juggle our strategies for living – allows us ultimately to escape from prison (to use a phrase from a writer he does not respect, J.R.R. Tolkien, for whom the twentieth century was a prison train bound for hell). What Moorcock may best be remembered for in the end is the (perhaps unique) interplay between modernism and postmodernism in his work. (But a plethora of discordant understandings makes these terms hard to use; so enough of them.) In the end, one might just say that Moorcock's work as a whole represents an extraordinarily multifarious execution of the fantasist's main task: which is to *get us out of here*.

Recent decades saw a continuation of the multifarious, but with a more intensely applied methodology. The late volumes of the long Elric saga, and the Second Ether sequence of meta-fantasies – *Blood: A Southern Fantasy* (1995), *Fabulous Harbours* (1995) and *The War Amongst the Angels: An Autobiographical Story* (1996) – brood on the real world and the multiverse through the lens of Chaos Theory: the closer you get to the world, the less you describe it. *The Metatemporal Detective* (2007) – a narrative in the Steampunk mode Moorcock had previewed as long ago as *The Warlord of the Air* (1971) and *The Land Leviathan* (1974) – continues the process, sometimes dizzyingly: as though the reader inhabited the eye of a camera increasing its focus on a closely observed reality while its bogey simultaneously wheels it backwards from the desired rapport: an old Kurasawa trick here amplified into a tool of conspectus, fantasy eyed and (once again) rejourneyed, this time through the lens of SF.

We reach the second decade of the twenty-first century, time still to make things new, but also time to sort. There are dozens of titles in *The Michael Moorcock Collection* that have not been listed in this short space, much less trawled for tidbits. The various avatars of the Eternal Champion – Elric, Kane of Old Mars, Hawkmoon, Count Brass, Corum, Von Bek – differ vastly from one another. Hawkmoon is a bit of a berk; Corum is a steely solitary at the End of Time: the joys and doleurs of the interplays amongst them can only be experienced through immersion. And the Dancers at the End of Time books, and the Nomad of the Time Stream books, and the Karl Glogauer books, and all the others. They are here now, a 100 books that make up one book. They have been fixed for reading. It is time to enter the multiverse and see the world.

September 2012

Introduction to
The Michael Moorcock Collection
Michael Moorcock

B Y 1964, AFTER I had been editing NEW WORLDS for some months and had published several science fiction and fantasy novels, including *Stormbringer*, I realised that my run as a writer was over. About the only new ideas I'd come up with were mini-ature computers, the multiverse and black holes, all very crudely realised, in *The Sundered Worlds*. No doubt I would have to return to journalism, writing features and editing. 'My career,' I told my friend J.G. Ballard, 'is finished.' He sympathised and told me he only had a few SF stories left in him, then he, too, wasn't sure what he'd do.

In January 1965, living in Colville Terrace, Notting Hill, then an infamous slum, best known for its race riots, I sat down at the typewriter in our kitchen-cum-bathroom and began a locally based book, designed to be accompanied by music and graphics. *The Final Programme* featured a character based on a young man I'd seen around the area and whom I named after a local green-grocer, Jerry Cornelius, 'Messiah to the Age of Science'. Jerry was as much a technique as a character. Not the 'spy' some critics described him as but an urban adventurer as interested in his psychic environment as the contemporary physical world. My influences were English and French absurdists, American noir novels. My inspiration was William Burroughs with whom I'd recently begun a correspondence. I also borrowed a few SF ideas, though I was adamant that I was not writing in any established genre. I felt I had at last found my own authentic voice.

I had already written a short novel, *The Golden Barge*, set in a nowhere, no-time world very much influenced by Peake and the surrealists, which I had not attempted to publish. An earlier auto-biographical novel, *The Hungry Dreamers*, set in Soho, was eaten by rats in a Ladbroke Grove basement. I remained unsatisfied with my style and my technique. *The Final Programme* took nine days to complete (by 20 January, 1965) with my baby daughters sometimes cradled with their bottles while I typed on. This, I should say, is my memory of events; my then wife scoffed at this story when I recounted it. Whatever the truth, the fact is I only believed I might be a serious writer after I had finished that novel, with all its flaws. But Jerry Cornelius, probably my most successful sustained attempt at unconventional fiction, was born then and ever since has remained a useful means of telling com-plex stories. Associated with the 60s and 70s, he has been equally at home in all the following decades. Through novels and novellas I developed a means of carrying several narratives and viewpoints on what appeared to be a very light (but tight) structure which dispensed with some of the earlier methods of fiction. In the sense that it took for granted the understanding that the novel is among other things an internal dialogue and I did not feel the need to repeat by now commonly understood modernist conven-tions, this fiction was post-modern.

Not all my fiction looked for new forms for the new century. Like many 'revolutionaries' I looked back as well as forward. As George Meredith looked to the eighteenth century for inspiration for his experiments with narrative, I looked to Meredith, popular Edwardian realists like Pett Ridge and Zangwill and the writers of the *fin de siècle* for methods and inspiration. An almost obsessive interest in the Fabians, several of whom believed in the possibility of benign imperialism, ultimately led to my Bastable books which examined our enduring British notion that an empire could be essentially a force for good. The first was *The Warlord of the Air*.

I also wrote my *Dancers at the End of Time* stories and novels under the influence of Edwardian humourists and absurdists like Jerome or Firbank. Together with more conventional generic books like *The Ice Schooner* or *The Black Corridor*, most of that work was done in the 1960s and 70s when I wrote the Eternal Champion supernatural adventure novels which helped support my own and others' experiments via NEW WORLDS, allowing me also to keep a family while writing books in which action and fantastic invention were paramount. Though I did them quickly, I didn't write them cynically. I have always believed, somewhat puritanically, in giving the audience good value for money. I enjoyed writing them, tried to avoid repetition, and through each new one was able to develop a few more ideas. They also continued to teach me how to express myself through image and metaphor. My Everyman became the Eternal Champion, his dreams and ambitions represented by the multiverse. He could be an ordinary person struggling with familiar problems in a contemporary setting or he could be a swordsman fighting monsters on a far-away world.

Long before I wrote *Gloriana* (in four parts reflecting the seasons) I had learned to think in images and symbols through reading John Bunyan's *Pilgrim's Progress*, Milton and others, understanding early on that the visual could be the most important part of a book and was often in itself a story as, for instance, a famous personality could also, through everything associated with their name, function as narrative. I wanted to find ways of carrying as many stories as possible in one. From the cinema I also learned how to use images as connecting themes. Images, colours, music, and even popular magazine headlines can all add coherence to an apparently random story, underpinning it and giving the reader a sense of internal logic and a satisfactory resolution, dispensing with certain familiar literary conventions.

When the story required it, I also began writing neo-realist fiction exploring the interface of character and environment, especially the city, especially London. In some books I condensed, manipulated and randomised time to achieve what I wanted, but in others the sense of 'real time' as we all generally perceive it was more suitable and could best be achieved by traditional nineteenth-century means. For the Pyat books I first looked back to the great German classic, Grimmelshausen's *Simplicissimus* and other early picaresques. I then examined the roots of a certain kind of moral fiction from Defoe through Thackeray and Meredith then to modern times where the picaresque (or rogue tale) can take the form of a road movie, for instance. While it's probably fair to say that Pyat and *Byzantium Endures* precipitated the end of my second marriage (echoed to a degree in *The Brothel in Rosenstrasse*), the late 70s and the 80s were exhilarating times for me, with *Mother London* being perhaps my own favourite novel of that period. I wanted to write something celebratory.

By the 90s I was again attempting to unite several kinds of fiction in one novel with my Second Ether trilogy. With Mandelbrot, Chaos Theory and String Theory I felt, as I said at the time, as if I were being offered a chart of my own brain. That chart made it easier for me to develop the notion of the multiverse as representing both the internal and the external, as a metaphor and as a means of structuring and rationalising an outrageously inventive and quasi-realistic narrative. The worlds of the multiverse move up and down scales or 'planes' explained in terms of mass, allowing entire universes to exist in the 'same' space. The result of developing this idea was the *War Amongst the Angels* sequence which added absurdist elements also functioning as a kind of mythology and folklore for a world beginning to understand itself in terms of new metaphysics and theoretical physics. As the cosmos becomes denser and almost infinite before our eyes, with black holes and dark matter affecting our own reality, we can explore them and observe them as our ancestors explored our planet and observed the heavens.

At the end of the 90s I'd returned to realism, sometimes with a dash of fantasy, with *King of the City* and the stories collected in *London Bone*. I also wrote a new Elric/Eternal Champion sequence, beginning with *Daughter of Dreams*, which brought the fantasy worlds of Hawkmoon, Bastable and Co. in line with my realistic and autobiographical stories, another attempt to unify all my fiction, and also offer a way in which disparate genres could be reunited, through notions developed from the multiverse and the Eternal Champion, as one giant novel. At the time I was finishing the Pyat sequence which attempted to look at the roots of the Nazi Holocaust in our European, Middle Eastern and American cultures and to ground my strange survival guilt while at the same time examining my own cultural roots in the light of an enduring anti-Semitism.

By the 2000s I was exploring various conventional ways of story-telling in the last parts of *The Metatemporal Detective* and through other homages, comics, parodies and games. I also looked back at my earliest influences. I had reached retirement age and felt like a rest. I wrote a 'prequel' to the Elric series as a graphic novel with Walter Simonson, *The Making of a Sorcerer*, and did a little online editing with FANTASTIC METROPOLIS.

By 2010 I had written a novel featuring Doctor Who, *The Coming of the Terraphiles*, with a nod to P.G. Wodehouse (a boyhood favourite), continued to write short stories and novellas and to work on the beginning of a new sequence combining pure fantasy and straight autobiography called *The Whispering Swarm* while still writing more Cornelius stories trying to unite all the various genres and sub-genres into which contemporary fiction has fallen.

Throughout my career critics have announced that I'm 'abandoning' fantasy and concentrating on literary fiction. The truth is, however, that all my life, since I became a professional writer and editor at the age of 16, I've written in whatever mode suits a story best and where necessary created a new form if an old one didn't work for me. Certain ideas are best carried on a Jerry Cornelius story, others work better as realism and others as fantasy or science fiction. Some work best as a combination. I'm sure I'll write whatever I like and will continue to experiment with all the ways there are of telling stories and carrying as many themes as possible. Whether I write about a widow coping with loneliness in her cottage or a massive, universe-size sentient spaceship searching for her children, I'll no doubt die trying to tell them all. I hope you'll find at least some of them to your taste.

One thing a reader can be sure of about these new editions is that they would not have been possible without the tremendous and indispensable help of my old friend and bibliographer John Davey. John has ensured that these Gollancz editions are definitive. I am indebted to John for many things, including his work at

Moorcock's Miscellany, my website, but his work on this edition has been outstanding. As well as being an accomplished novelist in his own right John is an astonishingly good editor who has worked with Gollancz and myself to point out every error and flaw in all previous editions, some of them not corrected since their first publication, and has enabled me to correct or revise them. I couldn't have completed this project without him. Together, I think, Gollancz, John Davey and myself have produced what will be the best editions possible and I am very grateful to him, to Malcolm Edwards, Darren Nash and Marcus Gipps for all the considerable hard work they have done to make this edition what it is.

Michael Moorcock

Contents

For Angus Wilson with great respect

Breakfast in the Ruins

Contents

Introduction

'Michael Moorcock' died of lung cancer, aged 31, in Birmingham last year. The whereabouts of Karl Glogauer are presently unknown.

– James Colvin,
Three Chimneys,
Raddon, Yorkshire
February 1971

Chapter One

In the Roof Garden:
1971: Scarlet Sin

Commonwealth immigrants to Britain were 22 per cent down
in April. There were 1,991 compared with 2,560 in April last year.

Guardian, 25 June, 1971

WHEN IN DOUBT, Karl Glogauer would always return to
Derry & Toms. He would walk down Kensington Church
Street in the summer sunshine, ignoring the boutiques and coffee
shops, until he reached the High Street. He would pass the first of
the three great department stores which stood side by side, stern
and eternal and bountiful, blotting out the sky, and would go
through the tall glass doors of the second store, Derry's. The
strongest of the citadels.

Weaving his way between the bright counters, piled with hats
and silks and paper flowers, he would reach the lifts with their late
art nouveau brasswork and he would take one of them up to the
third floor – a little journey through time, for here it was all art
deco and Cunard-style pastel plastics which he could admire for
their own sake as he waited for the special lift which would come
and bear him up into the paradise of the roof garden.

The gate would open to reveal something like a small conser-
vatory in which two pleasant middle-aged ladies stood to greet
the new arrivals and sell them, if required, tea-towels, postcards
and guide books. To one of these ladies Karl would hand his shil-
ling and stroll through into the Spanish Garden where fountains
splashed and well-tended exotic plants and flowers grew. Karl had
a bench near the central fountain. If it was occupied when he
arrived, he would stroll around for a while until it was free, then

9

he would sit down, open his book and pretend to read. The wall behind him was lined with deep, airy cages. Sometimes these cages were completely deserted but at other times they would contain a few parrots, parakeets, canaries, cockatoos, or a mynah bird. Occasionally pink flamingoes were present, parading awkwardly about the garden, wading through the tiny artificial streams. All these birds were, on the whole, decently silent, almost gloomy, offering hardly any reaction to the middle-aged ladies who liked to approach them and coo at them in pathetic, sometimes desperate, tones.

If the sunshine were warm and the number of visitors small Karl would sit in his seat for the best part of a morning or an afternoon before taking his lunch or tea in the roof garden restaurant. All the waitresses knew him well enough to offer a tight smile of recognition while continuing to wonder what a slightly seedy-looking young man in an old tweed jacket and rumpled flannels found to attract him in the roof garden. Karl recognised their puzzlement and took pleasure in it.

Karl knew why he liked to come here. In the whole of London this was the only place where he could find the peace he identified with the peace of his early childhood, the peace of ignorance (or 'innocence' as he preferred to call it). He had been born at the outbreak of the war, but he thought of his childhood as having existed a few years earlier, in the mid-thirties. Only lately had he come to understand that this peace was not really peace, but rather a sense of cosiness, the unique creation of a dying middle class. Vulgarity given a gloss of 'good taste'. Outside London there were a few other spots like it. He had found the right atmosphere in the tea-gardens of Surrey and Sussex, the parks in the richer suburbs of Dorking, Hove and Haywards Heath, all created during the twenties and thirties when, to that same middle class, comfiness had been a synonym for beauty. For all he knew too well that the urge which took him so frequently to the roof garden was both infantile and escapist, he tolerated it in himself. He would console himself sardonically that, of all his other infantile and escapist pursuits – his collection of children's books, his model soldiers – this was the cheapest. He no longer made any serious attempts to rid himself of these unmanly habits. He was their slave, just as much as he was the slave of his mother's childhood terrors; of the rich variety of horrors she had managed to introduce into his own childhood.

Thinking about his childhood as he sat in his usual place on a soft summer's day in June 1971, Karl wondered if his somewhat small creative gift was not, as most people would nowadays think, the result of his unstable upbringing at all. Perhaps, by virtue of his sensitivity, he had been unduly prone to his mother's influence. Such an influence could actually stunt talent, maybe. He did not like the drift of his thoughts. To follow their implications would be to offset the effects of the garden. He smiled to himself and leaned back, breathing in the heavy scent of snapdragons and tulips, believing, as he always did, that it was enough to admit a self-deception. It was what he called self-knowledge. He peered up at the blue uncluttered afternoon sky. The hum of the traffic in the street far below could almost be the sound of summer insects in a country garden. A country garden, long ago…

He leaned back on the bench a fraction more. He did not want to think about his mother, his childhood as it actually was, the failure of his ambitions. He became a handsome young aristocrat. He was a Regency buck relaxing from the wild London round of politics, gambling, duelling and women. He had just come down to his Somerset estate and had been greeted by his delightful young wife. He had married a sweet girl from these parts, the daughter of an old-fashioned squire, and she was ecstatic that he had returned home, for she doted on him. It did not occur to her to criticise the way he chose to live. As far as she was concerned, she existed entirely for his pleasure. What was her name? Emma? Sophy? Or something a little more Greek, perhaps?

The reverie was just beginning to develop into a full-scale fantasy when it was interrupted.

'Good afternoon.' The voice was deep, slightly hesitant, husky. It shocked him and he opened his eyes.

The face was quite close to his. Its owner was leaning down

and its expression was amused. The face was as dark and shining as ancient mahogany; almost black.

'Do you mind if I join you on this bench?' The tall black man sat down firmly.

Frustrated by the interruption Karl pretended an interest in a paving stone at his feet. He hated people who tried to talk to him here, particularly when they broke into his daydreams.

'Not at all,' he said, 'I was just leaving.' It was his usual reply. He adjusted the frayed cuff of his jacket.

'I'm visiting London,' said the black man. His own light suit was elegantly cut, a subtle silvery grey. Silk, Karl supposed. All the man's clothes and jewellery were evidently expensive. A rich American tourist, thought Karl (who had no ear for accents). 'I hadn't expected to find a place like this in the middle of your city,' the man continued. 'I saw a sign and followed it. Do you like it here?'

Karl shrugged.

The man laughed, removing the cover from his Rolleiflex. 'Can I take a picture of you here?'

And now Karl was flattered. Nobody had ever volunteered to take his picture before. His anger began to dissipate.

'It gives life to a photograph. It shows that I took it myself. Otherwise I might just as well buy the postcards, eh?'

Karl rose to go. But it seemed that the black man had misinterpreted the movement. 'You are a Londoner, aren't you?' He smiled, his deep-set eyes looking searchingly into Karl's face, Karl wondered for a moment if the question had some additional meaning he hadn't divined.

'Yes, I am.' He frowned.

Only now did the elegant negro seem to realise Karl's displeasure. 'I'm sorry if I'm imposing...' he said.

Again, Karl shrugged.

'It would not take a moment. I only asked if you were a Londoner because I don't wish to make the mistake of taking a picture of a typical Englishman and then you tell me you are French or something!' He laughed heartily. 'You see?'

Karl didn't much care for the 'typical', but he was disarmed by the man's charm. He smiled. The black man got up, put a hand on Karl's shoulder and guided him gently to the fountain. 'If you could sit on the rim for a moment...' He backed away and peered into his viewfinder, standing with his legs spread wide and his heels on the very edge of the flower bed, taking, from slightly different angles, a whole series of photographs. Karl was embarrassed. He felt that the situation was odd, but he could not define why it should seem so. It was as if the ritual of photography was a hint at a much more profound ritual going on at the same time. He must leave. Even the click and the whirr of the camera seemed to have a significant meaning.

'That's fine.' The photographer looked up. He narrowed his eyes against the sunlight. 'Just one more. I'm over here from Nigeria for a few days. Unfortunately it's more of a business visit than a pleasure trip: trying to get your government to pay a better price for our copper. What do you do?'

Karl waved a hand. 'Oh, nothing much. Look here, I must...'

'Come now! With a face as interesting as yours, you must do something equally interesting!'

'I'm a painter. An illustrator, really.' Again Karl was flattered by the attention. He had an impulse to tell the man anything he wanted to know – to tell him far more, probably, than he was prepared to listen to. Karl felt he was making a fool of himself.

'An artist! Very good. What sort of things do you paint?'

'I make my living doing military uniforms, mainly. People collect that sort of thing. It's a specialised craft. Sometimes I do work for the odd regiment which wants a picture to hang in the mess. Famous battles and stuff. You know...'

'So you're not a disciple of the avant-garde. I might have guessed. Your hair's too short! Ha ha! No cubism or action painting, eh?' The Nigerian snapped the case back on his camera. 'None of your "Which way up should I stand to look at it?"'

Karl laughed outright for the first time in ages. He was amused partly by the man's somewhat old-fashioned idea of the avant-garde, partly because he actually did paint stuff in his spare time which would fit the Nigerian's general description. All the same, he was pleased to have won the black man's approval.

'Not a revolutionary,' said the man, stepping closer. 'You're conventional, are you, in every respect?'

'Oh, hardly! Who is?'

'Who indeed? Have you had tea?' The black man took his arm, looking around him vaguely. 'I understand there's a café here.'

'A restaurant. On the other side.'

'Shall we cross?'

'I don't know…' Karl shivered. He didn't much care for people holding him like that, particularly when they were strangers, but a touch shouldn't make him shiver. 'I'm not sure…' Normally he could have walked away easily. Why should he mind being rude to a man who had so forcefully intruded on his privacy?

'You must have tea with me.' The grip tightened just a little. 'You have a bit of time to spare, surely? I rarely get the chance to make friends in London.'

Now Karl felt guilty. He remembered his mother's advice. Good advice, for a change. 'Never have anything to do with people who make you feel guilty.' She should have known! But it was no good. He did not want to disappoint the Nigerian. He felt rather faint suddenly. There was a sensation in the pit of his stomach which was not entirely unpleasurable.

They walked together through part of the Tudor Garden and through an archway which led into the Woodland Garden and there was the restaurant with its white wrought-iron tables and chairs on the verandah, its curve of glass through which the interior could be seen. The restaurant was quite busy today and was serving cucumber sandwiches and Danish pastries to little parties of women in jersey suits and silk frocks who were relaxing after their shopping. The only men present were one or two elderly husbands or fathers: tolerated because of their chequebooks. Karl and his new friend entered the restaurant and walked to the far end to a table by the window which looked out onto the lawns and willow trees skirting the miniature stream and its miniature wooden bridge. 'You had better order, I think,' said the Nigerian.

'I'm not much used to this sort of thing.' Again he smiled warmly. Karl picked up the menu.

'We might as well stick to the set tea,' said Karl. 'Sandwiches and cakes.'

'Very well.' The man's reply was vague, insouciant. He gave Karl the impression that, for all his politeness, he had weightier matters on his mind than the choice of food.

For a few moments Karl tried to signal a waitress. He felt embarrassed and avoided looking at his companion. He glanced about the crowded restaurant, at the pastel mauves and pinks and blues of the ladies' suits, the fluffy hats built up layer on layer of artificial petals, the Jaeger scarves. At last the waitress arrived. He didn't know her. She was new. But she looked like the rest. A tired woman of about thirty-five. Her thin face was yellow beneath the powder, the rouge and the lipstick. She had bags under her eyes and the deep crow's feet emphasised the bleakness of her expression. The skin on the bridge of her nose was peeling. She had the hands of a hag twice her age. One of them plucked the order pad from where it hung by a string against her dowdy black skirt and she settled her pencil heavily against the paper. It seemed that she lacked even the strength to hold the stub with only one hand.

'Two set teas, please,' said Karl. He tried to sound pleasant and sympathetic. But she paid attention neither to his face nor his tone.

'Thank you, sir.' She let the pad fall back without using it. She began to trudge towards the kitchen, pushing open the door as if gratefully entering the gates of hell.

Karl felt the pressure of his companion's long legs against his own. He tried, politely, to move, but could not; not without a violent tug. The black man seemed unaware of Karl's discomfort and leaned forward over the little table, putting his two elbows on the dainty white cloth and looking directly into Karl's eyes. 'I hope you don't think I've been rude, old chap,' he said.

'Rude?' Karl was trapped by the eyes.

'It occurred to me you might have better things to do than keep a bored tourist entertained.'

'Of course not,' Karl heard himself say. 'I'm afraid I don't know much about Nigeria. I'd like to know more. Of course, I followed the Biafran thing in the papers.' Had that been the wrong remark?

'Your Alfred had similar trouble with his "break-away" states, you know.'

'I suppose he did.' Karl wasn't sure who Alfred had been or what he had done.

The waitress came back with a mock silver tray on which stood a teapot, a milk jug and a hot-water jug, also of mock silver, together with cups and saucers and plates. She began to set her load down between the two men. The Nigerian leaned back but continued to smile into Karl's eyes while Karl murmured 'Thank you' every time the waitress placed something in front of him. These ingratiating noises were his usual response to most minor forms of human misery, as they had been to his mother when she had made it evident what it had cost her to prepare a meal for him.

'Shall I be mother?' said Karl and again the not unpleasant sensation of weakness swept through him. The Nigerian was looking away, vague once again, his handsome profile in silhouette as he took an interest in the garden. Karl repeated eagerly: 'Shall I –?' The Nigerian said: 'Fine.' And Karl realised that he was now desperate to please his companion, that he needed the man's whole attention, that he would do anything to ensure that he got it. He poured the tea. He handed a cup to his friend, who accepted it absently.

'We haven't introduced ourselves,' Karl said. He cleared his throat. 'I'm Karl Glogauer.'

The attention was regained. The eyes looked directly into Karl's, the pressure of the leg was deliberate. The Nigerian picked up the bowl nearest him and offered it to Karl.

'Sugar?'

'Thanks.' Karl took the bowl.

'You've got nice hands,' said the Nigerian. 'An artist's hands, of course.' Briefly, he touched Karl's fingers.

Karl giggled. 'Do you think so?' The sensation came again, but this time it was a wave and there was no doubt about its origin.

'Thank you.' He smiled suddenly because to remark on their hands and to pretend to read their palms was one of his standard ways of trying to pick up girls. 'Are you going to read my palm?'

The Nigerian's brows came together in a deep frown. 'Why should I?'

Karl's breathing was heavier. At last he understood the nature of the trap. And there was nothing he wished to do about it.

In silence, they ate their sandwiches. Karl was no longer irritated by the pressure of the man's leg on his.

A little later the Nigerian said: 'Will you come back with me?'

'Yes,' whispered Karl.

He began to shake.

What Would You Do? (1)

You are a passenger on a plane which is about to crash. The plane is not a jet and so you have a chance to parachute to safety. With the other passengers, you stand in line and take one of the parachutes which the crew hands out to you. There is one problem. The people ahead of you on the line are already jumping out. But you have a four-month-old baby with you and it is too large to button into your clothing. Yet you must have both hands free in order to (a) pull the emergency ripcord in the event of the parachute failing to open, (b) guide the chute to safety if you see danger below. The baby is crying. The people behind you are pressing forward. Someone helps you struggle into the harness and hands you back your baby. Even if you did hold the baby in both hands and pray that you had an easy descent, there is every possibility he could be yanked from your grip as you jumped.

There are a few more seconds to go before you miss your chance to get out of the plane.

Chapter Two

In the Commune:
1871: A Smile

Not only France, but the whole civilised world, was startled
and dismayed by the sudden success of the Red Republicans of
Paris. The most extraordinary, and perhaps the most alarming,
feature of the movement, was the fact that it had been brought
about by men nearly all of whom were totally unknown to
society at large. It was not, therefore, the influence, whether
for good or evil, of a few great names which might be supposed to exercise a species of enchantment on the uneducated
classes, and to be capable of moving them, almost without
thought, towards the execution of any design which the mas-
ter-minds might have determined on – it was not this which
had caused the convulsion. The outbreak was clearly due less
to individual persuasion, which in the nature of things is evan-
escent, than to the operation of deep-rooted principles such as
survive when men depart. The ideas which gave rise to the
Commune were within the cognisance of the middle and
upper classes of society; but it was not supposed that they had
attained such power, or were capable of such organised action.
A frightful apparition of the Red Republic had been momentarily visible in June, 1848; but it was at once exorcised by the
cannon and bayonets of Cavaignac. It was again apprehended
towards the close of 1851, and would probably have made itself
once more manifest, had not the coup d'état of Louis Napoleon prevented any such movement, not only at that time, but
for several years to come. Every now and then during the
period of the Second Empire, threatenings of this vague yet
appalling danger came and went, but the admirable organisation
of the Imperial Government kept the enemies of social order

in subjection, though only by a resort to means regrettable in themselves, against which the Moderate Republicans were perpetually directing their most bitter attacks, little thinking that they would soon be obliged to use the same weapons with still greater severity. Nevertheless, although the Emperor Napoleon held the Red Republic firmly down throughout his term of power, the principles of the extreme faction were working beneath the surface; and they only awaited the advent of a weaker Government, and of a period of social disruption, to glare upon the world with stormy menace.

– Anonymous,
History of the War Between France and Germany,
Cassell, Petter & Galpin, 1872

— *There you are, Karl.*

The black man strokes his head.

Karl has removed his clothes and lies naked on the double bed in the hotel suite. The silk counterpane is cool.

— *Do you feel any better now?*

— *I'm not sure.*

Karl's mouth is dry. The man's hands move down from his head to touch his shoulders. Karl gasps. He shuts his eyes.

Karl is seven years old. He and his mother have fled from their house as the Versailles troops storm Paris in their successful effort to destroy the Commune established a few months earlier. It is Civil War and it is savage. The more so, perhaps, because the French have received such an ignominious defeat at the hands of Bismarck's Prussians.

He is seven years old. It is the spring of 1871. He is on the move.

— *Do you like this?* asks the black man.

K ARL WAS SEVEN. His mother was twenty-five. His father was thirty-one, but had probably been killed fighting the Prussians at St Quentin. Karl's father had been so eager to join the National Guard and prove that he was a true Frenchman.

'Now, Karl.' His mother put him down and he felt the hard

cobble of the street beneath his thin shoes. 'You must walk a little. Mother is tired, too.'

It was true. When she was tired, her Alsatian accent always became thicker and now it was very thick. Karl felt ashamed for her.

He was not sure what was happening. The previous night he had heard loud noises and the sounds of running feet. There had been shots and explosions, but such things were familiar enough since the Siege of Paris. Then his mother had appeared in her street clothes and made him put on his coat and shoes, hurrying him from the room and down the stairs and into the street. He wondered what had happened to their maid. When they got into the street he saw that a fire had broken out some distance away and that there were many National Guardsmen about. Some of them were running towards the fires and others, who were wounded, were staggering in the other direction. Some bad soldiers were attacking them, he gathered, and his mother was afraid that the house would be burned down. 'Starvation – bombardment – and now fire,' she had muttered bitterly. 'I hope all the wretched Communards are shot!' Her heavy black skirts hissed as she led him through the night, away from the fighting.

By dawn, more of the city was burning and all was confusion. Ragged members of the National Guard in their stained uniforms rallied the citizens to pile furniture and bedding onto the carts which had been overturned to block the streets. Sometimes Karl and his mother were stopped and told to help the other women and children, but she gave excuses and hurried on. Karl was dazed. He had no idea where they were going. He was vaguely aware that his mother knew no better than he. When he gasped that he could walk no further, she picked him up and continued her flight, her sharp face expressing her disapproval at his weakness. She was a small, wiry woman who would have been reasonably pretty had her features not been set so solidly in a mask of tension and anxiety. Karl had never known her face to soften, either to him or to his father. Her eyes had always seemed fixed on some distant objective which, secretly and grimly, she had determined to reach.

That same look was in her eyes now, though much more emphatic, and the little boy had the impression that his mother's flight through the city was the natural climax to her life.

Karl tried not to cry out as he trotted behind his mother's dusty black skirts. His whole body was aching and his feet were blistered and once he fell on the cobbles and had to scramble up swiftly in order to catch her as she turned a corner.

They were now in a narrow side street not far from the Rue du Bac on the Left Bank. Twice Karl had caught a glimpse of the nearby Seine. It was a beautiful spring morning, but the sky was slowly being obscured by thick smoke from the many burning buildings on both sides of the river. Noticing this, his mother hesitated.

'Oh, the animals!' Her tone was a mixture of disgust and despair. 'They are setting fire to their own city!'

'May we rest now, Mother?' asked Karl.

'Rest?' She laughed bitterly. But she made no effort to continue on her way, though she cast about her in every direction, trying to decide where she could best expect to find safety.

Suddenly, from a couple of streets away, there came a series of explosions which shook the houses. There were shots and then a great angry cry, followed by individual screams and shouts. In the guise of addressing her son, she muttered to herself.

'The streets are not safe. The dogs are everywhere. We must try to find some government soldiers and ask their protection.'

'Are those the bad soldiers, Mother?'

'No, Karl, they are the good soldiers. They are freeing Paris of those who have brought the city to ruin.'

'The Prussians?'

'The Communists. We all knew it would come to this. What a fool your father was.'

Karl was surprised to hear the contempt in her voice. She had previously always told him to look up to his father. He began to cry. For the first time since leaving the house, he felt deeply miserable, rather than merely uncomfortable.

'Oh, my God!' His mother reached out and shook him.

'We don't need your weeping on top of everything else. Be quiet, Karl.'

He bit his lip, but he was still shaken by sobs.

She stroked his head. 'Your mother is tired,' she said. 'She has always done her duty.' A sigh. 'But what's the point?' Karl realised that she was not trying to comfort him at all, but herself. Even the automatic stroking of his hair was done in an effort to calm herself. There was no real sympathy in the gesture. For some reason this knowledge made him feel deep sympathy for her. It had not been easy, even when his father was alive, with no-one coming to buy clothes in the shop just because they had a German-sounding name. And she had protected him from the worst of the insults and beaten the boys who threw stones at him.

He hugged her waist. 'Have courage, Mother,' he whispered awkwardly.

She looked at him in astonishment. 'Courage? What does it gain us?' She took his hand. 'Come. We'll find the soldiers.'

Trotting beside her, Karl felt closer to her than he had ever felt, not because she had shown affection for him but because he had been able to show affection for her. Of late, he had begun to feel guilty, believing he might not love his mother as much as a good son should.

The two of them entered the somewhat broader street that was the Rue du Bac and here was the source of the sounds they had heard. The Communards were being beaten back by the well-trained Versailles troops. The Versaillese, having been so roundly defeated by the Prussians, were avenging themselves on their recalcitrant countrymen. Most of the Communards were armed with rifles on which were fixed bayonets. They had run out of ammunition and were using the rifles as spears. Most of them were dressed in ordinary clothes, but there was a handful of National Guardsmen among them, in soiled pale blue uniforms. Karl saw a torn red flag still flying somewhere. Many women were taking part in the fighting. Karl saw one woman bayonet a wounded Versaillese who lay on the ground. His mother pulled him away. She was trembling now. As they rounded a bend in the

Rue du Bac, they saw another barricade. Then there was an eruption and a roar and the barricades flew apart. Through the dust
and débris Karl saw bodies flung in every direction. Some of the
dead were children of his own age. A terrifying wailing filled the
street, a wailing which turned into a growl of anger. The remaining Communards began to fire at the unseen enemy. Another
eruption and another roar and the remains of the barricade went
down. For a second there was silence. Then a woman rushed
from a nearby house and screamed something, hurling a burning
bottle through an open window in her own cellar. Karl saw that a
house on the opposite side of the street was beginning to burn.
Why were the people setting fire to their own houses?

Now through the smoke and the ruins came the Versaillese in
their smart dark blue and red uniforms. Their eyes were red and
glaring, reflecting the flames. They frightened Karl far more than
the National Guardsmen. Behind them galloped an officer on a
black horse. He was screaming in the same high-pitched tone as
the woman. He was waving a sabre. Karl's mother took a step
towards the troops and then hesitated. She turned and began to
run in the other direction, Karl running with her.

There were several shots and Karl noticed that bullets were
striking the walls of the houses. He knew at once that he and his
mother were being fired at. He grinned with excitement.

They dashed down the next side street and had to wade through
piles of garbage to enter a ruined building, an earlier victim of the
first Siege. His mother hid behind a quaking wall as the soldiers
ran past. When they had gone she sat down on a slab of broken
stone and began to cry. Karl stroked her hair, wishing that he
could share her grief.

'Your father should not have deserted us,' she said.

'He had to fight, Mother,' said Karl. It was what she had said to
him when his father joined the guard. 'For France.'

'For the Reds. For the fools who brought all this upon us!'

Karl did not understand.

Soon his mother was sleeping in the ruins. He curled up beside
her and slept, too.

When they awakened that afternoon there was much more smoke. It drifted everywhere. On all sides buildings burned. Karl's mother staggered up. Without looking at him or speaking to him, she seized his hand in a grip which made him wince. Her boots slipping on the stones, her skirts all filthy and ragged at the hem, she dragged him with her to the street. A young girl stood there, her face grave. 'Good day,' she said.

'Are they still fighting?'

The girl could hardly understand his mother's accent, it had become so thick. The girl frowned.

'Are they still fighting?' his mother asked again, speaking in a peculiar, slow voice.

'Yes.' The girl shrugged. 'They are killing everyone. Anyone.'

'That way?' Karl's mother pointed towards the Seine. 'That way?'

'Yes. Everywhere. But more that way.' She pointed in the general direction of the Boulevard du Montparnasse. 'Are you a petrol-woman?'

'Certainly not!' Madame Glogauer glared at the girl. 'Are you?'

'I wasn't allowed,' said the girl regretfully. 'There isn't much petrol left.'

Karl's mother took him back the way they had come. The fires which had been started earlier were now out. It appeared that they had done little damage. Not enough petrol, thought Karl.

With her sleeves over her mouth, his mother picked her way through the corpses and crossed the ruins of the barricade. The other men and women who were searching for dead friends or relatives ignored them as they went by.

Karl thought there were more dead people than living people in the world now.

They reached the Boulevard Saint-Germain, hurrying towards the Quai d'Orsay. On the far side of the river monstrous sheets of flame sprang from a dozen buildings and smoke boiled into the clear May sky.

'I am so thirsty, Mother,' murmured Karl. The smoke and the dust filled his mouth. She ignored him.

Here again the barricades were deserted, save for the dead, the victors and the sightseers. Groups of Versaillese stood about, leaning on their rifles smoking and watching the fires, or chatting to the innocent citizens who were so anxious to establish their hatred of the Communards. Karl saw a group of prisoners, their hands bound with rope, sitting miserably in the road, guarded by the regular soldiers. Whenever a Communard moved, he would receive a harsh blow from a rifle butt or would be threatened by the bayonet. The red flag flew nowhere. In the distance came the sound of cannon-fire and rifle-fire.

'At last!' Madame Glogauer began to move towards the troops. 'We shall go home soon, Karl. If they have not burned our house down.'

Karl saw an empty wine bottle in the gutter. Perhaps they could fill it with water from the river. He picked it up even as his mother dragged him forward.

'Mother – we could...'

She stopped. 'What have you got there? Put the filthy thing down!'

'We could fill it with water.'

'We'll drink soon enough. And eat.'

She grabbed the bottle from his hand. 'If we are to remain respectable, Karl...'

She turned her head at a shout. A group of citizens were pointing at her. Soldiers began to run towards them. Karl heard the word 'pétroleuse' repeated several times. Madame Glogauer shook her head and threw the bottle down. 'It is empty,' she said quietly. They could not hear her. The soldiers stopped and raised their rifles. She stretched her hands towards them. 'It was an empty bottle!' she cried.

Karl tugged at her. 'Mother!' He tried to take her hand, but it was still stretched towards the soldiers. 'They cannot understand you, Mother.'

She began to back away and then she ran. He tried to follow, but fell down. She disappeared into a little alley. The soldiers ran past Karl and followed her into the alley. The citizens ran after the soldiers. They were shrieking with hysteria and bloodlust. Karl got up and ran behind them. There were some shots and some screams. By the time Karl had entered the little street the soldiers were coming back again, the citizens still standing looking at something on the ground. Karl pushed his way through them. They cuffed him and snarled at him and then they, too, turned away.

'The pigs use women and children to fight their battles,' said one man. He glared at Karl. 'The sooner Paris is cleansed of such scum the better.'

His mother lay sprawled on her face in the filth of the street. There was a dark, wet patch on her back. Karl went up to her and, as he had suspected, found that the patch was blood. She was still bleeding. He had never seen his mother's blood before. He tried hard to turn her over, but he was too weak. 'Mother?' Suddenly her whole body heaved and she drew in a great dry breath. Then she moaned.

The smoke drifted across the sky and evening came and the city burned. Red flames stained the night on every side. Shots boomed. But there were no more voices. Even the people who passed and whom Karl begged to help his wounded mother did not speak. One or two laughed harshly. With his help, his mother managed to turn herself over and sat with her back propped against the wall. She breathed with great difficulty and did not seem to know him, staring as fixedly and as determinedly into the middle distance as she had always done. Her hair was loose and it clung to her tight, anxious face. Karl wanted to find her some water, but he did not want to leave her.

At last he got up and blocked the path of a man who came walking towards the Boulevard Saint-Germain. 'Please help my mother, sir,' he said.

'Help her? Yes, of course. Then they will shoot me, too. That will be good, eh?' The man threw back his head and laughed heartily as he continued on his way.

'She did nothing wrong!' Karl shouted.

The man stopped just before he turned the corner. 'It depends how you look at it, doesn't it, young man?' He gestured into the boulevard. 'Here's what you need! Hey, there! Stop! I've got another passenger for you.' Karl heard the sound of something squeaking. The squeaking stopped and the man exchanged a few words with someone else. Then he disappeared. Instinctively Karl backed away with some idea of defending his mother. A filthy old man appeared next. 'I've just about got room,' he explained. He brushed Karl aside, heaved Madame Glogauer onto his shoulder and turned, staggering back down the street. Karl followed. Was the man going to help his mother? Take her to the hospital?

A cart stood in the street. There were no carthorses, for they had all been eaten during the Siege as Karl knew. Instead, between the shafts stood several ragged men and women. They began to move forward when they saw the old man appear again, dragging the squeaking cart behind them. Karl saw that there were people of all ages and sexes lying on top of one another in the cart. Most of them were dead, many with gaping wounds and parts of their faces or bodies missing. 'Give us a hand here,' said the old man and one of the younger men left his place at the front and helped heave Madame Glogauer onto the top of the pile. She groaned.

'Where are you taking her?' asked Karl.

They continued to ignore him. The cart squeaked on through the night. Karl followed it. From time to time he heard his mother moan.

He became very tired and could hardly see, for his eyes kept closing, but he followed the cart by its sound, hearing the sharp clack of clogs and the slap of bare feet on the road, the squeal of the wheels, the occasional cries and moans of the living passengers. By midnight they had reached one of the outlying districts of the city and entered a square. There were Versaillese soldiers here, standing about on the remains of a green. In the middle of the green was a dark area. The old man said something to the soldiers and then he and his companions began unloading the cart. Karl tried to see which one of the people was his mother. The ragged men and women carried their burdens to the dark area and dropped them into it. Karl could now see that it was a freshly dug pit. He peered in, certain that he had heard his mother's voice among the moans of the wounded as, indiscriminately, they were buried with the dead. All around the square shutters were closing and lights were being extinguished. A soldier came up and dragged Karl away from the graveside. 'Get back,' he said, 'or you'll go in with them.'

Soon the cart went away. The soldiers sat down by the graveside and lit their pipes, complaining about the smell, which had become almost overpowering, and passing a bottle of wine back and forth. 'I'll be glad when this is over,' said one.

Karl squatted against the wall of the house, trying to distinguish his mother's voice amongst those which groaned or cried out from the pit. He was sure he could hear her pleading to be let out.

By dawn, her voice had stopped and the cart came back with a fresh load. These were dumped into the pit and the soldiers got up reluctantly at the command of their officer, putting down their rifles and picking up shovels. They began to throw earth onto the bodies.

When the grave was covered, Karl got up and began to walk away.

The guards put down their shovels. They seemed more cheerful now and they opened another bottle of wine. One of them saw Karl. 'Hello, young man. You're up early.' He ruffled the boy's hair. 'Hoping for some more excitement, eh?' He took a pull on the bottle and then offered it to Karl. 'Like a drink?' He laughed.

Karl smiled at him.

Karl gasps and he writhes on the bed.

— What are you doing? he says.

— Don't you like it? You don't have to like it. Not everyone does.

— Oh, God, says Karl.

The black man gets up. His body gleams in the faint light from the window. He moves gracefully back, out of range of Karl's vision. — Perhaps you had better sleep. There is lots of time.

— No...

— *You want to go on?*
A pause.
— *Yes...*

What Would You Do? (2)

You have been brought to a room by the secret police.

They say that you can save the lives of your whole family if you will only assist them in one way.

You agree to help.

There is a table covered by a cloth. They remove the cloth and reveal a profusion of objects. There is a children's comforter, a Smith and Wesson .45, an umbrella, a big volume of *Don Quixote*, illustrated by Doré, two blankets, a jar of honey, four bottles of drugs, a bicycle pump, some blank envelopes, a carton of Sullivan's cigarettes, an enamelled pin with the word 1900 on it (blue on gold), a wristwatch, a Japanese fan.

They tell you that all you have to do is choose the correct object and you and your family will be released.

You have never seen any of the objects before. You tell them this. They nod. That is all right. They know. Now choose.

You stare at the objects, trying to divine their significance.

Chapter Three

Kaffee Klatsch in Brunswick:
1883: The Lowdown

Bismarck was very fond of enlarging on his favourite theory of the male and female European nations. The Germans themselves, the three Scandinavian peoples, the Dutch, the English proper, the Scotch, the Hungarians and the Turks, he declared to be essentially male races. The Russians, the Poles, the Bohemians, and indeed every Slavonic people, and all Celts, he maintained, just as emphatically, to be female races. A female race he ungallantly defined as one given to immense verbosity, to fickleness, and to lack of tenacity. He conceded to these feminine races some of the advantages of their sex, and acknowledged that they had great powers of attraction and charm, when they chose to exert them, and also a fluency of speech denied to the more virile nations. He maintained stoutly that it was quite useless to expect efficiency in any form from one of the female races, and he was full of contempt for the Celt and the Slav. He contended that the most interesting nations were the epicene ones, partaking, that is, of the characteristics of both sexes, and he instanced France and Italy, intensely virile in the North, absolutely female in the South; maintaining that the Northern French had saved their country times out of number from the follies of the 'Meridionaux'. He attributed the efficiency of the Frenchmen of the North to the fact that they had so large a proportion of Frankish and Norman blood in their veins, the Franks being a Germanic tribe, and the Normans, as their name implied, Northmen of Scandinavian, therefore also of Teutonic, origin. He declared that the fair-haired Piedmontese were the driving power of Italy, and that they owed their initiative to their descent from the Germanic hordes who invaded Italy under Alaric in the fifth century. Bismarck stoutly maintained that efficiency, wherever it was found, was due to Teutonic blood; a statement with which I will not quarrel.

As the inventor of 'Practical Politics' (*Real-Politik*), Bismarck had a supreme contempt for fluent talkers and for words, saying that only fools could imagine that facts could be talked away. He cynically added that words were sometimes useful for 'papering over structural cracks' when they had to be concealed for a time.

With his intensely overbearing disposition, Bismarck could not brook the smallest contradiction, or any criticism whatever. I have often watched him in the Reichstag – then housed in a very modest building – whilst being attacked, especially by Liebknecht the Socialist. He made no effort to conceal his anger, and would stab the blotting-pad before him viciously with a metal paper-cutter, his face purple with rage.

Bismarck himself was a very clear and forcible speaker, with a happy knack of coining felicitous phrases.

– Lord Frederick Hamilton,
The Vanished Pomps of Yesterday,
Hodder & Stoughton, 1920

There is a big colour TV in the suite.

The Nigerian walks up to it. His penis is still slightly stiff. — Do you want this on?

Karl is eight. It is 1883. Brunswick. He has a very respectable mother and father. They are kind but firm. It is very comfortable.

He shakes his head.

— Well, do you mind if I watch the news?

Karl is eight. It is 1948. There is a man in pyjamas in his mother's room.

It is 1883...

KARL WAS EIGHT. His mother was thirty-five. His father was forty. They had a large, modern house in the best part of Brunswick. His father's business was in the centre of town. Trade was good in Germany and particularly good in Brunswick. The Glogauers were part of the best society in Brunswick. Frau Glogauer belonged to the coffee circle which once a week met, in rotation, at the house of one of the members. This week the ladies were meeting at Frau Glogauer's.

Karl, of course, was not allowed into the big drawing room where his mother entertained. His nurse watched over him while he played in the garden in the hot summer sunshine. Through the French windows, which were open, he could just see his mother and her friends. They balanced the delicate china cups so elegantly and they leaned their heads so close together when they talked. They were not bored. Karl was bored.

He swung back and forth on his swing. Up and down and back and forward and up and down and back. He was dressed in his best velvet suit and he was hot and uncomfortable. But he always dressed in this way when it was his mother's turn to entertain the kaffee klatsch, even though he wasn't invited to join them. Usually he was asked to come in just before the ladies left. They would ask him the same questions they asked every time and they would compliment his mother on his looks and his size and his health and they would give him a little piece of gateau. He was looking forward to the gateau.

'Karl, you must wear your hat,' said Miss Henshaw. Miss Henshaw was English and her German was rather unfortunate in that she had learned it in a village. It was Low German and it made her sound like a yokel. Karl's parents and their friends spoke nothing but the more sophisticated High German. Low German sounded just like English, anyway. He didn't know why she'd bothered to learn it. 'Your hat, Karl. The sun is too hot.'

In her garishly striped blouse and her silly stiff grey skirt and her own floppy white hat, Miss Henshaw looked awful. How dowdy and decrepit she was compared to Mother who, corseted and bustled and covered in pretty silk ribbons and buttons and lace and brocade, moved with the dignity of a six-masted clipper. Miss Henshaw was evidently only a servant, for all her pretence at authority.

She stretched out her freckled arm, offering him the little sun hat. He ignored her, making the swing go higher and higher.

'You will get sunstroke, Karl. Your mother will be very angry with me.'

Karl shrugged and kicked his feet out straight, enjoying Miss Henshaw's helplessness.

'Karl! Karl!'

Miss Henshaw's voice was almost a screech.

Karl grinned. He saw that the ladies were looking out at him through the open window. He waved to his mother. The ladies smiled and returned to their gossip.

He knew it was gossip, about everyone in Brunswick, because once he had lain beside the window in the shrubs and listened before he had been caught by Miss Henshaw. He wished that he had understood more of the references, but at least he had got one useful tip – that Fritz Vieweg's father had been born 'the wrong side of the blanket'. He hadn't been sure of the meaning, but when he had confronted Fritz Vieweg with it, it had stopped Vieweg calling him a 'Jew-pig' all right.

Gossip like that was worth a lot.

'Karl! Karl!'

'Oh, go away, Fräulein Henshaw. I am not in need of my hat at present.' He chuckled to himself. When he talked like his father, she always disapproved.

His mother appeared in the doorway of the French window.

'Karl, dear. There is someone who would like to meet you. May we have Karl in with us for a moment, Miss Henshaw?'

'Of course, Frau Glogauer.' Miss Henshaw darted him a look of stern triumph. Reluctantly, he let the swing slow down and then jumped off.

Miss Henshaw took his hand and they walked across the ornamental pavement to the French windows. His mother smiled fondly and patted his head.

'Frau Spiegelberg is here and wants to meet you.'

He supposed, from his mother's tone, that he should know who Frau Spiegelberg was, that she must be an important visitor, not one of Frau Glogauer's regulars. A woman dressed in purple and white silk was towering behind his mother. She gave him quite a friendly smile. He bowed twice very deeply. 'Good afternoon, Frau Spiegelberg.'

'Good afternoon, Karl,' said Frau Spiegelberg.

'Frau Spiegelberg is from Berlin, Karl,' said his mother. 'She has met the great Chancellor Bismarck himself!'

Again Karl bowed.

The ladies laughed. Frau Spiegelberg said with charming, almost coquettish modesty, 'I must emphasise I am not on intimate terms with Prinz Bismarck!' and she gave a trilling laugh. Karl knew that all the ladies would be practising that laugh after she had gone back to Berlin.

'I would like to go to Berlin,' said Karl.

'It is a very fine city,' said Frau Spiegelberg complacently. 'But your Brunswick is very pretty.'

Karl was at a loss for something to say. He frowned and then brightened. 'Frau Spiegelberg –' he gave another little bow – 'have you met Chancellor Bismarck's son?'

'I have met both. Do you mean Herbert or William or –' Frau Spiegelberg glanced modestly at her companions again – 'Bill as he likes to be called.'

'Bill,' said Karl.

'I have attended several balls at which he has been present, yes.'

'So you – have touched him, Frau Spiegelberg?'

And again the trilling laugh. 'Why do you ask?'

'Well, Father met him once I believe when on business in Berlin…'

'So your father and I have an acquaintance in common. That is splendid, Karl.' Frau Spiegelberg made to turn away. 'A handsome boy, Frau –'

'And Father shook hands with him,' said Karl.

'Really? Well…'

'And Father said he drank so much beer that his hands were

always wet and clammy and he could not possibly live for long if he continued to drink that much. Father is, himself, not averse to a few tots of beer or glasses of punch, but he swears he has never seen anyone drink so much in all his life. Is Bill Bismarck dead yet, Frau Spiegelberg?'

His mother had been listening to him in cold horror, her mouth open. Frau Spiegelberg raised her eyebrows. The other ladies glanced at each other. Miss Henshaw took his hand and began to pull him away, apologising to his mother.

Karl bowed again. 'I am honoured to have met you, Frau Spiegelberg,' he said in his father's voice. 'I am afraid I have embarrassed you and so I will take my leave now.' Miss Henshaw's tugging became more insistent. 'I hope we shall meet again before you return to Berlin, Frau Spiegelberg...'

'It is time I left,' icily said Frau Spiegelberg to his mother.

His mother came out for a moment and hissed:

'You disgusting child. You will be punished for this. Your father shall do it.'

'But, Mother...'

'In the meantime, Miss Henshaw,' said Frau Glogauer in a terrible murmur, 'you have my permission to beat the boy.'

Karl shuddered as he caught a glint of hidden malice in Miss Henshaw's pale, grey eyes.

'Very well, madam,' said Miss Henshaw. As she led him away he heard her sigh a deep sigh of pleasure.

Already, he was plotting his own revenge.

— *You'll like it better when you get used to it. It's a question of your frame of mind.*

Karl sighs. — *Maybe.*

— *It's a matter of time, that's all.*

— *I believe you.*

— *You've got to let yourself go.*

They sip the dry, chilled champagne the black man has ordered. Outside, people are going into the theatres.

— *After all, says the black man, we are many people. There are a lot of different sides to one's personality. You mustn't feel that you've lost something. You have gained something. Another aspect is flowering.*

— *I feel terrible.*

— *It won't last. Your moment will come.*

Karl smiles. The black man's English is not always perfect.

— *There, you see, you are feeling more relaxed already.*

The black man reaches out and touches his arm. — How smooth your flesh is. What are you thinking?

— *I was remembering the time I found the air-raid warden in bed with my mother. I remember her explaining it to my father. My father was a patient man.*

— *Is your father still alive?*

— *I don't know.*

— *You have a great deal to learn, yet.*

What Would You Do? (3)

You are returning from the theatre after a pleasant evening with your sweetheart. You are in the centre of the city and you want a taxi. You decide to go to the main railway station and find a taxi there. As you come into a side entrance and approach a flight of steps you see an old man trying to ascend. He is evidently incapably drunk. Normally you would help him up the steps, but in this case there is a problem. His trousers have fallen down to his ankles, revealing his filthy legs. From his bottom protrude several pieces of newspaper covered in excrement. To help him would be a messy task, to say the least, and you are reluctant to spoil the previously pleasant mood of the evening. There is a second or two before you pass him and continue on your journey.

Chapter Four

Capetown Party:
1892: Butterflies

In the meantime let us not forget that if errors of judgement have been committed, they have been committed by men whose zeal and patriotism has never been doubted. We cannot refrain, however, from alluding here to the greatest of all lessons which this war has taught, not us alone, but all the world – the solidarity of the Empire. And for that great demonstration what sacrifice was not worth making.

– H.W. Wilson,
With the Flag to Pretoria,
Harmsworth Brothers, 1900

Karl emerges from the deep bath. Liquid drips from him. He stares in bewilderment at himself in the wall mirror opposite.

— Why did you make me do that?

— I thought you'd like it. You said how much you admired my body.

— I meant your physique.

— Oh, I see.

— I look like something out of a minstrel show. Al Jolson...

— Yes, you do rather. But you could pass for what? An Eurasian? The black man begins to laugh.

Karl laughs, too.

They fall into each other's arms.

— It shouldn't take long to dry, says the black man.

Karl is nine. It is 1892. He is at work now.

— I think I like you better like that, says the black man. He puts a palm on Karl's damp thigh. — It's your colour...

Karl giggles.
— There, you see, it has made you feel better.

KARL WAS NINE. His mother did not know her age. He did not know his father. He was a servant in a house with a huge garden. A white house. He was the punkah-wallah, the boy who operated the giant fan which swept back and forth over the white people while they were eating. When he was not doing this, he helped the cook in the kitchen. Whenever he could, however, he was out in the grounds with his net. He had a passion for butterflies. He had a large collection in the room he shared with the two other little houseboys and his companions were very envious. If he saw a specimen he did not own, he would forget everything else until he had caught it. Everyone knew about his hobby and that was why he was known as 'Butterfly' by everyone, from the master and mistress down. It was a kind house and they tolerated his passion. It was not everyone, even, who would employ a Cape Coloured boy, because most thought that half-breeds were less trustworthy than pure-blooded natives. The master had presented him with a proper killing jar and an old velvet-lined case in which to mount his specimens. Karl was very lucky.

Whenever the master saw him, he would say: 'And how's the young entomologist, today?' and Karl would flash him a smile. When Karl was older it was almost certain that he would be given a position as a footman. He would be the very first Cape Coloured footman in this district.

This evening it was very hot and the master and mistress were entertaining a large party of guests to dinner. Karl sat behind a screen and pulled on the string which made the fan work. He was good at his job and the motion of the fan was as regular as the swinging of a pendulum.

When his right arm became tired, Karl would use his left arm, and when his left arm was tired, he would transfer the string to the big toe of his right foot. When his right foot ached, he would use his left and by that time his right arm would be rested and he could begin again. In the meantime, he daydreamed, thinking of his lovely butterflies and of the specimens he had yet to collect. There was a very large one he wanted particularly. It had blue and yellow wings and a complicated pattern of zigzags on its body. He did not know its name. He knew few of the names because nobody could tell them to him. Someone had once shown him a book with some pictures of butterflies and the names underneath, but since he could not read he could not discover what the names were.

Laughter came from the other side of the screen. A deep voice said: 'Somebody will teach the Boers a lesson soon, mark my words. Those damned farmers can't go on treating British subjects in that high-handed fashion for ever. We've made their country rich and they treat us like natives!'

Another voice murmured a reply and the deep voice said loudly: 'If that's the sort of life they want to preserve, why don't they go somewhere else? They've got to move with the times.'

Karl lost interest in the conversation. He didn't understand it, anyway. Besides, he was more interested in butterflies. He transferred the string to his left toe.

When all the guests had withdrawn, a footman came to tell Karl that he might go to his supper. Stiffly Karl walked round the screen and hobbled towards the door. The dinner had been a long one.

In the kitchen the cook put a large plate of succulent scraps before him and said: 'Hurry up now, young man, I've had a long day and I want to get to my bed.'

He ate the food and washed it down with the half a glass of beer the cook gave him. It was a treat. She knew he had been working hard, too. As she let him out of the kitchen, she rumpled his hair and said: 'Poor little chap. How's your butterflies?'

'Very well, thank you, cook.' Karl was always polite.

'You must show them to me sometime.'

'I'll show them to you tomorrow, if you like.'

She nodded. 'Well, sometime... Goodnight, Butterfly.'

'Goodnight, cook.'

He climbed the back stairs high up to his room in the roof. The two houseboys were already asleep. Quietly, he lit his lamp and got out his case of butterflies. He would be needing another case soon.

Smiling tenderly, he delicately stroked their wings with the tip of his little finger.

For over an hour he looked at his butterflies and then he got into his bed and pulled the sheet over him. He lay staring at the eaves and thinking about the blue-and-yellow butterfly he would try to catch tomorrow.

There was a sound outside. He ignored it. It was a familiar sound. Feet creeping along the passage. Either one of the house-maids was on her way out to keep an assignation with her follower, or her follower had boldly entered the house. Karl turned over and tried to go to sleep.

The door of his room opened.

He turned onto his back again and peered through the gloom. A white figure was standing there, panting. It was a man in pyja-mas and a dressing gown. The man paused for a moment and then crept towards Karl's bed.

'There you are, you little beauty,' whispered the man. Karl rec-ognised the voice as the one he had heard earlier talking about the Boers.

'What do you want, sir?' Karl sat up in bed.

'Eh? Damn! Who the devil are you?'

'The punkah-boy, sir.'

'I thought this was where that little fat maid slept. What the devil!'

There was a crunch and the man grunted in pain, hopping about the room. 'Oh, I've had enough of this!'

Now the other two boys were awake. Their eyes stared in hor-ror at the hopping figure. Perhaps they thought it was a ghost.

The white man blundered back out of the room, leaving the door swinging on its hinges. Karl heard him go down the passage and descend the stairs.

Karl got up and lit the lamp.

He saw his butterfly case where he had left it beside the bed.

The white man had stepped on it and broken the glass. All the butterflies were broken, too.

— *Won't it wash off? asks Karl.*
  — *Do you want it to come off? Don't you feel more free?*
— *Free?*

What Would You Do? (4)

You are escaping from an enemy. You have climbed along the top of a sloping slate roof, several storeys up. It is raining. You slip and manage to hang on to the top of the roof. You try to get back, but your feet slip on the wet tiles. Below you, you can see a lead gutter. Will you risk sliding down the roof while there is still some strength left in your fingers and hope that you can catch the gutter as you go down and thus work your way to safety? Or will you continue to try to pull yourself back to the top of the roof? There is also the chance that the gutter will break under your weight when you grab it. Perhaps, also, your enemy has discovered where you are and is coming along the roof towards you.

Chapter Five

Liberation in Havana:
1898: Hooks

'You may fire when ready, Gridley.'

– Commodore Dewey,
1 May, 1898

— *There, it's dried nicely. The black man runs his nail down Karl's chest. — Are you religious, Karl?*

— *Not really.*

— *Do you believe in incarnation? Or what you might call 'transincarnation', I suppose.*

— *I don't know what you're talking about.*

The nail traces a line across his stomach. He gasps.

The black man bares his teeth in a sudden smile.

— *Oh, you do really. What's this? Wilful ignorance? How many people today suffer from that malaise!*

— *Leave me alone.*

— *Alone?*

Karl is ten, the son of a small manufacturer of cigars in Havana, Cuba. His grandfather had the cigar factory before his father. He will inherit the factory from his father.

— *Yes – alone... Oh, God!*

... The black man's tone becomes warmly sympathetic. — What's up?

Karl looks at him in surprise, hearing him speak English slang easily for the first time. The black man is changing.

Karl shudders. — You've – you've – made me cold...

— *Then we'd better tuck you into bed, old chap.*

— *You've corrupted me.*

— *Corrupted? Is that what you think turns me on? The Corruption of Ignorance! The black man throws back his handsome head and laughs heartily.*

Karl is ten...

The black man leans down and kisses Karl ferociously on the lips.

K ARL WAS TEN. His mother was dead. His father was fifty-one. His brother Willi was nineteen and, when last heard of, had joined the insurgents to fight against the Spaniards.

Karl's father had not approved of Willi's decision and had disowned his eldest son; that was why Karl was now the heir to the cigar factory. One day he would be master of nearly a hundred women and children who worked in the factory rolling the good cigars which were prized all over the world.

Not that business could be said to be good at present, with the American ships blockading the port. 'But the war is virtually over,' said Señor Glogauer, 'and things will be returning to normal soon enough.'

It was Sunday and the bells were ringing all over Havana. Big bells and little bells. It was almost impossible to hear anything else.

After church, Señor Glogauer walked with his son down the Prado towards Parque Central. Since the war, the beggars seemed to have multiplied to four or five times their previous number. Disdaining a carriage, Señor Glogauer led his son through the ragged clamourers, tapping a way through with his cane. Sometimes a particularly sluggish beggar would receive a heavy thwack for his pains and Señor Glogauer would smile to himself and put a little extra tilt on his beautifully white panama hat. His suit was white, too. Karl wore a coffee-coloured sailor suit and sweater. His father made a point of making this journey on foot every Sunday because he said Karl must learn to know the people and not fear them; they were all wretched cowards, even when you had to deal with a whole pack of them, as now.

This morning a brigade of volunteers had been lined up for inspection in the Prado. Their uniforms were ill-fitting and not all of them had rifles of the same make, but a little Spanish lieutenant strutted up and down in front of them as proudly as if he were Napoleon inspecting the Grand Army. And behind the marshalled volunteers a military band played rousing marches and patriotic tunes. The bells and the beggars and the band created such a cacophony that Karl felt his ears would close up against the noise. It echoed through the faded white grandeur of the street, from the elaborate stucco walls of the hotels and official buildings on both sides of the avenue, from the black and shining windows of the shops with their ornate gold, silver and scarlet lettering. And mingled with this noise were the smells – smells from sewers and beggars and sweating soldiers threatening to drown the more savoury smells of coffee and candy and cooking food.

Karl was glad when they entered the babble of the Café Inglaterra on the west side of the Parque Central. This was the fashionable place to come and, as always, it was crowded with the representatives of all nations, professions and trades. There were Spanish officers, businessmen, lawyers, priests. There were a number of ladies in colours as rich as the feathers of the jungle birds (from whom they had borrowed at least part of their finery), there were merchants from all the countries of Europe. There were English planters and even a few American journalists or tobacco-buyers. They sat at the tables, crowded tightly together, and drank beer or punch or whisky, talking, laughing, quarrelling. Some stood at the counters while upstairs others ate late breakfasts or early luncheons or merely drank coffee.

Señor Glogauer guided Karl into the café, nodding to acquaintances, smiling at friends, and found a seat for himself. 'You had better stand, Karl, until a seat becomes free,' he said. 'Your usual lemonade?'

'Thank you, Papa.' Karl wished he could be at home reading his book in the cool semi-darkness of the nursery.

Señor Glogauer studied the menu. 'The cost!' he exclaimed. 'I'll swear it has doubled since last week.'

The man sitting opposite spoke good Spanish but was evidently English or American. He smiled at Señor Glogauer. 'It's true what you people say – you're not being blockaded by the warships. You're being blockaded by the grocers!'

Señor Glogauer pursed his lips in a cautious smile. 'Our own people are ruining us, señor. You are quite right. The tradesmen are soaking the life out of us. They blame the Americans, but I know they had prepared for this – salting away their food knowing that if the blockade took effect they could charge anything they liked. It is hard for us at the moment, señor.'

'So I see,' said the stranger wryly. 'When the Americans get here things will be better, eh?'

Señor Glogauer shrugged. 'Not if La Lucha is correct. I was reading yesterday of the atrocities the American Rough Riders are committing in Santiago. They are drunk all the time. They steal. They shoot honest citizens at will – and worse.' Señor Glogauer glanced significantly at Karl. The waiter came up. He ordered a coffee for himself and a lemonade for Karl. Karl wondered if they ate children.

'I'm sure the reports are exaggerated,' said the stranger. 'A few isolated cases.'

'Perhaps.' Señor Glogauer put both his hands over the nob of his cane. 'But I fear that if they come here I – or my son – might be one of those "isolated cases". We should be just as dead, I think.'

The stranger laughed. 'I take your point, señor.' He turned in his chair and looked out at the life of the Parque. 'But at least Cuba will be master of her own fate when this is over.'

'Possibly.' Señor Glogauer watched the waiter setting down his coffee.

'You have no sympathy with the insurgents?'

'None. Why should I? They have disrupted my business.'

'Your view is understandable, señor. Well, I have work to do.' The stranger rose. Karl thought how ill and tired the man looked. He put on his own, slightly grubby, panama. 'It has been pleasant talking with you, señor. Good day.'

'Good day, señor.' Señor Glogauer pointed to the vacant chair and gratefully Karl went to it, sitting down. The lemonade was warm. It tasted of flies, thought Karl. He looked up at the huge electric fans rattling round and round on the ceiling. They had only been installed last year, but already there were specks of rust on their blades.

A little later, when they were leaving the Café Inglaterra, on their way across the Parque to where Señor Glogauer's carriage waited, a Spanish officer halted in front of them and saluted. He had four soldiers with him. They looked bored. 'Señor Glogauer?' The Spaniard gave a slight bow and brought his heels together.

'Yes.' Señor Glogauer frowned. 'What is it, captain?'

'We would like you to accompany us, if you please.'

'To where? For what?'

'A security matter. I do apologise. You are the father of Wilhelm Glogauer, are you not?'

'I have disowned my son,' said Karl Glogauer's father grimly. 'I do not support his opinions.'

'You know what his opinions are?'

'Vaguely. I understand he is in favour of a break with Spain.'

'I think he is rather more active a supporter of the insurgent cause than that, señor.' The captain glanced at Karl as if sharing a joke with him. 'Well, if you will now come with us to our headquarters, we can sort this whole thing out quickly.'

'Must I come? Can't you ask me your questions here?'

'No. What about the boy?'

'He will come with his father.' For a moment Karl thought that his father needed Karl's moral support. But that was silly, for his father was such a proud, self-reliant man.

With the soldiers behind them, they walked out of the Parque Central and up Obispo Street until they reached a gateway guarded by more soldiers. They went through the gate and into a courtyard. Here the captain dismissed the soldiers and gestured for Señor Glogauer to precede him into the building. Slowly, with dignity, Señor Glogauer ascended the steps and entered the foyer, one hand on his cane, the other grasping Karl's hand.

'And now this way, señor.' The captain indicated a dark passage with many doors leading off it on both sides. They walked down this. 'And down these steps, señor.' Down a curving flight of steps into the basement of the building. The lower passage was lit by oil lamps.

And another flight of steps.

'Down, please.'

And now the smell was worse even than the smell of the Prado. Señor Glogauer took out a pure white linen handkerchief and fastidiously wiped his lips. 'Where are we, señor captain?'

'The cells, Señor Glogauer. This is where we question prisoners and so on.'

'You are not – I am not –?'

'Of course not. You are a private citizen. We only seek your help, I assure you. Your own loyalty is not in question.'

Into one of the cells. There was a table in it. On the table was a flickering oil lamp. The lamp cast shadows which danced sluggishly. There was a strong smell of damp, of sweat, of urine. One of the shadows groaned. Señor Glogauer started and peered at it. 'Mother of God!'

'I am afraid it is your son, señor. As you see. He was captured only about twenty miles from the city. He claimed that he was a small planter from the other side of the island. But we found his name in his wallet and someone had heard of you – your cigars, you know, which are so good. We put two and two together and then you – thank you very much – confirmed that your son was an insurgent. But we wanted to be sure this was your son, naturally, and not someone who had managed merely to get hold of his papers. And again, we thank you.'

'Karl. Leave,' said Señor Glogauer, remembering his other son. His voice was shaking. 'At once.'

'The sergeant at the door,' said the officer, 'perhaps he will give you a drink.'

But Karl had already seen the dirty steel butcher's hooks on which Willi's wrists had been impaled, had seen the blue and yellow flesh around the wounds, the drying blood. He had seen Willi's poor, beaten face, his scarred body, his beast's eyes. Calmly, he came to a decision. He looked up the corridor. It was deserted.

When his father eventually came out of the cell, weeping and asking to be pardoned and justifying himself and calling upon God and cursing his son all at the same time, Karl had gone. He was walking steadily, walking on his little legs towards the outskirts of the city, on his way to find the insurgents still at liberty.

He intended to offer them his services.

— And why do you dislike Americans?

— I don't like the way some of them think they own the world.

— But didn't your people think that for centuries? Don't they still?

— It's different.

— And why do you collect model soldiers?

— I just do. It's relaxing. A hobby.

— Because you can't manipulate real people so easily?

— Think what you like. Karl turns over on the bed and immediately regrets it. But he lies there.

He feels the expected touch on his spine. — Now you are feeling altogether more yourself, aren't you, Karl?

Karl's face is pressed into the pillow. He cannot speak.

The man's body presses down on his and for a moment he smiles. Is this what they mean by the White Man's Burden?

— Sssssshhhhh, says the black man.

What Would You Do? (5)

You have three children.

One is eight years old. A girl.

One is six years old. A girl.

One is a few months old. A boy.

You are told that you can save any two of them from death, but not all three. You are given five minutes to choose.

Which one would you sacrifice?

Chapter Six

London Sewing Circle:
1905: A Message

One would have thought that the meaning of the word 'sweating' as applied to work was sufficiently obvious. But when 'the Sweating System' was inquired into by the Committee of the House of Lords, the meaning became suddenly involved. As a matter of fact the sweater was originally a man who kept his people at work for long hours. A schoolboy who 'sweats' for his examination studies for many hours beyond his usual working day. The schoolboy meaning of the word was originally the trade meaning.

But of late years the sweating system has come to mean an unhappy combination of long hours and low pay. 'The sweater's den' is a workshop – often a dwelling room as well – in which, under the most unhealthy conditions, men and women toil for from sixteen to eighteen hours a day for a wage barely sufficient to keep body and soul together.

The sweating system, as far as London is concerned, exists chiefly at the East End, but it flourishes also in the West, notably in Soho, where the principal 'sweating trade', tailoring, is now largely carried on. Let us visit the East End first, for here we can see the class which has largely contributed to the evil – the destitute foreign Jew – place his alien foot for the first time upon the free soil of England.

> – George R. Sims,
> *Living London,*
> Cassell & Co. Ltd, 1902

*

49

Karl turns onto his side. He is aching. He is weeping.

— Did I promise you pleasure? asks the tall, black man as he wipes his hands on a hotel towel and then stretches and then yawns. — Did I?

— No. Karl's voice is muffled and small.

— You can leave whenever you wish.

— Like this?

— You'll get used to it. After all, millions of others have...

— Have you known them all?

The black man parts the curtain. It is now pitch-dark outside and it is silent. — Now that's a leading question, he says. — The fact is, Karl, you are intrigued by all these new experiences. You welcome them. Why be a hypocrite?

— I'm not the hypocrite.

The black man grins and wags a chiding finger. — Don't take it out on me, man. That wouldn't be very liberal, would it?

— I never was very liberal.

— You've been very liberal to me. The black man rolls his eyes in a comic grimace. Karl has seen the expression earlier. He begins to tremble again. He looks at his own brown hands and he tries to make his brain see all this in a proper, normal light.

He is eleven. A dark, filthy room. Many little sounds.

The black man says from beside the window: — Come here, Karl.

Automatically Karl hauls himself from the bed and begins to make his way across the floor.

He remembers his mother and the tin of paint she threw at him which missed and ruined her wallpaper. You don't love me, she had said. Why should I? he had replied. He had been fourteen, perhaps, and ashamed of the question once he had asked it.

He is eleven. Many little regular sounds.

He approaches the black man. — That will do, Karl, says the black man.

Karl stops.

The black man approaches him. Under his breath he is humming 'Old Folks at Home'. Kneeling on the carpet, Karl begins to sing the words in an exaggerated minstrel accent.

KARL WAS ELEVEN. His mother was thirty. His father was thirty-five. They lived in London. They had come to London from Poland three years earlier. They had been escaping a pogrom. On their way, they had been robbed of most of their money by their countrymen. When they had arrived at the dockside, they had been met by a Jew who said he was from the same district as Karl's father and would help them. He had taken them to lodgings which had proved poor and expensive. When Karl's father ran out of money the man had loaned him a few shillings on his luggage and, when Karl's father could not pay him back, had kept the luggage and turned them out onto the street. Since then, Karl's father had found work. Now they all worked, Karl, his mother and his father. They worked for a tailor. Karl's father had been a printer in Poland, an educated man. But there was not enough work for Polish printers in London. One day Karl's father hoped that a job would become vacant on a Polish or Russian newspaper. Then they would become respectable again, as they had been in Poland.

At present, Karl, his mother and his father all looked rather older than their respective ages. They sat together at one corner of the long table. Karl's mother worked a sewing machine. Karl's father sewed the lapel of a jacket. Around the table sat other groups – a man and a wife, three sisters, a mother and daughter, a father and son, two brothers. They all had the same appearance, were dressed in threadbare clothes of black and brown. The women's mouths were tight shut. The men mostly had thin, straggly beards. They were not all Polish. Some were from other countries: Russia, Bohemia, Germany and elsewhere. Some could not even speak Yiddish and were therefore incapable of conversing with anyone not from their own country.

The room in which they worked was lit by a single gas-jet in the centre of the low ceiling. There was a small window, but it had been nailed up. The walls were of naked plaster through which could be seen patches of damp brick. Although it was winter, there was no fire in the room and the only heat came from the bodies of the workers. There was a fireplace in the room, but this was used to store the scraps of discarded material which could be re-used for padding. The smell of the people was very strong, but now few of them really noticed it, unless they left the room and came back in again, which was rarely. Some people would stay there for days at a time, sleeping in a corner and eating a bowl of soup someone would bring them, before starting work again.

A week ago, Karl had been there when they had discovered that the man whose coughing they had all complained about had not woken up for seven hours. Another man had knelt down and listened at the sleeping man's chest. He had nodded to the sleeping man's wife and sister-in-law and together they had carried him from the room. Neither the wife nor the sister-in-law came back for the rest of the day and it seemed to Karl that when they did return the wife's whole soul had not been in her work and her eyes were redder than usual, but the sister-in-law seemed much the same. The coughing man had not returned at all and, of course, Karl reasoned, it was because he was dead.

Karl's father laid down the coat. It was time to eat. He left the room and returned shortly with a small bundle wrapped in newspaper, a single large jug of hot tea. Karl's mother left her sewing machine and signed to Karl. The three of them sat in the corner of the room near the window while Karl's father unwrapped the newspaper and produced three cooked herrings. He handed one to each of them. They took turns to sip from the tea-jug. The meal lasted ten minutes and was eaten in silence. Then they went back to their place at the table, having carefully cleaned their fingers on the newspaper, for Mr Armfelt would fine them if he discovered any grease spots on the clothes they were making.

Karl looked at his mother's thin, red fingers, at his father's lined face. They were no worse off than the rest.

That was the phrase his father always used when he and his mother crawled into their end of the bed. Once he had prayed every night. Now that phrase was the nearest he came to a prayer.

The door opened and the room became a little more chill. The door closed. A short young man wearing a black bowler hat and a long overcoat stood there, blowing on his fingers. He spoke in Russian, his eyes wandering from face to face. Few looked up. Only Karl stared at him.

'Any lad like to do a job for me?' said the young man. 'Urgent. Good money.'

Several of the workers had his attention now, but Karl had already raised his hand. His father looked concerned, but said nothing.

'You'll do fine,' said the young man. 'Five shillings. And it won't take you long, probably. A message.'

'A message where?' Like Karl, Karl's father spoke Russian as well as he spoke Polish.

'Just down to the docks. Not far. I'm busy, or I'd go myself. But I need someone who knows a bit of English, as well as Russian.'

'I speak English,' said Karl in English.

'Then you're definitely the lad I need. Is that all right?' glancing at Karl's father. 'You've no objection?'

'I suppose not. Come back as soon as you can, Karl. And don't let anybody take your money from you.' Karl's father began to sew again. His mother turned the handle of the sewing machine a trifle faster, but that was all.

'Come on, then,' said the young man.

Karl got up.

'It's pelting down out there,' said the young man.

'Take the blanket, Karl,' said his father.

Karl went to the corner and picked up the thin scrap of blanket. He draped it round his shoulders. The young man was already clumping down the stairs. Karl followed.

Outside in the alley it was almost as dark as night. Heavy rain swished down and filled the broken street with black pools in which it seemed you could fall and drown. A dog leaned in a doorway, shivering. At the far end of the alley were the lights of the pub. Blinds were drawn in half the windows of the buildings lining both sides of the street. In some of the remaining windows could be seen faint, ghostly lights. A voice was shouting, but whether it was in this alley or the next one, Karl couldn't tell. The shouting stopped. He huddled deeper into the blanket.

'You know Irongate Stairs?' The young man looked rapidly up and down the alley.

'Where the boats come ashore?' said Karl.

'That's right. Well, I want you to take this envelope to someone who's landing from the *Solchester* in an hour or so. Tell no-one you have the envelope, save this man. And mention the man's name as little as you can. He may want your help. Do whatever he asks.'

'And when will you pay me?'

'When you have done the work.'

'How will I find you?'

'I'll come back here. Don't worry, I'm not like your damned masters! I won't go back on my word.' The young man lifted his head almost proudly. 'This day's work could see an end to what you people have to suffer.'

He handed Karl the envelope. On it, in Russian, was written a single word, a name: KOVRIN.

'Kovrin,' said Karl, rolling his 'r'. 'This is the man?'

'He's very tall and thin,' said his new employer. 'Probably wearing a Russian cap. You know the sort of thing people wear when they first come over. A very striking face, I'm told.'

'You've not met him?'

'A relative, come to look for work,' said the young man somewhat hastily. 'That's enough. Go, before you're too late. And tell no-one save him that you have met me, or there'll be no money for you. Get it?'

Karl nodded. The rain was already soaking through his blanket. He tucked the envelope into his shirt and began to trot along the alley, avoiding the worst of the puddles. As he passed the pub, a piano began to play and he heard a cracked voice singing:

> *Don't stop me 'arf a pint o' beer,*
> *It's the only fing what's keepin' me alive.*
> *I don't mind yer stoppin' of me coffee and me tea,*
> *But 'arf a pint o' beer a day is medicine to me.*

I don't want no bloomin' milk or eggs,
And to buy them I'll find it very dear.
If you want to see me 'appy and contented all me life,
Don't stop me 'arf a pint o' beer!

Now I'm a chap what's moderate in all I 'ave to drink,
And if that's wrong, then tell me what is right...

Karl did not hear all the words properly. Besides, such songs all sounded the same to him, with virtually the same tunes and the same sentiments. He found the English rather crude and stupid, particularly in their musical tastes. He wished he were somewhere else. Whenever he wasn't working, when he could daydream quite cheerfully as he sewed pads into jackets, this feeling overwhelmed him. He longed for the little town in Poland he could barely remember, for the sun and the cornfields, the snows and the pines. He had never been clear about why they had had to leave so hastily.

Water filled his ruined shoes and made the cloth of his trousers stick to his thin legs. He crossed another alley. There were two or three English boys there. They were scuffing about on the wet cobbles. He hoped they wouldn't see him. There was nothing that cheered bored English boys up so much as the prospect of baiting Karl Glogauer. And it was important that he shouldn't lose the letter, or fail to deliver it. Five shillings was worth nearly two days' work. In an hour he would make as much as he would normally make in thirty-six. They hadn't seen him. He reached the broader streets and entered Commercial Street which was crowded with slow-moving traffic. Everything, even the cabs, seemed beaten down by the grey rain. The world was a place of blacks and dirty whites, spattered with the yellow of gas-lamps in the windows of the pie-and-mash shops, the second-hand clothes shops, the pubs and the pawnshops. Plodding dray-horses threatened to smash their heads against the curved green fronts of the trams or the omnibuses; carters swore at their beasts, their rivals and themselves. Swathed in rubber, or canvas, or gaberdine, crouching beneath umbrellas, men and women stumbled into each other or stepped aside just in time. Through all these dodged Karl with his message in his shirt, crossing Aldgate and running down the dismal length of Leman Street, past more pubs, a few dismal shops, crumbling houses, brick walls which seemed to have no function but to block light from the street, a police station with a blue lamp gleaming over its door, another wall plastered with advertisements for meat-drinks, soaps, bicycles, nerve tonics, beers, money-lenders, political parties, newspapers, music halls, jobs (No Irish or Aliens Need Apply), furniture on easy terms, the Army. The rain washed them down and made some of them look fresh again. Across Cable Street, down Dock Street, through another maze of alleys, even darker than the others, to Wapping Lane.

When he reached the river, Karl had to ask his way, for, in fact, he had lied when he had told the man he knew Irongate Stairs. People found his guttural accent hard to understand and lost patience with him quickly, but one old man gave him the direction. It was still some distance off. He broke into a trot again, the blanket drawn up over his head, so that he looked like some supernatural creature, a body without a skull, running mindlessly through the cold streets.

When he reached Irongate Stairs, the first boats were already bringing the immigrants ashore, for the ship itself could not tie up at the wharf. He saw that it was the right ship, a mass of red and black, belching oily smoke over the oily river, smoke which also seemed pressed down by the rain and which would not rise. The *Solchester* was a regular caller at Irongate Stairs, sailing twice a week from Hamburg with its cargo of Jews and political exiles. Karl had seen many identical people in his three years in Whitechapel. They were thin and there was hunger in their eyes; bewildered, bare-headed women, with shawls round their shoulders more threadbare than Karl's blanket, dragged their bundles from the boats to the wharf, trying at the same time to keep control of their scrawny children. A number of the men were quarrelling with the boatman, refusing to pay the sixpence which was his standard charge. They had been cheated so often on their journey that they were certain they were being cheated yet again. Others were staring in miserable astonishment at the blurred and blotted line of wharves and grim buildings which seemed to make up the entire city, hesitating before entering the dark archway which protected this particular wharf. The archway was crowded with loafers and touts, all busily trying to confuse them, to seize their luggage, almost fighting to get possession of it.

Two policemen stood near the exit to Irongate Stairs, refusing to take part in any of the many arguments which broke out, unable to understand the many questions which the refugees put to them, simply smiling patronisingly and shaking their heads, pointing to the reasonably well-dressed man who moved anxiously amongst the people and asked questions in Yiddish or Lettish. Chiefly he wanted to know if the people had an address to go to. Karl recognised him. This was Mr Somper, the Superintendent of the Poor Jews' Temporary Shelter. Mr Somper had met them three years before. At that time Karl's father had been confident that he needed no such assistance. Karl saw that many of the newcomers were as confident as his father had been. Mr Somper did his best to listen sympathetically to all the tales they told him – of robbery at the frontier, of the travel agent who told them they would easily find a good job in England, of the oppression they had suffered in their own countries. Many waved pieces of crumpled paper on which addresses were written in English – the names of friends or relatives who had already settled in London. Mr Somper, his dark face clouded with care, saw to it that their baggage was loaded onto the waiting carts, assured those who tried to hang on to their bundles that they would not be stolen, united mothers with stray children and husbands with wives. Some of the people did not need his help and they looked as relieved as he did. These were going on to America and were merely transferring from one boat to another.

Karl could see no-one of Kovrin's description. He was jostled back and forth as the Germans and the Romanians and the Russians, many of them still wearing the embroidered smocks of their homeland, crowded around him, shrieking at each other, at the loafers and the officials, terrified by the oppressive skies and the gloomy darkness of the archway.

Another boat pulled in and a tall man stepped from it. He carried only a small bundle and was somewhat better dressed than those around him. He wore a long overcoat which was buttoned to the neck, a peaked Russian cap and there were high boots on his feet. Karl knew immediately that this was Kovrin. As the man moved through the crowd, making for the exit where the officials were checking the few papers the immigrants had, Karl ran up to him and tugged at his sleeve.

'Mr Kovrin?'

The man looked surprised and hesitated before answering. He had pale blue eyes and high cheekbones. There was a redness on his cheekbones which contrasted rather strangely with his pale skin. He nodded. 'Kovrin – yes.'

'I have a letter for you, sir.'

Karl drew the sodden envelope from his shirt. The ink had run, but Kovrin's name was still there in faint outline. Kovrin frowned and glanced about him before opening the envelope and reading the message inside. His lips moved slightly as he read. When he had finished, he looked down at Karl.

'Who sent you? Pesotsky?'

'A short man. He did not tell me his name.'

'You know where he lives?'

'No.'

'You know where this address is?' The Russian pointed at the letter.

'What is the address?'

Kovrin scowled at the letter and said slowly: 'Trinity Street and Falmouth Road. A doctor's surgery. Southwark, is it?'

'That's on the other side of the river,' said Karl. 'A long walk. Or you could get a cab.'

'A cab, yes. You speak English?'

'Yes, sir.'

'You will tell the driver where we wish to go?'

There were fewer of the immigrants on Irongate Stairs now. Kovrin must have realised that he was beginning to look conspicuous. He seized Karl's shoulder and guided him up to the exit, showing a piece of paper to the official there. The man seemed satisfied. There was one cab standing outside. It was old and the horse and driver seemed even older. 'There,' murmured Kovrin in Russian, 'that will do, eh?'

'It is a long way to Southwark, sir. I was not told...' Karl tried to break free of the man's grip. Kovrin hissed through his teeth and felt in the pocket of his greatcoat. He drew out half a sovereign and pushed it at Karl. 'Will that do? Will that pay for your valuable time, you urchin?'

Karl accepted the money, trying to disguise the light of elation which had fired his eyes. This was twice what the young man had offered him – and he would get that as well if he helped the Russian, Kovrin.

He shouted up to the cabby. 'Hey – this gentleman and I wish to go to Southwark. To Trinity Street. Get a move on, there!'

'Ye can pay, can ye?' said the old man, spitting. 'I've 'ad trouble wi' you lot afore.' He looked meaningfully around him at no-one. The rain fell on the sheds, on the patches of dirt, on the brick walls erected for no apparent purpose. Along the lane could just be seen the last of the immigrants, shuffling behind the carts which carried their baggage and their children. 'I'll want 'arf in advance.'

'How much?' Karl asked.

'Call it three bob – eighteenpence now – eighteenpence when we get there.'

'That's too much.'

'Take it or leave it.'

'He wants three shillings for the fare,' Karl told the Russian. 'Half now. Have you got it?'

Wearily and disdainfully Kovrin displayed a handful of change. Karl took three sixpences and gave them to the driver.

'All right – 'op in,' said the driver. He now spoke patronisingly, which was the nearest his tone could get to being actually friendly.

The hansom creaked and groaned as the cabby whipped his horse up. The springs in the seats squeaked and then the whole rickety contrivance was off, making quite rapid progress out of the dock area and heading for Tower Bridge, the nearest point of crossing into Southwark.

A boat was passing under the bridge, which was up. A line of traffic waited for it to be lowered again. While he waited Karl looked towards the West. The sky seemed lighter over that part of the city and the buildings seemed paler, purer, to him. He had only been to the West once and had seen the buildings of Parliament and Westminster Abbey in the sunshine. They were tall and spacious and he had imagined them to be the palaces of very great men. The cab jerked forward and began to move across the river, passing through a pall of smoke left behind by the funnel of the boat.

Doubtless the Russian, sitting in silence and glaring moodily out of the window, noticed no great difference between the streets on either side of the river, but Karl saw prosperity here. There were more food shops and there was more food sold in them. They went through a market where stalls sold shellfish, fried cod and potatoes, meat of almost every variety, as well as clothing, toys, vegetables, cutlery – everything one could possibly desire. With a fortune in his pocket, Karl's daydreams took a different turn as he thought of the luxuries they might buy; perhaps on Saturday after they had been to the synagogue. Certainly, they could have new coats, get their shoes repaired, buy a piece of meat, a cabbage...

The cab pulled up on the corner of Trinity Street and Falmouth Road. The cabby rapped on the roof with his whip. 'This is it.'

They pushed open the door and descended. Karl took another three sixpences from the Russian and handed them up to the driver who bit them, nodded, and was off again, disappearing into Dover Street, joining the other traffic. Karl looked at the building. There was a dirty brass plate on the wall by the door. He read: 'Seamen's Clinic.' He saw that the Russian was looking suspiciously at the plate, unable to understand the words. 'Are you a sailor?' Karl asked. 'Are you ill?'

'Be silent,' said Kovrin. 'Ring the bell. I'll wait here.' He put his hand inside his coat. 'Tell them that Kovrin is here.'

Karl went up the cracked steps and pulled the iron bell-handle. He heard a bell clang loudly. He had to wait some time before the door was opened by an old man with a long white forked beard and hooded eyes. 'What do you want, boy?' said the man in English.

Karl said, also in English: 'Kovrin is here.' He jerked a thumb at the tall Russian standing in the rain behind him.

'Now?' The old man smiled in unsuppressed delight. 'Here? Kovrin!'

Kovrin suddenly sprang up the steps, pushing Karl aside. After a perfunctory embrace, he and the old man went inside, speaking rapidly to each other in Russian. Karl followed them. He was hoping to earn another half-sovereign. He heard little of what they said, just a few words – 'St Petersburg' – 'prison' – 'commune' – 'death' – and one very potent word he had heard many times before, 'Siberia'. Had Kovrin escaped from Siberia? There were quite a few Russians who had. Karl had heard some of them talking.

In the house, he could see that it was evidently no longer a doctor's surgery. The house, in fact, seemed virtually derelict, with hardly any furniture but piles of paper all over the place. Many bundles of the same newspaper stood in one corner of the hall. Over these a mattress had been thrown and was serving someone as a bed. Most of the newspapers were in Russian, others were in English and in what Karl guessed was German. There were also handbills which echoed the headlines of the newspapers: PEASANTS REVOLT, said one. CRUEL SUPPRESSION OF DEMOCRATIC RIGHTS IN ST PETERSBURG, said another. Karl decided that these people must be political. His father had always told him to steer clear of 'politicals', they were always in trouble with the police. Perhaps he should leave?

But then the old man turned to him and smiled kindly. 'You look hungry. Will you eat with us?'

It would be foolish to turn down a free meal. Karl nodded.

They entered a big room warmed by a central stove. From the way in which the room was laid out, Karl guessed that this had been the doctor's waiting room. But now it, too, stored bales of paper. He could smell soup. It made his mouth water. At the same time there came a peculiar sound from below his feet. Growling, thumping, clanking: it was as if some awful monster were chained in the cellar, trying to escape. The room shook. The old man led Karl and Kovrin into what had once been the main surgery. There were still glass instrument-cases along the walls. Over in one corner they had installed a big, black cooking range and at this stood a woman, stirring an iron pot. The woman was quite pretty, but she looked scarcely less tired than Karl's mother. She ladled thick soup into an earthenware bowl. Karl's stomach rumbled. The woman smiled shyly at Kovrin whom she plainly did not know, but had been expecting. 'Who is the boy?' she asked.

'Karl,' said Karl. He bowed.

'Not Karl Marx, perhaps?' laughed the old man, nudging Karl on the shoulder. But Karl did not recognise the name. 'Karl Glogauer,' he said.

The old man explained to the woman: 'He's Kovrin's guide. Pesotsky sent him. Pesotsky couldn't come himself because he's being watched. To meet Kovrin would have been to betray him to our friends... Give the boy some soup, Tanya.' He took hold of Kovrin's arm. 'Now, Andrey Vassilitch, tell me everything that happened in Petersburg. Your poor brother I have already heard about.'

The rumbling from below grew louder. It was like an earthquake. Karl ate the tasty soup, sitting hunched over his bowl at the far end of the long bench. The soup had meat in it and several kinds of vegetables. At the other end of the bench Kovrin and the old man talked quietly together, hardly aware of their own bowls. Because of the noise from the cellar, Karl caught little of what they said, but they seemed to be speaking much of killing and torture and exile. He wondered why nobody else seemed to notice the noise.

The woman called Tanya offered him more soup. He wanted

to take more, but he was already feeling very strange. The rich food was hard to hold down. He felt that he might vomit at any moment. But he persisted in keeping it in his stomach. It would mean he would not need to eat tonight.

He summoned the courage to ask her what the noise was. 'Are we over an underground railway?'

She smiled. 'It is just the printing press.' She indicated a pile of leaflets on the bench. 'We tell the English people what it is like in our country – how we are ground under by the aristocrats and the middle classes.'

'They want to know?' Karl asked the question cynically. His own experience had given him the answer.

Again she smiled. 'Not many. The other papers are for our countrymen. They give news of what is going on in Russia and in Poland and elsewhere. Some of the papers go back to those countries...'

The old man looked up, putting a finger to his lips. He shook his head at Tanya and winked at Karl. 'What you don't hear won't harm you, young one.'

'My father was a printer in Poland,' Karl said. 'Perhaps you have work for him. He speaks Russian, Polish and Yiddish. He is an educated man.'

'There's little money in our work,' said Tanya. 'Is your father for the cause?'

'I don't think so,' said Karl. 'Is that necessary?'

'Yes,' said Kovrin suddenly. His red cheekbones burned a little more hotly. 'You must stop asking questions, boy. Wait a while longer. I think I will need to see Pesotsky.'

Karl didn't tell Kovrin that he didn't know where to find Pesotsky, because he might get another sum of money for taking Kovrin back to Whitechapel. Perhaps that would do. Also, if he could introduce his father to one of these people, they might decide to give him a job anyway. Then the family would be respectable again. He looked down at his clothes and felt miserable. They had stopped steaming and were now almost dry.

An hour later the noise from below stopped. Karl hardly noticed, for he was almost asleep with his head on his arms on the table. Someone seemed to be reciting a list to what had been the rhythm of the printing press.

'Elizelina Kralchenskaya – prison. Vera Ivanovna – Siberia. Dmitry Konstantinovitch – dead. Yegor Semyonitch – dead. Dukmasovs – all three dead. The Lebezyatnikovna sisters – five years prison. Klinevich, dead. Kudeyarov, dead. Nikolayevich, dead. Pervoyedov, dead. Petrovich, dead. And I heard they found Tarasevich in London and killed him.'

'That's so. A bomb. Every bomb they use on us confirms the police in their view. We're always blowing ourselves up with our bombs, aren't we?' The old man laughed. 'They've been after this place for months. One day a bomb will go off and the newspapers will report the accident – another bunch of Nihilists destroy themselves. It is easier to think that. What about Cherpanski? I heard he was in Germany...'

'They rooted him out. He fled. I thought he was in England. His wife and children are said to be here.'

'That's so.'

Karl fell asleep. He dreamed of respectability. He and his father and mother were living in the Houses of Parliament. But for some reason they were still sewing coats for Mr Armfelt.

Kovrin was shaking him. 'Wake up, boy. You've got to take me to Pesotsky now.'

'How much?' Karl said blearily.

Kovrin smiled bitterly. 'You're learning a good lesson, aren't you?' He put another half-sovereign on the table. Karl picked it up. 'You people...' Kovrin began, but then he shrugged and turned to the old man. 'Can we get a cab?'

'Not much chance. You'd best walk, anyway. It will be a degree safer.'

Karl pulled his blanket round him and stood up. He was reluctant to leave the warmth of the room but at the same time he was anxious to show his parents the wealth he had earned for them. His legs were stiff as he walked from the room and went to stand by the front door while Kovrin exchanged a few last words with the old man.

Kovrin opened the door. The rain had stopped and the night was very still. It must be very late, thought Karl.

The door closed behind them. Karl shivered. He was not sure where they were, but he had a general idea of the direction of the river. Once there he could find a bridge and he would know where he was. He hoped Kovrin would not be too angry when he discovered that Karl could not lead him directly to Pesotsky. They began to walk through the cold, deserted streets, some of which were dimly lit by gas-lamps. A few cats screeched, a few dogs barked and a few voices raised in anger came from the mean houses by which they passed. Once or twice a cab clattered into sight and they tried to hail it, but it was engaged or refused to stop for them.

Karl was surprised at how easily he found London Bridge. Once across the sullen blackness of the Thames he got his bearings and began to walk more confidently, Kovrin walking silently beside him.

In another half an hour they had reached Aldgate, brightened by the flaring lamps of the coffee stall which stood open all night, catering to the drunkards reluctant to go home, to the homeless, to the shift workers and even to some gentlemen who had finished sampling the low-life of Stepney and Whitechapel and were waiting until they could find a cab. There were a few women there, too – haggard, sickly. In the glare of the stall, their garishly painted faces reminded Karl of the ikons he had seen in the rooms of the Russians who lived on the same floor as his family. Even their soiled silks and their faded velvets had some of the quality of the clothes the people wore in the ikons. Two of the women jeered at Karl and Kovrin as they passed through the pool of light and entered the gash of blackness which was the opening to the warren of alleys where Karl lived.

Karl was anxious to get home now. He knew he had been away much longer than he had expected. He did not wish to give his parents concern.

He passed the dark and silent pub, Kovrin stepping cautiously behind him. He came to the door of the house. His parents might be sleeping now or they might still be working. They shared a room above the workroom.

Kovrin whispered: 'Is this Pesotsky's? You can go now.'

'This is where I live. Pesotsky said he would meet me here,' Karl told him at last. He felt relieved now that this confession was off his chest. 'He owes me five shillings, you see. He said he would come here and pay it. Perhaps he is waiting for us inside.'

Kovrin cursed and shoved Karl into the unlit doorway. Karl winced in pain as the Russian's hand squeezed his shoulder high up, near the neck. 'It will be all right,' he said. 'Pesotsky will come. It will be all right.'

Kovrin's grip relaxed and he gave a huge sigh, putting his hand to his nose and rubbing it, hissing a tune through his teeth as he considered what Karl had told him. Karl pressed the latch of the door and they entered a narrow passage. The passage was absolutely dark.

'Have you a match?' Karl asked Kovrin.

Kovrin struck a match. Karl found the stump of candle and held it out for Kovrin to light. The Russian just managed to light the wick before the match burned his fingers. Karl saw that Kovrin had a gun in his other hand. It was a peculiar gun with an oblong metal box coming down in front of the trigger. Karl had never seen a picture of a gun like it. He wondered if Kovrin had made it himself.

'Now where?' Kovrin said. He displayed the gun in the light of the guttering candle. 'If I think you've led me into a trap...'

'Pesotsky will come,' said Karl. 'It is not a trap. He said he would meet me here.' Karl pointed up the uncarpeted stairway. 'He may be there. Shall we see?'

Kovrin considered this and then shook his head. 'You go. See if he is there and if he is bring him down to me. I'll wait.'

Karl left the candle with Kovrin and began to grope his way up the two flights to the landing off which was the workroom. He had seen no lights at the window, but that was to be expected. Mr Armfelt knew the law and protected himself against it. Few factory inspectors visited this part of Whitechapel, but there was no point in inviting their attention. If they closed his business, where else would the people find work? Karl saw a faint light under the door. He opened it. The gas-jet was turned, if anything, a trifle lower. At the table sat the women and the children and the men, bent over their sewing. Karl's father looked up as Karl came in. His eyes were red and bleary. He could hardly see and his hands shook. It was plain that he had been waiting up for Karl. Karl saw that his mother was lying in the corner. She was snoring.

'Karl!' His father stood up, swaying. 'What happened to you?'

'It took longer than I expected, Father. I have got a lot of money and there is more to come. And there is a man I met who might give you a job as a printer.'

'A printer?' Karl's father rubbed his eyes and sat down on his chair again. It seemed he was finding it difficult to understand what Karl was saying. 'Printer? Your mother was in despair. She wanted to ask the police to find you. She thought – an accident.'

'I have eaten well, Father, and I have earned a lot of money.' Karl reached into his pocket. 'The Russian gave it to me. He is very rich.'

'Rich? You have eaten? Good. Well, you can tell me when we wake up. Go up now. I will follow with your mother.'

Karl realised that his father was too tired to hear him properly. Karl had seen his father like this before.

'You go, Father,' he said. 'I have slept, too. And I have some more business to do before I sleep again. That young man who came today. Has he returned?'

'The one who gave you the job?' His father screwed his eyes up and rubbed them. 'Yes, he came back about four or five hours ago, asking if *you* had returned.'

'He had come to pay me my money,' said Karl. 'Did he say he would be back?'

'I think he did. He seemed agitated. What is going on, Karl?'

'Nothing, Father.' Karl remembered the gun in Kovrin's hand. 'Nothing which concerns us. When Pesotsky comes back it will all be finished. They will go away.'

Karl's father knelt beside his mother, trying to wake her. But she would not wake up. Karl's father lay down beside his mother and was asleep. Karl smiled down at them. When they woke they would be very pleased to see the twenty-five shillings he would, by that time, have earned. And yet something marred his feeling of contentment. He frowned, realising that it was the gun he had seen. He hoped Pesotsky would return soon and that he and Kovrin would go away for good. He could not send Kovrin off somewhere, because then Pesotsky would not pay him the five shillings. He had to wait.

He saw that a few of the others at the table were staring at him almost resentfully. Perhaps they were jealous of his good fortune. He stared back and they resumed their concentration on their work. He felt at that point what it must be like to be Mr Armfelt. Mr Armfelt was scarcely any richer than the people he employed, but he had power. Karl saw that power was almost as good as money. And a little money gave one a great deal of power. He stared in contempt around the room, at the mean-faced people, at his sprawled, snoring parents. He smiled.

Kovrin came into the room. The hand which had held the gun was now buried in his greatcoat pocket. His face seemed paler than ever, his red cheekbones even more pronounced. 'Is Pesotsky here?'

'He is coming.' Karl indicated his sleeping father. 'My father said so.'

'When?'

Karl became amused by Kovrin's anxiety. 'Soon,' he said.

The people at the table were all looking up again. One young woman said: 'We are trying to work here. Go somewhere else to talk.'

Karl laughed. The laughter was high-pitched and unpleasant. Even he was shocked by it. 'We will not be here much longer,' he said. 'Get on with your work, then.'

The young woman grumbled but resumed her sewing.

Kovrin looked at them all in disgust. 'You fools,' he said, 'you will always be like this unless you do something about it. You are all victims.'

The young woman's father, who sat beside her, stitching the seam of a pair of trousers, raised his head and there was an unexpected gleam of irony in his eyes. 'We are all victims.'

Kovrin glanced away. 'That's what I said.' He was disconcerted. He stepped to the door. 'I'll wait on the landing,' he told Karl.

Karl joined him on the landing. High above, a little light filtered through a patched fanlight. Most of the glass had been replaced with slats of wood. From the room behind them the small sounds of sewing continued, like the noises made by rats as they searched the tenements for food.

Karl smiled at Kovrin and said familiarly: 'He's mad, that old man. I think he meant you were a victim. But you are rich, aren't you, Mr Kovrin?'

Kovrin ignored him.

Karl went and sat on the top stair. He hardly felt the cold at all. Tomorrow he would have a new coat.

He heard the street door open below. He looked up at Kovrin, who had also heard it. Karl nodded. It could only be Pesotsky. Kovrin pushed past Karl and swiftly descended the stairs. Karl followed.

But when they reached the passage, the candle was still flickering and it was plain that no-one was there. Kovrin frowned. His hand remained in the pocket of his coat. He peered into the back of the passage, behind the stairs. 'Pesotsky?'

There was no reply.

And then the door was flung open suddenly and Pesotsky stood framed in it. He was hatless, panting, wild-eyed. 'Christ! Is that Kovrin?' he gasped.

Kovrin said quietly. 'Kovrin here.'

'Now,' said Karl. 'My five shillings, Mr Pesotsky.'

The young man ignored the outstretched hand as he spoke rapidly to Kovrin. 'All the plan's gone wrong. You shouldn't have come here...'

'I had to. Uncle Theodore said you knew where Cherpanski was hiding. Without Cherpanski, there is no point in –' Kovrin broke off as Pesotsky silenced him.

'They have been following me for days, our friends. They don't know about Cherpanski, but they do know about Theodore's damned press. It's that they want to destroy. But I am their only link. That's why I've been staying away. I heard you'd been at the press and had left for Whitechapel. I was followed, but I think I shook them off. We'd better leave at once.'

'My five shillings, sir,' said Karl. 'You promised.'

Uncomprehending, Pesotsky stared at Karl for a long moment, then he said to Kovrin: 'Cherpanski's in the country. He's staying with some English comrades. Yorkshire, I think. You can get the train. You'll be safe enough once you're out of London. It's the presses they're chiefly after. They don't care what we do here as long as none of our stuff gets back into Russia. Now, you'll want Kings Cross Station...'

The door opened again and two men stood there, one behind the other. Both were fat. Both wore black overcoats with astrakhan collars and had bowler hats on their heads. They looked like successful businessmen. The leader smiled.

'Here at last,' he said in Russian. Karl saw that his companion carried a hatbox under his arm. It was incongruous; it was sinister. Karl began to retreat up the stairs.

'Stop him!' called the newcomer. From the shadows of the next landing stepped two men. They had revolvers. Karl stopped halfway up the stairs. Here was an explanation for the sound of the door opening which had brought them down.

'This is good cover, Comrade Pesotsky,' said the leader. 'Is that your name, these days?'

Pesotsky shrugged. He looked completely dejected. Karl wondered who the well-dressed Russians could be. They acted like policemen, but the British police didn't employ foreigners, he knew that much.

Kovrin laughed. 'It's little Captain Minsky, isn't it? Or have you changed your name, too?'

Minsky pursed his lips and came a few paces into the passage. It was obvious that he was puzzled by Kovrin's recognition. He peered hard at Kovrin's face.

'I don't know you.'

'No,' said Kovrin quietly. 'Why have they transferred you to the foreign branch? Were your barbarities too terrible even for St Petersburg?'

Minsky smiled, as if complimented. 'There is so little work for me in Petersburg these days,' he said. 'That is always the snag for a policeman. If he is a success, he faces unemployment.'

'Vampire!' hissed Pesotsky. 'Aren't you satisfied yet? Must you drink the last drop of blood?'

'It is a feature of your kind, Pesotsky,' said Minsky patiently, 'that everything must be coloured in the most melodramatic terms. It is your basic weakness, if I might offer advice. You are failed poets, the lot of you. That is the worst sort of person to choose a career in politics.'

Pesotsky said sulkily: 'Well, *you've* failed this time, anyway. This isn't the printing press. It's a sweatshop.'

'I complimented you once on your excellent cover,' said Minsky. 'Do you want another compliment?'

Pesotsky shrugged. 'Good luck in your search, then.'

'We haven't time for a thorough search,' Minsky told him. He signed to the man with the hatbox. 'We, too, have our difficulties. Problems of diplomacy and so on.' He took a watch from within his coat. 'But we have a good five minutes, I think.'

Karl was almost enjoying himself. Captain Minsky really did believe that the printing press was hidden here.

'Shall we begin upstairs?' Minsky said. 'I understand that's where you were originally.'

'How could a press be upstairs,' Pesotsky said. 'These rotten boards wouldn't stand the weight.'

'The last press was very neatly distributed through several rooms,' Minsky told him. 'Lead on, please.'

They ascended the stairs to the first landing. Karl guessed that the occupants of these rooms were probably awake and listening behind their doors. He once again experienced a thrill of superiority. One of the men who had been on the landing shook his head and pointed up the next flight of stairs.

The seven of them went up slowly. Captain Minsky had his revolver in his gloved hand. His three men also carried their revolvers, trained on the wretched Pesotsky and the glowering Kovrin. Karl led the way. 'This is where my father and mother work,' he said. 'It is not a printer's.'

'They are disgusting,' said Minsky to his lieutenant with the hatbox. 'They are so swift to employ children for their degraded work. There's a light behind that door. Open it up, boy.'

Karl opened the door of the workroom, fighting to hide his grin. His mother and father were still asleep. The young woman who had complained before looked up and glared at him. Then all seven had pushed into the room.

Minsky said: 'Oh, you do look innocent. But I know what you're really up to here. Where's the press?'

Now everyone put down their work and looked at him in astonishment as he kicked at the wall in which the fireplace was set. It rang hollow, but that was because it was so thin. There was an identical room on the other side. But it satisfied Minsky. 'Put that in here,' he told the man with the hatbox. 'We must be leaving.'

'Have you found the press, then?' Karl grinned openly.

Minsky struck him across the mouth with the barrel of his revolver. Karl moaned as blood filled his right cheek. He fell back over the sleeping bodies of his parents. They stirred.

Kovrin had drawn his gun. He waved it to cover all four members of the Secret Police. 'Drop your weapons,' he shouted. 'You – pick that hatbox up again.'

The man glanced uncertainly at Minsky. 'It's already triggered. We have a few moments.'

Karl realised there was a bomb in the box. He tried to wake his father to tell him. Now the people who had been working were standing up. There was a noisy outcry. Children were weeping, women shrieking, men shouting.

Kovrin shot Minsky.

One of Minsky's men shot Kovrin. Kovrin fell back through the door and Karl heard him fall to the landing outside. Pesotsky flung himself at the man who had shot Kovrin. Another gun went off and Pesotsky fell to the floor, his fists clenched, his stomach pulsing out blood.

Karl's father woke up. His eyes widened at what they saw. He clutched Karl to him. Karl's mother woke up. She whimpered. Karl saw that Minsky was dead. The other three men hurried from the room and began to run downstairs.

An explosion filled the room.

Karl was protected by his parents' bodies, but he felt them shudder and move as the explosion hit them. He saw a little boy strike the far wall. He saw the window shatter. He saw the door collapse, driven out into the darkness of the stairwell. He saw fire send tendrils in all directions and then withdraw them. The workbench had come to rest against the opposite wall. It was black and broken. The wall was naked brick and the brick was also black. Something was roaring. His vision was wiped out and he saw only whiteness.

He closed his eyes and opened them again. His eyes stung but he could see dimly, even though the gas-jet had been blown out. Throughout the room there was a terrible silence for a second or two. Then they began to groan.

Soon the room was filled with their groaning. Karl saw that the floor sloped where it had not sloped before. He saw that part of the outer wall had split. Through this great crack came moonlight. Black things shifted about on the floor.

Now the entire street outside was alive with noise. Voices came from below and from above. He heard feet on the stairs. Someone shone a lamp onto the scene and then retreated with a gasp. Karl stood up. He was unhurt, although his skin was stinging and he had some bruises. He saw that his father had no right hand any more and that blood was oozing from the stump. He put his head to his father's chest. He was still breathing. His mother held her face. She told Karl that she was blind.

Karl went out onto the landing and saw the crowd on both the upper and the lower stairs. The man with the lamp was Mr Armfelt. He was in his nightshirt. He looked unwell and was staring at the figure who leaned on the wall on the opposite side of the door. It was Kovrin. He was soaked in blood, but he was breathing and the strange gun was still in his right hand. Karl hated Kovrin, whom he saw as the chief agent of this disaster. He went and looked up into the tall Russian's eyes. He took the pistol from Kovrin's limp hand. As if the pistol had been supporting him, Kovrin crashed to the floor as soon as it was removed from his grasp. Karl looked down at him. Kovrin was dead. None of the watchers spoke. They all looked on as if they were the audience at some particularly terrifying melodrama.

Karl took the lamp from Mr Armfelt and returned to the room.

Many of the occupants were dead. Karl saw that the young woman was dead, her body all broken and tangled up with that of her father, the man who had said 'We are all victims'. Karl sniffed. Minsky's body had been blown under the shattered bench, but Pesotsky had been quite close to the recess where Karl and his parents had lain. Although wounded, he was alive. He was chuckling. With every spasm, more blood gushed from his mouth. He said thickly to Karl: 'Thanks – thanks.' He waited for the blood to subside. 'They've blown up the wrong place, thanks to you. What luck!'

Karl studied the gun he had taken from Kovrin. He assumed that it was basically the same as a revolver and contained at least another five bullets. He held it in both hands and, with both his index fingers on the trigger, squeezed. The gun went off with a bang and a flash and Karl's knuckles were driven back into his face, cutting his lip again. He lowered the gun and picked up the lamp which he had placed on the floor. He advanced to Pesotsky and held the lamp over the body. The bullet had driven through one of Pesotsky's eyes and Pesotsky was dead. Karl searched through Pesotsky's blood-soaked clothes and found two shillings and some coppers. He counted it. Three shillings and eightpence in all. Pesotsky had lied to him. Pesotsky had not possessed five shillings. He spat on Pesotsky's face.

At the sound of the shot, the people on the stairs had withdrawn a few paces. Only Mr Armfelt remained where he was. He was talking rapidly to himself in a language Karl did not recognise. Karl tucked the gun into the waistband of his trousers and turned Kovrin's corpse over. In the pockets of the greatcoat he found about ten pounds in gold. In an inner pocket he found some documents, which he discarded, and about fifty pounds in paper money. Carrying the lamp high he shone it on the blind face of his mother and on the pain-racked face of his father. His father was awake and saying something about a doctor.

Karl nodded. It was sensible that they should get a doctor as soon as possible. They could afford one now. He held out the money so that his father could see it all, the white banknotes and the bright gold. 'I can look after you both, Father. You will get better. It doesn't matter if you cannot work. We shall be respectable.'

He saw that his father could still not quite understand. With a shake of his head, Karl crouched down and put a kindly hand on his father's shoulder. He spoke clearly and gently, as one might address a very young child who had failed to gather it was about to receive a birthday present and was not showing proper enthusiasm.

'We can go to *America*, Father.'

He inspected the wrist from which most of the hand had been blown. With some of the rags, he bandaged it, stopping the worst of the bleeding.

And then the sobs began to come up from his stomach. He did not know why he was crying, but he could not control himself. The sobs made him helpless. His body was shaken by them and the noise he made was not very loud but it was the worst noise any of the listeners had heard that night. Even Mr Armfelt, absorbed in his hysterical calculations, was dimly aware of the noise and he became, if anything, even more depressed.

— *What do you think it can be? Something you ate? Do you want some aspirin?*

— *Aspirin won't do anything for me. I don't know what causes a migraine. A combination of things, maybe.*

MICHAEL MOORCOCK

— *Or merely a useful evasion, Karl. Like some forms of gout or consumption. One of those subtle diseases whose symptoms can only be transmitted by word of mouth.*

— *Thanks for your sympathy. Can I sleep now?*

— *What a time to get a headache. And you were just beginning to enjoy yourself, too.*

What Would You Do? (6)

You live in a city.

A disaster has resulted in the collapse of society as you know it.

Public amenities, such as gas, electricity, telephones and postal services no longer exist. There is no piped water. Rats and other vermin proliferate in the piles of garbage which, uncollected, contaminate the city. Disease is rife. You have heard that things are equally bad in the country. There, strangers are attacked and killed if they try to settle. In some ways it is more dangerous in the country than it is in the city where gangs of predatory men and women roam the streets.

You are used to city life. You have a house, a car and you have obtained several guns from a gunshop you broke into. You raid shops and garages for fuel and food. You have a water purifier and a camp-stove. You have a wife and three young children.

Do you think it would be better to go out into the country and take your chances in the wild, or would you try to work out a way of living and protecting yourself and your family in a city with which you are familiar?

Chapter Seven

Calcutta Flies:
1911: Doing Business

Ten years ago, an observer going to India with a fresh mind for
its problems saw two great engines at work. One was the British Government, ruling the country according to its own
canons of what would be best for the people. Its system of
education in Western science and thought was shaking the old
beliefs and social traditions. By securing justice and enforcing
peace, it had set men's minds free to speculate and criticise.
For India's future it had no definite plan; its ambitions, to all
outward seeming, were confined to a steady growth of administrative efficiency. The other engine was the awakening of a
national consciousness. It was feeding on the Western ideas
provided by the British Government and the noble army of
Christian missionaries, adapting them to its own purposes, and
building on them a rising demand that the people should be
given a larger share in their own destiny. Our observer could
not help being impressed by how far the two engines were
from working in parallel. There was friction and a general feeling of unsettlement. In 1908 a cautious measure of political
advance had been offered when Lord Minto was Viceroy and
Lord Morley was his 'opposite number' in Whitehall. It was
tainted, however, with an air of unreality which disquieted the
officials and irritated the Indian politician. The cry grew loud
for more rapid progress, 'colonial self-government' was the slogan, and the professional classes (chiefly the lawyers) with an
English education were busy in a wide-spread movement for a
change in the methods of government. As in all nationalist
movements, there was an extreme wing, which leaned to direct
action, rather than the slower constitutional modes of

agitation. In Eastern hyperbole they wrote and harangued about British tyranny and the duty of patriots to rise and become martyrs for freedom. What they thus conceived in poetic frenzy was translated into sinister prose by others. Anarchists are never lacking in any crowded population, especially when hunger is the bedfellow of so many. In India the section of violence had got into touch with revolutionary camps in Europe and the United States, and sporadic outbursts from 1907 onwards, including attempts on the life of two Viceroys and a Lieutenant-Governor, indicated the existence of subterranean conspiracy. Public opinion condemned it, but did little to check vehemence of language which continued to inflame weak minds. The whole position was one of anxiety. Would it ever be possible to reconcile the two forces which were rapidly moving towards conflict?

– The Rt Hon. Lord Meston, KCSI, LLD,
The Dominions and Dependencies of the Empire: India,
Collins, 1924

— *There! That's more like it, Karl! Ah! Better! Better! Now you're moving!*

Karl bucks and bounces, gasps and groans. His muscles ache, but he forces his body to make dramatic responses to every tiny stimulus. The black man cheers him on, yelling with delight.

— *Ah! sings Karl.* — *Oh!*

Ah! Oh!

Up and down and from side to side, whinnying like a proud stallion, he carries the black man round the hotel room on his back. His back is wet, but not from sperm or sweat, for, in spite of all his shouts of pleasure, the black man has not had an orgasm as far as Karl can tell. His back is wet with just a drop or two of blood.

— *Now you're moving! Now you're moving! shouts the black man again.* — *Hurrah!*

Karl is twelve. An orphan. Half-German, half-Indian. In Calcutta. In 1911.

— Faster! Faster! The black man has produced a riding crop and with it he flicks Karl's bouncing buttocks. — Faster!

When Karl was fifteen, he left home to become a great painter. He returned home three months later. He had been turned down by the art school. His mother had been very sympathetic. She could afford to be.

— Faster! That's it! You're learning, Karl!

Karl is twelve. The red sun rises over red ships. Calcutta...

The riding crop cracks harder and Karl gallops on.

KARL WAS TWELVE. His mother was dead. His father was dead. His two sisters were sixteen and seventeen and he did not often see them. He embarrassed them. Karl was in business for himself and, all things considered, he was doing pretty well.

He worked the docks along the Hooghly. He described himself as an agent. If something was wanted by the sailors or the passengers off the ships, he would either get it for them or take them somewhere where they might obtain it. He did better than the other boys in the same trade, for he was quite light-skinned and he wore a European suit. He spoke English and German perfectly and was fairly fluent in most other languages, including a fair number of Indian dialects. Because he knew when to be honest and who to bribe, he was popular both with customers and suppliers, and people coming from the big red steamers would ask after him when they landed, having been recommended to them by friends. Because he was well-mannered and discreet, he was tolerated by most of the Indian and British policemen on the docks (and he had done several of them good turns in his time, for he knew the importance of keeping in with the authorities). Karl was rumoured to be a millionaire (in rupees), but, because of his overheads, he was, in fact, worth only about a thousand rupees, which he banked with his friend in Barrackpore, some fifteen miles away, because it was safer. He was content with his relatively small profit and had worked out that by the time he was twenty he would be quite rich enough to set himself up in a respectable business of some kind in central Calcutta.

Karl's only concession to his Indian mother was his turban. His turban was virtually his trademark and he was recognised by it throughout Calcutta. It was a black turban, of gleaming silk. Its single decoration was a small pin – an enamelled pin he had been given by a rather eccentric English lady who had sought his services a year or two back. The pin was white, gold and red and showed a crown with a scroll over it. On the scroll was written *Edward VII*. It had been made, the lady had told Karl, to commemorate the Coronation. The pin was therefore quite old and might be valuable. Karl felt it a fitting decoration for his black silk turban.

Earlier that morning, Karl had been contacted by a young sailor who had offered to buy all the hemp Karl could procure by that afternoon. He had offered a reasonable price – though not an especially good one – and Karl had agreed. He knew that the young sailor had a customer in one of the European ports and that once his hemp arrived in Europe it would be several times more valuable than it was in Calcutta. But Karl was not worried. He would make his profit and it would be satisfactory. Everyone would be happy. The young sailor was English, but he was working on a French boat, the *Juliette* currently taking on grain and indigo down at Kalna. The young sailor, whose name was Marsden, had come up on one of the river-steamers.

Through the confusion of the dock strode Karl, walking as quickly as was sensible in the midday heat, dodging bicycles and donkeys and carts and men who were scarcely visible for the huge bundles on their backs. Karl was proud of his city, enjoying the profusion of different racial types, the many contrasts and paradoxes of Calcutta. When he was cursed, as he often was, he would curse back in the same language. When he was greeted by acquaintances he would give a little bow and salute them with cheeky condescension, apeing the manner of the Lieutenant-Governor on one of his ceremonial processions through the city.

Karl swaggered a little as he crossed Kidderpore Bridge and walked across the Maidan. He imagined that London must look very much like this and had heard the Maidan compared to Hyde Park, although the Maidan was much bigger. The trees were mainly of the English variety and reminded Karl of the pictures he had seen of the English countryside. He passed close to the cathedral, with its Gothic spire emerging from a mass of greenery and a large sheet of water in the foreground. One of his customers, whom he had taken on a tour of the city the year before, had said it recalled exactly the view over Bayswater from the bridge spanning the Serpentine. One day Karl would visit London and see for himself.

He swaggered a little as he crossed the Maidan. He always felt more relaxed and at home in the better part of town. Near Government House, he hailed a rickshaw with a lordly wave and told the boy to take him to the junction of Armenian Street and Bhubab Road. It was really not much further to walk, but he felt in an expansive mood. He leaned back in his seat and breathed the spiced air of the city. He had told Marsden, the sailor, that he could get him a hundred pounds' worth of hemp if he wanted it. Marsden had agreed to bring a hundred pounds to Dalhousie Square that afternoon. It would be one of the largest single business deals Karl had pulled off. He hoped that his friend in Armenian Street would be able to supply him with all the hemp he needed.

His friend worked for one of the big shipping firms in Armenian Street. This friend was a messenger and made a number of trips in and out of Calcutta during the week. Almost every one of these trips yielded a certain supply of hemp which Karl's friend then stored in a safe place until contacted by Karl.

The rickshaw stopped at the corner of Bhubab Road and Karl descended to the pavement, giving the rickshaw boy – a man of about fifty – a generous tip.

The bustle in this part of town was of a different quality to that nearer the docks. It was more assured, more muted. People didn't push so much, or bellow at one, or shout obscene insults. And here, too, there were fewer people sharing considerably more money. Karl was considering Armenian Street as the site for his business when he opened it. It would probably be an import–export business of some kind. He began to walk, sighing with pleasure at the thought of his future. The bright sunshine and the blue sky served as a perfect background to the solid, imposing Victorian buildings, making them all the more imposing. Karl strolled in their shade, reading off their dignified signs as he passed. The signs were beautifully painted in black script, or Gothic gold or tasteful silver. There was nothing vulgar here.

Karl entered the offices of a well-known shipping company and asked for his friend.

When he had completed his business in Armenian Street, Karl took out his steel railway watch and saw he had plenty of time to lunch before meeting the young sailor. Dalhousie Square was only a short distance away. Karl had, in fact, decided on one of his regular meeting-places in St Andrew's Church – the Red Church as the Indians called it – which would be deserted that afternoon. He had chosen a spot not too far from Armenian Street because it was unwise to carry a full case of hemp around for too long. There was always the risk of an officious policeman deciding to find out what was in his case. On the other hand, St Andrew's was almost next door to the police headquarters and therefore one of the least likely places, so Karl hoped the police would reason, to choose for an illegal transaction.

Karl lunched at the small hotel called the Imperial Indian Hotel in Cotton Street. It was run by a Bengali friend of his and served the most delicious curries in Calcutta. Karl had brought many a customer here and his enthusiastic recommendations were always genuine. The customers, too, were well-pleased. In return for this service, Karl could eat at the Imperial Indian Hotel whenever he wished.

He finished his lunch and passed the time of day with the manager of the restaurant before leaving. It was nearly three o'clock. Karl had arranged to meet Marsden at seven minutes past three. Karl always arranged to meet people at odd minutes past the hour. It was one of his superstitions.

The curry had settled well on his stomach and he moved unhurriedly through the city of his birth. His suit was as clean and as well-pressed as ever. His shirt was white and crisp and his black silk turban gleamed on his head like a fat sleek cat. In fact Karl himself was almost purring. In a short time he would have a hundred pounds in his pocket. Fifty of that, of course, would go immediately to his friend in Armenian Street. Then there were a few other expenses, such as the one he had just incurred during his chat with the manager of the hotel restaurant, but there would at the end of the day be about forty pounds to bank with his friend in Barrackpore. A worthwhile sum. His own business was not too far away now.

Dalhousie Square was one of Karl's favourite spots in the city. He would often come here simply for pleasure but when he could he mixed business with pleasure and became an unofficial tourist guide. As this was one of the oldest parts of Calcutta, he could show people everything they expected. The original Fort William had once stood here and part of it was now the Customs House. Karl particularly enjoyed pointing out to the European ladies where the guardroom of the Fort had been. This guardroom had, in 1756, become the infamous Black Hole. Karl could describe the sufferings of the people more than adequately. He had had the satisfaction, more than once, of seeing sensitive English ladies faint away during his descriptions.

St Andrew's Scottish Presbyterian Church stood in its own wooded grounds in which there were two large artificial ponds (in common with the Anglo-Indians, Karl called them 'tanks') and the one drawback of the place was that it was infested with mosquitoes virtually all the year round. As Karl walked up the paved path between the trees, he saw a great cloud of flies swarming in the bars of light between the Graecian columns of the portico. The clock on the 'Lal Girja's' tower stood at six minutes past three.

Karl opened the iron gate in the fence and went up the steps, swatting at mosquitoes as he did so. He killed them in a rather chiding, friendly way.

He entered the relatively cool and almost deserted church. There was no service today and the only other occupant, standing awkwardly in the aisle between the pews of plain, polished wood, was the young sailor, Marsden. His face was red and sticky with sweat. He was wearing a pair of cream-coloured shorts, and a somewhat dirty white shirt. His legs and his arms were bare and the mosquitoes were delighted.

Marsden plainly had not wanted to make a noise in the church for fear of attracting someone's attention, so he had not slapped at the mosquitoes which covered his face, arms, hands and legs. Instead he was vainly trying to brush them off him. They would fly up in a cloud and settle immediately, continuing their feast.

'Good afternoon, Mr Marsden, sir,' said Karl, displaying the carpet bag containing the drug. 'One hundred pounds' worth, as promised. Have you the money?'

'I'm glad to see you,' said Marsden. 'I'm being eaten alive in here. What a place to choose. Is it always like this?'

'Usually, I'm afraid to say.' Karl tried to sound completely English, but to his annoyance he could still detect a slight lilt in his voice. The lilt, he knew, betrayed him.

The sailor held out his hand for the bag. Karl saw that red lumps were rising on virtually every spot of the man's bare skin. 'Come on, then, old son,' said Marsden, 'let's see if it's the genuine article.'

Karl smiled ingratiatingly. 'It is one hundred per cent perfect stuff, Mr Marsden.' He put the bag at his feet and spread his hands. 'Can I say the same about your cash, sir?'

'Naturally you can. Of course you can. Don't say you don't trust me, you little baboo! It's me should be worrying.'

'Then let me see the money, sir,' Karl said reasonably. 'I am sure you are an honourable man, but...'

'You're damned right I am! I won't have a bloody darkie...' Marsden looked round nervously, realising he had raised his voice and it was echoing through the church. He whispered: 'I'll not have a bloody darkie telling me I'm a welsher. The money's back at the ship. I'd have been a fool to come here alone with a hundred quid on me, wouldn't I?'

Karl sighed. 'So you do not have the money on your person, Mr Marsden?'

'No I don't!'

'Then I must keep the bag until you bring the money,' Karl told him. 'I am sorry. Business is business. You agreed.'

'I know what we agreed,' said Marsden defensively. 'But I've got to be certain. Show me the stuff.'

Karl shrugged and opened the bag. The aroma of hemp was unmistakeable.

Marsden leaned forward and sniffed. He nodded.

'How much money do you have with you?' said Karl. He was beginning to see that Marsden had been exaggerating when he had said he would buy as much as Karl could find.

Marsden shrugged. He put his hands in his pockets. 'I don't know. It's mainly in rupees. About four pounds ten.'

Karl sniggered. 'It is not a hundred pounds.'

'I can get it. Back at the ship.'

'The ship is nearly fifty miles away, Mr Marsden.'

'I'll give it you tomorrow.'

When Marsden jumped forward and grabbed up the bag, Karl didn't move. When Marsden pushed him aside and ran with the bag up the aisle, Karl sat down in one of the pews. If Marsden really did have four pounds ten, then at least Karl would have lost nothing on the deal. He would return the bag to his friend in Armenian Street and wait until he had a proper customer.

A short while later the young Sikh from Delhi came into the church. He was holding the bag. The Sikh had been staying at the Imperial Indian Hotel and had had trouble paying his bill. The manager of the restaurant had told Karl this and Karl had told the Sikh how he could earn the money to pay for his room. The Sikh evidently did not relish working for Karl, but he had no choice. He handed Karl the bag.

'Did he have enough money?' Karl asked.

The Sikh nodded. 'Is that all?'

'Excellent,' Karl told him. 'Where is Marsden now?'

'In the tank. He was probably drunk and fell in there. It happens to sailors, I hear, in Calcutta. He may drown. He may not.'

'Thank you,' said Karl.

He waited for the Sikh to leave and remained in the church for some minutes, watching the mosquitoes dancing in the light from the windows. He was a little disappointed, he had to admit. But sooner or later another deal would come, even if he had to work a trifle harder, and there was no doubt that his savings would increase, that his ambitions would be realised.

A priest appeared from behind the altar. He saw Karl and smiled at him. 'You're early, laddie, if you've come for the choir practice.'

— *You're learning, says the black man lasciviously.* — *You see, I said you would.*

Karl smiles up at him and stretches. — *Yes, you said I would. It's funny…*

— *You were saying about that girlfriend of yours. The black man changes the subject.* — *How she became pregnant?*

— *That's right. Before the abortion reforms. It cost me the best part of two hundred pounds. Karl smiles.* — *A lot of uniforms.*

— *But the other two were cheaper? The two before?*

— *They got those done themselves. I was always unlucky. I couldn't use those rubber things, that was the trouble. I'd just lose interest if I tried to put one on.*

— *None of your children were born?*

— *If you put it like that, no.*

— *Let the next one be born. The black man puts his hand on the muscles of Karl's upper forearm.*

Karl is astonished at this apparent expression of human feeling. — *You're against abortion, then?*

The black one rolls over and reaches for his cigarettes on the bedside table. They are Nat Sherman's Queen-Size Cigaretellos, an obscure American brand which Karl hasn't seen before. Earlier he has studied the packet with some interest. He accepts one of the slim, brown cigarettes and lights up from the tip of the black man's. He enjoys the taste.

— *You're against abortion, then? Karl repeats.*

— *I'm against the destruction of possibilities. Everything should be*

*allowed to proliferate. The interest lies in seeing which becomes domin-
ant. Which wins.*

*— Ah, says Karl, I see. You want as many pieces on the board as you
can get.*

— Why not?

What Would You Do? (7)

You are a refugee fleeing from a government which will kill you
and your family if they catch you.

You reach the railway station and in a great deal of confusion
manage to get your wife and children onto the train, telling them
to find a seat while you get the luggage on board.

After a while you manage to haul your luggage into the train as
it is leaving the station. You settle it in the corridor and go to look
for your family.

You search both ends of the train and they are not there. Someone tells you that only half the train left, that the other half is
going to another destination.

Could they have got into the other half by mistake?

What will you do?

Pull the communication cord and set off back to the station,
leaving your luggage on the train?

Wait until you reach the next station, leave your luggage there
and catch the next train back?

Hope that your family will remain calm and follow you to your
ultimate destination on the next available train?

Chapter Eight

Quiet Days in Thann:
1918: Mixed Meat

Never, probably in the history of the world, not even in the last years of the Napoleonic domination, has there taken place such a display of warlike passion as manifested itself in the most civilised countries of Europe at the beginning of August, 1914. Then was seen how frail were the commercial and political forces on which modern cosmopolitanism had fondly relied for the obliteration of national barriers. The elaborate system of European finance which, in the opinion of some, had rendered war impossible no more availed to avert the catastrophe than the Utopian aspirations of international socialism, or the links with which a common culture had bound together the more educated classes of the Continent. The world of credit set to work to adapt itself to conditions which seemed, for a moment, to threaten it with annihilation. The voices of the advocates of a world-wide fraternity and equality were drowned in a roar of hostile preparation. The great gulfs that separate Slav, Latin, Teuton, and Anglo-Saxon were revealed; and the forces which decide the destinies of the world were gauntly expressed in terms of racial antagonism.

> *History of the War, Part One,*
> published by *The Times*, 1915

— It's your turn now, says the black man. — If you like...
— I'm tired, says Karl.
— Oh, come now! Tired! Psychological tiredness, that's all! The black man pats him on the back. He gives Karl an encouraging grin, offering him the riding crop.

— *No, says Karl.* — *Please, no…*

— *Well, I offered.*

Karl is thirteen. His mother is twenty-nine. His father is dead, killed at Verdun in 1916. His mother has gone to live with her sister in a village near Thann, in Alsace…

— *Leave me alone, says Karl.*

— *Of course. I don't want to influence you.*

When Karl was thirteen he met a man who claimed to be his father. It was in a public lavatory somewhere in West London. 'I'm your dad,' the man had said. His stiff penis had been exposed. 'Are you still at school, lad?' Karl had mumbled something and run out of the lavatory. He regretted his decision later because the man could have been his father, after all.

— *Leave me in peace.*

— *You're a very moody chap, young Karl, laughs the black man.*

He brings the riding crop down with a crack on Karl's back. Karl yells. He scrambles out of the bed and begins to get dressed. — *That's it, he says.*

— *I'm sorry, says the black man.* — *Please forgive me.*

Karl is thirteen. He is now the provider for his mother and his aunt. The war continues not too far away. While it continues, Karl will survive…

— *I misinterpreted you, that's all, says the black man.* — *Please stay just a short while longer, eh?*

— *Why should I?*

But Karl is weakening again.

KARL WAS THIRTEEN. His mother was twenty-nine. His father was dead, killed in the war. His mother's sister was twenty-six, also a widow. Where they lived there were many reminders of the war. It had been fought around here for a while. Broken fences, smashed trees, craters filled with water, old trenches and ruins. Ploughmen did not like to plough the ground, for they always found at least one corpse.

Karl had found a gun. It was a good French rifle. He had found plenty of ammunition in the belt of the soldier. He had tried to get the soldier's boots, but the flesh inside them had swollen up too much. Besides, Karl was perfectly satisfied with the gun. With it, he was now able to earn a decent living. Few people in the villages around Thann could do that at present.

In a thick corduroy jacket and tweed knickerbockers secured below the knee with an English soldier's puttees, with a large German knapsack over his shoulder and the French rifle in the crook of his arm, Karl sat comfortably on a slab of masonry and smoked a cigarette, waiting.

It was close to sunrise and he had arrived at the ruined farmhouse about an hour earlier. Dawn was a yellow line on the horizon. He unpacked his German field glasses and began to scan the surrounding ground – mud, tree-stumps, ditches, trenches, craters, ruins... all were shadowy, all still. Karl was looking for movement.

He saw a dog. It was quite big, but thin. It sauntered along the edge of a ditch, wagging its feathery tail. Karl put down his field glasses and picked up his rifle. He adjusted the sliding rearsight, tucked the stock firmly into his shoulder, braced his feet on the mound of brick, took precise aim and squeezed the trigger of the rifle. The stock banged into his shoulder and the gun jumped. There was a report and smoke. Karl lowered the rifle and took out his field glasses. The dog was not quite dead. He stood up, a thumb hooked into the strap of the knapsack. By the time he reached it, the dog would be dead.

As he skinned the animal, Karl kept his eyes peeled for other quarry. It was thin on the ground, these days. But, if anyone could get it, Karl could. He sawed off the head with the bayonet he carried for the purpose. The butcher in Thann did not ask questions when he bought Karl's loads of 'mixed meat', but he did not like to be reminded too closely of the type of animal he was buying.

A little later Karl shot two rats and the cat which had been hunting them. He was amused by this exploit.

He wished he could have told someone of it. But his mother and aunt were squeamish. They preferred to believe he was hunting pigeons. Sometimes he did shoot a pigeon. He would take that home and give it to his mother to cook. 'Part of the bag,' he would say. It was just as well to keep up appearances.

By midday Karl had done well. His knapsack was so heavy that he had trouble carrying it. He lay in a trench which was overgrown with a rich variety of weeds and grasses and smelled delicious. The early-autumn day was warm and Karl had been amazed to see a pair of hares. He had killed one, but the other had fled. He was hoping it would reappear. When he had it, he would go home. He had not eaten that morning and was both tired and hungry.

The rims of the glasses were beginning to irritate his eyes when he caught a movement to the south and adjusted the focus quickly. At first he was disappointed. It wasn't the hare, only a man.

The man was running. Sometimes he fell down, but picked himself up again immediately, running on. His back was bowed and he waved his arms loosely as he ran. Karl could now see that he was in uniform. The uniform was probably grey. It was covered in mud. The man was hatless and had no weapons. Karl hadn't seen a soldier in this part of the world for well over a year. He had heard the gunfire, as had everyone else, but otherwise his particular village had seen no action for ages.

The German soldier came closer. He was unshaven. His eyes were red. He gasped as he moved. He seemed to be running away. Surely the Allies had not broken through the German line? Karl had been certain it would hold for ever. It seemed to have been holding for almost as long as he could remember. The thought unsettled him. He had been happy with the status quo and wasn't sure if he looked forward to any change.

More likely the German soldier was a deserter. A silly place to desert, round here. Still...

Karl yawned. Another quarter of an hour and he'd leave. He hung his field glasses round his neck and picked up his rifle. He sighted down the barrel, aiming at the German soldier. He pretended he was in the war and that this was an attack on his trench. He cocked the bolt of the rifle. There were thousands of them attacking now. He squeezed the trigger.

Although he was surprised when the German threw up his arms and shouted (he could hear the shout from where he lay) he did not regret his action. He raised his field glasses. The bullet had struck the soldier in the stomach. A careless shot. But then he hadn't been aiming properly. The soldier fell down in the long grass and Karl saw it waving. He frowned. The waving stopped. He wondered whether to go home or whether to cross the field and have a look at the soldier. Morally, he should look at the soldier. After all, it was the first time he had killed a human being. He shrugged and left his bag of mixed meat where it was. The soldier might have something useful on him, anyway.

With his rifle over his shoulder, he began to plod towards the spot where his man had fallen.

— *Is it morning yet? asks Karl, yawning.*
  — *No. A long time until morning, Karl.*
  — *The night seems to be lasting for ever.*
  — *Aren't you glad?*
  He feels a strong hand in his crotch. It squeezes him gently but firmly. Karl's lips part a little.
  — *Yes, says Karl, I'm glad.*

What Would You Do? (8)

You are a white man in a town where the people are predominantly black.

Because of indignities and insufficient representation of their cause, the black people, militant and angry, seize control of the town.

They are met with violence from some of the whites and they respond in turn, lynching two white officials against whom they have particular grievances.

But now the people have become a mob and are out for white blood. The mob is approaching your part of the town, smashing and burning and beating whites. Some of the whites have been beaten to death.

You cannot contact your black friends and ask for their help because you don't know exactly where they are.

Would you hide in the house and hope that the mob didn't bother you?

Would you try to take your chances on the street and hope to find a black friend who would vouch for you?

Would you go to the aid of other white people defending themselves against the mob? Would you then try to make everyone calm down?

Or would you simply help your fellow white people kill the black people attacking them?

Or would you join the black people attacking the whites and hope to win acceptance that way?

Chapter Nine

The Downline to Kiev:
1920: Shuffling Along

Official verification came to hand yesterday of the report recently published of the ex-Tsar's violent end at Ekaterinburg at the hands of his Red Guards. The message has been transmitted as follows through the wireless stations of the Russian Government:

Recently Ekaterinburg, the capital of the Red Ural, was seriously threatened by the approach of the Czecho-Slovak bands. At the same time a counter-revolutionary conspiracy was discovered, having for its object the wresting of the ex-Tsar from the hands of the Council's authority by armed force. In view of this fact the Council decided to shoot the ex-Tsar. This decision was carried out on July 16. The wife and son of Romanoff have been sent to a place of security. Documents concerning the conspiracy, which were discovered, have been forwarded to Moscow by a special messenger. It had been recently decided to bring the ex-Tsar before a tribunal to be tried for his crimes against the people and only later occurrences led to delay in adopting this course. The Russian Executive Council accept the decision of the Rural Regional Council as being regular. The Central Executive Committee has now at its disposal extremely important material and documents concerning the Nicholas Romanoff affair – his own diary, which he kept almost to the last day, diaries of his wife and children, his correspondence, amongst which are letters by Gregory Rasputin to Romanoff and his family. All these materials will be examined and published in the near future.

News of the World, 21 July, 1918

*

Seated before the mirror, Karl examines his flesh. Neither the harsh neon light over the mirror, nor the mirror itself, is flattering. Karl pouts his lips and rolls his eyes.

— I don't think you're a Nigerian at all, now. Your accent changes all the time.

— We all change our accents to suit our circumstances. In the mirror their eyes meet. Karl feels cold.

We are all victims.

He is fourteen. His mother and his father were killed in an explosion in a café in Bobrinskaya.

Karl's friend puts friendly hands on Karl's shoulders. — What would you like to do now?

He is fourteen. Sitting on a flat-car, hanging on for dear life as the train roars across the plain. The plain is dead. It consists of nothing but the blackened stalks of what was once wheat. The wheat has been deliberately burned.

The sky is huge and empty.

Karl shivers.

— Any ideas?

The train moves to meet the sullen bank of grey cloud on the horizon. It is like the end of the world. The train carries death. It goes to find more death. That is its cargo, its destiny.

At several points on the train – on the locomotive bellowing ahead, on the rocking carriages, the bucking open trucks – black flags flap like the wings of settling crows.

It is the Ukraine.

And Karl shivers.

KARL WAS FOURTEEN. His mother and father had been thirty-five when they were killed by the bomb. They came from Kiev but had been driven out during one of the pogroms. They had thought it safer to stay with their relatives in Bobrinskaya. Someone had set a bomb off in a café and Karl had gone to Alexandria where he had met the army of Bekov, the Nihilist. He had joined that army. He had been in several battles since then and now he had a machine gun of his own to look after. He loved the machine gun. He had secured the stand to the flat-car with big horseshoe nails. It was an English machine gun, a Lewis. His greatcoat was English, too. It was leather and had a special pocket in front shaped like a revolver. During their last battle, near Golta, he had managed to acquire a revolver. They had been beaten at that battle. They were now making for Kiev because the railway line direct to Alexandria had been blown up to cut off their retreat. Bekov's black banners flew everywhere on the train. Some of the banners bore his slogan: Anarchy Breeds Order. But most were plain. Bekov had been in a bad mood since Golta.

Over the rattle of the train and the roar of the locomotive came the sounds of laughter, of song, of an accordion's whine. Bekov's army lounged on every available surface. Young men, mainly, their clothes were evidence of a hundred successful raids. One wore a tall silk hat decorated with streaming red and black ribbons. His body was swathed in a sleeveless fur coat with the skirt hacked off to give his legs freedom. He wore green Cossack breeches tucked into red leather boots. Over his coat were criss-crossed four bandoliers of bullets. In his hands was a rifle which, intermittently, he would fire into the air, laughing all the time. At his belt was a curved sabre and stuck in the belt were a Mauser automatic pistol and a Smith and Wesson .45 revolver. Bottles were passed from hand to hand as they thundered along. The young man in the top hat flung back his head and poured wine over his bearded face and down his throat, breaking into song as the accordion began to play the army's familiar melody, 'Arise young men!' Karl himself joined in with the sad, bold last lines. 'Who lies under the green sward?' sang the man in the top hat. 'We heroes of Bekov,' sang Karl, 'saddle rugs for shrouds.'

There was a great cheer and peaked caps, sheepskin hats, derby hats, stocking caps and the caps of a dozen different regiments were waved or thrown through the steam from the engine. Karl was proud to be of this reckless company which cared nothing for death and very little for life. The cause for which they fought might be doomed but what did it matter? The human race was doomed. They at least would have made their gesture.

There was not a man on the train who was not festooned with weapons. Sabres and rifles and pistols were common to all. Some sported ornate antique weapons, broadswords, officers' dress swords, pistols inlaid with gold, silver and mother-of-pearl. They wore boaters, solar topees, extravagant German helmets, wide-brimmed felt hats, panamas and every variety of clothing. Near Karl and manning one of the other machine guns, a fat Georgian was stripped to the waist, wearing only a pair of gentleman's blue riding breeches and boots decorated with silver thread. Around his neck he had wound a long feather boa. He was hatless, but had on a pair of smoked glasses with gold rims. At his belt were two military holsters containing matched revolvers. The Georgian claimed that they had belonged to the Emperor himself. Sharing a bottle with the Georgian was a sailor from Odessa, his vest open to the navel, displaying a torso completely covered in pink and blue tattoos showing dragons, swords and half-dressed ladies all mixed up together. The freshest of the tattoos ran across his breastbone, a Nihilist slogan – Death to Life. A boy, younger than Karl, wearing a torn and bloodstained surplice, clutching a cooked chicken in one hand, jumped down from the top of the boxcar behind them and swayed towards the sailor, offering him half the chicken in exchange for the rest of the wine. In his other hand he held an enormous butcher's cleaver. The boy was already nine parts drunk. He was a Ukrainian Jew called Pyat.

The train hooted.

Balancing on the carriage ahead, an old man, with a student cap perched on his white hair, hooted back. He steadied himself by means of a Cossack lance around which was tied a torn black skirt. Painted on the skirt was a yellow sunrise. The old man hooted again, before falling on his side and rolling dangerously close to the edge of the roof. The lance remained where he had stuck it. The old man lost his cap and began to laugh. The train took a bend. The old man fell off. Karl saluted the tumbling figure as it disappeared down a bank.

On the curve, Karl could see the front section of the train where Bekov himself sat. The flat-wagons on both sides of him were piled with gun carriages, their dirty steel and brasswork shining dully beneath a sun which now only made occasional appearances through the looming clouds. A truck near to the engine was full of shaggy horses, their backs covered by Jewish prayer-shawls in place of blankets. Bekov's chosen Heroes sat all around their leader, their feet dangling over the sides of the wagons, but none sat near him. Karl had an impression of nothing but legs. There were legs in riding boots, legs in puttees made from silk dresses or red plush or green baize ripped from a billiard table, feet in yellow silk slippers with velvet pom-poms bouncing on them, in felt shoes, in laced boots, in sandals and in brogues, or some completely naked, scratched, red, horny, dirty. No songs came from Bekov's guard. They were probably all too drunk to sing.

On Bekov's wagon a huge, gleaming black landau had been anchored. The landau's door was decorated with the gilded coat of arms of some dead aristocrat. The upholstery was a rich crimson morocco leather. The shafts of the landau stuck up into the air and on each shaft flapped a black banner of Nihilism. On each corner of the wagon was placed a highly polished machine gun and at each machine gun squatted a man in a white Cossack cap and a black leather greatcoat. These four were not drunk. Bekov himself was probably not drunk. He lay against the leather cushions of the landau and laughed to himself, tossing a revolver high into the air and catching it again, his feet in their shining black boots crossed indolently on the coach-box.

Feodor Bekov was dying. Karl realised it suddenly. The man was small and sickly. His face was the grey face of death. The black Cossack hat and the gay, embroidered Cossack jacket he wore emphasised the pallor of his features. Over his forehead hung a damp fringe of hair which made him look a little like some pictures of Napoleon. Only his eyes were alive. Even from where he sat Karl could see the eyes – blazing with a wild and malevolent misery.

Feodor Bekov tossed the revolver up again and caught it. He tossed it and caught it again.

Karl saw that they were nearing a station. The train howled.

The platform was deserted. If there were passengers waiting for a train, they were hiding. People normally hid when Bekov's army came through. Karl grinned to himself. This was not an age in which the timid could survive.

The train slowed as it approached the station. Did Bekov intend to stop for some reason?

And then, incongruously, a guard appeared on the platform. He was dressed in the uniform of the railway line and he held a green flag in his right hand. What a fool he was, thought Karl, still sticking to the rule book while the world was being destroyed around him.

The guard raised his left hand to his head in a shaky salute. There was a terrified grin on his face, an imploring, placatory grin.

The front part of the train was by now passing through the station. Karl saw Bekov catch his revolver and cock it. Then, casually, as his landau came level with the guard, the Nihilist fired. He did not even bother to aim. He had hardly glanced at the guard. Perhaps he had not really intended to hit the man. But the guard fell, stumbling backwards on buckling legs and then crumpling against the wall of his office, his whole body shuddering as he dropped his flag and grasped at his neck. His chest heaved and blood vomited from between his lips.

Karl laughed. He swung his machine gun round and jerked the trigger. The gun began to sing. The bullets smashed into the walls and made the body of the guard dance for a few seconds. Karl saw that the placatory smile was still on the dead man's face. He pulled the trigger again and raked the whole station as they went through. Glass smashed, a sign fell down, someone screamed.

The name of the station was Pomoshnaya.

Karl turned to the young Ukrainian who had opened a fresh bottle of vodka and was drinking from it in great gulps. He had hardly noticed Karl's action. Karl tapped him on the shoulder.

'Hey, Pyat – where the hell is Pomoshnaya?'

The Ukrainian shrugged and offered Karl the bottle.

The station was disappearing behind them. Soon it had vanished.

The tattooed sailor, his arm around a snub-nosed girl with cropped hair, a Mauser in her hand, took the bottle from Pyat and placed it against the girl's thin lips. 'Drink up,' he said. He peered at Karl. 'What was that, youngster?'

Karl tried to repeat his question, but the train entered a tunnel and thick smoke filled their lungs, stung their eyes and they could see nothing. Everyone began to cough and to curse.

'It doesn't matter,' said Karl.

— *You're still looking a bit pale, says Karl's friend, fingering his own ebony skin.* — *Maybe you could do with another bath?*

Karl shakes his head. — *It'll be hard enough getting this lot off. I've got to leave here sometime, you know. It's going to be embarrassing.*

— *Only if you let it be. Brazen it out. After all, you're not the only one, are you?*

Karl giggles. — *I bet you say that to all the boys.*

What Would You Do? (9)

You have been told that you have at most a year to live.

Would you decide to spend that year:

(a) enjoying every possible pleasure?
(b) doing charitable works?
(c) in some quiet retreat, relishing the simpler pleasures of life?
(d) trying to accomplish one big thing that you will be remembered for in times to come?
(e) putting all your resources into finding a cure for the illness you have?

or would you simply kill yourself and get the whole thing over with?

Chapter Ten
Hitting the High Spots on W. Fifty-Sixth:
1929: Recognition

Trapped at sea in a violent thunderstorm, the U.S.S. *Akron*, largest and finest dirigible airship in the world, crashed off the Barnegat Lightship at 12:30 o'clock this morning with 77 officers and men aboard. Among them was Rear Admiral William A. Moffett, chief of the Bureau of Aeronautics.

Only 4 of the 77 were known to have been saved at 5 o'clock this morning. At that time the wreckage of the stricken airship was out of sight in the storm and darkness from the German oil tanker *Phoebus*, which first reported the catastrophe. A northwest wind blowing about 45 miles an hour was blowing the wreckage off shore and made rescue operations doubly difficult.

No hint of the cause of the disaster was contained in the fragmentary and frequently confusing reports received from the *Phoebus*, but it was considered highly likely that the great airship was struck by lightning.

New York Times, 4 April, 1933

— *You were bound to get depressed after all that excitement, says Karl's friend.* — *What about some coffee? Or would you rather I sent down for some more champagne?*

He grins, making an expansive gesture.

— *Name your poison!*

Karl sighs and chews at his thumbnail. His eyes are hooded. He won't look at the black man.

— *All right, then how can I cheer you up?*

— *You could fuck off, says Karl.*

— *Take it easy, Karl.*

— *You could fuck off.*

— *What good would that do?*

— *I didn't know you were interested in doing good.*

— *Where did you get that idea? Don't you feel more a person now than you felt before you came with me through the door? More real?*

— *Maybe that's the trouble.*

— *You don't like reality?*

— *Yes, maybe that's it.*

— *Well, that isn't my problem.*

— *No.*

— *It's your problem.*

— *Yes.*

— *Oh, come on now! You're starting a new life and you can't manage even a tiny smile!*

— *I'm not your slave, says Karl. — I don't have to do everything you say.*

— *Who said you had to? Me? The black man laughs deridingly. — Did I say that?*

— *I thought that was the deal.*

— *Deal? Now you're being obscure. I thought you wanted some fun. Karl is fifteen. Quite a little man now.*

— *Fuck off, he says. — Leave me alone.*

— *In my experience, the black man sits down beside him, that's what people always say when they think they're not getting enough attention. It's a challenge, in a way. 'Leave me alone.'*

— *Maybe you're right.*

— *Darling, I'm not often wrong. The black man once again puts his arm around Karl's shoulders.*

Karl is fifteen and in his own way pretty good-looking.

He's dating the sweetest little tomato in the school.

— *Oh, Jesus!*

Karl begins to weep.

— *Now that's enough of that, says his friend.*

K ARL WAS FIFTEEN. His mom was forty. His dad was forty-two. His dad had done all right for himself in his business and just recently had become president of one of the biggest investment trusts in the nation. He had, to celebrate, increased Karl's allowance at his fifteenth birthday and turned a blind eye when Karl borrowed his mother's car when he went out on a date. Karl was a big boy for his age and looked older than fifteen.

In his new tuxedo and with his hair gleaming with oil, Karl could have passed for twenty easily. That was probably why Nancy Goldmann was so willing to let him take her out.

As they left the movie theatre (*Gold Diggers of Broadway*), he whistled one of the tunes from the film while he gathered his courage together to suggest to Nancy what he had been meaning to suggest all evening.

Nancy put her arm through his and saved him the worst part: 'Where to now?' she asked.

'There's a speakeasy I know on West Fifty-Sixth.' He guided her across the street while the cars honked on all sides. It was getting dark and the lights were coming on all down Forty-Second Street. 'What do you say, Nancy?' They reached his car. It was a new Ford Coupe. His dad had a Cadillac limousine which he hoped to borrow by the time he was sixteen. He opened the door for Nancy.

'A speakeasy, Karl? I don't know…' She hesitated before getting into the car. He glanced away from her calves. His eyes would keep going to them. It was the short, fluffy skirt. You could almost see through it.

'Aw, come on, Nancy. Are you bored with speakeasies? Is that it?'

She laughed. 'No! Will it be dangerous? Gangsters and bootleggers and shooting and stuff?'

'It'll be the dullest place in the world. But we can get a drink there.' He hoped she would have a drink, then she might do more than hold his hand and kiss him on the way home. He had only a vague idea of what 'more' meant. 'If you want one, of course.'

'Well, maybe just one.'

He could see that Nancy was excited.

All the way up to W. Fifty-Sixth Street she chattered beside him, talking about the movie mostly. He could tell that she was unconsciously seeing herself as Ann Pennington. Well, he didn't mind that. He grinned to himself as he parked the car. Taking his hat and his evening coat from the back, he walked round and opened the door for Nancy. She really was beautiful. And she was warm.

They crossed Seventh Avenue and were nearly bowled over by a man in a straw hat who mumbled an apology and hurried on. Karl thought it was a bit late in the year to be wearing a straw hat. He shrugged and then, on impulse, leaned forward and kissed Nancy's cheek. Not only didn't she resist, she blew him a kiss back and laughed her lovely trilling laugh. 'Did anyone ever tell you you looked like Rudy Vallee?' she said.

'Lots of people.' He smirked in a comic way and made her laugh again.

They came to a gaudy neon sign which flashed on and off. It showed a pink pyramid, a blue-and-green dancing girl, a white camel. It was called the Casa Blanca.

'Shall we?' said Karl, opening the door for her.

'This is a restaurant.'

'Just wait and see!'

They checked their hats and coats and were shown by an ingratiating little waiter to a table some distance from the stand where a band was backing someone who looked and sounded almost exactly like Janet Gaynor. She was even singing 'Keep Your Sunny Side Up'.

'What happens next?' said Nancy. She was beginning to look disappointed.

The waiter brought the menus and bowed. Karl had been told what to say by his friend Paul who had recommended the place. 'Could we have some soft drinks, please?' he said.

'Certainly, sir. What kind?'

'Uh – the strong kind, please.' Karl looked significantly at the waiter.

'Yes, sir.' The waiter went away again.

Karl held Nancy's hand. She responded with a funny little spasm and grinned at him. 'What are you going to eat?'

'Oh, anything. Steak Diane. I'm mad about Steak Diane.'

'Me, too.' Under the table, his knee touched Nancy's and she didn't move away. Of course, there was always the chance that she thought his knee was a table leg or something. Then, when she looked at him, she moved her chin up in a way that told him she knew it was his knee. He swallowed hard. The waiter arrived with the drinks. He ordered two Steak Dianes 'and all the trimmings'. He lifted his glass and toasted Nancy. They sipped together.

'They've put a lot of lemon in it,' said Nancy. 'I guess they have to. In case of a raid or something.'

'That's it,' said Karl, fingering his bow tie.

He saw his father just as his father saw him. He wondered if his father would take the whole thing in good part. The band struck up and a couple of thinly dressed lady dancers began to Charleston. He saw that the lady dining with his father was not his mother. In fact she looked too young to be anybody's mother, in spite of the make-up. Karl's father left his place and came over to Karl. 'Get out of here at once and don't tell your mother you saw me here tonight. Who told you about this place?' He had to speak loudly because the band was now in full swing. A lot of people were clapping in time to the music.

'I just knew about it, Dad.'

'Did you? Do you come here often, then? Do you know what kind of a place this is? It's a haunt of gangsters, immoral women, all kinds of riff-raff!'

Karl looked at his father's young friend.

'That young lady is the daughter of a business associate,' said Mr Glogauer. 'I brought her here because she said she wanted to see some New York nightlife. It is not the place for a boy of fifteen!'

Nancy got up. 'I think I'll get somebody to call me a cab,' she said. She paused, then took her drink and swallowed it all down. Karl ran after her and caught her at the checking desk. 'There's another place I know, Nancy,' he said.

She stopped, pulling on her hat and giving him a calculating look. Then her expression softened. 'We could go back to my place? My mom and pop are out.'

'Oh, great!'

On the way back to Nancy's place in the car she put her arms round his neck and nibbled his ear and ruffled his hair.

'You're just a little boy at heart, aren't you?' she said.

His knees shook. He had heard that line earlier tonight and he could guess what it meant.

He knew he would always remember this day in September.

— Thanks. Karl accepts the cup of coffee his friend hands him. — How long have I been asleep?

— Not long.

Karl remembers their scene. He wishes it hadn't happened. He was behaving like some little fairy, all temperament and flounce. Homosexual relationships didn't have to be like that now. It was normal, after all. Between normal people, he thought. That was the difference. He looked at his friend. The man was sitting naked on the edge of a chest of drawers, swinging his leg lazily as he smoked a cigarette. His body really was beautiful. It was attractive in itself. It was very masculine. Oddly, it made Karl feel more masculine, too. That was what he found strange. He had thought things would be different. He kept being reminded of some quality he had always felt in his father when his father had been at home.

— Did you dream anything? asked the black man.

— I don't remember.

What Would You Do? (10)

You are married with a family and you live in a small apartment in the city, reasonably close to your work.

You learn that your mother has become very ill and can no longer look after herself.

You hate the idea of her coming to live with you in your already cramped conditions, particularly since she is not a very nice old woman and tends to make the children nervous and your wife tense. Your mother's house is larger, but in a part of the world which depresses you and which is also a long way from your work. Yet you have always sworn that you will not let her go into an old people's home. You know it would cause her considerable misery. Any other decision, however, would mean you changing your way of life quite radically.

Would you sell your mother's house and use the money to buy a larger flat in your own area? Or would you move away to a completely different area, perhaps somewhere in the country, and look for a new job?

Or would you decide, after all, that it would be best for everyone if she did go into a retirement home?

Chapter Eleven
Shanghai Sally:
1932: Problems of Diplomacy

In Shanghai is one of the most extraordinarily gruesome sights in the world. I have never seen anything to approach it. Parts of Chapei and Hongkew, where fighting was hottest, are in ruins paralleling those of the Western front in France. The Japanese looted this area, which comprises several square miles, not merely of furniture, valuables, and household possessions, but of every nail, every window wire, every screw, bolt, nut, or key, every infinitesimal piece of metal they could lay hands on. Houses were ripped to pieces, then the whole region set on fire. No one lives in this charred ruin now. No one could. The Japanese have, however, maintained street lighting; the lighted avenues protrude through an area totally black, totally devoid of human life, like phosphorescent fingers poking into a grisly void.

What is known as the Garden Bridge separates this Japanese-occupied area with one rim of the International Settlement proper. Barbed wire and sandbags protect it. Japanese sentries representing army, navy, and police stand at one end. British sentries are at the other. I have seen these tall Englishmen go white with rage as the Japanese, a few feet away, kicked coolies or slapped old men. The Japanese have life-and-death power over anyone in their area. Chinese, passing the Japanese sentries, have to bow ceremoniously, and doff their hats. Yet the Japanese – at the same time they may playfully prod a man across the bridge with their bayonets – say that they are in China to make friends of the Chinese people!

Lest it be thought that I exaggerate I append the following Reuter dispatch from Shanghai of date 30 March, 1938:

'Feeling is running high in British military circles here today as a result of an incident which occurred this morning on a bridge over the Soochow Creek ... Japanese soldiers set upon and beat an old Chinese man who happened to be on the bridge, and then threw him over into the water. The whole action was in full view of sentries of the Durhams, who were on duty, at one end of the bridge. The British soldiers, unable to leave their posts, were compelled helplessly to watch the old man drown, while the Japanese soldiers laughed and cheered.'

– John Gunther,
Inside Asia,
Hamish Hamilton, 1939

— We protect ourselves in so many foolish ways, says Karl's friend. — But let the defences drop and we discover that we are much happier.

— I don't feel much happier.

— Not at present, perhaps. Freedom, after all, takes some getting used to.

— I don't feel free.

— Not yet.

— There is no such thing as freedom.

— Of course there is! It's often hard to assimilate a new idea, I know.

— Your ideas don't seem particularly new.

— Oh, you just haven't understood yet, that's all!

Karl is sixteen. Shanghai is the largest city in China. It is one of the most exciting and romantic cities in the world. His mother and father came here to live two years ago. There are no taxes in Shanghai. Great ships stand in the harbour. Warships stand a few miles out to sea. Anything can happen in Shanghai.

— Why do people always need a philosophy to justify their lusts? Karl says spitefully. — What's so liberating about sex of any kind?

— It isn't just the sex.

Black smoke boils over the city from the north. People are complaining.

— No, it's power.

— Oh, come, come, Karl! Take it easy!

Karl Glogauer is sixteen. Although a German by birth, he attends the British school because it is considered to be the best.

— Who do you like best! asks Karl. — Men or women?

— I love everyone, Karl.

KARL WAS SIXTEEN. His mother was forty-two. His father was fifty. They all lived in the better part of Shanghai and enjoyed many benefits they would not have been able to afford in Munich.

Having dined with his father at the German Club, Karl, feeling fat and contented, ambled through the revolving glass doors into the bright sunshine and noisy bustle of the Bund, Shanghai's main street and the city's heart. The wide boulevard fronted the harbour and offered him a familiar view of junks and steamers and even a few yachts with crisp, white sails, sailing gently up towards the sea. As he creased the crown of his cream-coloured hat he noticed with dissatisfaction that there was a spot of dark grease on the cuff of his right sleeve. He adjusted the hat on his head and with the fingers of both hands turned down the brim a little. Then he looked out over the Bund to see if his mother had arrived yet. She had arranged to meet him at three o'clock and take him home in the car. He searched the mass of traffic but couldn't see her. There were trams and buses and trucks and cars, rickshaws and pedicabs, transport of every possible description, but no Rolls-Royce. He was content to wait and watch the passing throng. Shanghai must be the one place in the world where one never tired of the view. He could see people on the Bund of virtually every race on Earth: Chinese from all parts of China, from beautifully elegant businessmen in well-tailored European suits, mandarins in flowing silks, singing girls in slit skirts, flashily dressed gangster types, sailors and soldiers, to the poorest coolies in smocks or loincloths. As well as the Chinese, there were Indian merchants and clerks, French industrialists with their wives, German ship-brokers, Dutch, Swedish, English and American factory-owners or their employees, all moving along in the twin tides that swept back and forth along the Bund. As well as the babble of a hundred languages, there was the rich, satisfying smell of Shanghai, a mixture of human sweat and machine oil, of spices and drugs and stimulants, of cooking food and exhaust fumes. Horns barked, beggars whined, street-sellers shouted their wares. Shanghai.

Karl smiled. If it were not for the present trouble the Japanese were having in their sector of the International District, Shanghai would offer a young man the best of all possible worlds. For entertainment there were the cinemas, theatres and clubs, the brothels and dance halls along the Szechwan Road. You could buy anything you wanted – a piece of jade, a bale of silk, embroideries, fine porcelain, imports from Paris, New York and London, a child of any age or sex, a pipe of opium, a limousine with bulletproof glass, the most exotic meal in the world, the latest books in any language, instruction in any religion or aspect of mysticism. Admittedly there was poverty (he had heard that an average of 29,000 people starved to death on the streets of Shanghai every year) but it was a price that had to be paid for so much colour and beauty and experience. In the two years that he had been here he had managed to sample only a few of Shanghai's delights and, as he neared manhood, the possibilities of what he could do became wider and wider. No-one could have a better education than to be brought up in Shanghai.

He saw the Rolls pull in to the curb and he waved. His mother, wearing one of her least extravagant hats, leaned out of the window and waved back. He sprang down the steps and pushed his way through the crowd until he got to the car. The Chinese chauffeur, whose name Karl could never remember and whom he always called 'Hank', got out and opened the door, saluting him. Karl gave him a friendly grin. He stepped into the car and stretched out beside his mother, kissing her lightly on the cheek. 'Lovely perfume,' he said. He flattered her as a matter of habit, but she was always pleased. It hardly occurred to him to dislike anything she chose to do, wear or say. She was his mother, after all. He was her son.

'Oh, Karl, it's been terrible today.' Frau Glogauer was Hungarian and spoke German, as she spoke French and English, with a soft, pretty accent. She was very popular with the gentlemen in all the best European circles of the city. 'I meant to do much more shopping, but there wasn't time. The traffic! That's why I was late, darling.'

'Only five minutes, Mama.' Karl looked at his Swiss watch. 'I always give you at least half an hour, you know that. Do you want to finish your shopping before we go home?' They lived in the fashionable Frenchtown area to the west, not too far from the racecourse, in a large Victorian Gothic house which Karl's father had purchased very reasonably from the American who had previously owned it.

His mother shook her head. 'No. No. I get irritable if I can't do everything at my own pace and it's impossible this afternoon. I wish those Japanese would hurry up and restore order. A handful of bandits can't cause that much trouble, surely? I'm sure if the Japanese had a free hand, the whole city would be better run. We ought to put them in charge.'

'There'd be fewer people to manage,' said Karl dryly. 'I'm afraid I don't like them awfully. They're a bit too heavy-handed in their methods, if you ask me.'

'Do the Chinese understand any other methods?' His mother hated being contradicted. She shrugged and pouted out of the window.

'But perhaps you're right,' he conceded.

'Well, see for yourself,' she said, gesturing into the street. It was true that the usual dense mass of traffic was if anything denser, was moving more slowly, with less order, hampered by even more pedestrians than was normal at this hour. Karl didn't like the look of the lot of them. Really villainous wretches in their grubby smocks and head-rags. 'It's chaos!' his mother continued. 'We're having to go halfway round the city to get home.'

'I suppose it's the refugees from the Japanese quarters,' said Karl. 'You could blame the Japs for the delays, too, Mother.'

'I blame the Chinese,' she said firmly. 'In the end, it always comes down to them. They are the most inefficient people on the face of the Earth. And lazy!'

Karl laughed. 'And devious. They're terrible scamps, I'll agree. But don't you love them, really? What would Shanghai be without them?'

'Orderly,' she said, but she was forced to smile back at him, making fun at herself for her outburst, 'and clean. They run all the vice rings, you know. The opium dens, the dance halls...'

'That's what I meant!'

They laughed together.

The car moved forward a few more inches. The chauffeur sounded the horn.

Frau Glogauer hissed in despair and flung herself back against the upholstery, her gloved fingers tapping the arm of the seat.

Karl pulled the speaking tube towards him. 'Could you try another way, Hank? This seems impassable.'

The Chinese, in his neat grey uniform, nodded but did nothing. There were carts and rickshaws packing the street in front of him and a large truck blocking his way back. 'We could walk,' said Karl.

His mother ignored him, her lips pursed. A moment later she took out her handbag and opened the flap so that she could look into the mirror set inside it. She brushed with her little finger at the right eyelid. It was a gesture of withdrawal. Karl stared out of the window. He could see the skyscrapers of the Bund looming close behind them still. They had not gone far. He studied the shops on both sides. For all that the street was crowded, nobody seemed to be doing much business. He watched a fat Indian in a linen suit and a white turban pause outside a shop selling the newspapers of a dozen countries. The Indian picked his nose as he studied the papers, then he selected an American pulp magazine from another rack and paid the proprietor. Rolling the magazine up, the Indian walked rapidly away. It seemed to Karl that some more mysterious transaction must have taken place. But then every transaction seemed like that in Shanghai.

The Rolls rolled a few more feet. Then the chauffeur saw an opening in a side street and turned down it. He managed to get halfway before a nightsoil cart – the 'honey-carts' as the Chinese called them – got in his way and he was forced to brake quite sharply. The driver of the cart pretended not to notice the car. One wheel of his cart mounted the sidewalk as he squeezed past. Then they were able to drive into the side street which was barely wide enough to accommodate the big Phantom.

'At least we're moving,' said Frau Glogauer, putting her compact back into her bag and closing the clasp with a snap. 'Where are we?'

'We're going all round the world,' said Karl. 'The river's just ahead, I think. Is that a bridge?' He craned forward trying to get his bearings. 'Now, that must be north... My God!'

'What?'

'Chapei. They must have set fire to it. The smoke. I thought it was clouds.'

'Will it mean trouble – here, I mean?' asked his mother, taking hold of his arm.

He shook his head. 'I've no idea. We're pretty close to the Japanese concession now. Maybe we should go back and speak to Father?'

She was silent. She liked to make the decisions. But the political situation had never interested her. She always found it boring. Now she had no information on which to base a decision. 'Yes, I suppose so,' she said reluctantly. 'That was gunfire, wasn't it?'

'It was something exploding.' Karl suddenly felt an intense hatred for the Japanese. With all their meddling, they could ruin Shanghai for everybody. He took up the speaking tube. 'Back to the Bund, Hank, as soon as you can get out of here.'

They entered a wider thoroughfare and Karl saw the crowds part as if swept back by invisible walls. Through the corridors thus created a Chinese youth came running. Hank had pulled out into the street and now the car was blocking the youth's progress.

Behind the youth came three little Japanese policemen with clubs and pistols in their hands. They were chasing him. The youth did not appear to see the car and he struck it in the way that a moth might strike a screen door. He fell backwards and then tried to scramble up. He was completely dazed. Karl wondered what to do.

The Japanese policemen flung themselves onto the youth, their clubs rising and falling.

Karl started to wind down the window. 'Hey!'

His mother buried her face in his shoulder. He saw a smear of powder on his lapel. 'Oh, Karl!'

He put his arm around his mother's warm body. The smell of her perfume seemed even stronger. He saw blood well out of the bruises on the Chinese boy's face and back. Hank was trying to turn the car into the main street. A tug went past on the river, its funnel belching white smoke which contrasted sharply with the oily black smoke rising over Chapei. It was strange how peaceful the rest of the tall city looked. The New York of the Orient.

The clubs continued to rise and fall. His mother snuffled in his shoulder. Karl turned his eyes away from the sight. The car began to reverse a fraction. There was a tap on the window. One of the Japanese policemen stood there, bowing and smiling and saluting with his bloody club. He made some apology in Japanese and grinned widely, shaking his free hand as if to say, 'Such things happen in even the best-run city.' Karl leaned over and wound the window right up. The car pulled away from the scene. He didn't look back.

As they drove towards the Bund again, Karl's mother sniffed, straightened up and fumbled in her handbag for a handkerchief. 'Oh, that awful man,' she said. 'And those policemen! They must have been drunk.'

Karl was happy to accept this explanation. 'Of course,' he said. 'They were drunk.'

The car stopped.

— *There is certainly something secure, says Karl, about a world which excludes women. Which is not to say that I deny their charms and their virtues. But I can understand, suddenly, one of the strong appeals of the homosexual world.*

— *Now you're thinking of substituting one narrow world for another, warns his friend. — I spoke earlier of broadening your experience. That's quite different.*

— What if the person isn't up to being broadened? I mean, we all have a limited capacity for absorbing experience, surely? I could be, as it were, naturally narrow.

Karl feels euphoric. He smiles slowly.

— No-one but a moron could be that, says the black man, just a trifle prudishly.

What Would You Do? (11)

A girl you know has become pregnant.

You are almost certainly the father.

The girl is not certain whether she wants the baby or not. She asks you to help her to decide.

Would you try to convince her to have an abortion?

Would you try to convince her to have the baby?

Would you offer to support her, if she had the baby?

Would you deny that the baby was yours and have nothing further to do with the girl?

If she decided to have an abortion and it had to be done privately, would you offer to pay the whole cost?

Would you tell her that the decision was entirely up to her and refuse to be drawn into any discussion?

Chapter Twelve
Memories of Berlin:
1935: Dusty

King Alexander of Yugoslavia was assassinated at Marseilles yesterday. M. Barthou, the French Foreign Minister, who had gone to the port to greet the King, was also murdered.

The assassin jumped on the running board of the car in which the King, who had only just landed, was driving with M. Barthou, General Georges, and Admiral Berthelot, and fired a series of shots. The General and the Admiral were both wounded. The murderer, believed to be a Croat, was killed by the guard.

King Alexander was on his way to Paris for a visit of great political importance. It was to have been the occasion of an attempt to find means, through French mediation, of improving relations between Yugoslavia, the ally of France, and Italy, as preliminary to a Franco-Italian rapprochement.

The Times, 10 October, 1934

A policy of keeping the United States 'unentangled and free' was announced here today by President Roosevelt in his first public utterance recognising the gravity of war abroad...

The general advance of the Italian armies from Eritrea has begun. At dawn today 20,000 men in four columns crossed the Mareb River which forms the Ethiopian boundary. Groups of light tanks operating ahead covered the crossing. Airplanes hovered overhead and long range guns fired occasional shells to discourage opposition. Italian planes bombed Adowa and Adigrat...

New York Times, 2 & 3 October, 1935

'The Italian government is capable of almost any kind of treason.'

– Adolf Hitler,
9 August, 1943

He looks up into the cloudy eyes of his friend. — You seem quite pale, he says. — Why doesn't anything happen? Karl wipes his lips.

— That's none of your business, says the black man. — I feel like a drink. Do you want one? He turns and goes to the table where the waiter has arranged a variety of drinks. — What do you like?

I don't drink much. A lemonade will do.

— A glass of wine?

— All right.

Karl accepts the glass of red wine. He holds it up to a beam of moonlight. — I wish I could help you, he says.

— Don't worry about that.

— If you say so. Karl sits down on the edge of the bed, swinging his legs and sipping his wine. — Do you think I'm unimaginative?

— I suppose you are. But that's nothing to do with it.

— Maybe that's why I never made much of a painter.

— There are lots of different kinds of imagination.

— Yes. It's a funny thing. Imagination is Man's greatest strength and yet it's also his central weakness. Imagination was a survival trait at first, but when it becomes overdeveloped it destroys him, like the tusks of a mammoth growing into its own eyes. Imagination, in my opinion, is being given far too much play, these days.

— I think you're talking nonsense, says the black man. It is true that he looks paler. Perhaps that is the moonlight, too, thinks Karl.

— Probably, agrees Karl.

— Imagination can allow Man to become anything he wants to be. It gives us everything that is human.

— And it creates the fears, the bogeymen, the devils which destroy us. Unreasoning terror. What other beast has fears like ours?

The black man gives him an intense glare. For a moment his eyes seem to shine with a feral gleam. But perhaps that is the moonlight again.

Karl is seventeen. A dupe of the Duce. Escaped from Berlin and claiming Italian citizenship, he now finds himself drafted into the Army. You can't win in Europe these days. It's bad. There is pain...

There is heat.

— Are you afraid, then? asks Karl's friend.

— Of course. I'm guilty, fearful, unfulfilled...

— Forget your guilts and your fears and you will be fulfilled.

— And will I be human?

— What are you afraid of?

K ARL WAS SEVENTEEN. His mother had gone. His father had gone. His uncle, an Italian citizen, adopted him in 1934. Almost immediately Karl had been conscripted into the Army. He had no work. He had been conscripted under his uncle's new name of Giombini, but they knew he was a Jew really.

He had guessed he would be going to Ethiopia when all the lads in the barracks had been issued with tropical kit. Almost everyone had been sure that it would be Ethiopia.

And now, after a considerable amount of sailing and marching, here he was, lying in the dust near a burning mud hut in a town called Adowa with the noise of bombs and artillery all around him and a primitive spear stuck in his stomach, his rifle stolen, his body full of pain and his head full of regrets. His comrades ran about all round him, shooting at people he couldn't see. He didn't bother to call out. He would be punished for losing his rifle to a skinny brown man wearing a white sheet. He hadn't even had a chance to kill somebody.

He regretted first that he had left Berlin. Things might have quietened down there eventually, after all. He had left only because of his parents' panic after the shop had been smashed. In Rome he had never been able to get used to the food. He remembered the Berlin restaurants and wished he had had a chance to eat one good meal before going. He regretted, too, that he had not been able to realise his ambitions, once in the Army. A clever lad could rise rapidly to an important rank in wartime, he knew. A bomb fell near by and the force of it stirred his body a little. Dust began to drift over everything. The yells and the shots and the sounds of the planes, the whine of the shells and the bombs, became distant. The dust made his throat itch and he used all his strength to stop himself from coughing and so make the pain from his wound worse. But he coughed at last and the spear quivered, a sharp black line against the dust which made everything else look so vague.

He watched the spear, forcing his eyes to focus on it. It was all he had.

You were supposed to forget about worldly ambitions when you were dying. But he felt cheated. He had got out of Berlin at the right time. Really, there was no point in believing otherwise. Friends of his would be in camps now, or deported to some frightful dungheap in North Africa. Italy had been a clever choice. Anti-Semitic feeling had never meant much in Italy. The fools who had gone to America and Britain might find themselves victims of pogroms at any minute. On the other hand the Scandinavian countries had seemed to offer an alternative. Perhaps he should have tried his luck in Sweden, where so many people spoke German and he wouldn't have felt too strange. A spasm of pain shook him. It felt as if his entrails were being stirred around by a big spoon. He had become so conscious of his innards. He could visualise them all – his lungs and his heart and his ruined stomach, the yards and yards of offal curled like so many pink, grey and yellow sausages inside him; then his cock, his balls, the muscles in his strong, naked legs; his fingers, his lips, his eyes, his nose and his ears. The black line faded. He forced it back into focus. His blood, no longer circulating smoothly through his veins and arteries, but pumping out of the openings around the blade of the spear, dribbled into the dust. Nothing would have happened in Germany after the first outbursts. It would have died down, the trouble. Hitler and his friends would have turned their attention to Russia, to the real enemies, the Communists. A funny little flutter started in his groin, below the spear blade. It was as if a moth were trying to get into the air, using his groin as a flying field, hopping about and beating its wings and failing to achieve take-off. He tried to see, but fell back. He was thirsty. The line of the spear shaft had almost disappeared and he didn't bother to try to focus on it again.

The distant noises seemed to combine and establish close rhythms and counter-rhythms coupled with the beating of his heart. He recognised the tune. Some American popular song he had heard in a film. He had hummed the same song for six months after he had seen the film in Berlin. It must have been four years ago. Maybe longer. He wished that he had had a chance to make love to a woman. He had always disdained whores. A decent man didn't need whores. He wished that he had been to a whore and found out what it was like. One had offered last year as he walked to the railway station.

The film had been called *Sweet Music*, he remembered. He had never learned all the English words, but had made up words to sound like them.

> There's a tavern in the town, in the town,
> When atroola setsen dahn, setsen dahn,
> Und der she sits on a luvaduvadee,
> Und never never sinka see.
> So fairdeewell mein on tooday...

He had had ambitions to be an opera singer and he had had ambitions to be a great writer.

The potential had all been there, it was just a question of choosing. He might even have been a great general.

His possible incarnations marched before him through the dust.

And then he was dead.

— *You could be anything you wanted to be. His friend kisses his shoulder.*

— *Or nothing. Could I be a woman and give birth to five children? Karl bites the black man.*

The black man leaps up. He is a blur. For a moment, in the half-light, Karl thinks that his friend is a woman and white and then an animal of some kind, teeth bared. The black man glowers at him. — Don't do that to me!

And Karl wipes his lips.

He turns his back on his friend. — Okay. You taste funny, anyway.

What Would You Do? (12)

You are a priest, devoutly religious, you are made miserable by the very idea of violence. You are, in every sense, a man of peace.

One morning you are cutting bread in the small hall attached to your church. You hear screams and oaths coming from the church itself. You hurry into the church, the knife still in your hand.

The soldier of the enemy currently occupying your country is in the act of raping a girl of about thirteen. He has beaten her and torn her clothes. He is just about to enter her. She whimpers. He grunts. You recognise the girl as a member of your parish. Doubtless she came to the church for your help. You shout, but the soldier pays no attention. You implore him to stop, to no avail.

If you kill the soldier with your knife it will save the young girl from being hurt further. It might even save her life. Nobody knows the soldier has entered the church. You could hide the body easily.

If you merely knock him out – even if that's possible – he will almost certainly take horrible reprisals on you, your church and its congregation. It has happened before, in other towns. Yet you want to save the girl.

What would you do?

Chapter Thirteen
At the Auschwitz Ball:
1944: Strings

The war in Europe has been won; but the air of Europe smells of blood. Nazis and Fascists have been defeated; but their leaders have not yet been destroyed. It is still touch-and-go even now, whether the surviving Nazis are to have another chance of power, or whether they can be made harmless for ever by their swift arraignment as war criminals. And make no mistake this is not simply a matter for self-evident criminals such as Goering, Rosenberg and those others guilty of outstanding crimes, or responsible for the orders which caused major atrocities.

I have before me about twenty dossiers from small, unimportant French villages, and some from better-known places. They are unemotional accounts based on the evidence of named witnesses, of events which occurred during the German occupation. The Massacre of Dun Les Plages on June 26, 1944; the destruction of the village of Manlay on July 31, 1944; the treatment and murder in the Gestapo barracks at Cannes – and so it goes on. Sometimes the names of the local Nazis responsible have been discovered and named; often not.

The full horror of these cold indictments are revealed by the photographs which accompany them. It is difficult to describe them. Two or three of the mildest only are reproduced here. The Nazis took delight in having themselves photographed with their victims while these were in their agony of outrage and torture. It is not a simple crime that is depicted, but a terrible degradation of man. All the most horrible instincts which survive in our subconscious have come brutally out into the open. It is no relapse into savagery, because no savages ever behaved with such cold, unfeeling, educated brutality and shamelessness.

These dossiers are French. But the same story is repeated in every country the Germans occupied, and also from those countries which allied themselves with the Nazis. Arrests, deportations, questionings and punishment were all carried out with a deliberate maximum of brutality accompanied by every conceivable carnal licence. Like the concentration camps, these methods aimed at the destruction of confidence in democratic values; at inducing a total surrender to the Nazi terror.

They succeeded for a time – probably more than most people who have never lived under Nazi domination care to believe. That fear and horror of the Nazi bully has not yet been eradicated. The war will not be over until all the outraged millions of once-occupied Europe enjoy full confidence that democratic Governments can protect their rights, and that those who have offended are punished and broken. The Nazis mobilised the *Untermensch*, the sub-human, into their ranks. The wickedness he worked is a vivid memory, and it must be exorcised before Europe can have peace.

Picture Post, 23 June, 1945

— *Don't try that with me, you little white bastard! Karl displays his arms.*

— *I'm a black bastard now.*

— *We can soon change that.*

— *Oh, hell, I'm sorry, says Karl.* — *It was just an impulse.*

— *Well, says his friend grimly, you're certainly losing your inhibitions now, aren't you.*

Karl is eighteen. He is very lucky, along with the other members of the orchestra. His mother told him there was a point to learning, that you never knew when it came in useful, fiddle-playing. And it was beautifully warm in the barracks. He hoped they would dance all night.

— *Come back to bed, says Karl.* — *Please...*

—*I thought you were a nice, simple, uncomplicated sort of chap, says the black man. — That's what attracted me to you in the first place. Ah, well – it was my own fault, I suppose.*

Karl is eighteen and playing Johann Strauss. How beautiful. How his mother would have loved it. There are tears in his eyes. He hoped they would dance for ever! The Oswiecim Waltz!

—*Well, I'm not at my best, says Karl. — I wasn't when you met me. That's why I was in the roof garden.*

—*It's true, says his friend, that we hardly know each other yet.*

K ARL WAS EIGHTEEN. His mother had been given an injection some time ago and she had died. His father had probably been killed in Spain. Karl sat behind the screen with the other members of the orchestra and he played the violin.

That was his job in Auschwitz. It was the plum job and he had been lucky to get it. Others were doing much less pleasant work and it was so cold outside. The big barrack hall was well-heated for the Christmas dance and all the guards and non-commissioned officers, their sweethearts and wives, were enjoying themselves thoroughly, in spite of rations being so short.

Karl could see them through a gap in the screen as he and the others played *The Blue Danube* for the umpteenth time that evening. Round and round went the brown and grey uniforms; round and round went the skirts and the dresses. Boots stamped on the uncarpeted boards of the hall. Beer flowed. Everyone laughed and joked and sang and enjoyed themselves. And behind the leather-upholstered screen borrowed for the occasion the band played on.

Karl had two pullovers and a pair of thick corduroy trousers, but he hardly needed the second pullover, it was so warm. He was much better off than when he had first come to the camp with his mother. Not that he had actually seen his mother at the camp, because they had been segregated earlier on. It had been awful at first, seeing the faces of the older inmates, feeling that you were bound to become like them, losing all dignity. He had suffered the humiliation while he summed up the angles and, while a rather poor violinist, had registered himself as a professional. It had done the trick. He had lost a lot of weight, of course, which was only to be expected. Nobody, after all, was doing very well, this winter. But he had kept his dignity and his life and there was no reason why he shouldn't go on for a long while as he was. The guards liked his playing. They were not very hot on Bach and Mozart and luckily neither was he. He had always preferred the lighter gayer melodies.

He shut his eyes, smiling as he enjoyed his own playing.

When he opened his eyes, the others were not smiling. They were all looking at him. He shut his eyes again.

— *Would you say you were a winner? asks Karl's friend.*

— *No. Everything considered, I'd say I was a loser. Aren't we all?*

— *Are we? With the proper encouragement you could be a winner. With my encouragement.*

— *Oh, I don't know. I'm something of a depressive, as you may have noticed.*

— *That's my point. You've never had the encouragement. I love you, Karl.*

— *For myself?*

— *Of course. I have a lot of influence. I could get your work sold for good prices. You could be rich.*

— *I suppose I'd like that.*

— *If I got you a lot of money, what would you do?*

— *I don't know. Give it back to you?*

— *I don't mean my money. I mean if your work sold well.*

— *I'd buy a yacht, I think. Go round the world. It's something I've always wanted to do. I went to Paris when I was younger.*

— *Did you like it?*

— *It wasn't bad.*

What Would You Do? (13)

You own a dog. It is a dog you inherited from a friend some years ago. The friend asked you to look after it for a short while and never returned.

Now the dog is getting old. You have never cared much for it, but you feel sympathetic towards it. It has become long in the tooth, it makes peculiar retching noises, it has difficulty eating and sometimes its legs are so stiff you have to carry it up and down stairs.

The dog is rather curlike in its general demeanour. It has never had what you would call a noble character. It is nervous, cowardly and given to hysterical barking.

Because of the stiffness in its legs you take it to the veterinary clinic.

The dog has lived several years beyond its expected life-span. Its eyes are failing and it is rather deaf.

You have the opportunity to ask the veterinary to destroy the dog. And yet the dog is in no pain or any particular discomfort most of the time. The vet says that it will go on quite happily for another year or so. You hate the idea of witnessing the dog's last agonies when its time does come to die. You have only a faint degree of affection for it. It would really be better if the vet got it over with now.

What would you say to the vet?

Chapter Fourteen
The Road to Tel Aviv:
1947: Traps

ATIYAH: I have three comments to make. First, concerning what Reid said about Palestine having belonged to the Turks. Under Turkish suzerainty the Arabs were not a subject people, but partners with the Turks in the empire. Second, on what I considered was the false analogy – when Crossman said the Jews were unlucky in that they were, as he put it, the last comers into the fields of overseas settlement. He mentioned Australia. I would point out that the Arabs in Palestine do not belong to the same category as the aborigines of Australia. They belong to what was once a highly-civilised community, and before what you call overseas settlement in Palestine by the Jews was begun, the Arabs were reawakening into a tremendous intellectual and spiritual activity after a period of decadence, so there can be no comparison between the two cases.

CROSSMAN: Tom, what do you think were the real mistakes of British policy which led up to what we all agree is an intolerable situation?

REID: The British Government during the first World War had induced the Arabs, who were in revolt against the Turks, to come in and fight on the Allied side. We made them a promise in the McMahon Declaration and then, without their knowledge, invited the Jews to come in and establish a national home. That was unwise and wicked. As I understand it, the idea of the British Government was that the Jews should come in and gradually become a majority. That was a secret understanding and was doubly wicked.

Picture Post,
'Palestine: Can deadlock be broken?'
Discussion between Edward Atiyah,
Arab Office; Thomas Reid, MP;
R.H.S. Crossman, MP, and Prof.
Martin Buber, Prof. Sociology,
Jerusalem University, 12 July, 1947

— *What does money mean to you, Karl?*

— *Well, security, I suppose, first and foremost.*

— *You mean it can buy you security. A house, food, the obvious comforts, power over others.*

— *I'm not sure about power over others. What has that to do with security?*

— *Oh, it must have something to do with it.*

At nineteen, Karl is bent on vengeance and the regaining of his rights. He has a .303 Lee-Enfield rifle, some hand grenades, a bayonet and a long dagger. He wears a khaki shirt and blue jeans. On his head is a burnoose. He stands on the bank overlooking the winding road to Tel Aviv. He lifts his head proudly into the sun.

— *You can keep yourself to yourself, says Karl with a grin. — Can't you?*

— *As long as others do. The dweller in the suburbs, Karl, must pursue a policy of armed neutrality.*

— *I was brought up in the suburbs. I never saw it like that. I don't know what things are like in Nigeria, mind you...*

At nineteen, Karl has a girl whom he has left behind in Joppa. There are five friends with him on the road. He sees a dust cloud approaching. It must be the jeep. With the veil of his burnoose, Karl covers his mouth against the dust.

— *Much the same, says Karl's friend. — Much the same.*

KARL WAS NINETEEN. His mother had been gassed, his father had been gassed. At least, that was as far as he knew. He had been lucky. In 1942 he and his uncle had managed to sneak into

Palestine and had not been caught as illegal immigrants. But Karl had soon realised the injustice of British rule and now he belonged to the Irgun Tsva'i Leumi, pledged to drive the British out of Palestine if they had to kill every single British man, woman or child to do it. It was time the Jews turned. There would never be another pogrom against the Jews that was not answered in kind. It was the only way.

He squinted against the glare of the sun, breathing with some difficulty through the gauze of his headdress. The air was dry, dusty and stale. There was no doubt about the single jeep droning along the road from Abid to Tel Aviv. It was British. He gestured down to his friend David. David, too, was masked. David, too, had a Lee-Enfield rifle. He handed up the field glasses to Karl. Karl took them, adjusted them, saw that there were two soldiers in the jeep – a sergeant and a corporal. They would do.

Further along the road, in the shade of a clump of stunted palms, waited the rest of the section. Karl signalled to them. He swept the surrounding hills with his glasses to check that there was no-one about. Even a goatherd could prove an embarrassment, particularly if he were an Arab. The parched hills were deserted.

You could hear the jeep quite clearly now, its engine whining as it changed gear and took an incline.

Karl unclipped a grenade from his belt.

The others left the shade of the palms and got into the ditch behind the bank, lying flat, their rifles ready. Karl looked at David. The boy's dark eyes were troubled. Karl signalled for David to join him. He pulled the pin from the grenade. David imitated him, unclipping a grenade, pulling out the pin, holding down the safety.

Karl felt his legs begin to tremble. He felt ill. The heat was getting to him. The jeep was almost level. He sprang up, steadied himself on the top of the bank and threw the grenade in a gentle, graceful curve. It was a beautiful throw. It went straight into the back seat of the jeep. The soldiers looked astonished. They glanced back. They glanced at Karl. The jeep's pace didn't slacken. It blew up.

There was really no need for the second grenade which David threw and which landed in the road behind the remains of the jeep.

The two soldiers had been thrown out of the wreckage. They were both alive, though broken and bleeding. One of them was trying to draw his side arm. Karl walked slowly towards him, his .303 cocked. With a casual movement of his foot he kicked the pistol from the sergeant's hand as the man tried to get the hammer back. The sergeant's face was covered in blood. Out of the mess stared two blue eyes. The ruined lips moved, but there were no words. Near by, the corporal sat up.

The rest of the group joined Karl.

'I'm glad you weren't killed,' Karl said in his guttural English.

'Aaah!' said the corporal. 'You dirty Arab bastards.' He hugged his broken right arm.

'We are Jews,' said David, ripping his mask down.

'I don't believe it,' said the corporal.

'We are going to hang you,' said Karl, pointing at the palms, visible beyond the bank.

David went to look at the jeep. The whole back section was buckled and one of the wheels was off. Some piece of machinery still gasped under the bonnet. David reached into the jeep and turned the engine off. There was a smell of leaking petrol. 'It's not much use to us,' said David.

'What do you bloody mean?' said the corporal in horror. 'What the fuck do you bloody mean?'

'It's a message,' said Karl, 'from us to you.'

— *I've made up my mind, says Karl's friend as he busily massages Karl's buttocks. — I'm going to take you with me when I go home. You'll like it. It isn't everyone I meet I'd do that for.*

Karl makes no reply. He is feeling rather detached. He doesn't remember when he felt so relaxed.

What Would You Do? (14)

You are very attracted to a girl of about seventeen who is the daughter of one of your parents' friends. The girl lives with her parents in the country. You take every opportunity to see her (you are not much older than her, yourself) but although you take her out to formal parties a couple of times and to the cinema once, you can't be sure how she feels towards you. The more you see of her the more you want to make love to her. But you realise she is quite young and you don't want to see yourself in the rôle of the seducer. You would feel perfectly happy about it if she made the first move. But she is shy. She plainly likes you. Probably she is waiting for you to make the first move. You are passing through the part of the world where she and her parents live and you decide to visit the house and ask if you can stay the night, as it's quite late. You rather hope that, at last, you will be able to find an opportunity to make love to the girl.

You arrive at the house. The door is opened by the girl's mother, an attractive woman in her early forties. She is very welcoming. You tell her your story and she says that of course you can stay, for as long as you like. She regrets that you will not be able to see her husband because he is away for some days on a business trip. Her daughter is out – 'with one of her boyfriends'. You feel disappointed.

You have dinner with the mother and you and she drink quite a lot of wine. The mother makes no doubt about the fact that she finds you attractive. After dinner, sitting together on a couch, you find that you are holding hands with her.

You have a mixture of feelings. She is attractive and you do feel that you want to make love, but you're rather afraid of her experience. Secondly, you feel that if you sleep with her, it will complicate the situation so much that you will never have an opportunity to make love to her daughter, whom you feel you could easily fall in love with. You also need the mother's good will.

Would you get up from the couch and make an excuse in order

to go to bed? Would you make love to the mother up to a point and then claim that you were too drunk to go further? Would you pretend to be ill? Would you give in completely to your desires of the moment and sleep with the mother, in spite of the inevitable situation which this would lead to? Would you hope that the daughter would be so intrigued by your having slept with her mother that she would make it clear that she, too, wanted to sleep with you (you have heard that such things happen)? Or would you feel that the whole problem was too much, leave the house and resolve never to see any member of the family ever again?

Chapter Fifteen

Big Bang in Budapest:
1956: Leaving Home

In the Troodos hills in the west of Cyprus, the job is being carried out by Number 45 Commando of the Royal Marines, together with two companies of the Gordon Highlanders. The Commando arrived in Cyprus last September; its headquarters are now in Platres, near Troodos. Its commanding officer, Lt.-Col. N.H. Tailyour, DSO, recalled its record to date. 'In early November we took the first haul of EOKA arms. We shot and captured the brother of the Bishop of Kyrenia (who was deported with the Archbishop) while he was trying to break through a cordon with some important documents ... So far we have killed two men ... We have been ambushed seven times, and lost one marine killed and seven wounded.' A lot more has happened since then.

Picture Post, 7 April, 1956

'My daughter was one of the ten people who went into the Radio building. They were asked to wait on the balcony while the business was discussed. The students below thought they had been pushed out. They tried to crush through the door and the police opened fire. I did not see my daughter fall down. They said she fell and the security police carried her away. She may not be dead. Perhaps it were better she were.'

Hungarian woman,
Picture Post, 5 November, 1956

Picture Post brings you this week the most dramatic exclusive of the war in Egypt – the first documentary record of life behind the Egyptian lines after the invasion of Port Said. How this story was obtained by correspondent William Richardson and photographer Max Scheler is in itself one of the remarkable stories of the campaign. While the fires at Port Said still burned, Richardson was at the British front line at El Cäp watching the Egyptians dig in 1,000 yards south. Three weeks later he stood at those same Egyptian positions watching the British across the lines and getting a briefing on the campaign from Brigadier Anin Helmini, one of Nasser's most brilliant young generals. Yet to negotiate that 1,000 yards between the British and Egyptian lines Richardson had to travel some 5,600 times that distance, flying from Port Said to Cyprus and from there to Athens and Rome. There the Egyptian Embassy granted him a visa after he told them he had been in Port Said and wanted to see both sides. In a month, he was accredited to three forces – British, Egyptian and United Nations, a total of 12 nationalities in uniform.

Picture Post, 17 December, 1956

— *Is your only pleasure making me feel pleasure? Karl asks.*

— *Of course not.*

— *Well, you don't seem to be getting any fun out of this. Not physical, anyway.*

— *Cerebral pleasures can be just as nice. It depends what turns you on, surely?*

Karl turns over. — *There's something pretty repressed about you, he says.* — *Something almost dead.*

— *You know how to be offensive don't you? A short time ago you were just an ordinary London lad. Now you're behaving like the bitchiest pansy I ever saw.*

— *Maybe I like the rôle.*

Karl is twenty. He scents escape at last. He has survived through the

war, through the Communist takeover. Now there is a way out. He prays
that nothing will happen to frustrate his plans this time...

— And maybe I don't. When I said you could have anything you
wanted I didn't mean a bra and suspender belt. The black man turns
away in disgust.

— You said anything was worth trying, didn't you? I think I'd look
rather nifty. A few hormone jabs, a pump or two of silicone in my chest.
I'd be a luscious, tropical beauty. Wouldn't you love me more?

Karl is twenty. His brain is sharp. He tears up his party membership
card. Time for a change.

— Stop that! orders Karl's friend. — Or I won't bother. You can leave
now.

— Who's being narrow-minded, then!

Karl was twenty. Both his mother and his father had been killed in the pre-war pogroms. He had survived in Budapest by changing his name and keeping undercover until the war was over. When the new government was installed, he became a member of the Communist party, but he didn't tell his friends. That would have been pointless, since part of his work involved making discreet enquiries for the Russian-controlled security department on the Westbahnhof.

Now he was working out his best route to the Austrian border. He had joined with his fellow students in the least aggressive of the demonstrations against the Russians and had established himself as a patriot. When the Russians won – as they must win – he would be in Vienna on his way to America. Other Hungarians would vouch for him – a victim, like themselves, of Russian imperialism.

Earlier that day he had contacted the hotel where the tourists were staying. They told him that there were some cars due to leave for Austria in the afternoon by the big suspension bridge near the hotel. He had described himself as a 'known patriot' whom the secret police were even now hunting down. They had been sympathetic and assured him of their help.

Lenin Street was comparatively quiet after the fighting

which, yesterday, had blasted it into ruins. He picked his way through the rubble, ducking behind a fallen tree as a Russian tank appeared, its treads squeaking protest as they struck obstacle after obstacle.

Karl reached the riverside. A few people came running up the boulevard but there didn't seem to be anyone behind them. Karl decided it was safe to continue. He could see the bridge from here. Not far to go.

There came the sudden slamming cacophony of automatic cannon a few blocks to the east; a howl from a hundred throats at least; the decisive rattle of machine guns; the sound of running feet. From out of a street opposite him Karl saw about fifty free-dom fighters, most of them armed with rifles and a few with tommy guns, dash like flushed rats onto the boulevard, glance around and then run towards the bridge. He cursed them. Why couldn't they have fled in the other direction?

But he decided to follow them, at a distance.

On the suspension bridge he saw some tanks. He hoped they had been immobilised. Bodies were being thrown over the side into the Danube. He hoped they were Russian bodies. He began to look for the cars. A new Citroën, green, one of the tourists had told him, and a Volkswagen. He peered through the gaps in the ranks of the running men. He began to run himself.

And then the automatic cannon started once more. This time it was directly ahead and it was joined by the guns of the tanks. The freedom fighters fell down. Some got up and crawled into doorways, firing back. Karl fell flat, rolling to the railings and looking to see if there was a way down to the river. He might be able to swim the rest of the distance. He looked across the Dan-ube. He could still make it. He would survive.

Tanks came towards him, he made a vain attempt to get through the railings and then lay still, hoping they would think him dead.

More rifle and tommy-gun fire. More Russian gunfire. A shout. A strangled scream.

Karl opened his eyes. One of the tanks was on fire, its

camouflaged sides scorched, its red star smeared with blood. The tank's driver had tried to get out of his turret and had been shot to pieces. The other tanks rumbled on. The fighting became more distant. Karl glanced at his watch. Not more than five minutes before the cars left.

He got cautiously to his feet.

A Russian's head appeared in the turret behind the corpse of the driver. The man's flat features were tormented. He was doubtless badly wounded. He saw Karl. Karl put up his hands to show that he was unarmed. He smiled an ingratiating smile. The Russian aimed a pistol at him. Karl tried to think what to do.

He felt the impact as the bullet struck his skull. He went back against the railings and collapsed without seeing the Danube again.

— *You seem to think I'm trying to corrupt your morals or something. You've got hold of the wrong end of the stick. I was simply talking about expanding your range of choices. I don't know what to make of you, Karl.*

— *Then we're even.*

— *I might have to change my mind about you. I'm sorry, but that's the way it is. If I'm to adopt you, it will be on very strict terms. I don't want you to embarrass me.*

— *That goes for me, too.*

— *Now, don't be insolent, Karl.*

What Would You Do? (15)

You live in a poor country, though you yourself are comparatively rich.

There is a famine in the country and many of the people are starving. You want to help them. You can afford to give the local people in the village about fifty pounds. But the number of people in the village is at least two hundred. If each receives part of the money you have, it will buy them enough to live on for perhaps another four days.

Would you give them the money on condition it was spent on the people most in need? Or on condition that it was spent on the children? Or would you select a handful of people you thought deserved the money most? Or would you hand it over to them and ask them to divide as they saw fit?

Chapter Sixteen
Camping in Kenya:
1959: Smoke

Here is the grim record as far as it can be added up in figures: more than a thousand Africans hanged for serious crimes, 9,252 Mau Mau convicts jailed for serious offences, and 44,000 'detainees', guilty of lesser Mau Mau offences, in rehabilitation prison camps. In these camps, in carefully graded groups, Mau Mau adherents are re-educated as decent citizens ... To make return possible mental attitudes have to be changed ... Perhaps 'soul-washing' is not too strong a word for an organised process aimed at teaching civilised behaviour and the duties, as well as the rights, of citizenship...

Soldiers and police have won the long battle of the bush against ill-armed men fighting for what they believe to be a good cause. All but the broken remnants, under their broken leader Dedan Kimathi, have been killed or rounded up. The battle to turn Mau Mau adherents into decent citizens goes well.

But the battle to remove the underlying causes, social and economic, of the anti-white hate that created Mau Mau, will go on for long years. There, too, a hopeful beginning has been made. Princess Margaret's visit marks not just the end of a long nightmare, but the beginning of a new era of multi-racial integration – and of fairer shares for the African – in lovely Kenya.

Picture Post, 22 October, 1956

If the Malayan and Korean campaigns had drawn most attention during the early part of the 1950s, the British Army had

had much to do elsewhere. In Kenya the Mau Mau gangs, recruited from the Kikuyu tribe, had taken to the dense rain forests from which they made sorties to attack Europeans and Africans. The Kikuyu were land hungry. Their discontent was used to further the aspirations of urban Africans for political independence. Over eight years, 1952–60, British battalions, batteries and engineer squadrons, supported by small but intensely-worked communications and administrative teams, broke the movement in alliance with a devoted police and civil government organisation, many of them Africans or Asian settlers. Only when this had been done was the cause of Kenyan independence advanced.

– Brig. Anthony H. Farrar-Hockley, DSO, MBE, MC,
Ch. 32: 'After the War', *History of the British Army*,
ed. Brig. Peter Young & Lt.-Col. J.P. Lawford,
Arthur Baker, 1970

— *You're right. There's no such thing as innocence, says Karl.*
— *Absolutely. It's as abstract as 'justice' and 'virtue' – or, for that matter, 'morality'.*
— *Right. There's certainly no justice!*
— *And far too much morality!*
They laugh.
— *I didn't realise you had blue eyes, says Karl, astonished.*
— *They're only blue in some lights. Look, I'll turn my head. See?*
— *They're still blue.*
— *What about this? Green? Brown?*
— *Blue.*
Karl had reached his majority. He's twenty-one. Signed on for another seven years' stint in the Mob. There's no life like it!
— *You're just telling me that, says his friend anxiously. — How about now?*
— *Well, I suppose you could say they looked a bit greenish, says Karl kindly.*
— *It's envy, old chap, at your lovely big bovine brown tones.*

— Give us a kiss.

Twenty-one and the world his oyster. Cyprus, Aden, Singapore. Wherever the British Army's needed. Karl is a sergeant already. And he could do the officer exam soon. He's used to commanding, by now. Twice decorated? No sweat!

— Where?

— Don't make me laugh.

KARL WAS TWENTY-ONE. His mother was forty-five. His father was forty-seven. They lived in Hendon, Middlesex, in a semi-detached house which Karl's father, who had never been out of work in his life, had begun to buy just before the war. His father had been doing indispensable war work and so had not had to serve in the Army (he was a boiler engineer). His father had thoughtfully changed his name to Gower in 1939, partly because it sounded too German, partly because, you never knew, if the Germans won, it sounded too Jewish. Not, of course, that it was a Jewish name. Karl's dad denied any such suggestion vehemently. It was an old Austrian name, resembling a name attached to one of the most ancient noble houses in Vienna. That's what Karl's grandfather had said, anyway. Karl had been called after his grand-dad. Karl's father's name was English – Arnold.

Karl had been in the Army since he had joined up as a boy-entrant in 1954. He had seen a lot of service since then. But for the past two years he'd been out in Kenya, clearing up the Mau Mau business, which seemed to drag on for ever. Off duty, it was a smashing life. The worst of the terrorism was over and it wasn't nearly so dangerous as it had been. Karl had an Indian girlfriend in Nairobi and he got there as often as he could to fuck the shit out of her. She was a hot little bitch though he had a sneaking suspicion she'd given him his last dose of crabs. You could never tell with crabs, mind you, so he gave her the benefit of the doubt. What a muff! What tits! It gave you a hard-on just thinking about them. Lovely!

The jeep pulled up at the gates of the compound. Another day's work was beginning. Karl was part of the special intelligence team working closely with the Kenya Police in this area, where there was still a bit of Mau Mau mischief. Privately, Karl thought it would go on for ever. They didn't have a hope in hell of governing themselves. He looked at the inmates behind the barbed wire. It made you smile to think about it. Offering it, that was different, if you had to keep them under control. Of course you can have independence – in two million bloody years! Ho, ho, ho!

He scratched his crotch with his swagger stick and grinned to himself as his driver presented their pass. The jeep bumped its way over the uneven mud track into the compound.

The Kikuyu prisoners stood, or sat, or leaned around, looking with dull eyes at the jeep as it pulled up outside the main intelligence hut. Some distance away, squatting on the ground, were about a hundred natives listening to Colonel Wibberley giving them their usual brainwashing (or what would be a brainwashing if they had any brains to wash, thought Karl. He knew bloody well that you released the buggers as decontaminated only to get half of them back sooner or later with blood on their bloody hands). Oh, what a horrible lot they were, in their reach-me-down flannel shorts, their tattered shirts, their old tweed jackets, their bare scabby feet, some of them with silly grins all over their ugly mugs. He saluted Private Peterson who was on guard outside the hut as usual. He already felt like an officer.

'Morning, sarge,' said Peterson as he passed. Bastard!

Corporal Anderson, all red and sweaty as usual, was on duty at the desk when Karl entered. Anderson always looked as if he'd just been caught in the act of pulling his plonker – shifty, seedy.

'You are an unwholesome little sod, Corporal Anderson,' said Karl by way of greeting. Corporal Anderson tittered. 'What's new, then? Blimey, couldn't you get a stronger bulb, I can't see for looking.'

'I'll put a chit in, sarge.'

'And hurry up about it. Is old Lailu ready to talk yet?'

'I haven't been in there this morning, sarge. The lieutenant...'

'What about the bleeding lieutenant?'

'He's away, sarge. That's all.'

'Bloody good fucking thing, too, little shit-faced prick, little upper-class turd,' mumbled Karl to himself as he went through the papers on his desk. Same problem as yesterday. Find out what Lailu knew about the attack on the Kuanda farm a week ago. Lailu had been in the raid, all right, because he'd been recognised. And he'd used to work at the farm. He claimed to have been in his own village, but that was a lie. Who could prove it? And he'd been in the camp more than once. He was a known Mau Mau. And he was a killer. Or knew who the killers were, which was the same thing.

'I'll have a word with him, I think,' said Karl, sipping the tea the corporal brought him. 'I'll have to get unpleasant today if he don't open his fucking mouth. And I'll have him all to my fucking self, won't I, corp?'

'Yes, sarge,' said corp, his thick lips writhing, his hot, shifty eyes seething, as if Karl had caught him out at some really nasty form of self-abuse.

'Ugh, you are horrible,' said Karl, automatically.

'Yes, sarge.'

Karl snorted with laughter. 'Go and tell them to take our little black brother into the special room, will you?'

'Yes, sarge,' Corporal Anderson went through the door into the back of the hut. Karl heard him talking to the guards. A bit later Anderson came back.

'He's ready, sarge.'

'Thank you, corporal,' said Karl in his crisp, decisive voice. He put his cigarettes and matches in the top pocket of his shirt, picked up his swagger stick and crossed the mud floor to the inner door. 'Oh,' he said, hesitating before entering, 'if our good lieutenant should come calling, let me know would you, corporal?'

'Yes, sarge, I get you.'

'And don't pick your nose while I'm gone, will you, corporal?'

'No, sarge.'

Karl thought about that little Indian bint in Nairobi. He'd give a lot to be taking her knickers down at this moment, getting her legs open and fucking the arse off of her. But duty called.

He whistled as he walked along the short, dark passage to the special room. It was bleeding hot in here, worse than a bloody native hut. It stank of fucking Kikuyu.

He gave the guard at the door of the special room his officer's salute, with the swagger stick touching the peak of his well-set cap.

He went into the special room and turned on the light.

Lailu sat on the bench, his bony knees sticking up at a peculiar angle, his eyes wide and white. There was a lot of sweat in his thin moustache.

'Hello, Mr Lailu,' said Karl with his cold grin, 'how are you feeling this fine summer morning? A bit warm? Sorry we can't open a window for you, but you can see for yourself, there isn't one. That's probably against fire regulations. You could complain about that. Do you want to complain to me, Mr Lailu?'

Lailu shook his black head.

'Because you've got your rights, you know. Lots and lots of rights. You've heard the lectures? Yes, of course you have, more than once, because you've been here more than once, haven't you, Mr Lailu?'

Lailu made no response at all to this. Karl went up to him and stood very close, looking down on him. Lailu didn't look back. Karl grabbed the man's ear and twisted it so that Lailu's lips came together tightly. 'Because I remember my trademark, you see, Mr Lailu. That little scar, that's not a tribal scar, is it, Mr Lailu? That little scar isn't a Mau Mau scar, is it? That is a Sergeant Gower scar, eh?'

'Yes, boss,' said Lailu. 'Yes, boss.'

'Good.'

Karl stepped back and leaned against the door of the special room. 'We're going to keep everything informal, Mr Lailu. You know your rights, don't you?'

'Yes, boss.'

'Good.'

Karl grinned down on Lailu again. 'You were at the Kuanda farm last week, weren't you?'

'No, boss.'

'Yes you were!' Karl began to breathe quickly, the swagger stick held firmly in his two hands. 'Weren't you?'

'No, boss. Lailu not Mau Mau, boss. Lailu good boy, boss.'

'Yes, a good little liar.' The swagger stick left Karl's right hand almost without him thinking about it. It struck Lailu on the top of his head. Lailu whimpered. 'Now I won't do that again, Lailu, because that's not the way I work, is it?'

'Don't know, boss.'

'Is it?'

'No, boss.'

'Good.' Karl took out his packet of Players and selected one. He put the cigarette between his lips and he put the packet carefully back into his pocket. He took out his matches and he lit the cigarette so that it was burning just right. He put the matches back in his pocket and neatly he buttoned the pocket. He drew a deep puff on the cigarette. 'Smoke, Lailu?'

Lailu trembled all over. 'No, boss. Please.'

'Shit, Lailu? You look as if you feel like one. Use the pot over there. Get them manky pants down, Lailu.'

'Please, boss.'

Karl moved quickly. It was always best to move quickly. He grabbed the top of the Kikuyu's shorts and ripped them down to his knees, exposing the shrivelled, scarred genitals.

'Oh, I have been here before, haven't I, Lailu?'

— That's better, says Karl.

— You're insatiable, says his friend admiringly. — I've got to admit it, for all your faults.

— What's the time? Karl asks. — My watch has stopped.

— It must be coming up for morning, says his friend.

What Would You Do? (16)

You and your sister have been captured by your enemies. They are brutal enemies.

They want information from you concerning your friends. They say they will make you responsible for your sister's safety. If you tell them all they wish to know she will go free. If you do not they will humiliate, terrorise and torture her in every way they know.

You are aware that should they catch your friends they will do the same thing to at least some of them, perhaps all of them.

Whom will you betray?

Chapter Seventeen

So Long Son Lon:
1968: Babies

Quite apart from the enormous present importance of South Vietnam and our actions there, I have often reflected – as one who was tempted to become a professional historian – that the story of Vietnam, of South-East Asia, and of American policy there forms an extraordinarily broad case history involving almost all the major problems that have affected the world as a whole in the past 25 years. For the strands of the Vietnam history include the characteristics of French colonial control compared to colonial control elsewhere, the end of the colonial period, the inter-relation and competition of nationalism and Communism, our relation to the Soviet Union and Communist China and their relationships with each other, our relation to the European colonial power – France – and at least since 1954 – the relation of Vietnam to the wider question of national independence and self-determination in South-East Asia and indeed throughout Asia...

... So all over South-East Asia there is today a sense of confidence – to which Drew Middleton again testified from his trip. Time has been bought, and used. But that confidence is not solid or secure for the future. It would surely be disrupted if we were, in President Johnson's words, to permit a Communist takeover in South Vietnam either through withdrawal or 'under the cloak of a meaningless agreement'. If, on the contrary, we proceed on our present course – with measured military actions and with every possible non-military measure, and searching always for an avenue to peace – the prospects for a peaceful and secure South-East Asia now appear brighter than they have been at any time since the nations of the area were established on an independent basis.

– William P. Bundy,
'The Path to Vietnam': An address given before
the National Student Association convention held
at the University of Maryland, 15 August, 1967,
United States Information Service, American Embassy,
London, August 1967

'We were all psyched up, and as a result when we got there the shooting started, almost as a chain reaction. The majority of us had expected to meet VC combat troops, but this did not turn out to be so ... After they got in the village, I guess you could say that the men were out of control.'

– G.I. Dennis Conti

'They just kept walking towards us ... You could hear the little girl saying, "No, no..." All of a sudden, the GIs opened up and cut them down.'

– Ron Haeberle, reporter

'It's just that they didn't know what they were supposed to do; killing them seemed like a good idea, so they did it. The old lady who fought so hard was probably a VC. Maybe it was just her daughter.'

– Jay Roberts, reporter,
'My Lai 4: a Report on the Massacre and Its Aftermath'
by Seymour M. Hersh,
Harper's Magazine, May 1970

Mr Daniel Ellsberg will surrender tomorrow in Boston where he lives. He was charged on Friday with being unlawfully in possession of secret documents, and a warrant was issued for his arrest. Since he was named on June 16, by a former reporter of the 'New York Times', as the man who provided the paper with its copy of a Pentagon report, Mr Ellsberg and his wife have been in hiding. The Pentagon is about to hand over its Vietnam study to congress for confidential perusal. On Saturday the Justice Department sought to convince the court that indiscriminate publication of further documents from the study would endanger troops in South Vietnam and prejudice the procedures for obtaining the release of prisoners.

Guardian, 28 June, 1971

— You're not slow, are you? says Karl's friend. — And to think I was worried. Now I think I'll get some sleep.

— Not yet, says Karl.

— Yes, now. I'm not feeling too well, as it happens.

— You are looking a big grey. Karl inspects the black man's flesh. Compared with his own skin, it is quite pale.

Karl is twenty-two and it's his last few months in the Army. The past five months have been spent in Vietnam. Although he's seen only one VC in that time, he's tired and tense and fearful. He jokes a lot, like his buddies. There is heat, sticky sweat, jungle, mud, flies, poverty, death, but no Viet Cong. And this is a place reputedly thick with them.

— I'll be all right when I've rested, says Karl's friend. — You've worn me out, that's all.

Karl reaches out the index finger of his right hand and traces his nail over his friend's lips. — You can't be that tired.

Twenty-two and weary. A diet of little more than cold C-rations for weeks at a stretch. No change of clothing. Crashing around in the jungle. For nothing. It wasn't like the John Wayne movies. Or maybe it was. The shit and the heat – and then the action coming fast and hard. The victory. The tough captain proving he was right to drive the men so hard, after all. The bowed heads as they honoured dead buddies. Not many could stop the tears... But so far all they had was the shit and the heat.

Karl's friend opens his lips. Karl hasn't noticed before that his friend's teeth are rather stained.

—Just let me rest a little.

K ARL WAS TWENTY-TWO. His mother was forty-five. His father was forty-four. His father managed a hardware store in Phoenix, Arizona. His mother was a housewife.

Karl was on a big mission at last. He felt that if he survived the mission then it would all be over and he could look forward to going home, back to his job as his father's assistant. It was all he wanted.

He sat shoulder to shoulder with his buddies in the shivering chopper as it flew them to the combat area. He tried to read the tattered *X-Men* comic book he had brought along, but it was hard to concentrate. Nobody, among the other members of his platoon, was talking much.

Karl's hands were sweating and there was dark grease on them from the helicopter, from his rifle. The grease left his fingerprints on the pages of the comic book. He tucked the book into his shirt and buttoned it up. He smoked a joint handed to him by Bill Leinster who, like two thirds of the platoon, was black. The joint didn't do anything for him. He shifted the extra belt of M16 ammo to a more comfortable position round his neck. He was overloaded with equipment. It would almost be worth a battle to get rid of some of the weight of cartridges he was carrying.

He wondered what would be happening in Son Lon now. The hamlet had already been hit by the morning's artillery barrage and the gunships had gone in ahead. The first platoon must have arrived already. Karl was in the second platoon of four. Things would be warming up by the time he landed.

The note of the chopper's engine changed and Karl knew they were going down. He thought he heard gunfire. He wiped the grease off his hands onto the legs of his pants. He took a grip on his M16. Everyone else was beginning to straighten up, ready themselves. None of the faces showed much emotion and Karl hoped that his face looked the same.

'After what they did to Goldberg,' said Bill Leinster in a masculine growl, 'I'm going to get me a lot of ears.'

Karl grinned at him.

The chopper's deck tilted a little as the machine settled. Sergeant Grossman got the door open. Now Karl could hear the firing quite clearly, but he could only see a few trees through the door. 'Okay, let's go,' said Sergeant Grossman grimly. He sprayed a few rounds into the nearby trees and jumped out. Karl was the fifth man to follow him. There were eight other helicopters on the ground, a patch of mud entirely surrounded by trees. Karl could see four big gunships firing at something ahead. Two more big black transports were landing. The noise of their rotors nearly drowned the noise of the guns. It seemed that the first platoon was still in the landing zone. Karl saw Sergeant Grossman run across to where Lieutenant Snider was standing with his men. They conferred for a few moments and then Grossman ran back. Snider's platoon moved off into the jungle. After waiting a moment or two Grossman ordered his men forward, entering the line of trees to the left and at an angle to where Snider's men had gone in. Karl assumed that the VC in this area had either been killed or had retreated back to the hamlet. There was no firing from the enemy as yet. But he kept himself alert. They could be anywhere in the jungle and they could attack in a dozen different ways. He suddenly got a craving for a Coors. Only a Coors in a giant-size schooner, the glass misted with frost. And a Kool, enjoyed in that downtown bar where his father's friends always drank on Saturday nights. That was what he'd have when he got home. The firing in front intensified. The first platoon must have met head-on with the VC. Karl peered through the trees but could still see nothing. Sergeant Grossman waved at them to proceed with increased caution. The comic book was scratching his stomach. He regretted putting it in there. He glanced back at Bill Leinster. Leinster had the only grenade launcher in this team. Karl wondered if Leinster shouldn't be ahead of them, with the machine gunner and the sergeant. On the other hand, their rear might not be protected by the squad supposed to be flanking them and there was no cover on either side, as far as he knew, though technically there should have been. You could be hit from anywhere. He began to inspect the ground for mines, walking carefully in the footprints of the man in front of him. Sergeant Grossman paused and for a second they halted. Karl could now see a flash of red brick through the trees. They had reached the hamlet of Son Lon. There was a lot of groundfire.

Suddenly Karl was ready. He knew he would do well on this mission. His whole body was alert.

They moved into the hamlet.

The first thing they saw were VC bodies in black silk pyjamas and coolie hats. They were mostly middle-aged men and some women. There didn't seem to be too many weapons about. Maybe these had been collected up by the first platoon.

Two or three hootches were burning fitfully where they had been blasted by grenades and subsequently set on fire. A couple of the red-brick houses bore evidence of having been in the battle. Outside one of them lay the bloody corpse of a kid of around eight or nine. That was the worst part, when they used kids to draw your fire, or even throw grenades at you. More firing came from the left; Karl turned, ducking and ready, his rifle raised, but no attack came. They proceeded warily into the village. Leinster, on command from Grossman, loaded his grenade launcher and started firing into the huts and houses as they passed, in case any VC should still be in there. It was menacingly safe, thought Karl, wondering what the VC were waiting for. Or maybe there hadn't been as many slopes in the hamlet as Captain Heffer had anticipated. Or maybe they were in the paddy fields on the left and right of the village.

Karl really wanted to fire at something. Just one VC would do. It would justify everything else.

They entered the centre of the village, the plaza. Lieutenant Snider and his men were already there, rounding up civilians. There were a lot of bodies around the plaza, mainly women and children. Karl was used to seeing corpses, but he had never seen so many. He was filled with disgust for the Vietnamese. They really had no human feelings. They were just like the Japs had been, and the Chinese in Korea. What was the point of fighting for them?

One of the kids in the group which had been rounded up ran forward. He held a Coke bottle in his hand, offering it to the nearest soldier. The soldier was Henry Tabori. Karl knew him.

Tabori backed away from the boy and fired his M16 from the hip. The M16 was an automatic. The boy got all of it, staggering backwards and falling into the gang of villagers. Some of the women and old men started to shout. Some fell to their knees, wringing their hands. Karl had seen pictures of them doing that. Lieutenant Snider turned away with a shrug. Tabori put a new magazine into his rifle. By this time the other five men were firing into the ranks of civilians. They poured scores of rounds into them. Blood appeared on the jerking bodies. Bits of chipped bone flew.

Karl saw Sergeant Grossman watching the slaughter. Grossman's face was thoughtful. Then Grossman said: 'Okay, Leinster. Give it to 'em.' He indicated the huts which had so far not been blasted. Leinster loaded his grenade launcher and began sending grenades through every doorway he could see. People started to run out. Grossman shot them down as they came. His machine gunner opened up. One by one the other boys started firing. Karl dropped to a kneeling position, tucked his rifle hard against his shoulder, set the gun to automatic, and sent seventeen rounds into an old man as he stumbled from his hootch, his hands raised in front of his face, his legs streaming with blood. He put a fresh magazine into the rifle. The next time he fired he got a woman. The woman, with a dying action, rolled over onto a baby. The baby wasn't much good without its mother. Karl stepped closer and fired half his magazine into the baby. All the huts and houses were smoking, but people kept running out. Karl killed some more of them. Their numbers seemed to be endless.

Grossman shouted for them to cease firing, then led them at a run out of the plazas and along a dirt road. 'Get 'em out of the huts,' Grossman told his men. 'Round the bastards up.'

Karl and a negro called Keller went into one of the huts and kicked the family until they moved out into the street. There were two old men, an old woman, two young girls, a boy and a woman with a baby. Karl and Keller waved their rifles and made the family join the others in the street. They did not wait for Grossman's orders to fire.

Some of the women and the older girls and boys tried to put themselves between the soldiers and the smaller children. The soldiers continued to fire until they were sure they were all dead. Leinster began to giggle. Soon they were all giggling. They left the pile of corpses behind them and some of them swaggered as they walked. 'We sure have got a lot of VC today,' said Keller, wiping his forehead with a rag.

Karl looked back. He saw a figure rising from the pile of corpses. It was a girl of about thirteen, dressed in a black smock and black pyjamas. She looked bewildered. Her eyes met Karl's. Karl turned away. But he could still see her eyes. He whirled, dropped to one knee, took careful aim, and shot her head off. He thought: They've all got to die now. What have they got to live for, anyway? He was putting them out of their misery. He thought: If I don't shoot them, they'll see that it was me who shot the others. He reached up and pulled his helmet more firmly over his eyes. It was not his fault. They had told him he would be shooting VC. It was too late, now.

They left the hamlet and were on a road. They saw a whole lot of women and children in a ditch between the road and a paddy field. Karl was the first to fire at them. Leinster finished them off with his grenades. Only Karl and Leinster had bothered to fire that time. Nobody looked at anybody else for a moment. Then

Grossman said: 'It's a VC village. All we're doing is stopping them from growing up to be VC.'

Leinster snorted. 'Yeah.'

'It's true,' said Sergeant Grossman. He looked around him at the paddy fields as if addressing the hundreds of hidden VC he thought must be there. 'It's true. We've got to waste them all this time.'

Another group of men emerged on the other side of the paddy field. They had two grenade launchers which they were firing at random into the ground and making the mud and plants gout up.

Karl looked at the corpses in the ditch. They were really mangled.

They went back into the village. They found a hut with three old women in it. They wasted the hut and its occupants. They found a two-year-old kid, screaming. They wasted him. They found a fifteen-year-old girl. After Leinster and another man called Aitken had torn her clothes off and raped her, they wasted her. Karl didn't fuck her because he couldn't get a hard-on, but he was the one who shot her tits to ribbons.

'Jesus Christ!' grinned Karl as he and Leinster paused for a moment. 'What a day!'

They both laughed. They wasted two water buffalo and a cow. Leinster blew a hole in the cow with his launcher. 'That's a messy cow!' said Karl.

Karl and Leinster went hunting. They were looking for anything which moved. Karl was haunted by the faces of the living. These, and not the dead, were the ghosts that had to be exorcised. He would not be accused by them. He kicked aside the corpses of women to get at their babies. He bayoneted the babies. He and Leinster went into the jungle and found some wounded kids. They wasted the kids as they tried to stumble away.

They went back to the village and found Lieutenant Snider talking to Captain Heffer. They were laughing, too. Captain Heffer's pants were covered in mud to the thigh. He had evidently been in one of the paddies.

The gunships and communications choppers were still thundering away overhead. Every two or three minutes you heard gunfire from somewhere. Karl couldn't see any more gooks. For a moment he had an impulse to shoot Lieutenant Snider and Captain Heffer. If they had turned and seen him, he might have done so. But Leinster tapped him on the shoulder, as if he guessed what he was thinking, and jerked his thumb to indicate they should try the outlying hootches. Karl went with him part of the way, but he had begun to feel tired. He was hoping the battle would be over soon. He saw an unshattered Coke bottle lying on the ground. He reached out to pick it up before it occurred to him that it might be booby-trapped. He looked at it for a long time, struggling with his desire for a drink and his caution.

He trudged along the alley between the ruined huts, the sprawled and shattered corpses. Why hadn't the VC appeared? It was their fault. He had been geared to fight. The sound of gunfire went on and on and on.

Karl found that he had left the village. He thought he had better try to rejoin his squad. They ought to retain military discipline. It was the only way to make sense of this. He tried to go back, but he couldn't. He dropped his rifle. He leaned down to pick it up. On either side of him the rice paddies gleamed in the sun. He reached out for the rifle, but his boot caught it by accident and it fell into a ditch. He climbed into the ditch to get the rifle. He found it. It was covered in slime. He knew it would take him an age to clean it. He realised that he had begun to cry. He sat in the ditch and he shook with weeping.

A little later Grossman found him.

Grossman knelt at the side of the ditch and patted Karl's shoulder. 'What's the matter, boy?'

Karl couldn't answer.

'Come on, son,' said Grossman kindly. He picked Karl's slimy rifle out of the ditch and slung it over his own shoulder. 'There isn't much left to do here.' He helped Karl to his feet. Karl drew a deep, shuddering breath.

'Don't worry, kid,' said Grossman. 'Please...'

He seemed to be begging Karl, as if Karl were reminding him of something he didn't want to remember.

'Now, you stop all that, you hear? It ain't manly.' He spoke gruffly and kept patting Karl's shoulder, but there was an edge to his voice, too.

'Sorry,' said Karl at last as they moved back to the village.

'Nobody's blaming you,' said the sergeant. 'Nobody's blaming nobody. It's what happens, that's all.'

'I'm sorry,' said Karl again.

— But we have got to blame somebody sooner or later, says Karl. — We need victims. Somebody's got to suffer. 'Now lieutenant, will you kindly tell the Court just what you had to do with the Human Condition? We are waiting, lieutenant? Why are we not as happy as we might be, lieutenant? Give your answer briefly and clearly.'

— What the hell are you talking about? says his friend, waking up and yawning.

— I didn't say anything, says Karl. — You must have been dreaming. Do you feel better?

— I'm not sure.

— You don't look it.

What Would You Do? (17)

You have been travelling in the desert.

There has been an accident. Your car has overturned and the friend with whom you were travelling has been badly hurt. He is almost certain to die.

Would you remain with him and hope that rescue would come soon?

Would you leave him what water you have, making him as comfortable as possible and setting off to find help, knowing he will probably be dead by the time you return?

Would you decide that, since he was as good as dead, you might as well take the water and food with you, as it will give you a better chance?

Would you remain in the shade of the wreck, knowing that this would be the wisest thing to do, but deciding not to waste your water on your dying friend?

Chapter Eighteen
London Life:
2020: City of Shadows

One of the happiest answers recorded of living statesmen was that in which a well known minister recommended to an alarmed interrogator the 'study of large maps'. The danger which seems so imminent, so ominous, when we read about it in a newspaper article or in the report of a speech, grows reassuringly distant when considered through the medium of a good sized chart.

– Walter Richards,
Her Majesty's Army: Indian and Colonial
Forces: A Descriptive Account,
J.S. Virtue & Co., 1890

If SNCC had said Negro Power or Colored Power, white folks would've continued sleeping easy every night. But BLACK POWER! Black! That word. BLACK! And the visions came of alligator-infested swamps arched by primordial trees with moss dripping from the limbs and out of the depths of the swamp, the mire oozing from his skin, came the black monster and fathers told their daughters to be in by nine instead of nine-thirty. The visions came of big BLACK bucks running through the streets, raping everything white that wore a dress, burning, stealing, killing. BLACK POWER! My God, the niggers were gon' start paying white folks back. They hadn't forgotten 14-year-old Emmett Till being thrown into the Tallahatchie River. (We know what you and that chick threw off the Talla-hatchie bridge, Billy Joe) with a gin mill tied around his ninety-pound body. They hadn't forgotten the trees bent low with the weight of black bodies on a lynching rope. They hadn't forgotten the black women walking down country roads who were shoved into cars, raped, and then pushed out, the threat of death ringing in their ears, the pain of hateful sex in their pelvis. The niggers hadn't forgotten and they wanted power. BLACK POWER!

– Julius Lester,
Look Out, Whitey! Black Power's Gon' Get Your Mama,
Grove Press, 1969

— *It's dawn, says Karl. — At last! I'm starving!*

— *You're beautiful, says his friend. — I want you for always.*

— *Well...*

— *Always.*

— *Let's have some breakfast. What's the time? Do they serve it yet?*

— *They serve it whenever you want it, whatever you want.*

— *That's service.*

— *Karl?*

— *What?*

— *Please stay with me.*

— *I think I'll just have something simple. Boiled eggs and toast. Christ, can you hear my stomach rumbling?*

Karl is eighty-one. Lonely. All as far as he can see, the ruins stretch away, some black, some grey, some red, outlined against a cold sky. The world is over.

Karl's friend seizes him by the wrist. The grip hurts Karl, he tries to break free. Karl blinks. The pain swims through him, confusing him.

An old eighty-one. A scrawny eighty-one. And what has he survived for? What right has he had to survive when others have not? There is no justice...

— *Karl, you promised me, last night.*

— *I don't remember much of last night. It was a bit confused, last night, wasn't it?*

— *Karl! I'm warning you.*

Karl smiles, taking an interest in his fine, black body. He turns one of his arms this way and that as the dawn sunshine glints on the rich, shiny skin. — That's nice, he says.

— After all I've done for you, says his friend, almost weeping.

— There's no justice, says Karl. — Or maybe there is a very little. Maybe you have to work hard to manufacture tiny quantities of justice, the way you get gold by panning for it. Eh?

— There's only desire! His friend hisses through savage, stained teeth. His eyes are bloodshot. — Karl! Karl! Karl!

— You're looking even worse in the daylight, says Karl. — You could do with some breakfast as much as me. Let's order it now. We can talk while we eat.

K ARL WILL BE EIGHTY-ONE. His mother will have been dead long since, of cancer. His father will have been dead for nine years, killed in the Wolverhampton riots of 2011. Karl will be unemployed.

He will sit by the shattered window of his front room on the ground floor of the house in Ladbroke Grove, London. He will look out into the festering street. There will be nobody there but the rats and the cats. There will be only a handful of other human beings left in London, most of them in Southwark, by the river.

But the wars will be over. It will be peaceful.

Peaceful for Karl, at any rate. Karl will have been a cannibal for two of the years he has been home, having helped in the destruction of Hong Kong and served as a mercenary in Paris, where he will have gained the taste for human flesh. Anything will be preferable to the rats and the cats. Not that, by this time, he will be hunting his meat himself; he will have lost any wish to kill the few creatures like him who will haunt the diseased ruins of the city.

Karl will brood by the window. He will have secured all other doors and windows against attack, though there will have been no attack up to that time. He will have left the wide window open, since it will command the best view of Ladbroke Grove.

He will have been burning books in the big fireplace to keep himself warm. He will not, any longer, be reading books. They will all depress him too much. He will not, as far as it will be possible, think any more. He will wish to become only a part of whatever it will be that he is part of.

From the corners of his eyes he will see fleeting shadows which he will think are people, perhaps even old friends, who will have come, seeking him out. But they will only be shadows. Or perhaps rats. Or cats. But probably only shadows. He will come to think of these shadows in quite an affectionate way. He will see them as the ghosts of his unborn children. He will see them as the women he never loved, the men he never knew.

Karl will scratch his scurvy, unhealthy body. His body will be dying much faster now that the cans have run out and he will no longer be able to find the vitamins he has used before.

He will not fear death.

He will not understand death, just as he will not understand life.

One idea will run together with another.

Nothing will have a greater or a lesser value than another thing. All will have been brought to the same state. This will be peace of a particular kind. This will be security and stability of a particular kind. There will be no other kind. All things will flow together. There will be no past, no present. No future.

Later Karl will lie like a lizard, unmoving on the flat table, his rifle forgotten beside him, and he will stare out at the ruins as if he has known them all his life, as if they, like him, are eternal.

They eat breakfast.

— It's a lovely morning, says Karl.

— I am very rich, says his friend. — I can let you have all you want. Women, other men, anyone. Power. You can satisfy every desire. And I will be whatever you want me to be. I promise. I will serve you. I will be like a genie from the lamp bringing you your heart's every whim! It is true, Karl! The sickly eyes burn with a fever of lust.

— I'm not sure I want anything at the moment. Karl finishes his coffee.

— Stay with me, Karl.

Karl feels sorry for his friend. He puts down his napkin.
— I'll tell you what we'll do today. We'll go back to the roof garden.
What about it?
— If that's what you want.
— I'm very grateful to you, in a way, says Karl.

What Would You Do? (18)

Your father has been to hospital at his doctor's request, because he has been suffering pain in his chest, his stomach and his throat. The hospital has told him that he has a form of rheumatism and prescribes certain kinds of treatment.

You receive a request from your father's doctor to visit him.

The doctor tells you that your father is actually suffering from inoperable cancer. He has cancer of the lung, of the stomach and of the throat. He has at very most a year to live.

The doctor says that the decision whether to tell your father of this is up to you. He, the doctor, can't accept the responsibility.

Your father loves life and he fears death.

Would you tell your father the whole truth?

Would you offer him part of the truth and tell him that he has a chance of recovering?

Would you think it better for your father's peace of mind that he know nothing?

Chapter Nineteen

In the Roof Garden:
1971: Happy Day

The prosecution today won its fight to try Capt. Ernest
L. Medina on murder charges, but decided not to seek the
death penalty.

International Herald Tribune, 26 & 27 June, 1971

K ARL AND HIS friend stood together by the railing, looking at
the view over London. It was a beautiful, warm day. Karl
breathed in the scents of the flowers, of the store below, of the
traffic beyond. He felt contented.

His friend's pale, blue eyes were troubled. He looked thin and
his silk suit hardly seemed to fit any longer. He had put on several
rings and, when he tapped his fingers nervously on the rails, they
seemed to be the only part of him that had any life.

'Are you sure you know what you're doing, Karl?' said his
friend.

'I think so. Honestly, it would be for the best now. It couldn't
last.'

'I could do so much for you still. If you knew who I really was,
you'd believe me.'

'Oh, I've seen your pictures. I didn't want to put you out by
mentioning it. I didn't recognise you at first, that was all.'

'I offered you an empire, and you've chosen a cabbage patch.'

Karl grinned. 'It's more my style, boss.'

'You can always change your mind.'

'I know. Thank you.'

Karl's friend was reluctant to say goodbye, but he was too

miserable to attempt to summon any further strength and try to persuade Karl.

Karl adjusted the hat he had bought for himself on the way up. 'I think I'll go down and buy a suit somewhere now,' he said. 'Adios!'

The white man nodded and turned away without saying goodbye.

'Look after yourself,' said Karl. 'Get some sleep.' With a spring in his step, he walked through the Woodland Garden to the exit. The two middle-aged ladies were there as usual. A fat tourist came out of the lift and bumped into him. The tourist cursed him and then apologised almost at the same time. He was evidently embarrassed.

'Don't worry, boss,' said Karl, flashing him a grin. 'That's okay.'

He took the lift down, changed as usual at the third floor, went down to the ground floor, bought himself a newspaper and studied the lists of runners for the day's races.

A middle-aged man in a check suit and wearing a smart bowler, with a white handlebar moustache, smelling of tobacco, asked: 'What are you planning to do?' He was genuinely interested. He had his own paper open at the racing page. 'Any tips?'

'I'm feeling lucky today.' Karl ran his slender brown finger down the lists. 'What about Russian Roulette, two-thirty, Epsom?'

'Right. And thank you very kindly.'

'It's all right, man.'

The punter laughed heartily and slapped Karl on the back. 'I'll say that for you fellows, you know how to keep cheerful. Cheerio!'

Karl saluted and left the store, crossing the High Street and walking up Church Street, enjoying the morning. At Notting Hill he stopped and wondered if he should go straight back to Ladbroke Grove. The suit he wanted had just taken shape in his mind.

The Time Dweller

D USK HAD COME to the universe, albeit the small universe inhabited by Man. The sun of Earth had dimmed, the moon had retreated and salt clogged the sluggish oceans, filled the rivers that toiled slowly between white, crystalline banks, beneath darkened, moody skies that slumbered in eternal evening.

Of course, in the sun's long life this stage was merely one interlude. In perhaps a few thousand years, it would flare to full splendour again. But for the meantime it kept its light in close rein, grumbling in its mighty depths and preparing itself for the next step in its evolution.

It had taken time in its fading and those few creatures who had remained on its planets had managed to adapt. Among them was Man, indefatigable; undeserving, really, considering the lengths he had gone to, in previous epochs, to dispose of himself. But here he was, in his small universe consisting of one planet without even the satellite which had slid away into space long since and, in its passing, left legends on his lips.

Brown clouds, brown light, brown rocks and brown ocean flecked with white. A pale rider on a pale beast thumping along the shore, the dry taste of ocean salt in his mouth, the stink of a dead oozer in his nostrils.

His name was the Scar-faced Brooder, son of the Sleepy-eyed Smiler, his father, and the Pinch-cheeked Worrier, his mother. The seal-beast he rode was called Urge. Its glossy coat was still sleek with the salt-rain that had recently ceased, its snout pointed eagerly forward and its two strong leg-fins thwacked the encrusted shore as it galloped along, dragging its razor-edged tail with scant effort. The Scar-faced Brooder was supported on his steed's sloping back by a built-up saddle of polished silicon that flashed whenever it reflected the salt-patches studding the ground like worn teeth. In his hand, held at its butt by a stirrup grip, was his long gun, the piercer with an everlasting ruby as its life. He was dressed in sealskin dyed in sombre rust-red and dark yellow.

Behind him, the Scar-faced Brooder heard the sound of another rider, one whom he had tried to avoid since morning.

Now, as evening quietly flowed brown and misty into black night, she still followed. He turned his calm face to look, his mouth tight and white as the scar which rose from its corner to follow his left cheekbone. She was in the distance, still, but gaining.

He increased his speed.

Brown clouds boiled low like foam across the dark sand of the flat, and their seals slapped loudly over the damp shore as she neared him.

He came to a pool of salt-thick water and Urge splashed into it. It was warm. Still she followed him, even into the water, so that he turned his steed and waited, half-trembling, until she rode up, a tall, well-formed woman with light brown hair long and loose in the breeze.

'Dearest Tall Laugher,' he told his sister, 'for me there is no amusement in this game.'

Frowning, she smiled.

He pressed his point, disturbed, his calm face earnest in the fading brown light that was all the clouds would let pass.

'I wish to ride alone.'

'Where would you go, alone, when together we might be carried to more exotic adventure?'

He paused, unwilling and unable to answer.

'Will you come back?'

'I would prefer not to.'

A cold, silent wind began to buffet them as it came in suddenly from the sea. Urge moved nervously.

'You fear what the Chronarch might do?'

'The Chronarch has no love for me – but neither has he hatred.

He would prefer me gone from Lanjis Liho, to cross the great salt plains of the west and seek my fortune in the land of fronds. He would not trust me with a small part of the Future, as you know, nor give a fraction of the Past into my safe-keeping. I go to shape my own destiny!'

'So – you sulk!' she cried as the wind began to mewl. 'You sulk because the Chronarch delegates no honours. Meanwhile, your loving sister aches and is miserable.'

'Marry the Big-brained Boaster! He has trust of Past and Future both!'

He forced his restless seal-beast through the thick water and into the night. As it moved, he reached into the saddle sheath and took out his torch to light his way. He depressed its grip and it blazed out, illuminating the surrounding beach for several yards around. Turning, he saw her for a moment in the circle of light, motionless, her eyes aghast as if he had betrayed her.

Oh, I am lonely now, he thought, as the wind blew cold and strong against his body.

He headed inland, over the salt-rocks, towards the west. He rode all night until his eyes were heavy with tiredness, but still he rode, away from Lanjis Liho where the Chronarch, Lord of Time, ruled past and present and watched the future come, away from family, home and city, his heart racked with the strain of the breaking, his mind fevered fire and his body all stiff from the demands he made of it.

Into the night, into the west, with his torch burning in his saddle and loyal Urge responding to his affectionate whispering. To the west, until dawn came slowly up from behind him and covered the barren land with soft light.

A little further through the morning he heard a sound as of cloth flapping in the wind and when he turned his head he saw a green tent pitched beside a shallow crevasse, its front flap dancing. He readied his long piercer and halted Urge.

Drawn out, perhaps, by the noise of the seal-beast's movement, a man's head poked from the tent like a tortoise emerging from the recesses of its shell. He had a beak of a nose and a fishlike pecker of a mouth, his large eyes were heavy-lidded and a tight-fitting hood hid hair and neck.

'Aha,' said the Scar-faced Brooder in recognition.

'Hmm,' said the Hooknosed Wanderer, also recognising the mounted man confronting him. 'You are some distance from Lanjis Liho. Where are you bound?'

'For the land of fronds.'

He resheathed his piercer and clambered down from the high saddle. He passed the tent, its occupant's head craning round to follow him, and stared into the crevasse. It had been widened and deepened by human tools, revealing pieces of ancient wreckage. 'What's this?'

'Nothing but the remains of a crashed spaceship,' replied the Hooknosed Wanderer in such obvious disappointment that he could not have been lying. 'My metal diviner found it and I had hoped for a capsule with books or film.'

'There were never many of those. I'd say they had all been gathered by now.'

'That's my belief, too, but one hopes. Have you breakfasted?'

'No. Thank you.'

The hooded head withdrew into the tent and a thin hand held back the flap. The Scar-faced Brooder bent and entered the cluttered tent. There was a great deal of equipment therein; the Hooknosed Wanderer's livelihood, for he sustained himself by bartering some of the objects he found with his metal diviner and other instruments.

'Apparently, you have no riding animal,' said the Scar-faced Brooder as he sat down and crossed his legs between a soft bundle and an angular statuette of steel and concrete.

'It was necessary to abandon her when my water was exhausted and I could find none to replace it. That is why I was heading for the sea. I am exceedingly thirsty, am suffering from salt-deficiency since I have no liking for the salt which grows in these parts.'

'I have plenty in my saddle barrel,' he said. 'Help yourself – good salt water, slightly diluted with fresh, if that suits your taste.'

He leaned back on the bundle as the Wanderer, nodding sharply, scrambled up, clasping a canteen, and left the tent.

He returned smiling. 'Thanks. I can last for several days, now.' He pushed aside his clutter of antiques, discovering a small stove. He activated it, placed a pan on top and began frying the leg-fish he had trapped recently.

'Which city was your destination, Brooder? Only two are in easy reach from here – and both lie still many leagues hence. Is it Barbart or Piorha?'

'Barbart in the land of fronds, I think, for I should like to see green vegetation instead of grey or brown. And the ancient places thereabouts have, I must admit, romantic connotations for me. I should like to go and wallow in racial memory, sense the danger of uncontrolled Past, insignificant Present and random Future…'

'Some feel it as that,' the Wanderer smiled, shuffling the leg-fish onto plates. 'Especially those from Lanjis Liho where the Chronarchy holds sway. But remember, much will be in your mind. You may see Barbart and the land of fronds, but its significance will be decided by you, not by it. Try to do as I do – make no judgements or descriptions of this world of ours. Do that, and it will treat you better.'

'Your words seem wise, Wanderer, but I have no precedents by which to judge them. Perhaps when I have placed some of the Future in the Past, I will know.'

'You seem tired,' said the Wanderer when they were finished eating, 'would you like to sleep?'

'I would. Thanks.' And while the Hooknosed Wanderer went about his business, the Brooder slept.

He rose in the mellow afternoon, roused Urge who had taken advantage of his master's slumber to rest also, and wished the Wanderer goodbye.

'May your blood stay thick,' said the Wanderer formally, 'and your mind remain open.'

He rode away and by dusk had come to the moss which was primarily grey and brown, but tinted in places with patches of light green. He took out his torch and fixed it in its saddle bracket, unwilling to sleep at night because of the potential danger of predatory life.

Once the light from his torch showed him a school of oozers, moving at right angles to his path. They were far inland for their kind, these great white slug-creatures that raised their heads to observe him. He felt he could hear them sniffing at his body salt as perhaps their leech ancestors had sniffed out the blood of his own forefathers. Urge, without prompting, increased his speed.

As he left them, he felt that the oozers represented the true native of Earth now. Man's place was no longer easy to define, but it seemed that he had been superseded. By remaining alive on the salt-heavy Earth he was outstaying his welcome. If there was another home for Man, it did not lie here but in some other region; perhaps not even the region of space at all but in dimensions where natural evolution could not affect him.

Brooding, as was his bent, he continued to ride for Barbart and, by the following day, had reached the delicate frond forests that waved golden green in the soft sunlight, all silence and sweet scent. Urge's bounding gait became almost merry as they fled over the cushions of moss between the shaded spaces left by the web-thin fronds waving and flowing in the gusts of air which occasionally swept the forest.

He dismounted soon and lay back on a bank of comfortable moss, breathing the scented breeze in luxurious self-indulgence. His mind began to receive disjointed images, he heard his sister's voice, the sonorous tones of the Chronarch denying him a function in the House of Time – a function which he had expected as of right, for had not his grand-uncle been the previous Chronarch? He saw the twisting many-dimensioned Tower of Time, that wonder-work of an ancient architect with its colours and strange, moving angles and curves. And then he slept.

When he awoke it was night and Urge was hooting at him to wake. He got up sleepily and hauled himself into the saddle, settled himself, reached for his torch and adjusting it rode through what seemed to be a network of black and stirring threads that were the fronds seen in the cold torchlight.

The next morning he could see the low-roofed houses of Barbart lying in a valley walled by gentle hills. High above the roofs, a great contrivance of burnished brass glowered like rich red gold. He speculated momentarily upon its function.

Now a road became evident, a hard track winding among the moss dunes and leading towards the city. As he followed it he heard the muffled thud of a rider approaching and, somewhat wary for he knew little of Barbart or its inhabitants, reined in Urge, his piercer ready.

Riding towards him on a heavy old walrus came a young man, long-haired and pleasant-featured in a jerkin of light blue that matched his eyes. He stopped the walrus and looked quizzically at the Scar-faced Brooder.

'Stranger,' he said cheerfully, 'it is a pleasant morning.'

'Yes it is – and a pleasant land you dwell in. Is that city Barbart?'

'Barbart, certainly. There's none other hereabouts. From where are you?'

'From Lanjis Liho by the sea.'

'I had the inkling that men from Lanjis Liho never travelled far.'

'I am the first. My name is the Scar-faced Brooder.'

'Mine is Domm and I welcome you to Barbart. I would escort you there save for the fact that I have a mission from my mother to seek herbs among the fronds. I am already late, I fear. What time is it?'

'Time? Why the present, of course.'

'Ha! Ha! But the hour – what is that?'

'What is "the hour"?' asked the Brooder, greatly puzzled.

'That's my question.'

'I am afraid your local vernacular is beyond me,' said the Brooder politely, but nonplussed. The lad's question had been strange to begin with, but now it had become incomprehensible.

'No matter,' Domm decided with a smile. 'I have heard you

people of Lanjis Liho have some peculiar customs. I will not delay you. Follow the road and you should be in Barbart in less than an hour.'

'Hour' – the word again. Was it some division of the league used here? He gave up wondering and wished the youth 'thick blood' as he rode on.

The mosaiced buildings of Barbart were built in orderly geometric patterns about the central quadrangle in which lay the towering machine of burnished brass with its ridges and knobs and curlicues. Set in the centre of the machine was a great round plaque, divided into twelve units with each unit of twelve divided into a further five units. From the centre arose two pointers, one shorter than the other and the Scar-faced Brooder saw them move slowly. As he rode through Barbart, he noticed that facsimiles of this object were everywhere and he judged, at last, that it was some holy object or heraldic device.

Barbart seemed a pleasant place, though with a somewhat restless atmosphere epitomised by the frantic market place where men and women rushed from stall to stall shouting at one another, tugging at bales of bright cloth, fingering salt-free fruits and vegetables, pawing meats and confectioneries amid the constant babble of the vendors crying their wares.

Enjoying the scene, the Scar-faced Brooder led his seal-beast through the square and discovered a tavern in one of the side plazas. The plaza itself contained a small fountain in its centre and benches and tables had been placed close by outside the tavern. The Brooder seated himself upon one of these and gave his order to the fat girl who came to ask it.

'Beer?' she said, folding her plump, brown arms over her red bodice. 'We have only a little and it is expensive. The fermented peach juice is cheaper.'

'Then bring me that,' he said pleasantly and turned to watch the thin fountain water, noting that it smelled of brine hardly at all.

Hearing, perhaps, a strange accent, a man emerged from the

shadowy doorway of the tavern and, tankard in hand, stood looking down at the Scar-faced Brooder, an amiable expression on
his face.

'Where are you from, traveller?' he asked.

The Brooder told him and the Barbartian seemed surprised.
He seated himself on another bench.

'You are the second visitor from strange parts we have had here
in a week. The other was an emissary from Moon. They have
changed much, those Moonites, you know. Tall, they are, and thin
as a frond with aesthetic faces. They dress in cloth of metal. He
told us he had sailed space for many weeks to reach us...'

At this second reference to the unfamiliar word 'week', the
Brooder turned his head to look at the Barbartian. 'Forgive me,'
he said, 'but as a stranger I am curious at certain words I have
heard here. What would you mean by "week" exactly?'

'Why – a week – seven days – what else?'

The Brooder laughed apologetically. 'There you are, you see.
Another word – days. What is a days?'

The Barbartian scratched his head, a wry expression on his
face. He was a middle-aged man with a slight stoop, dressed in a
robe of yellow cloth. He put down his tankard and raised his
hand. 'Come with me and I will do my best to show you.'

'That would please me greatly,' said the Brooder gratefully. He
finished his wine and called for the girl. When she appeared he
asked her to take care of his steed and to make him up a bed since
he would be staying through the next darkness.

The Barbartian introduced himself as Mokof, took the Brooder's arm and led him through the series of squares, triangles and
circles formed by the buildings, to come at length to the great
central plaza and stare up at the pulsing, monstrous machine of
burnished bronze.

'This machine supplies the city with its life,' Mokof informed
him. 'And also regulates our lives.' He pointed at the disc which
the Brooder had noted earlier. 'Do you know what that is, my
friend?'

'No. I am afraid I do not. Could you explain?'

'It's a *clock*. It measures the hours of the day,' he broke off, noting the Brooder's puzzlement. 'That is to say it measures time.'

'Ah! I am with you at last. But a strange device, surely, for it cannot measure a great deal of time with that little circular dial. How does it note the flow…?'

'We call a period of sunlight "day" and a period of darkness "night". We divide each into twelve hours –'

'Then the period of sunlight and the period of darkness are equal? I had thought…'

'No, we call them equal for convenience, since they vary. The twelve divisions are called hours. When the hands reach twelve, they begin to count around again…'

'Fantastic!' The Brooder was astounded. 'You mean you recycle the same period of time round and round again. A marvellous idea. Wonderful! I had not thought it possible.'

'Not exactly,' Mokof said patiently. 'However, the hours are divided into sixty units. These are called minutes. The minutes are also divided into sixty units, each unit is called a second. The seconds are…'

'Stop! Stop! I am confounded, bewildered, dazzled! How do you control the flow of time that you can thus manipulate it at will? You must tell me. The Chronarch in Lanjis Liho would be overawed to learn of your discoveries!'

'You fail to understand, my friend. We do not *control* time. If anything, it controls us. We simply measure it.'

'You don't control… but if that's so why –?' The Brooder broke off, unable to see the logic of the Barbartian's words. 'You tell me you recycle a given period of time which you divided into twelve. And yet you then tell me you recycle a shorter period and then an even shorter period. It would soon become apparent if this were true, for you would be performing the same action over and over again and I see you are not. Or, if you were using the same time without being in its power, the sun would cease to move across the sky and I see it still moves. Given that you can release yourself from the influence of time, why am I not conscious of it since that instrument,' he pointed at the *clock*, 'exerts its influence over the entire city. Or, again, if it is a natural talent, why are we in Lanjis Liho so busily concerned with categorising and investigating our researches into the flow if you have mastered it so completely?'

A broad smile crossed the face of Mokof. He shook his head. 'I told you – we have no mastery over it. The instrument merely tells us what time it is.'

'That is ridiculous,' the Brooder said, dazed. His brain fought to retain its sanity. 'There is only the present. Your words are illogical!'

Mokof stared at his face in concern. 'Are you unwell?'

'I'm well enough. Thank you for the trouble you have taken, I will return to the tavern now, before I lose all hold of sanity!'

The clutter in his head was too much. Mokof made a statement and then denied it in the same breath. He decided he would cogitate it over a meal.

When he reached the tavern he found the door closed and no amount of banging could get those inside to open it. He noticed that his saddle and saddlebags were resting outside and he knew he had some food in one of the bags, so he sat on the bench and began to munch on a large hunk of bread.

Suddenly, from above him, he heard a cry and looking up he saw an old woman's head regarding him from a top-storey window.

'Ah!' she cried. 'Aah! What are you doing?'

'Why, eating this piece of bread, madam,' he said in surprise.

'Filthy!' she shrieked. 'Filthy, immoral pig!'

'Really, I fail to –'

'Watch! Watch!' the old woman cried from the window.

Very swiftly, three armed men came running into the plaza. They screwed up their faces in disgust when they saw the Scarfaced Brooder.

'A disgusting exhibitionist as well as a pervert!' said the leader.

They seized the startled Brooder.

'What's happening?' he gasped. 'What have I done?'

'Ask the judge,' snarled one of his captors and they hauled him towards the central plaza and took him to a tall house which appeared to be their headquarters.

There he was flung into a cell and they went away.

An overdressed youth in the next cell said with a grin: 'Greetings, stranger. What's your offence?'

'I have no idea,' said the Brooder. 'I merely sat down to have my lunch when, all at once...'

'Your lunch? But it is not lunch-time for another ten minutes!'

'Lunch-time. You mean you set aside a special period to *eat* – oh, this is too much for me.'

The overdressed youth drew away from the bars and went to the other side of his cell, his nose wrinkling in disgust. 'Ugh – you deserve the maximum penalty for a crime like that!'

Sadly puzzled, the Brooder sat down on his bench, completely mystified and hopeless. Evidently the strange customs of these people were connected with their *clock* which seemed to be a virtual deity to them. If the hands did not point to a certain figure when you did something, then that act became an offence. He wondered what the maximum penalty would be.

Very much later, the guards came to him and made him walk through a series of corridors and into a room where a man in a long purple gown wearing a metallic mask was seated at a carved table. The guards made the Brooder sit before the man and then they went and stood by the door.

The masked man said in a sonorous voice: 'You have been accused of eating outside the proper hour and of doing it in a public place for all to see. A serious charge. What is your defence?'

'Only that I am a stranger and do not understand your customs,' said the Brooder.

'A poor excuse. Where are you from?'

'From Lanjis Liho by the sea.'

'I have heard rumours of the immoralities practised there. You will learn that you cannot bring your filthy habits to another city and hope to continue with them. I will be lenient with you, however, and sentence you to one year in the antique mines.'

'But it is unjust!'

'Unjust, is it? Watch your tongue or I will extend the sentence!'

Depressed and without hope, the Brooder allowed the guards to take him back to his cell.

The night passed and morning came and then the guards arrived. 'Get up,' said the leader, 'the judge wishes to see you again!'

'Does he intend to increase my sentence, after all?'

'Ask him.'

The judge was tapping his desk nervously as the Brooder and his guards entered.

'You know of machines in Lanjis Liho, do you not? You have some strange ones, I've heard. Do you wish to be released?'

'I wish to be released, of course. Yes, we know something of machines, but...'

'Our Great Regulator is out of control. I would not be surprised if your crime did not provide the shock which caused it to behave erratically. Something has gone wrong with its life-core and we may have to evacuate Barbart if it cannot be adjusted. We have forgotten our old knowledge of machines. If you adjust the Great Regulator, we shall let you go. Without it, we do not know when to sleep, eat or perform any of our other functions. We shall go mad if we lose its guidance!'

Scarcely understanding the rest of the judge's statement, the Brooder heard only the fact that he was to be released if he mended their machine. On the other hand, he had left Lanjis Liho for the very reason that the Chronarch would not give him trust of any instruments. He had little experience, yet, if it meant his release, he would try.

When he arrived again in the central plaza, he noted that the machine of burnished bronze – the Great Regulator, they called it – was making a peculiar grumbling noise and shaking mightily. Around it, trembling in unison, stood a dozen old men, waving their hands.

'Here is the man from Lanjis Liho!' called the guard. They looked anxiously at the Scar-faced Brooder.

179

'The life-core. It must certainly be the life-core,' said an ancient, tugging at his jerkin.

'Let me see,' said the Scar-faced Brooder, not at all sure that he could be of help.

They wound off several of the machine's outer plates and he stared through thick glass and looked at the luminous life-core. He had seen them before and knew a little about them. He knew enough, certainly, to understand that this should not be glowing bright purple and showering particles with such constancy.

He knew, suddenly, that in an exceedingly short space of time – one of these people's 'minutes', perhaps – the life-core would reach a critical state, it would swell and burst from its confines and its radiation would destroy everything living. But, he ignored their shouts as he became lost in the problem, he would need considerably longer than that if he was to deal with it.

Soon, he realised helplessly, they would all be dead.

He turned to tell them this, and then it struck him. Why could not he, as he had guessed these citizens capable of, *recycle* that moment, personally?

Since the previous day, his mind had been trying to see the logic in what Mokof had told him and, using parts of things the Chronarch had told him, he had constructed an idea of what the process must be like.

Experimentally, he eased himself *backwards* in time. Yes, it worked. The core was now as he had first seen it.

He had never thought of doing this before, but now he saw that it was easy, requiring merely a degree of concentration. He was grateful for the Barbartians, with their weird time device, for giving him the idea.

All he had to do was to remember what the Chronarch had taught him about the nature of time – how it constantly and imperceptibly to ordinary beings re-formed its constituents to give it the apparently forward movement which affected, so broadly, the organisation of matter.

Shifting himself into the time-area he had occupied a short while before, he began to study the temporal co-ordinates of the life-core. He could think of no physical means of stopping it, but if he could, in some manner, lock it in time, it would then cease to be a danger. But he would still have to work speedily, since, sooner or later, the temporal structure would fail to hold and he would sweep onwards, losing time continuously, until he was brought to the moment when the life-core began to spread its radiation.

Again and again he let himself drift up almost to the ultimate moment, shifting himself backwards, losing a few grains of time with every shift.

Then, at last, he understood the temporal construction of the core. With an effort of will he reduced the temporal co-ordinates to zero. It could not progress through time. It was frozen and no longer a danger.

He fell back into his normal time stream, his body wet with sweat. They crowded about him, questioning in shrill, excited voices.

'What have you done? What have you done? Are we safe?'

'You are safe,' he said.

They seized him, thanking him with generous words, his earlier crime forgotten. 'You must be rewarded.'

But he scarcely heard them, as they bore him back to the judge, for he was brooding on what he had just accomplished.

As a man might step backwards to regain lost ground, he had stepped backwards to regain lost time. He had his reward. He was most grateful to these people now, for with their weird ideas about time, they had shown him that it was possible to exist at will in a point in time – just as it was possible to exist in a point in space. It was, he realised, merely a matter of *knowing* such a thing was possible. Then it became easy.

The judge had doffed his mask and smiled his gratitude. 'The wise men tell me that you worked a miracle. They saw your body flickering like a candle flame, disappearing and appearing constantly. How did you achieve this?'

He spread his hands: 'It was extraordinarily simple. Until I came to Barbart and saw the thing you call *clock*, I did not realise the possibilities of moving through time as I could move through space. It seemed to me that since you appeared capable of recycling the same period of time, I could do likewise. This I did. Then I studied the life-core and saw that, by manipulation of its time structure, I could fix it in a certain point, thus arresting its progress. So simple – and yet it might never have occurred to me if I had not come here.'

The judge passed a hand over his puzzled eyes. 'Ah...' he said.

'And now,' the Brooder said cheerfully, 'I thank you for your hospitality. I intend to leave Barbart immediately, since I shall obviously never understand your customs. I return to Lanjis Liho to tell the Chronarch of my discoveries. Farewell.'

He left the courtroom, crossed the plaza through crowds of grateful citizens, and was soon saddling Urge and riding away from Barbart in the land of fronds.

Two days later he came upon the Hooknosed Wanderer grubbing in a ditch he had just dug.

'Greetings, Wanderer,' he called from the saddle.

The Wanderer looked up, wiping salty earth from his face.

'Oh, 'tis you, Brooder. I thought you had decided to journey to the land of fronds.'

'I did. I went to Barbart and there –' briefly the Brooder explained what had happened.

'Aha,' nodded the Wanderer. 'So the Chronarch is educating his people well, after all. I frankly considered what he was doing impossible. But you have proved me wrong.'

'What do you mean?'

'I think I can tell you. Come into my tent and drink some wine.'

'Willingly,' the Brooder said, dismounting.

From a plastic flask, the Wanderer poured wine into two cut-glass goblets.

'Lanjis Liho,' he said, 'was founded in ancient times as an experimental village where newborn children were taken and educated according to the teachings of a certain philosopher called Rashin. Rashin regarded people's attitude towards time as being imposed on their consciousness by their method of record-ing and measuring it – by the state of mind which said 'the past is the past and cannot be changed', 'we cannot know what the future holds' and so forth. Our minds, he decided, were biased and while we continued to think in this way we should never be free of the shackles of time. It was, he felt, the most necessary shackle to cast off. He said, for instance, that when the temperature becomes too hot, a man devises a means of keeping himself cool. When it rains he enters a shelter or devises a shelter he can trans-port with him. If he comes to a river, he builds a bridge, or if to the sea – a boat. Physical difficulties of a certain intensity can be over-come in a physical way. But what if the difficulties intensify to the degree where physical means can no longer work against them?'

The Brooder shrugged. 'We perish – or find some means other than physical to combat them.'

'Exactly. Rashin said that if time moves too swiftly for a man to accomplish what he desires he accepts the fact passively. Rashin thought that with re-education Man might rid himself of his pre-conception and take as easily to adjusting time to his requirements as he adjusts nature. A non-physical means, you see.'

'I think I understand a little of what you mean,' said the Scar-faced Brooder. 'But why is it necessary, I wonder?' The question was rhetorical, but the Wanderer chose to answer.

'On this world,' he said, 'we must admit it, Man is an anachron-ism. He has adapted to a degree but not sufficiently to the point where he could sustain himself without artifice. The planet has never been particularly suitable for him, of course, but it has never been so inhospitable as now.

'The Chronarchy, as I have said, is a conscious experiment. Time and Matter are both ideas. Matter makes a more immediate impression on Man, but Time's effects are longer-lasting. There-fore the Chronarchy, down the ages, has sought to educate its people into thinking of Time in a similar way as they think of Matter. In this way it has been possible to produce a science of time, like the science of physics. But it has only been possible to study time until now – not manipulate it.

'We may soon master time as we once mastered the atom. And our mastery will give us far greater freedom than did our nuclear science. Time may be explored as our ancestors explored space. Your descendants, Scar-faced Brooder, shall be heir to continents of time as we have continents of space. They shall travel about in time, the old view of Past, Present and Future abolished. Even now you regard these in an entirely different light – merely as convenient classifications for the study of time.'

'That is true,' he nodded, 'I had never considered them anything else. But now I am unsure what to do, for I fled to Barbart originally to settle and forget Lanjis Liho where I went unhonoured.'

The Wanderer smiled a little. 'I do not think you will go unhonoured now, my friend,' he said.

The Brooder saw the point and smiled also. 'Perhaps not,' he agreed.

The Wanderer sipped his wine. 'Your journeyings in space are all but ended, anyway. For space is becoming increasingly hostile to Man and will soon refuse to sustain him, however much he adapts physically. You and your like must enter the new dimensions you've discovered and dwell there. Go back to Lanjis Liho of your birth and tell the Chronarch what you did in Barbart, *show* him what you did and he will welcome you. Your reason for leaving no longer exists. You are the first of the Time Dwellers and I salute you as the salvation of mankind.' The Wanderer drained his glass.

Somewhat overwhelmed by this speech, the Brooder bade the Wanderer farewell and thick blood, left the tent and climbed upon the back of Urge.

The Wanderer stood beside the tent, smiling at him. 'One day you must tell me how you did it,' he said.

'It is such a simple thing – you just live through the same period of time instead of different ones. Perhaps this is just the start and soon I will be able to explore further abroad – or is the word "a-time"? But now I will be off for I'm impatient to tell my news to the Chronarch!'

The Wanderer watched him ride away, feeling a trifle as the last dinosaur must have felt so many millions of years before.

Once again, the Scar-faced Brooder rode along the seashore staring over the sluggish waves at the brown sky beyond.

Salt shone everywhere across the land, perhaps heralding an age where crystalline life forms would develop in conditions absolutely unsuitable for animal life as he knew it.

Yes, the period when Man must change his environment radically had come, if Man were to survive at all.

The Earth would cease to support him soon, the sun cease to warm him. He had the choice of living for a while in artificial conditions such as the Moonites already did, or of completely changing his environment – from a physical one to a temporal one!

Definitely, the latter was the better choice. As the sky darkened over the sea, he took out his torch, depressed the handle and sent a great blaze of light spreading across the inhospitable Earth.

The first of the Time Dwellers goaded his seal-beast into a faster pace, impatient to tell the Chronarch his welcome news, impatient to begin the exploration of a new environment.

Escape from Evening

O N MOON IT was white like ice. An endless series of blocks and spikes, like an ancient cubist painting. But white; glaring, though the sun was almost dead, a red featureless disc in the dark sky.

In his artificial cavern, full of synthetic, meaningless things that contained no mythology or mood, Pepin Hunchback bent over his book so that the tears from his eyes fell upon the plastic pages and lay there glistening.

Of all the things that the glass cavern contained – pumps and pipes and flinching dials – only Pepin had warmth. His twisted body was a-throb with life and large emotions. His imagination was alive and active as each word in the book sparked off great chords of yearning within him. His narrow face, utterly pale save for the bright black eyes, was intense. His clumsy hands moved to turn the pages. He was dressed, as were all his fellow Moonites, in cloth-of-metal which, with a helmet fitted to its hauberk, protected his life from an impossibility – the threat of the System collapsing.

The System was Moon's imitation of life. It aped an older Earth than that which now existed far away, barely visible in space. It aped its plants and its animals and its elements – for the System was Moon's artificial ecology. Moon was a planet of goodish size – had been for centuries since it had ceased to be Earth's satellite and had drifted into the asteroids and attracted many of them to itself.

And Pepin hated the System for what it was. Pepin was a throwback, unsuited to his present Time or Space. Pepin's life was not the System, for with just that he would have died. It was his imagination, his sorrow and his ambition, fed by his few old books.

He read the familiar pages and realised again that the intellect had triumphed over the spirit, and both had conquered emotion. The men of Moon, at least, had become as barren as their accident of a planet.

Pepin knew much of Earth as his people's traders had described it. Knew that it was changing and was no longer as it was when his books were written. Yet still he yearned to go there and see if he could find some trace of what he needed – though he would only know what he needed when he found it.

For some time he had planned to visit Earth and his people were willing that he should go, if he did not return, for he discomforted them. His name – his true name – was on the list, close to the top. Soon a ship would be ready for him. His true name was P Karr.

Now he thought of the ship and decided to go to the list. He went to the list infrequently for in his atavism he was superstitious and believed completely that the more he looked at it, the less chance there would be of his name being at the top.

Pepin jerked his body off his stool and slammed the book shut. On the hushed world of Moon, he made as much noise as he could.

He limped, more evidently high-shouldered now that he was moving, towards the door section of his dome. He took down his helmet and fitted it onto his shoulders, activated the door section, and crossed the sharp, bright ground covering the distance between himself and the city. By choice, and to the relief of his people, he lived outside the city.

On the surface, there was little to see of the city. Merely a storey or two, perhaps three in places. All the prominences were square and transparent, to absorb as much energy from the waning sun as possible.

Another door section in one of the buildings opened to him and he went inside, hardly realising that he had left the surface. He entered a funnel containing a disc-shaped platform and the platform began to fall downwards, slowing as it reached the bottom.

Here the light was completely artificial and the walls were of metal – plain, undecorated tubes twice the height of a tall, thin Moonite. Pepin was not typical of his race.

He limped along this tube for a short distance, until the floor began to move. He let it carry him through the labyrinthine intestines of the city until he came to the hall he wanted.

The hall was quite unpopulated until Pepin entered. It had a domed ceiling and was covered by screens, charts, indicators, conveying every item of information which a citizen might require to know in the day-to-day life of the city. Pepin went to the list, craning his head to look at it. He started at the bottom and followed the list of names up.

His name was at the top. He must go immediately to Ship Controller and apply for his ship. If he did not, his name would go back to the bottom, according to regulations.

As he turned to leave the hall, another Moonite entered. His helmet was flung back, lying against his shoulder blades. His golden hair was long and his thin face smiled.

This was G Nak, the greatest of the trader-pilots, and he did not need to look at the list, for he had a permanent ship of his own. The population of Moon was small, and G Nak knew Pepin as well as anyone.

He stopped sharply, arms akimbo, and contemplated the list.

'So you journey to Earth, P Karr. You will find it decadent and unpleasant. Take plenty of food – you will not like their salty grub.'

'Thank you,' bobbed Pepin as he left.

As if mutated by their constant contact with the mother planet, only the ships of Moon had character. They were burnished and patterned with fancifully wrought images. Ancient animals prowled along their hulls, gargoyles glowered from indentations created by heavily moulded figures of famous men, tentacled hands curled themselves over the curves like the arms of wrecked sailors clinging to spars, or else like the protective hands of a she-baboon about her young. The ships were so heavily decorated that in the light they looked like frozen lava, all lumps and gullies in obsidian or brass.

Pepin, luggage on back, paused before he put foot on the short, moving ramp which would deliver him to the entrance of his allotted ship. He allowed himself time to study the raised images, then stepped upon the ramp and was whisked up to the airlock which opened for him.

The inside of the ship was very cramped and consisted mainly of cargo space. The cargo, which would go with Pepin and be delivered to an Earth-city called Barbart, was already stowed. Pepin lowered himself onto the couch where he would spend the journey. After Pepin and cargo had been delivered, the ship would return, as it had left, automatically.

A whisper of noise, hushed like all Moon sounds, warned him that the ship was about to take off. He braced himself; felt no sensation as the ship rose on course for Earth.

The bright ship sped through the soft darks of weary space, a bold spark intruding the blackness. It flickered along its path until at length Pepin's screen picked up the growing globe of Earth – brown, yellow and white, turning slowly in the scant warmth of the dormant sun.

The planet seemed vaguely unreal, perhaps because it was imperfectly focused on the screen, yet the stuff of space seemed to drift through it as if the planet's very fabric was worn thin. Pepin felt the hard metal rocket would not stop when it reached Earth, but tear through it easily and continue on into empty space where more vital stars pulsed. At one time, Pepin knew, the universe had been even thicker with bright stars, and even his own sun had possessed more than the three planets that now circled it.

Silently, the ship went into orbit, easing itself by stages into the atmosphere, down through the clear, purple sky, down into the brown cloud banks that hung close to the ground, through the clouds until it had levelled out again and moved with decreasing speed across sluggish seas and wastes of dark yellow, brown and black, studded by great white patches of salt. Much further inland, grey moss became apparent, and later the waving light green of the fragile fronds that marked what Earth's inhabitants called the Land of Fronds. In the Land of Fronds were two principal cities, two towns and a village. Barbart, the trading port between Moon and Earth, lay in a gentle valley. The hills were covered in fronds that from above seemed like a rolling sea – more sealike than the salt-heavy waters far to the east.

Barbart was laid out precisely, in quadrangles, triangles and star-shaped plazas. The roofs of the low houses were of dark green and brick-brown, yet seemed brightly coloured compared with their surroundings. The ship passed over the huge red-gold machine which rose high above the other buildings. This, Pepin knew, was called the Great Regulator and supplied necessary power to the city. Behind the Great Regulator, in the city's central plaza, was a cradlepad ready for his ship. It hovered and then dropped down onto the cradlepad.

Pepin shivered suddenly and did not rise immediately but watched his screen as people began to enter the plaza, moving speedily towards the ship.

Barbart was the city most like those he had read about in his books. It was considerably smaller than the Golden Age cities had been and resembled best a medieval Italian city. From the ground, even the frond-covered hills might be a forest of oaks and elms if they were not looked at closely. Also Pepin knew that the folk of Barbart were quite similar to the ancient folk of Earth. Yet he could not convince himself, though he tried, that he had returned to the Earth of his books. For one thing the light was fainter, the air darker, the drifting brown clouds unlike any that had existed in Earth's past. Pepin was not as disappointed as he expected. Whatever deficiencies existed here, at least the planet was *natural* and Pepin placed much value on the naturalness of things.

The airlock had opened and the Barbartians grouped themselves outside it, waiting for the pilot to appear.

Pepin took up his luggage from beside the couch, swung his

well-shaped legs to the floor and limped out of the cabin and through the airlock.

The heavy, brine-laden air half-choked him. The smell of salt was so marked that he felt faintly sick. He swung his helmet up so that it enclosed his head. He turned on his emergency oxygen supply, deciding to give himself time to adjust.

The merchants of Barbart stood around the ramp leading from the cradlepad. They looked at him eagerly.

'May we inspect the cargo, Pilot?' enquired a heavy-shouldered man with broad cheekbones and a flaking skin half-invisible beneath his thick, black beard. He wore a quilted coat, belted at his chest. This was a rusty black. A white stock was tied at his throat and he wore baggy yellow trousers tucked into furry boots.

Pepin looked at him, wanting to greet him in some manner that would convey the pleasure he felt at seeing a human being of heavy build, with muscles and flaws on his skin.

'Pilot?' said the merchant.

Pepin began to limp slowly down the ramp. He stood aside to let the bulky merchant move up it and duck his head to enter the airlock. Three others followed him, glancing rather quizzically at the silent Moonite.

A man smaller than Pepin with the narrow face of a reptile, dressed in dull red and black, sidled up clutching a handwritten list. Fascinated, Pepin looked at it, not understanding the words. He would like to have taken off his gauntlets and fingered the parchment, but he would wait for a little.

'Pilot? When do you return?'

Pepin smiled. 'I do not return. I have come to live here.'

The man was startled. He took the parchment back and turned his head, did not see what he looked for and gazed up the ramp towards the open airlock.

'Then be welcome,' he said absently, still not looking at Pepin. He excused himself and walked with short, rapid steps back to the warehouse at the side of the plaza.

Pepin waited until the merchant and his friends reappeared. They looked satisfied and were nodding to one another. The black-bearded merchant bustled down the ramp and slapped Pepin's arm.

'I admit it,' he grinned, 'a very generous cargo. We have the best of this month's bargain, I think. Gold and alcohol for our fertilisers. May I begin unloading?'

'As you wish,' Pepin said courteously, wondering at this man who could delight in receiving such useless things in return for valuable fertilisers.

'You are new,' said the merchant, taking Pepin's arm and leading him towards the warehouse where the other man had gone. 'What do you think of our city?'

'It is wonderful,' sighed Pepin. 'I admire it. I should like to live here.'

'Ha! Ha! With all those marvels and comforts in Moon you have. You'd miss them after a while, Pilot. And every year we hear of cities dying, populations shrinking, fewer children than ever being born. No, I envy you Moonites with your safety and stability – you don't have to worry about the future, for you can plan efficiently. But we here can make no plans – we merely hope that things will not alter too much in our own lifetimes.'

'At least you are part of the natural order, sir,' Pepin said hesitantly. 'You might adapt further as the Earth changes.'

The merchant laughed again. 'No – we of Earth will all be dead. We accept this, now. The human race has had a long run. No-one would have expected us to last this time, but soon the point will be reached where we can adapt no longer. It is already happening in less fortunate areas. Man is dying out on Earth. Yet while you have your System, that is not possible on Moon.'

'But our System is artificial – your planet is natural.'

They reached the warehouse. Men were already folding back the heavy doors. The casks of fertiliser were stacked in a cool, dark corner of the place. The man with the reptile face glanced at Pepin as he counted the casks.

'There is the matter of the pilot's gift,' said the merchant. 'The traditional gift of gratitude to the man who brings the cargo safely to us. Is there anything we have which you desire?'

Traditionally, the pilot asked for a small token gift of no great value and Pepin knew what was expected of him.

'You mine antiques in Barbart, I believe?' he said politely.

'Yes. It provides employment for our criminals. Forty cities have stood where Barbart now stands.'

Pepin smiled with pleasure. Such history!

'I am fond of books,' he said.

'Books?' The merchant frowned. 'Why, yes, we have a stack of those somewhere. Have the folk of Moon taken to reading? Ha! ha!'

'You do not read them yourselves?'

'A lost art, Pilot. Those ancient languages are impossible. We have no scholars in Barbart, save for our elders – and their wisdom comes from here,' he tapped his head, 'not from any books. We've little use for the old knowledge – it was a knowledge suitable for a younger Earth.'

Though Pepin understood, he felt a pang of sorrow and disappointment. Intellectually he had known that the folk of Earth would not be like his idealised picture of them, yet emotionally he could not accept this.

'Then I would like some books,' he said.

'As many as your ship has room for when our cargo's loaded!' promised the merchant. 'What language do you read in? I'll let you sort them out for yourself.'

'I read in all the ancient tongues,' said Pepin proudly. His fellows thought his a useless skill and it probably was, but he did not care.

He added: 'And there is no need to load them. I shall not be returning with the ship. That will go back to Moon automatically.'

'You'll not be –? Are you then to be some sort of permanent representative of Moon on Earth?'

'No. I wish to live on Earth as one of her folk.'

The merchant scratched his nose. 'Aha, I see. Aha...'

'Is there reason why I should not be welcome?'

'Oh, no – no – I was merely astonished that you should elect to stay with us. I gather you Moonites regard us as primitives, doomed to die with the planet.' His tone was now mildly resentful. 'Your regulations admitting no-one of Earth to Moon have been strict for centuries. No Earthman has visited Moon, even. You have your stability to consider, of course. But why should you *elect* to suffer the discomforts of our wasted planet?'

'You will note,' said Pepin carefully, 'that I am not like other Moonites. I am, I suppose, some sort of romantic throwback – or it may be that my original difference has fostered mental differences, I do not know. However, I alone amongst my race have an admiration for Earth and the folk of Earth. I have a yearning for the past whereas my people look always to the future – a future which they are pledged to keep stable and as much like the present as possible.'

'I see...' The merchant folded his arms. 'Well, you are welcome to stay here as a guest – until you wish to return to Moon.'

'I never wish to return.'

'My friend,' the merchant smiled. 'You will wish to return soon enough. Spend a month with us – a year – but I warrant you'll stay no longer.'

He paused before saying: 'You'll find plenty of signs of the past here – for the past is all we have. There is no future for Earth.'

The clock, centrepiece of the Great Regulator, had measured off six weeks before Pepin Hunchback became restless and frustrated by the uncaring ignorance of the Barbartians. The citizens were pleasant enough and treated him well considering their covert antipathy towards the Moonites. But he made no friends and found no sympathisers.

He rejoiced in those books which were not technical manuals or technical fiction. He enjoyed the poetry and the legends and the history books and the adventure stories. But there were fewer than he had expected and did not last him long.

He lived in a room at an inn. He grew used to the heavy, briny air and the dull colours, he began to enjoy the gloom which shadowed the Earth, for it mirrored something of his own mood. He would go for walks over the hills and watch the heavy brown clouds course towards him from the horizon, smell the sweetish scent of the frond forests, climb the crumbling rocks that stood against the purple sky, worn by the wind and scoured by the salt.

Unlike Moon, this planet still lived, still held surprises in the sudden winds that blew its surface, the odd animals which crawled over it.

Pepin was afraid only of the animals, for these had become truly alien. The principal life form other than Man was the oozer – a giant leech which normally prowled the bleak seashores but which was being seen increasingly further inland. If Man's time was ending, then the time of the oozer was beginning. As Man died out, the oozer multiplied. They moved in schools varying from a dozen to a hundred, depending on the species – they grew from two feet to ten feet long. Some were black, some brown, some yellow – but the most disgusting was the white variety which was also the largest and most ferocious, a great grub of a thing capable of fast speeds, able to outdistance a running man and bring him down. When this happened, the oozer, like its leech ancestor, fed off the blood and body salt of its prey and could leave the body drained and dry.

Pepin saw a school moving through a glade once as he sat on a rock staring down into the frond forest.

'The new tenants,' he said aloud, after he'd conquered his nausea, 'are arriving – and the Earth ignores Man. She is not hostile, she is not friendly. She no longer supports him. She has forgotten him. Now she fosters new children.'

Pepin was given to talking to himself. It was the only time when words came easily – when he was alone.

Pepin tried to talk with Kop the merchant and his fellow residents at the inn, but though they were polite enough, his questions, his statements and his arguments made them frown and puzzle and excuse themselves early.

One fellow resident, a mild-mannered and friendly man called Mokof, middle-aged with a slight stoop, made greater attempts to understand Pepin, but was incapable, rather than unwilling, of helping him.

'With your talk of the past and philosophy, you would be happier in that odd city of Lanjis Liho by the sea,' he said pleasantly one day as they sat outside the inn, tankards at their sides, watching the fountain play in the plaza.

Pepin had heard Lanjis Liho mentioned, but had been so curious about other matters that he had not asked of the city before. Now he raised one fair, near-invisible eyebrow.

'I once knew a man from Lanjis Liho,' Mokof continued in answer. 'He had a strange name which I forget – it was similar to your last name in type. He had a scar on his face. Got into trouble by eating his food at the wrong time, saved himself by fixing the Great Regulator for us. We know nothing of these machines these days. He believed that he could travel in time, though I saw little evidence of this while he was here. All the folk of Lanjis Liho are like him, I hear – bizarre, if you follow me – they know nothing of clocks, for instance, have no means of measuring the hours. Their ruler is called Chronarch and he lives in a palace called the House of Time, though only an oozer knows why they should emphasise Time when they can't even *tell* it.'

Mokof could tell Pepin very little more that was not merely opinion or speculation, but Lanjis Liho by the sea sounded an interesting place. Also Pepin was attracted by the words 'time travel' – for his true wish was to return to Earth's past.

During the seventh week of his stay in Barbart, he decided to journey eastwards towards Lanjis Liho by the sea.

Pepin Hunchback set off on foot for Lanjis Liho. Mokof in particular tried to dissuade him – it was a long journey and the land was dangerous with oozers. He could easily lose his direction without a good steed.

But he had tried to ride the seal-beasts which were the mounts of most Earthmen. These creatures, with their strongly muscled forefins and razor-sharp tails, were reliable and fairly fast. They had built-up saddles of silicon to give the rider a straight seat. Part of their equipment also included a long gun, called a piercer, which fired a ray from its ruby core, and a torch fed by batteries which supplied the traveller with light in the moonless, near-starless night.

Pepin Hunchback took a torch and balanced a piercer over his shoulder. He liked the feeling both gave him. But he did not trust himself to a seal-beast.

He left in the dark morning, with food and a flask in the pack on his back, still dressed in his cloth-of-metal suit.

The citizens of Barbart, like those of Moon, were not regretful when he had gone. He had disturbed them when they believed they had conquered all disturbances within themselves. For seven weeks he had interrupted their purpose and the purpose they wished to transmit to any children they might have.

That purpose was to die peacefully and generously on an Earth which no longer desired their presence.

Pepin was disappointed as he limped away from Barbart in the Land of Fronds. He had expected to find dynamic vitality on Earth – people prepared for change, but not for death. Somewhere on the planet – possibly in Lanjis Liho by the sea – he would find heroes. From what Mokof had hinted, he might even find a means of travelling into the past. This is what he wanted most, but he had never expected to achieve it.

The moss of the frond forests was springy and helped his walking, but by evening it was beginning to give way to hard, brown earth over which dust scurried. Ahead of him, ominous in the waning light, was a barren plain, cracked and almost featureless. Here and there chunks of rock stood up. He selected one as his goal, realising, even as night fell, cold and pitch-dark, that to sleep would be to risk his life. Oozers, he had been told, only slept when they had fed – and there was little to feed on save Man.

He depressed the grip of his torch and its light illuminated a distance of a few yards round him. He continued to walk, warm enough in his suit. As he walked, his mind became almost blank. He was so weary that he could not tell how long he had marched by the degrees of weariness. But when a silhouette of rock became apparent in the torchlight, he stopped, took off his pack, leaned his back against the rock and slid down it. He did not care about the oozers and he was fortunate because no oozers scented his blood and came to care about him.

Dawn came dark brown, the muddy clouds streaming across the sky, blocking out much of the sun's dim light. Pepin opened his pack and took out the flask of specially distilled fresh water. He could not drink the salt water which the folk of Earth drank. They, in turn, had adapted to the extent where they could not bear to drink fresh water. He took two tablets from a box and swallowed them. Having breakfasted, he heaved his aching body up, adjusted the pack on his back, slung the torch into its sheath at his side, shouldered the piercer and looked about him.

In the west, the frond forests were out of sight and the plain looked as endless in that direction as it did in the other. Yet the plain to the east was now further broken by low hills and many more rocks.

He set off eastwards. *In the east*, he reflected, *our ancestors believed Paradise lay. Perhaps I will find my Paradise in the east.*

If Paradise existed, and Pepin was entitled to enter, he came very close to entering two days later as he collapsed descending a salt-encrusted hill and rolled many feet down it, knocking himself unconscious.

As it was, the Hooknosed Wanderer saved him from this chance of Paradise.

The Hooknosed Wanderer was a burrower, a gossiper, a quester after secrets. Amongst all the Earth folk he was perhaps the only aimless nomad. No-one knew his origin, no-one thought to ask. He was as familiar in Barbart as he was in Lanjis Liho. His knowledge of Earth, past and present, was extensive, but few ever availed themselves of it. He was a short man with a huge nose, receding chin, and a close-fitting hood and jerkin which made him resemble a beaked turtle.

He saw the fallen tangle that was Pepin Hunchback at much the same time as the school of oozers scented Pepin's blood.

He was riding a big, fat seal-beast and leading another on which was heaped a preposterous burden of rolled fabric, digging equipment, a small stove, angular bundles – in fact the Hooknosed Wanderer's entire household tied precariously to the seal-beast's back. The seal-beast seemed mildly pleased with itself that it was capable of carrying this load.

In the Hooknosed Wanderer's right hand, borne like a lance resting in a special grip on his stirrup, was his piercer. He saw Pepin, he saw the oozers.

He rode closer, raised his piercer, pressed the charger and then the trigger-stud. The concentrated light was scarcely visible, but it bit into the oozer school instantaneously. They were of the black variety. The Hooknosed Wanderer moved the piercer about very gradually and burned every oozer to death. It gave him satisfaction.

Then he rode up to where Pepin lay and looked down at him. Pepin was not badly hurt, he was even beginning to stir on the ground. The Hooknosed Wanderer saw that he was a Moonite by his dress. He wondered where Pepin had got the piercer and torch which lay near him.

He dismounted and helped the Moonite to his feet. Pepin rubbed his head and looked rather nervously at the Hooknosed Wanderer.

'I fell down,' he said.

'Just so,' said the Hooknosed Wanderer. 'Where is your spaceship? Has it crashed nearby?'

'I have no spaceship,' Pepin explained, 'I was journeying from Barbart, where I landed some seven weeks ago, to Lanjis Liho, which I am told lies close to the shores of the sea.'

'You were foolish to go on foot,' said the Wanderer. 'It is still a long way.'

He continued eagerly: 'But you must guest with me and we will talk about Moon. I should be happy to add to my knowledge.'

Pepin's head was aching. He was glad that this odd stranger had come upon him. He agreed willingly and even tried to help the Wanderer raise his tent.

When the tent was finally erected and the Wanderer's goods distributed about it, Pepin and he went inside.

The Wanderer offered him leg-fish and salt-water, but Pepin refused politely and swallowed his own food.

Then he told the Wanderer of his coming from Moon to Earth, of his stay in Barbart, of his frustration and disappointment, and of his ambition. The Wanderer listened, asking questions that showed he was more interested in Moon than Pepin.

Listlessly, Pepin replied to these questions and then asked one of his own.

'What do you know of Lanjis Liho, sir?'

'Everything but the most recent events,' said the Wanderer with a smile. 'Lanjis Liho is very ancient and has its origin in an experimental village where a philosopher tried to educate people to regard Time as they regard Matter – something that can be moved through, manipulated and so on. From this, the Chronarchy was formed and it became traditional in Lanjis Liho to investigate time and little else. Perhaps by mutation, perhaps by the awakening of some power we have always possessed, a race of people exists in Lanjis Liho who can *move themselves through Time*!

'I had the good fortune to know the young man who first discovered this talent within himself and trained others in its use. A man called the Scar-faced Brooder – he is the present Chronarch.'

'He can travel into the past?'

'And future, so I hear. Once the chronopathic talent is released in Man, he can move through time at will.'

'But the past,' said Pepin excitedly. 'We can journey back to Earth's Golden Age and not worry about natural death or artificial living. We can *do* things!'

'Um,' said the Wanderer. 'I share your love for the past, Pepin Hunchback – my tent is full of antiques I have excavated – but is it possible to return to the past? Would not that act change the future – for there is no record in our history of men from the future settling in the past?'

Pepin nodded. 'It is a mystery – yet surely *one* man, who did not admit he was from the future, could settle in the past?'

The Hooknosed Wanderer smiled. 'I see what you mean.'

'I realise now,' said Pepin seriously, 'that I have little in common with either my own people or the folk of Earth. My only hope is to return to the past where I shall find the things I need to exist fully. I am a man out of my time.'

'You are not the first. Earth's ancient history is full of such men.'

'But I shall be the first, perhaps, able to find the age which most suits him.'

'Perhaps,' said the Hooknosed Wanderer dubiously. 'But your wishes are scarcely constructive.'

'Are they not? What, then, has this Earth to offer mankind? We on Moon live an artificial life, turning year by year into machines less perfect than those which support us. And you here accept death passively – are only concerned with the business of facing extinction "well"! My race will not be human within a century – yours will not exist. Are we to perish? Are the values of humanity to perish – have the strivings of the last million years been pointless? Is there no escape from Earth's evening? I will not accept that!'

'You are not logical, my friend,' smiled the Wanderer. 'You take the least positive line of all – by refusing to face the future – by your desire to return to the past. How will that benefit the rest of us?'

Pepin clutched his head. 'Ah,' he murmured. 'Ah...'

The Hooknosed Wanderer continued. 'I have no wish to survive the evening. You have seen something of the horrors which will multiply as Earth's evening turns to night.'

Pepin did not reply. He had become inarticulate with emotion.

The Hooknosed Wanderer took him outside and pointed into the east. 'That way lies Lanjis Liho and her chronopaths,' he said. 'I pity you, Pepin, for I think you will find no solution to your problem – and it *is* your problem, not humanity's.'

Pepin limped from weariness as well as deformity. He limped along a beach. It was morning and the dull, red sun was rising slowly from the sea as he moved down the dark shore towards Lanjis Liho. It was cold.

Grey-brown mist hung over the sea and drifted towards the bleak landscape that was dominated by the solid black outline of cliffs to his right. The brown beach glistened with patches of hard salt and the salt-sluggish sea was motionless, for there was no longer a nearby moon to move it.

Pepin still considered his conversation with the strange Wanderer. Was this the end of Earth, or merely one phase in a cycle? Night must come – but would it be followed by a new day? If so, then perhaps the future was attractive. Yet the Earth had slowly destroyed the greater part of the human race. Would the rest die before the new morning?

Suddenly, Pepin slipped into a pool of thick water. He floundered in the clinging stuff, dragging himself back by clutching a spur of hardened salt, but the salt wouldn't bear his weight and he fell into the pool again. Finally he crawled back to dry land. Everything was crumbling or changing.

He continued along the shore more carefully. Leg-fish scuttled away as he approached. They sought the deeper shadow of the crags of rock which rose from the beach like jagged teeth, corroded by wind-borne salt. They hid and were silent and the whole shore was quiet. Pepin Hunchback found no peace of mind here, but the solitude seemed to absorb his tangled thoughts and eased his brain a little.

The disc of the sun took a long time to rise above the horizon, and brought little light with it, and even less warmth. He paused and turned to stare over the sea which changed from black to brown as the sun came up. He sighed and looked at the sun which caught his face in its dull glow and stained it a deep pink, bringing a look of radiance to his native pallor.

Later, he heard a sound which he first took to be the squawking of fighting leg-fish. Then he recognised it as a human voice. Without moving his head, he listened more intently.

Then he turned.

A tiny figure sat a seal on the cliff above. Jutting upwards from it like a lance was the barrel of a long piercer. The figure was half-shadowed by the ruin of an ancient watchtower and, as he looked, jerked at the reins impatiently, disappeared into the whole shadow and was gone.

Pepin frowned and wondered if this could be an enemy. He readied his own piercer.

Now the rider had descended the cliff and was nearing him. He heard the distant thwack of the beast's fins against the damp beach. He levelled the gun.

The rider was a woman. A woman from out of his books.

She was tall, long-legged, with the collar of her seal-leather jacket raised to frame her sharp-jawed face. Her brown hair drifted over it and flew behind. One hand, protected by a loose-fitting glove, clutched the pommel of her high, silicon saddle. The other held her beast's reins. Her wide, full-lipped mouth seemed pursed by the cold, for she held it tight.

Then her seal entered a deep pool of sluggish water and began swimming through it with great difficulty. The strong smell of the brine-thick liquid came to his awareness then and he saw her as a woman out of mythology – a mermaid astride a seal. Yet, she frightened him. She was unexpected.

Was she from Lanjis Liho? It was likely. And were they all like her?

Now, as she reached firm ground again, she began to laugh in rhythm with the seal's movement. It was rich, delightful laughter, but as she came towards him, the heavy drops of water rolling slowly from her mount, his stomach contracted in panic. He backed away a few paces.

At this moment she seemed to personify the bleak insanity of the dying planet.

She halted her beast close to him. She lowered her chin and opened her grey-green eyes. She still smiled.

'Stranger, you are from Moon by your garb. Are you lost?'

He put the piercer over his shoulder. 'No. I seek Lanjis Liho.'

She pointed backwards up the beach. 'You are close to our city. I am Tall Laugher, sister to the Scar-faced Brooder, Chronarch of the City of Time. I will take you there.'

'I am Pepin Hunchback, without kin or rank.'

'Climb up on my seal-beast's back, hang on to my saddle and we will soon be in Lanjis Liho.'

He obeyed her, clinging desperately to the slippery silicon as she wheeled the seal about and sped back the way she had come.

She called to him once or twice on the journey up the salty beach, but he could not make out the sense.

It had begun to rain a little before they reached Lanjis Liho.

Built upon a huge and heavy cliff, the city was smaller even than Barbart, but its houses were towerlike – slim and ancient with conical roofs and small windows. Lanjis Liho was dominated by the Tower of Time which rose from a building called, according to Tall Laugher's shouted description, the Hall of Time, palace of the Chronarch.

Both Hall and Tower were impressive, though puzzling. Their design was an impossibility of curves and angles, bright colours bordering on the indefinable, and creating an emotion in Pepin similar to the emotion created in him by pictures of Gothic architecture – though whereas Gothic took the mind soaring upwards, this took the mind in all directions.

The pale sun shone down on the city streets and the salt-rain fell, washing the gleaming salt deposits off the walls and roofs and leaving fresh ones. The drops even fell between the blades and domes of the Hall and Tower of Time.

There were few people in the streets, and yet there seemed to be an air of activity about the city – almost as if the people were preparing to abandon it.

Although quite similar in their various types to the folk of Barbart, these people seemed livelier – eager.

Pepin wondered if he had arrived at a festival time, as Tall Laugher reined in her beast on the corner of a narrow street.

He clambered down, his bones throbbing. She also dismounted and pointed at the nearest house. 'This is where I live. Since you claimed no rank, I gather you have come here as a visitor and not as an official emissary from Moon. What do you seek in Lanjis Liho?'

'Transport to the past,' he said at once.

She paused. 'Why should you want that?'

'I have nothing in common with the present.'

She looked at him through her cool, intelligent eyes. Then she smiled. 'There is nothing in the past that would attract you.'

'Let me decide.'

'Very well,' she shrugged, 'but how do you propose to find the past?'

'I –' his momentary confidence disappeared – 'I had hoped for your help.'

'You will have to speak with the Chronarch.'

'When?'

She looked at him, frowning slightly. She did not seem unsympathetic. 'Come,' she said, 'we will go to the Hall of Time now.'

As Pepin followed the girl, walking quickly to keep up with her long strides, he wondered if perhaps the people of Lanjis Liho were bent on keeping the secrets of time to themselves.

Though they glanced at him curiously as they passed him, the citizens did not pause. The mood of hurried activity seemed even stronger as they reached the spiralling steps which led upwards to the great gates of the hall.

The guards did not challenge them as they entered an echoing corridor, the tall walls of which were decorated with peculiar cryptographs inlaid in silver, bronze and platinum.

Ahead of them were double doors of yellow gold. Tall Laugher pushed against these and they entered a large, oblong hall with a high ceiling. At the far end, on a dais, was a seated man talking to a couple of others who turned as Tall Laugher and Pepin Hunchback entered.

The seated man smiled calmly as he saw Tall Laugher. He murmured to the other two who left by a door at the side of the dais. The man's pale face bore a scar running from the left corner of his mouth along his cheekbone. His black hair swept from a widow's peak to his wide shoulders. He wore clothes that did not suit him – evidently the clothes of his office. His shirt was of yellow cloth and his cravat, knotted high at his chin, was black. He wore a long-sleeved jacket of quilted blue velvet and breeches of wine-red. His feet were shod in black slippers.

The hall itself was strange. At regular intervals the walls were set alternately with symbolic mosaics and computers. Behind the seated man, close to the far wall, which was blank, was a metal bench bearing the ancient tools of alchemy. They seemed in bizarre contrast to the rest of the hall.

'Well, Tall Laugher,' said the man, 'who is this visitor?'

'He is from Moon, Brooder – and seeks to journey into the past!'

The Scar-faced Brooder, Chronarch of Lanjis Liho, laughed and then, looking sharply at Pepin, stopped.

Pepin said eagerly: 'I have heard that you can travel in time at will. This is true?'

'Yes,' said the Brooder, 'but...'

'Do you plan to go backward or forward?'

The Scar-faced Brooder seemed nonplussed. 'Forward, I suppose – but what makes you think you have the ability for travelling in time?'

'Ability?'

'It is a special skill – only the folk of Lanjis Liho possess it.'

'Have you no *machines*?' Pepin demanded, his spirits sinking.

'We do not *need* machines. Our skill is natural.'

'But I must return to the past – I *must*!' Pepin limped towards the dais, ignoring the restraining hand of the Tall Laugher. 'You want no-one else to share your chance of escape! You must know much about time – you must know how to help me return to the past!'

'It would do you no good if you went back.'

'How do you know?'

'We know,' said the Chronarch bleakly. 'My friend, give up this obsession. There is nothing we can do for you in Lanjis Liho.'

'You are lying!' Pepin changed his tone and said more levelly: 'I beg you to help me. I – I need the past as others need air to survive!'

'You speak from ignorance.'

'What do you mean?'

'I mean that the secrets of time are more complex than you believe.' The Chronarch stood up. 'Now I must leave you. I have a mission in the future.'

He frowned, as if concentrating – and vanished.

Pepin was startled. 'Where has he gone?'

'Into the future – to join others of our folk. He will return soon, I hope. Come, Pepin Hunchback, I will take you to my house and let you eat and rest there. After that, if you'll accept my advice, you had best arrange to go back to Moon.'

'You must be able to construct a machine!' he shouted. 'There must be a way! I must return!'

'Return?' she said, raising an eyebrow. 'Return? How can you return to somewhere you have never been? Come.' She led the way out of the hall.

Pepin Hunchback had calmed down by the time he had eaten a little of the salty food in Tall Laugher's house. They sat in a small room with a bay window which overlooked the street. He sat on one side of a table, she on the other. He did not speak. His mood had become apathetic. She seemed sympathetic and he was attracted to her for the qualities which he had first noted on the beach, and for her warm womanliness, but his despair was greater. He stared at the table, his twisted body bent over it, his hands stretched out in front of him.

'Your yearning, Pepin Hunchback, is not for the past as it was,' she was saying softly. 'It is for a world that never existed – a Paradise, a Golden Age. Men have always spoken of such a time in history – but such an idyllic world is a yearning for childhood, not the past, for lost innocence. It is childhood we wish to return to.'

He looked up and smiled bitterly. 'My childhood was not idyllic,' he said. 'I was a mistake. My birth was an accident. I had no friends, no peace of mind.'

'You had your wonderment, your illusion, your hopes. Even if you could return to Earth's past – you would not be happy.'

'Earth's present is decadent. Here the decadence is part of the process of evolution, on Moon it is artificial, that is all. Earth's past was never truly decadent.'

'One cannot recapture the past.'

'An old saying – yet your ability disproves that.'

'You do not know, Pepin Hunchback,' she said almost sadly. 'Even if you used the ship, you could not...'

'Ship?'

'A time craft, an earlier, cruder experiment we abandoned. We have no need of such devices now.'

'It still exists?'

'Yes – it stands behind the Hall of Time,' she spoke vaguely, her thoughts on something else.

Afraid that she would soon guess what was in his mind, Pepin changed the subject.

'Maybe you are right, Tall Laugher. Old Earth has none to love her any longer – her appearance does not inspire love. If I am the last who loves Earth, then I should stay with her.' Part of him meant what he said, he realised. The words had come spontaneously, he had never considered this before.

She had only half-heard his words. She gave him a slightly startled look as he spoke. She rose from the table. 'I will show you to your room,' she said. 'You need sleep.'

He pretended to agree and followed her out. There would be no sleep now. He must seize his opportunity. Outside, in the fading light of evening, lay a time craft. Soon, perhaps, he could return to the past, to security, to a green, golden Earth, leaving this tired ball of salt for ever!

There was enough light coming from the houses to show him the way through the twisting streets to the Tower of Time. He was unobserved as he circled around the great building, searching for the ship which Tall Laugher had said was there.

At last, half-seen in shadows, he noticed a shape lying in a small square at the back of the Tower.

Resting in davits was a ship of cold, blue metal. It could only be the time craft. It was large enough to contain three or four men.

Several other machines stood nearby, showing signs of neglect. Pepin limped cautiously forward until he stood by the ship. He touched it. It swayed slightly and the davits squealed. Pepin tried to steady it, looking nervously around him, but no-one had noticed. The ship was roughly egg-shaped, with a small airlock in its side. Running his hand over it, Pepin found a stud which he pressed. The outer door slid open.

With considerable difficulty, Pepin managed to heave himself into the violently swinging ship. The noise of the squealing davits was ghastly. He shut the door and crouched in the utter blackness of the interior as it swayed back and forth.

It was likely that a light-stud was near the door. His searching hand found a projection and hesitated. Then, risking the possibility that it was not for the light, he pressed it.

The light came on. It was a bluish, mellow light, but it served adequately to show the interior of the ship. There were no seats and most of the machinery seemed hidden behind squat casings. At the centre of the ship was a column on which were set, at hand height, four controls. The ship was still swaying as Pepin went over to the controls and inspected them. His life on Moon had made him very familiar with all kinds of machinery, and he noted that the system of measurement was the same. The largest dial was in the middle. A division on the right was marked with a minus sign and on the left with a plus sign – obviously indicating past and future. Yet Pepin had expected such a control to be marked off with dates. There was none. Instead there were figures – units from one to ten. One trip, however, was all he would need in order to equate these numbers with the actual period of time they measured.

Another dial seemed to indicate speed. Another was marked 'Emergency Return' and another, mysteriously, 'Megaflow Tuner'.

Now all Pepin had to discover was whether the ship was still powered.

He limped over to another bank of instruments. There was a lever set into it. At the moment the indicator on its handle said

OFF. His heart beating rapidly, Pepin pushed the lever down. A light flashed on the indicator and now it read ON. An almost inaudible humming came from the bank of instruments as needles swung and screens gleamed. Pepin returned to the column and put his large hand on the central dial. It moved easily to the right. He left it at –3.

The ship no longer swung on its davits. There was no sensation of speed, but the banks of instruments began to click and whirr noisily and Pepin felt suddenly dizzy.

The ship was moving backwards in time.

Soon, he would be in the past at last!

Perhaps it was something to do with the ship's motion, the eruptions of colour which blossomed and faded on the screens, or the weird sounds of the instruments that made Pepin become almost hysterical. He began to laugh with joy. He had succeeded! His ambition was close to fruition!

At last the sounds died down, the sensation of sickness left him, the ship no longer seemed to move.

Pepin trembled as he raised his helmet and set it over his head. He knew enough to realise that the air of an earlier Earth would probably be too rich for him at first. This action saved his life.

He went to the door and pressed the stud to open it. The door moved backwards slowly and Pepin stepped into the airlock. The door closed. Pepin opened the outer door.

He looked out at absolutely nothing.

A lightless void lay around the ship. No stars, no planets – nothing at all.

Where was he? Had the ship's instruments been faulty? Had he been borne into an area of space so far away from any material body?

He felt vertigo seize him, backed into the airlock for as far as he could go, frightened that the vacuum would suck him into itself. He closed the outer door and returned to the ship.

In panic he went to the control column and again twisted the dial. This time to −8. Again the screens filled with colour, again lights blinked and needles swung, again he felt sick. Again the ship came to a stop.

More cautiously, he opened the inner door, closed it, opened the outer door.

Nothing.

Shouting inarticulately, he hurried back into the ship and turned the dial to −10. The same sensations. Another stop.

And outside was the same featureless pit of empty space.

There was only one thing left to do to test the ship. Set the dial for the future and see what lay there. If it was the same, he could switch to Emergency Return.

He swung the dial right round to +2.

The humming rose to a shrill. Lightning exploded on the screens, the needles sped around the dials and Pepin flung himself to the floor in panic as his head began to ache horribly. The ship seemed to be tossed from side to side and yet he remained in the same position on the floor.

At last the ship came to a halt. He got up slowly, passed through the airlock.

He saw *everything*.

He saw gold-flecked bands of blue spiralling away into infinity. He saw streamers of cerise and violet light. He saw heaving mountains of black and green. He saw clouds of orange and purple. Shapes formed and melted. It seemed he was a giant at one moment and a midget at the next. His mind was not equipped to take in so much.

Quickly, he shut the airlock.

What had he seen? A vision of chaos? The sight seemed to him to have been metaphysical rather than physical. But what had it signified? It had been the very opposite of the vacuum – it had been space filled with everything imaginable, or the components of everything. The ship could not be a time craft after all, but a vessel for journeying – where? Another dimension? An alternate universe? But why the plus and minus signs on the controls? Why had Tall Laugher called this a time ship? Had he been tricked?

He pushed back his helmet and wiped the sweat from his face. His eyes felt sore and his headache was worse. He was incapable of logical thought.

He was tempted to turn the dial marked 'Emergency Return', but there was still the mysterious dial marked 'Megaflow Tuner'. Filled with hysterical recklessness, he turned it and was flung back as the ship jerked into normal motion. On the screens he saw a little of what he had observed outside.

All kinds of images appeared and disappeared. Once human figures – like golden shadows – were seen for a moment. His eyes fixed insanely on the screens, Pepin Hunchback could only stare.

Much, much later, he fell back to the floor. He had fainted.

At the sound of Tall Laugher's voice, he opened his eyes. His initial question was scarcely original, but it was the thing he most needed to know.

'Where am I?' he said, looking up at her.

'On the megaflow,' she replied. 'You are a fool, Pepin Hunchback. The Brooder and I have had a considerable amount of difficulty locating you. It is a wonder you are not insane.'

'I think I am. How did you get here?'

'We travelled up the megaflow after you. But your speed was so great we wasted a great deal of energy catching you. I see from the instruments that you went into the past. Were you satisfied?'

He got up slowly. 'Was that – that vacuum the *past*?'

'Yes.'

'But it was not Earth's past?'

'It is the only past there is.' She was at the controls, manipulating them. He turned his head and saw the Chronarch standing, head bowed, at the back of the ship.

He looked up and pursed his lips at Pepin.

'I attempted to explain – but I knew you would not believe me.

It is a pity that you know the truth, for it will not console you, my friend.'

'What *truth*?'

The Scar-faced Brooder sighed. He spread his hands. 'The only truth there is. The past is nothing but limbo – the future is what you have observed – chaos, save for the megaflow.'

'You mean Earth only has existence in the *present*?'

'As far as we are concerned, yes.' The Brooder folded his arms across his chest. 'It means little to us of Lanjis Liho – but I knew how it would affect you. We are Time Dwellers, you see – you are still a Space Dweller. Your mind is not adjusted to understand and exist in the dimensions of time-without-space.'

'Time without space is an impossibility!' Pepin shouted.

The Brooder grimaced. 'Is it? Then what do you think of the future – of the megaflow? Admittedly something exists here, but it is not the stuff of space as you would understand it. It is – well, the physical manifestation of time-without-space.' He sighed as he noted Pepin's expression. 'You will never properly understand, my friend.'

Tall Laugher spoke. 'We are nearly at Present, Brooder.'

'I will explain further when we return to Earth,' said the Chronarch kindly. 'You have my sympathy, Pepin Hunchback.'

In the Hall of Time, the Scar-faced Brooder walked up to his dais and lowered himself into his chair. 'Sit down, Pepin,' he said, indicating the edge of the dais. Dazedly, Pepin obeyed.

'What do you think of the past?' said the Chronarch ironically, as Tall Laugher joined them. Pepin looked up at her and then at her brother. He shook his head.

Tall Laugher put her hand on his shoulder. 'Poor Pepin...'

He did not have enough emotion left to feel anything at this. He rubbed his face and stared at the floor. His eyes were full of tears.

'Do you want the Chronarch to explain, Pepin?' she asked. Looking into her face, he saw that she, too, seemed extraordinarily sad. Somehow she could understand his hopelessness. If only she were normal, he thought, and we had met in different circumstances. Even here, life would be more than bearable with her. He had never seen such a look of sympathy directed at him before. She was repeating her question. He nodded.

'At first we were as astonished as you at the true nature of time,' said the Chronarch. 'But, of course, it was much easier for us to accept it. We are capable of moving through time as others move through space. Time is now our natural element. We have adapted in a peculiar way – we are able to journey into the past or future merely by an effort of will. We have reached the stage where we no longer need space to exist. In time-with-space our physical requirements are manifold and increasingly hard to meet on this changing planet. But in time-without-space these physical requirements no longer exist.'

'Brooder,' put in Tall Laugher, 'I do not think he is interested in us. Tell him why he found only limbo in the past.'

'Yes,' said Pepin, turning to stare at the Chronarch. 'Tell me.'

'I'll try. Imagine time as a straight line along which the physical universe is moving. At a certain point on that line the physical universe exists. But if we move away from the present, backward or forward, what do we find?'

Again Pepin shook his head.

'We find what you found – for by leaving the present, we also leave the physical universe. You see, Pepin, when we leave our native time stream, we move into others which are, in relation to us, *above* time. There is a central stream along which our universe moves – we call this the megaflow. As it moves it absorbs the stuff of time – absorbs the chronons, as we call them, but leaves nothing behind. Chronons constitute the future – they are infinite. The reason you found nothing in the past is because, in a sense, space *eats* the chronons but cannot replace them.'

'You mean Earth absorbs this – this temporal energy but emits none herself – like a beast prowling through time gobbling it up but excreting nothing.' Pepin spoke with a faint return of interest. 'Yes, I understand.'

The Chronarch leaned back. 'So when you came to me asking

to return to the past, I almost told you this, but you would not have believed me. You did not want to. You cannot return to Earth's past because, simply, it no longer exists. Neither is there a future in terms of space, only in terms of the chronon-constituted megaflow and its offshoots. We have managed to move ourselves where we wish, individually absorbing the chronons we need. Thus, the human race will continue – possibly we shall be immortal, ranging the continents of time at will, exploring, acquiring knowledge which will be useful to us.'

'While the rest of us die or turn into little better than machines,' said Pepin flatly.

'Yes.'

'Now I have no hope at all,' said Pepin, rising. He limped up to Tall Laugher. 'When do you leave for good?'

'Shortly.'

'I thank you for your sympathy and courtesy,' he said.

He left them standing silently in the Hall of Time.

Pepin walked along the beach, still moving towards the east, away from Lanjis Liho by the sea. The morning was a brown shroud covering the endlessness of sluggish sea and salt-frosted land, illuminated by a dying sun, blown by a cold wind.

Ah, he thought, *this is a morning for tears and self-contempt. Loneliness sits upon me like a great oozer with its mouth at my throat, sucking me dry of optimism. If only I could give myself up to this pitiless morning, let it engulf me, freeze me, toss me on its frigid wind and sink me in its slow-yielding sea, to lose sight of sun and sky, such as they are, and return to Mother Earth's ever-greedy womb...*

Oh, this alien Earth!

And yet he did not envy the Time Dwellers. Like the Moonites, they were renouncing their humanity. At least he still had his.

He turned as he heard his name called – a thin cry like that of an ancient seabird.

Tall Laugher was riding towards him, waving to him. She rode beneath the brown and heaving sky, her back straight and a smile on her lips and for some reason it seemed to him that she was riding to him out of the past, as when he had first seen her, a goddess from an age of mythology.

The red disc of the sun glowed behind her and again he noticed the strong smell of brine.

He waited by the edge of the thick, salt sea and, as he waited, he knew that his journey had been worthwhile.

A Dead Singer

In memory, among others, of Smiling Mike and John the Bog

Chapter One

'IT'S NOT THE speed, Jimi,' said Shakey Mo, 'it's the H you got to look out for.'

Jimi was amused. 'Well, it never did me much good.'

'It didn't do you no harm in the long run.' Mo laughed. He could hardly hold on to the steering wheel.

The big Mercedes camper took another badly lit bend. It was raining hard against the windscreen. He switched on the lamps. With his left hand he fumbled a cartridge from the case on the floor beside him and slotted it into the stereo. The heavy, driving drumming and moody synthesisers of Hawkwind's latest album made Mo feel much better. 'That's the stuff for energy,' said Mo.

Jimi leaned back. Relaxed, he nodded. The music filled the camper.

Mo kept getting speed hallucinations on the road ahead. Armies marched across his path; Nazis set up roadblocks; scampering children chased balls; big fires suddenly started and ghouls appeared and disappeared. He had a bad time controlling himself enough to keep on driving through it all. The images were familiar and he wasn't freaked out by them. He was content to be driving for Jimi. Since his comeback (or resurrection, as Mo privately called it) Jimi hadn't touched a guitar or sung a note, preferring to listen to other people's music. He was taking a long while to recover from what had happened to him in Ladbroke Grove. Only recently his colour had started to return and he was still wearing the white silk shirt and jeans in which he'd been

219

dressed when Mo first saw him, standing casually on the cowling of the Imperial Airways flying boat as it taxied towards the landing stage on Derwent Water. What a summer that had been, thought Mo. Beautiful.

The tape began to go round for the second time. Mo touched the stud to switch tracks, then thought better of it. He turned the stereo off altogether.

'Nice one.' Jimi was looking thoughtful again. He was almost asleep as he lay stretched out over the bench seat, his hooded eyes fixed on the black road.

'It's got to build up again soon,' said Mo. 'It can't last, can it? I mean, everything's so dead. Where's the energy going to come from, Jimi?'

'It's where it keeps going to that bothers me, man. You know?'

'I guess you're right.' Mo didn't understand.

But Jimi had to be right.

Jimi had known what he was doing, even when he died. Eric Burdon had gone on TV to say so. 'Jimi knew it was time to go,' he'd said. It was like that with the records and performances. Some of them hadn't seemed to be as tight as others; some of them were even a bit rambling. Hard to turn on to. But Jimi had known what he was doing. You had to have faith in him.

Mo felt the weight of his responsibilities. He was a good roadie, but there were better roadies than him. More together people who could be trusted with a big secret. Jimi hadn't spelled it out but it was obvious he felt that the world wasn't yet ready for his return. But why hadn't Jimi chosen one of the really ace roadies? Everything had to be prepared for the big gig. Maybe at Shea Stadium or the Albert Hall or the Paris Olympia? Anyway, some classic venue. Or at a festival? A special festival celebrating the resurrection. Woodstock or Glastonbury. Probably something new altogether, some new holy place. India, maybe? Jimi would say when the time came. After Jimi had contacted him and told him where to be picked up, Mo had soon stopped asking questions. With all his old gentleness, Jimi had turned the questions aside. He had been kind, but it was clear he hadn't wanted to answer.

Mo respected that.

The only really painful request Jimi had made was that Mo stop playing his old records, including 'Hey, Joe' the first single. Previously there hadn't been a day when Mo hadn't put something of Jimi's on. In his room in Lancaster Road, in the truck when he was roading for Light and later the Deep Fix, even when he'd gone to the House during his short-lived conversion to Scientology he'd been able to plug his earbead into his cassette recorder for an hour or so. While Jimi's physical presence made up for a lot and stopped the worst of the withdrawal symptoms, it was still difficult. No amount of mandrax, speed or booze could counter his need for the music and, consequently, the shakes were getting just a little bit worse each day. Mo sometimes felt that he was paying some kind of price for Jimi's trust in him. That was good karma so he didn't mind. He was used to the shakes anyway. You could get used to anything. He looked at his sinewy, tattooed arms stretched before him, the hands gripping the steering wheel. The world snake was wriggling again. Black, red and green, it coiled slowly down his skin, round his wrist and began to inch towards his elbow. He fixed his eyes back on the road.

Chapter Two

JIMI HAD FALLEN into a deep sleep. He lay along the seat behind Mo, his head resting on the empty guitar case. He was breathing heavily, almost as if something were pressing down on his chest.

The sky ahead was wide and pink. In the distance was a line of blue hills. Mo was tired. He could feel the old paranoia creeping in. He took a fresh joint from the ledge and lit it, but he knew that dope wouldn't do a lot of good. He needed a couple of hours' sleep himself.

Without waking Jimi, Mo pulled the truck into the side of the road, near a wide, shallow river full of flat, white limestone rocks. He opened his door and climbed slowly to the grass. He wasn't sure where they were; maybe somewhere in Yorkshire. There were hills all around. It was a mild autumn morning but Mo felt cold. He clambered down to the bank and knelt there, cupping his hands in the clear water, sucking up the river. He stretched out and put his tattered straw hat over his face. It was a very heavy scene at the moment. Maybe that was why it was taking Jimi so long to get it together.

Mo felt much better when he woke up. It must have been noon. The sun was hot on his skin. He took a deep breath of the rich air and cautiously removed his hat from his face. The black Mercedes camper with its chrome trimming was still on the grass near the road. Mo's mouth felt dry. He had another drink of water and rose, shaking the silver drops from his brown fingers. He trudged slowly to the truck, pulled back the door and looked over the edge of the driver's seat. Jimi wasn't there, but sounds came from behind the partition. Mo climbed across the two seats and slid open the connecting door. Jimi sat on one of the beds. He had erected the table and was drawing in a big red notebook. His smile was remote as Mo entered.

'Sleep good?' he asked.

Mo nodded. 'I needed it.'

'Sure,' said Jimi. 'Maybe I ought to do a little driving.'

'It's okay. Unless you want to make better time.'

'No.'

'I'll get some breakfast,' said Mo. 'Are you hungry?'

Jimi shook his head. All through the summer, since he had left the flying boat and got into the truck beside Mo, Jimi appeared to have eaten nothing. Mo cooked himself some sausages and beans on the little Calor stove, opening the back door so that the smell wouldn't fill the camper. 'I might go for a swim,' he said as he brought his plate to the table and sat as far away from Jimi as possible, so as not to disturb him.

'Okay,' said Jimi, absorbed in his drawing.

'What you doing? Looks like a comic strip. I'm really into comics.'

Jimi shrugged. 'Just doodling, man. You know.'

Mo finished his food. 'I'll get some comics next time we stop on the motorway. Some of the new ones are really far out, you know.'

'Yeah?' Jimi's smile was sardonic.

'Really far out. Cosmic wars, time warps. All the usual stuff but different, you know. Better. Bigger. More spectacular. Sensational, man. Oh, you want to see them. I'll get some.'

'Too much,' said Jimi distantly but it was obvious he hadn't been listening. He closed the notebook and sat back against the vinyl cushions, folding his arms across his white silk chest. As if it occurred to him that he might have hurt Mo's feelings, he added: 'Yeah, I used to be into comics a lot. You seen the Jap kind? Big fat books. Oh, man – they are *really* far out. Kids burning. Rape. All that stuff.' He laughed, shaking his head. 'Oh, man!'

'Yeah?' Mo laughed hesitantly.

'Right!' Jimi went to the door, placing a hand either side of the frame and looking into the day. 'Where are we, Mo? It's a little like Pennsylvania. The Delaware Valley. Ever been there?'

'Never been to the States.'

'Is that right?'

'Somewhere in Yorkshire, I think. Probably north of Leeds. That could be the Lake District over there.'

'Is that where I came through?'

'Derwent Water.'

'Well, well.' Jimi chuckled.

Jimi was livelier today. Maybe it was taking him time to store up all the energy he'd need when he finally decided to reveal himself to the world. Their driving had been completely at random. Jimi had let Mo decide where to go. They had been all over Wales, the Peaks, the West Country, most parts of the Home Counties, everywhere except London. Jimi had been reluctant to go to London. It was obvious why. Bad memories. Mo had been into town a few times, leaving the Mercedes and Jimi in a suburban lay-by and walking and hitching into London to get his mandies and his speed. When he could he scored some coke. He liked to get behind a snort or two once in a while. In Finch's on the corner of Portobello Road he'd wanted to tell his old mates about Jimi, but Jimi had said to keep quiet about it, so when people had asked him what he was doing, where he was living these days, he'd had to give vague answers. There was no problem about money. Jimi didn't have any but Mo had got a lot selling the white Dodge convertible. The Deep Fix had given it to him after they'd stopped going on the road. And there was a big bag of dope in the truck, too. Enough to last two people for months, though Jimi didn't seem to have any taste for that, either.

Jimi came back into the gloom of the truck. 'What d'you say we get on the road again?'

Mo took his plate, knife and fork down to the river, washed them and stashed them back in the locker. He got into the driver's seat and turned the key. The Wankel engine started at once. The Mercedes pulled smoothly away, still heading north, bumping off the grass and back onto the asphalt. They were on a narrow road suitable only for one-way traffic, but there was nobody behind them and nobody ahead of them until they left this road and turned onto the A65, making for Kendal.

'You don't mind the Lake District?' Mo asked.

'Suits me,' said Jimi. 'I'm the mad Gull Warrior, man.' He smiled. 'Maybe we should make for the ocean?'

'It's not far from here.' Mo pointed west. 'Morecambe Bay?'

Chapter Three

THE CLIFF-TOPS WERE covered in turf as smooth as a fairway. Below them the sea sighed. Jimi and Mo were in good spirits, looning around like kids.

In the distance, round the curve of the bay, were the towers and funfairs and penny arcades of Morecambe, but here it was deserted and still, apart from the occasional cry of a gull.

Mo laughed, then cried out nervously as Jimi danced so near to the cliff edge it seemed he'd fall over.

'Take it easy, Jimi.'

'Shit, man. They can't kill me.'

He had a broad, euphoric smile on his face and he looked really healthy. 'They can't kill Jimi, man!'

Mo remembered him on stage. In total command. Moving through the strobes, his big guitar stuck out in front of him, pointing at each individual member of the audience, making each kid feel that he was in personal touch with Jimi.

'Right!' Mo began to giggle.

Jimi hovered on the edge, still flapping his outstretched arms. 'I'm the boy they boogie to. Oh, man! There ain't nothing they can do to me!'

'Right!'

Jimi came zooming round and flung himself down on the turf next to Mo. He was panting. He was grinning. 'It's coming back, Mo. All fresh and new.'

Mo nodded, still giggling.

'I just know it's there, man.'

Mo looked up. The gulls were everywhere. They were screaming. They took on the aspect of an audience. He hated them. They were so thick in the sky now.

'Don't let them fucking feathers stick in your throat,' said Mo, suddenly sullen. He got up and returned to the truck.

'Mo. What's the matter with you, man?'

Jimi was concerned as ever, but that only brought Mo down more. It was Jimi's kindness which had killed him the first time. He'd been polite to everyone. He couldn't help it. Really hung-up people had got off on him. And they'd drained Jimi dry.

'They'll get you again, man,' said Mo. 'I know they will. Every time. There isn't a thing you can do about it. No matter how much energy you build up, you know, they'll still suck it out of you and moan for more. They want your blood, man. They want your sperm and your bones and your flesh, man. They'll take you, man. They'll eat you up again.'

'No. I'll – no, not this time.'

'Sure.' Mo sneered.

'Man, are you trying to bring me down?'

Mo began to twitch. 'No. But...'

'Don't worry, man, okay?' Jimi's voice was soft and assured.

'I can't put it into words, Jimi. It's this, sort of, premonition, you know.'

'What good did words ever do for anybody?' Jimi laughed his old, deep laugh. 'You *are* crazy, Mo. Come on, let's get back in the truck. Where do you want to head for?'

But Mo couldn't reply. He sat at the steering wheel and stared through the windscreen at the sea and the gulls.

Jimi was conciliatory. 'Look, Mo, I'll be cool about it, right? I'll take it easy, or maybe you think I don't need you?'

Mo didn't know why he was so down all of a sudden.

'Mo, you stay with me, wherever I go,' said Jimi.

Chapter Four

O UTSIDE CARLISLE THEY saw a hitch-hiker, a young guy who
looked really wasted. He was leaning on a signpost. He had
enough energy to raise his hand. Mo thought they should stop for
him. Jimi said: 'If you want to,' and went into the back of the
truck, closing the door as Mo pulled in for the hitch-hiker.

Mo said: 'Where you going?'

The hitch-hiker said: 'What about Fort William, man?'

Mo said: 'Get in.'

The hitch-hiker said his name was Chris. 'You with a band,
man?' He glanced round the cabin at the old stickers and the stereo, at Mo's tattoos, his faded face-paint, his Cawthorn T-shirt, his
beaded jacket, his worn jeans with washed-out patches on them,
the leather cowboy boots which Mo had bought at the Emperor
of Wyoming in Notting Hill Gate last year.

'Used to road for the Deep Fix,' said Mo.

The hitch-hiker's eyes were sunken and the sockets were red.
His thick black hair was long and hung down to his pale face. He
wore a torn Wrangler denim shirt, a dirty white Levi jacket and
both legs of his jeans had holes in the knees. He had moccasins on
his feet. He was nervous and eager.

'Yeah?'

'Right,' said Mo.

'What's in the back?' Chris turned to look at the door. 'Gear?'

'You could say that.'

'I've been hitching for three days, night and day,' said Chris. He
had an oil- and weather-stained khaki pack on his lap.

'D'you mind if I get some kip sometime?'

'No,' said Mo. There was a service station ahead. He decided to
pull in and fill the Merc up. By the time he got to the pumps Chris
was asleep.

As he waited to get back into the traffic, Mo crammed his mouth full of pills. Some of them fell from his hand onto the floor. He didn't bother to pick them up. He was feeling bleak.

Chris woke when they were going through Glasgow.

'Is this Glasgow?'

Mo nodded. He couldn't keep the paranoia down. He glared at the cars ahead as they moved slowly through the streets. Every window of every shop had a big steel mesh grille on it. The pubs were like bunkers. He was really pissed off without knowing why.

'Where you going yourself?' Chris asked.

'Fort William?'

'Lucky for me. Know where I can score any grass in Fort William?'

Mo reached forward and pushed a tobacco tin along the edge towards the hitch-hiker. 'You can have that.'

Chris took the tin and opened it. 'Far out! You mean it? And the skins?'

'Sure,' said Mo. He hated Chris, he hated everybody. He knew the mood would pass.

'Oh, wow! Thanks, man.' Chris put the tin in his pack.

'I'll roll one when we're out of the city, okay?'

'Okay.'

'Who are you working for now?' said Chris. 'A band?'

'No.'

'You on holiday?'

The kid was too speedy. Probably it was just his lack of sleep. 'Sort of,' he said.

'Me, too. Well, it started like that. I'm at university. Exeter. Or was. I decided to drop out. I'm not going back to that shit heap. One term was enough for me. I thought of heading for the Hebrides. Someone I know's living in a commune out there, on one of the islands. They got their own sheep, goats, a cow. Nobody getting off on them. You know. Really free. It seems okay to me.'

Mo nodded.

Chris pushed back his black, greasy hair. 'I mean compare

something like that with a place like this. How do people stand it, man? Fucking hell.'

Mo didn't answer. He moved forward, changing gear as the lights changed.

'Amazing,' said Chris. He saw the case of cartridges at his feet. 'Can I play some music?'

'Go ahead,' said Mo.

Chris picked out an old album, *Who's Next*. He tried to slide it into the slot the wrong way round. Mo took it from his hand and put it in the right way. He felt better when the music started. He noticed, out of the corner of his eye, that Chris tried to talk for a while before he realised he couldn't be heard.

Mo let the tape play over and over again as they drove away from Glasgow. Chris rolled joints and Mo smoked a little, beginning to get on top of his paranoia. By about four in the afternoon, he was feeling better and he switched off the stereo. They were driving beside Loch Lomond. The bracken was turning brown and shone like brass where the sun touched it. Chris had fallen asleep again, but he woke up as the music stopped. 'Far out.' He dug the scenery. 'Fucking far out.' He wound his window down. 'This is the first time I've been to Scotland.'

'Yeah?' said Mo.

'How long before we reach Fort William, man?'

'A few hours. Why are you heading for Fort William?'

'I met this chick. She comes from there. Her old man's a chemist or something.'

Mo said softly, on impulse: 'Guess who I've got in the back.'

'A chick?'

'No.'

'Who?'

'Jimi Hendrix.'

Chris's jaw dropped. He looked at Mo and snorted, willing to join in the joke. 'No? Really? Hendrix, eh? What is it, a refrigerated truck?' He was excited by the fantasy. 'You think if we thaw him out he'll play something for us?' He shook his head, grinning.

'He is sitting in the back there. Alive. I'm roading for him.'

'Really?'

'Yeah.'

'Fantastic.' Chris was half convinced. Mo laughed. Chris looked at the door. After that, he was silent for a while.

Something like a half an hour later, he said: 'Hendrix was the best, you know. He was the king, man. Not just the music, but the style, too. Everything. I couldn't believe it when I heard he died. I still can't believe it, you know.'

'Sure,' said Mo. 'Well, he's back.'

'Yeah?' Again Chris laughed uncertainly. 'In there? Can I see him?'

'He's not ready, yet.'

'Sure,' said Chris.

It was dark when they reached Fort William. Chris staggered down from the truck. 'Thanks, man. That's really nice, you know. Where are you staying?'

'I'm moving on,' said Mo. 'See you.'

'Yeah. See you.' Chris still had that baffled look on his face.

Mo smiled to himself as he started the camper, heading for Oban. Once they were moving the door opened and Jimi clambered over the seats to sit beside him.

'You told that kid about me?'

'He didn't believe me,' said Mo.

Jimi shrugged.

It began to rain again.

Chapter Five

THEY LAY TOGETHER in the damp heather looking out over the hills. There was nobody for miles; no roads, towns or houses. The air was still and empty save for a hawk drifting so high above them it was almost out of sight.

'This'll do, eh?' said Mo. 'It's fantastic.'

Jimi smiled gently. 'It's nice,' he said.

Mo took a Mars bar from his pocket and offered it to Jimi who shook his head. Mo began to eat the Mars bar.

'What d'you think I am, man?' said Jimi.

'How d'you mean?'

'Devil or angel? You know.'

'You're Jimi,' said Mo. 'That's good enough for me, man.'

'Or just a ghost,' said Jimi. 'Maybe I'm just a ghost.'

Mo began to shake. 'No,' he said.

'Or a killer?' Jimi got up and struck a pose. 'The Sonic Assassin. Or the messiah, maybe.' He laughed. 'You wanna hear my words of wisdom?'

'That's not what it's about,' said Mo, frowning. 'Words. You just have to be there, Jimi. On the stage. With your guitar. You're above all that stuff – all the hype. Whatever you do – it's right, you know.'

'If you say so, Mo.' Jimi was on some kind of downer. He lowered himself to the heather and sat there cross-legged, smoothing his white jeans, picking mud off his black patent leather boots. 'What is all this *Easy Rider* crap anyway? What are we doing here?'

'You didn't like *Easy Rider*?' Mo was astonished.

'The best thing since *Lassie Come Home*.' Jimi shrugged. 'All it ever proved was that Hollywood could still turn 'em out, you know. They got a couple of fake freaks and made themselves a lot of money. A rip-off, man. And the kids fell for it. What does that make me?'

'You never ripped anybody off, Jimi.'

'Yeah? How d'you know?'

'Well, you never did.'

'All that low energy shit creeping in everywhere. Things are bad.' Jimi had changed the subject, making a jump Mo couldn't follow. 'People all over the Grove playing nothing but fake fifties crap, Simon and Garfunkel. Jesus Christ! Was it ever worth doing?'

'Things go in waves. You can't be up the whole time.'

'Sure,' Jimi sneered. 'This one's for all the soldiers fighting in Chicago. And Milwaukee. And New York... And Vietnam. Down with War and Pollution. What was all that about?'

'Well...' Mo swallowed the remains of the Mars bar. 'Well – it's important, man. I mean, all those kids getting killed.'

'While we made fortunes. And came out with a lot of sentimental shit. That's where we were wrong. You're either in the social conscience business or show business. You're just foolish if you think you can combine them like that.'

'No, man. I mean, you can say things which people will hear.'

'You say what your audience wants. A Frank Sinatra audience gets their shit rapped back to them by Frank Sinatra. Jimi Hendrix gives a Jimi Hendrix audience what they want to hear. Is that what I want to get back into?'

But Mo had lost him. Mo was watching the tattoos crawl up his arms. He said vaguely: 'You need different music for different moods. There's nothing wrong with the New Riders, say, if you're trying to get off some paranoia trip. And you get up on Hendrix. That's what it's like. Like uppers and downers, you know.'

'Okay,' said Jimi. 'You're right. But it's the other stuff that's stupid. Why do they always want you to keep saying things? If you're just a musician that's all you should have to be. When you're playing a gig, anyway, or making a record. Anything else should come out of that. If you wanna do benefits, free concerts, okay. But your opinions should be private. They want to turn us into politicians.'

'I tol' you,' said Mo, staring intensely at his arms. 'Nobody asks that. You do what you want to do.'

'Nobody asks it, but you always feel you got to give it to 'em.' Jimi rolled over and lay on his back, scratching his head. 'Then you blame them for it.'

'Not everyone thinks they owe anything to anyone,' said Mo mildly as his skin undulated over his flesh.

'Maybe that's it,' said Jimi. 'Maybe that's what kills you. Jesus Christ. Psychologically, man, you know, that means you must be in one hell of a mess. Jesus Christ. That's suicide, man. Creepy.'

'They killed you,' said Mo.

'No, man. It was suicide.'

Mo watched the world snake crawl. Could this Hendrix be an imposter?

Chapter Six

'So what you going to do, then?' said Mo. They were on the road to Skye and running low on fuel.

'I was a cunt to come back,' said Jimi. 'I thought I had some kind of duty.'

Mo shrugged. 'Maybe you have, you know.'

'And maybe I haven't.'

'Sure.' Mo saw a filling station ahead. The gauge read Empty and a red light was flashing on the panel. It always happened like that. He'd hardly ever been stranded. He glanced in the mirror and saw his own mad eyes staring back at him. Momentarily he wondered if he should turn the mirror a little to see if Jimi's reflection was there too. He pushed the thought away. More paranoia. He had to stay on top of it.

While the attendant was filling the truck, Mo went to the toilet. Among the more common bits of graffiti on the wall was the slogan 'Hawkwind is Ace'. Maybe Jimi was right. Maybe his day was over and he should have stayed dead. Mo felt miserable. Hendrix had been his only hero. He did up his flies and the effort drained off the last of his energy. He staggered against the door and began to slide down towards the messy floor. His mouth was dry; his heart was thumping very fast. He tried to remember how many pills he'd swallowed recently. Maybe he was about to O.D.

He put his hands up to the door handle and hauled himself to his feet. He bent over the lavatory bowl and shoved his finger down his throat. Everything was moving. The bowl was alive. A greedy mouth trying to swallow him. The walls heaved and moved in on him. He heard a whistling noise. Nothing came up. He stopped trying to vomit, turned, steadied himself as best as he could, brushed aside the little white stick-men who tried to grab at him, dragged the door open and plunged through. Outside, the attendant was putting the cap back on the tank. He wiped his big hands on a piece of rag and put the rag back into his overalls, saying something. Mo found some money in his back pocket and gave it to him. He heard a voice:

'You okay, laddie?'

The man had offered him a genuine look of concern.

Mo mumbled something and clambered into the cab.

The man ran up as Mo started the engine, waving money and green stamps.

'What?' said Mo. He managed to wind the window down. The man's face changed to a malevolent devil's mask. Mo knew enough not to worry about it. 'What?'

He thought he heard the attendant say: 'Your friend's already paid.'

'That's right, man,' said Jimi from beside him.

'Keep it,' said Mo. He had to get on the road quickly. Once he was driving he would be more in control of himself. He fumbled a cartridge at random from the case. He jammed it into the slot. The tape started halfway through a Stones album. Jagger singing 'Let It Bleed' had a calming effect on Mo. The snakes stopped winding up and down his arms and the road ahead became steady and clearer. He'd never liked the Stones much. A load of wankers, really, though you had to admit Jagger had a style of his own which no-one could copy. But basically wankers like the rest of the current evil-trippers, like Morrison and Alice Cooper. It occurred to him he was wasting his time thinking about nothing but bands, but what else was there to think about? Anyway how else could you see your life? The mystical thing didn't mean much to him. Scientology was a load of crap. At any rate, he couldn't see anything in it. The guys running all that stuff seemed to be more hung-up than the people they were supposed to be helping. That was true of a lot of things. Most people who told you they wanted to help you were getting off on you in some way. He'd met pretty much every kind of freak by now. Sufis, Hare Krishnas, Jesus freaks, Meditators, Processors, Divine Lighters. They could all talk better than him, but they all seemed to need more from him than they could give. You got into people when you were tripping. Acid had done a lot for him that way. He could suss out the hype-merchants so easily these days. And by that test Jimi couldn't be a fake. Jimi was straight. Fucked up now, possibly, but okay.

The road was long and white and then it became a big boulder. Mo couldn't tell if the boulder was real or not. He drove at it, then changed his mind, braking sharply. A red car behind him swerved and hooted as it went past him through the boulder which disappeared. Mo shook all over. He took out the Stones tape and changed it for the Grateful Dead's *American Beauty*, turned down low.

'You okay, man?' said Hendrix.

'Sure. Just a bit shakey.' Mo started the Merc up.

'You want to stop and get some sleep?'

'I'll see how I feel later.'

It was sunset when Jimi said: 'We seem to be heading south.'

'Yeah,' said Mo. 'I need to get back to London.'

'You got to score?'

'Yeah.'

'Maybe I'll come in with you this time.'

'Yeah?'

'Maybe I won't.'

Chapter Seven

B Y THE TIME Mo had hitched to the nearest Tube station and reached Ladbroke Grove he was totally wasted. The images were all inside his head now: pictures of Jimi from the first time he'd seen him on TV playing 'Hey, Joe' (Mo had still been at school then), pictures of Jimi playing at Woodstock, at festivals and gigs all over the country. Jimi in big, feathered hats, bizarre multicoloured shirts, several rings on each finger, playing that white Strat, flinging the guitar over his head, plucking the strings with his teeth, shoving it under his straddled legs, making it wail and moan and throb, doing more with a guitar than anyone had done before. Only Jimi could make a guitar come alive in that way, turning the machine into an organic creature, simultaneously a prick, a woman, a white horse, a sliding snake. Mo glanced at his arms, but they were still. The sun was beginning to set as he turned into Lancaster Road, driven more by a mixture of habit and momentum than any energy or sense of purpose. He had another image in his head now, of Jimi as a soul thief, taking the energy away from the audience. Instead of a martyr, Jimi became the vampire. Mo knew that the paranoia was really setting in and the sooner he got hold of some uppers the better. He couldn't blame Jimi for how he felt. He hadn't slept for two days. That was all it was. Jimi had given everything to the people in the audience, including his life. How many people in the audience had died for Jimi?

He crawled up the steps of the house in Lancaster Road and rang the third bell down. There was no answer. He was shaking badly. He held on to the concrete steps and tried to calm himself, but it got worse and he thought he was going to pass out.

The door behind him opened.

'Mo?'

It was Dave's chick, Jenny, wearing a purple brocade dress. Her hair was caked with wet henna.

'Mo? You all right?'

Mo swallowed and said: 'Hullo, Jenny. Where's Dave?'

'He went down the Mountain Grill to get something to eat. About half an hour ago. Are you all right, Mo?'

'Tired. Dave got any uppers?'

'He had a lot of mandies in.'

Mo accepted the news. 'Can you let me have a couple of quid's worth?'

'You'd better ask him yourself, Mo. I don't know who he's promised them to.'

Mo nodded and got up carefully.

'You want to come in and wait, Mo?' said Jenny.

Mo shook his head. 'I'll go down the Mountain. See you later, Jenny.'

'See you later, Mo. Take care, man.'

Mo shuffled slowly up Lancaster Road and turned the corner into Portobello Road. He thought he saw the black-and-chrome Merc cross the top of the street. The buildings were all crowding in on him. He saw them grinning at him, leering. He heard them talking about him. There were fuzz everywhere. A woman threw something at him. He kept going until he reached the Mountain Grill and had stumbled through the door. The café was crowded with freaks but there was nobody there he knew. They all had evil, secretive expressions and they were whispering.

'You fuckers,' he mumbled, but they pretended they weren't listening. He saw Dave.

'Dave? Dave, man!'

Dave looked up, grinning privately. 'Hi, Mo. When did you get back to town?' He was dressed in new, clean denims with fresh patches on them. One of the patches said 'Star Rider'.

'Just got in.' Mo leaned across the tables, careless of the intervening people, and whispered in Dave's ear. 'I hear you got some mandies.'

Dave's face became serious. 'Sure. Now?'

Mo nodded.

Dave rose slowly and paid his bill to the dark, fat lady at the till. 'Thanks, Maria.'

Dave took Mo by the shoulder and led him out of the café. Mo wondered if Dave was about to finger him. He remembered that Dave had been suspected more than once.

Dave said softly as they went along. 'How many d'you need, Mo?'

'How much are they?'

Dave said: 'You can have them for ten a piece.'

'I'll have five quid's worth. A hundred, yeah?'

'Fifty.'

They got back to Lancaster Road and Dave let himself in with two keys, a Yale and a mortise. They went up a dark, dangerous stairway. Dave's room was gloomy, thick with incense, with painted blinds covering the window. Jenny sat on a mattress in the corner listening to Ace on the stereo. She was knitting.

'Hi, Mo,' she said. 'So you found him.'

Mo sat down on the mattress in the opposite corner. 'How's it going, Jenny?' he said. He didn't like Dave, but he liked Jenny. He made a big effort to be polite. Dave was standing by a chest of drawers, dragging a box from under a pile of tasselled curtains. Mo looked past him and saw Jimi standing there. He was dressed in a hand-painted silk shirt with roses all over it. There was a jade talisman on a silver chain round his throat. He had the white Strat in his hands. His eyes were closed as he played it. Almost immediately Mo guessed he was looking at a poster.

Dave counted fifty mandies into an aspirin bottle. Mo reached into his jeans and found some money. He gave Dave a five-pound note and Dave gave him the bottle. Mo opened the bottle and took out a lot of the pills, swallowing them fast. They didn't act right away, but he felt better for taking them. He got up.

'See you later, Dave.'

'See you later, man,' said Dave. 'Maybe in Finch's tonight.'

'Yeah.'

Chapter Eight

M O COULDN'T REMEMBER how the fight started. He'd been sitting quietly in a corner of the pub drinking his pint of bitter when that big fat fart who was always in there causing trouble decided to pick on him. He remembered getting up and punching the fat fart. There had been a lot of confusion then and he had somehow knocked the fat fart over the bar. Then a few people he knew pulled him away and took him back to a basement in Oxford Gardens where he listened to some music.

It was *Band of Gypsys* that woke him up. Listening to 'Machine Gun' he realised suddenly that he didn't like it. He went to the pile of records and found other Hendrix albums. He played *Are You Experienced*, the first album, and *Electric Ladyland*, and he liked them much better. Then he played *Band of Gypsys* again.

He looked round the dark room. Everyone seemed to be totally spaced out.

'He died at the right time,' he said. 'It was over for him, you know. He shouldn't have come back.'

He felt in his pocket for his bottle of mandies. There didn't seem to be that many left. Maybe someone had ripped them off in the pub. He took a few more and reached for the bottle of wine on the table, washing them down. He put *Are You Experienced* on the deck again and lay back. 'That was really great,' he said. He fell asleep. He shook a little bit. His breathing got deeper and deeper. When he started to vomit in his sleep nobody noticed. By that time everyone was right out of it. He choked quietly and then stopped.

Chapter Nine

About an hour later a black man came into the room. He was tall and elegant. He radiated energy. He wore a white silk shirt and white jeans. There were shiny patent leather boots on his feet. A chick started to get up as he came into the room. She looked bemused.

'Hi,' said the newcomer. 'I'm looking for Shakey Mo. We ought to be going.'

He peered at the sleeping bodies and then looked closer at one which lay a little apart from the others. There was vomit all over his face and over his shirt. His skin was a ghastly, dirty green. The black man stepped across the others and knelt beside Mo, feeling his heart, taking his pulse.

The chick stared stupidly at him. 'Is he all right?'

'He's O.D.'d,' the newcomer said quietly. 'He's gone. D'you want to get a doctor or something, honey?'

'Oh, Jesus,' she said.

The black man got up and walked to the door.

'Hey,' she said. 'You look just like Jimi Hendrix, you know that?'

'Sure.'

'You can't be – you're not, are you? I mean, Jimi's dead.'

Jimi shook his head and smiled his old smile. 'Shit, lady. They can't kill Jimi.' He laughed as he left.

The chick glanced down at the small, ruined body covered in its own vomit. She swayed a little, rubbing at her thighs. She frowned. Then she went as quickly as she could from the room, hampered by her long cotton dress, and into the street. It was nearly dawn and it was cold. The tall figure in the white shirt and jeans didn't seem to notice the cold. It strode up to the big Mercedes camper parked near the end of the street.

The chick began to run after the black truck as it started up and rolled a little way before it had to stop on the red light at the Ladbroke Grove intersection.

'Wait,' she shouted. 'Jimi!'

But the camper was moving before she could reach it.

She saw it heading north towards Kilburn.

She wiped the clammy sweat from her face. She must be freaking. She hoped when she got back to the basement that there wouldn't really be a dead guy there.

She didn't need it.

London Flesh

Chapter One

D ANIEL DEFOE WAS the first to write about 'London Flesh', the legendary meat of the hern supposed to 'confer Magical Powers upon those who Partook of it'. Defoe, in fact, invested money in its unsuccessful commercial production. Perhaps that was why he wrote his famous pamphlet which, while pretending scepticism, actually gave the impression that the meat, sold mostly in the form of a paste, had supernatural properties.

De Quincey, Lamb, Dickens, and Grossmith all claimed to have sampled London Flesh, usually in pies, sausages, or patés, but only Lamb was convinced that he had briefly become invisible and known the power of flight (over Chelsea Gardens). The Flesh was rumoured, of course, to be human, and Dickens raised the name of Sweeney Todd in *Household Words*, but Doctor 'Dog' Donovan of Guy's was convinced that the meat was 'undoubtedly that of the female hern'. That said, the rumour persisted.

The hern was never abundant. The last pair in the London area was seen in Kew in 1950. Legend had it they were raised in captivity in Hackney Marshes up until the Second World War. Patrick Hamilton and Gerald Kersh both claimed to have been taken to a hern farm (Kersh was blindfolded) and seen dozens of the creatures penned in cages hidden behind trees and bushes, where they were offered hern paté on cream crackers. 'London Flesh,' reports Hamilton, 'as sweet and smooth as your mother's cheeks.'

'There's a book in heaven,' said Coleridge, who was convinced that the Flesh was human, 'in which is recorded the names of all who dishonour the Dead. Graveyard Desecrations and any form of Cannibalism, including the eating of London Flesh.'

London believes it remembers the horrible story of the cannibal tramwaymen of Hampstead Heath and how they devoured on Christmas Day the passengers and crew of the Number 64 tram which mysteriously returned empty to the Tudor Hamlets terminus. This is the true story of that event.

No complete list of passengers has ever been made, but we do know that a party of some dozen revellers left the Red Mill public house on Tufnell Hill and made their way to the tram stop to board the 64. Witnesses saw and heard them, commenting on their cheerful drunkenness and the somewhat lewd behaviour of the young women who, removing hats and veils, bared their entire heads at passers-by. We also know that the vicar of St Alban's, Brookgate, was last seen boarding at the Tessie O'Shea stop, because his brother walked him there. A young mother with three rather boisterous children also boarded, though it was possible they disembarked before the 64 began its crossing of the Heath. The night was foggy. The gas was out across a fairly wide area, due to air in the pipes at Highgate, the GLC said. Indeed the Gas Light and Coke Co. were held partially responsible for police officers not at once investigating after the tram failed to reach Tudor Hamlets. The gas being restored, the tram mysteriously returned to its own terminus. All that was found aboard was a leverman's uniform cap and two ladies' hats, which told their own grim story.

At that time there was no fashion for elaborate headgear or, indeed, the casual doffing of it as there is today. At least two young women had been aboard, yet at first the police tried to treat the case as one of simple abandonment. They thought the overhead power rail had come adrift from its connector and passengers had decided to walk home. But neither the leverman nor the conductor reported for duty. The Home Office decided to investigate the mystery and sent Sir Seaton Begg and his friend Dr 'Taffy' Sinclair relatively late on Boxing Day. Unhappy at being called away from their festivities, the two men came together at Tudor

Hamlets, in the office of Mr Thorn, the regional manager of the Universal Transport Company.

Thorn was a red-faced, anxious man whose perspiration made dark stains on his scarlet, gold and white uniform. He was somewhat in awe of Begg and Sinclair, their reputations being familiar to all who followed the news.

'It will be my head on the block, gentlemen,' he reminded them, 'if the UTC determine negligence here. Of course, we are used to tram robbers on the Heath, but in all my years we have only known one killing and that was when a barker went off by accident. It has always been prudent of levermen to obey a command when they receive one, especially since we are insured for material loss but not for the death of our employees. Guild tramwaymen never do more than wound. Those flintlock pistols they affect allow for little else. It is to everyone's advantage that their guild, formed in 1759, laid down strict regulations as to weaponry, masks, mounts, uniforms, and so on. Do you have any suspicions, gentlemen?'

Removing his wide-brimmed slouch hat Sir Seaton Begg brushed at the brim with his sleeve. 'It's rare for a tramwayman to disobey his own strict codes. They would sooner lose the good will of Londoners and therefore their guarantees of secrecy and shelter. Nor is it like them to abduct women and children. Either this was a gang feigning to be real tramway thieves or we are dealing with rogues who hold their guild honour at nought.'

'It would be yet another sign of the times,' murmured the tall Welshman, the detective's lifelong friend and amanuensis. 'When tramwaymen go against their traditions, then the next thing we'll see will be the looting of graves.'

'Quite so,' said Begg, taking out an enormous briar, filling it with black shag and lighting it from a vesta he struck against the bricks of the terminus. Soon heavy black smoke filled the hall as, puffing contemplatively, he paced back and forth across the stone flags.

'Remarkable,' offered Sinclair, 'that no passengers were reported missing.'

'And only the leverman's wife called in to say he had not come home.' Begg paused frowning. 'The conductor lived alone?'

'A widower,' said Mr Thorn. 'His mother is in Deal with relatives.'

'Young women? A mother with children?' Sir Seaton drew thoughtfully on his briar. 'Could they all have disembarked before the terminus?'

'It's not unheard of, sir.'

'But unlikely, I'm sure you'll agree. I think it's probably time we took a tram back to the Red Mill. Can you spare us a leverman, Mr Thorn?'

'We're still on a skeleton schedule for the holidays, but in these circumstances...' Guild rules usually demanded that every tram carry both a driver and a conductor. 'I can't see anyone objecting here if only the leverman takes out the Special. I'll give the appropriate instructions. We should have her connected in fifteen minutes.'

Chapter Two

G REY CLOUDS REGATHERED over the Heath as the Special began her long climb up Tufnell Hill. The Red Mill's tethered sails strained against air, bending foliage across the horizon like mourners in procession.

Snow had melted into the grass, and mud puddles reflected the sky. Crows called with mysterious urgency, and there was a strong, fecund smell. Dr Sinclair remarked on the unseasonable warmth. Only a few roofs and the steeple of St Valentine's, Hampstead Vale, could be seen below until the Mill was reached. There they looked onto Tudor Hamlets and the suburbs beyond Highgate, red roofs, green cedars and pines, the bones of elms supporting untidy nests, all gauzed in smoke from the chimneys.

Disembarking, Begg strolled up the path, through the ornamental metal gates and began to ascend worn granite steps to the Red Mill. Sinclair, examining the soft ground, bent to frown over something. 'Hello! That's odd for this time of the year!' He straightened, now giving his attention to something on the other side of the path. 'I wonder why –?'

A bass voice greeted them from the door of the hostelry attached to the Mill. 'I'm sorry, gents, but we're closed until New Year's Eve.' Sinclair looked up to see the large red-bearded publican standing there.

'Except for guests who ride hunters, it seems.' Dr Sinclair smiled and pointed to the evidence. 'One doesn't have to be a High Mobsman to know that tramway thieves always convene here for the holidays.'

Sir Seaton shared his friend's humour. 'Don't worry, Mr O'Dowd,' he told the publican, 'we're neither peelers nor wildsmen and have no direct business to discuss with your guests.

Would I be wrong if I understood Captain Anchovy to be stabling his horse here for the Season?'

A cheerful, handsome face appeared behind O'Dowd's broad shoulder as, with his famous dashing grace, a man in the white wig and elaborate long waistcoat of a guild member stepped forward, lowering and uncocking a huge horse pistol, the traditional tool of his trade.

'Festive greetings to ye, Sir Seaton. I trust you and your companion will take a glass with us?' He smiled as he shook hands with the detectives. Together they entered the heat of a public bar filled with tobymen of every rank. Any suspicion of the newcomers was swiftly dispelled, and within moments the two investigators were imbibing goblets of mulled wine while Captain Anchovy and his men volunteered their aid in solving the mystery. Their own honour, they said, was at stake.

Tom Anchovy in particular was inflamed with disgust. 'My dear Sir Seaton, that 64 was indeed our intended prize as she came up Tufnell Hill. But it was Boxing Day, and we had no intention of stealing anything but the hearts of the ladies aboard. All were brought here. Three children were given presents, and old men of pleasant humour were presented with a glass of wine. Only a few refused our hospitality – the mother of the children, a good-hearted reverend gentleman whose abstinence we respected – and that sour fellow who had refused to quit the Inn on our arrival and refused to share his vitalls with us. On any other occasion we might have taken him for ransom.'

'And he was –?' Sir Seaton lifted the beaker to his lips.

'Henry Marriage, sir. A humourless walking cadaver if ever I met one. Yet even he was permitted to retain his valuables. I don't mind tellin' ye, Sir Seaton, that had it not been Christmas, I would have had his last stitch *and* kept him for ransom!'

'Is that Marriage of Marriage's Opiates by the river?' asked Dr Sinclair, placing his finished beaker on the bar and nodding with approval as O'Dowd refilled it. 'The millionaire who lives in a house on his own wharf?'

'The same, Doctor Sinclair. Do ye know him?'

'Only by reputation,' replied the doctor. 'A solitary individual, they say. A dabbler in the alchemist's art. He's published an inter- esting book or two. No charlatan, but no great scientist, either. Many of his findings and experiments have been discredited. He's considered a mere amateur by the medical and scientific guilds.'

'I understand nothing of such things, sir. But I'll swear to this – when that tram left last evening he was safe and sound, as was every living soul aboard. Though he chose to go with them, all but Henry Marriage were as cheerful as when they had embarked. If that 64 was taken, then it would have been on the high stretch of track below the ruined village.'

'Why so?' Begg enquired.

'Because we watched her lights until they were out of sight, and young Jaimie Gordon here was on his way to join us, taking the low road up the Vale. He'd have spotted anything untoward.'

Sir Seaton was already slamming down his glass and cramming his hat onto his handsome, aquiline head. 'Then I can guess where the tram was stopped. Come on, Taffy, let's board our Special. I'm much obliged to you, Captain Anchovy.'

'Delighted to have helped, sir.'

After a further quick word with the tramwayman, the two metatemporal investigators were again on their way.

Chapter Three

A BLÉRIOT 'BAT', no doubt taking the day's mail to France,
flew high overhead as the 64 rattled to a stop below the ruins
of Hampstead Model Village which lay on the brow of the hill
above the tramline whose branches had once serviced the inhabitants of Lady Hecate Brown's failed evangelical dream of a healthy
environment where a good Christian life and enlightened working conditions would be the antidote to all the ills of city life. Her
failure to supply the model village with familiar recreations, public houses and fried fish shops caused even the most enlightened
artisans to view her idealistic community as a kind of prison. The
village had flourished as a middle-class enclave until, without servants or city facilities, the bourgeoisie chose the suburbs of Tudor
Hamlets and Lyonne's Greene. The tram service had been discon-
tinued, though the tracks were intact, lost beneath the encroaching
weeds and brambles.

As Begg and Sinclair disembarked, the sky clouded darker and
it began to rain heavily. Peering with difficulty through the ever-
thickening mist, Begg quickly saw that his intuition had been right.

Sinclair was the first to observe how the track had been cleared
through the swampy ground leading up to the ruins. 'Look, Begg.
There's the shine of brass. A tram was diverted at this very spot and
went up Ham Hill towards the old village. What do you make of it?'

'The best place to take a tram off the usual routes, Taffy. The
emptied vehicle was sent back on its way, perhaps to divert attention from whatever dark deed was done here. Let us pray we are
in time to save those poor souls – victims, no doubt, of some
rogue band caring nought for the rules and habits of an old guild!'

With difficulty, they followed the line up the muddy terrain,
their boots sinking and sliding in ground normally frozen hard.

As the rain let up, Ham Hill's ruins were seen bleak beneath a lowering sky. The air was unseasonably muggy; thunder rolled closer. Melted snow left pools so that the hill might have been the remains of Hereward's Romney fastness. Sinclair suppressed a shiver as a sudden chill crept up his spine. The afternoon's gloom was illuminated by a sudden sheet of lightning throwing the ruins into vivid silhouette.

'Press on, Taffy,' murmured Seaton Begg, clapping his friend on his sturdy shoulder. 'I sense we're not far from solving this mystery!'

'And maybe perishing as a consequence.' The mordant Welshman spoke only half in jest.

Making some remark about the 'dark instincts of the Celtic soul', Begg tramped on until they at last stood regarding the outskirts of the ruins, looking down at Tufnell Vale whose yellow lights offered distant reassurance.

No such friendly gas burned in the ruins of Hampstead Model Village, yet a few guttering brands lit the remaining glass in the low church chapel, said now to harbour all manner of pagan ritual and devil worship. The nearby Anglican church had been desanctified on orders from Southwark, but the ragged walls remained. Close to the church blazed three or four bonfires built from the wood of old pews and other religious furniture.

Begg and Sinclair kept to the cover of fallen walls and shrubbery. Human figures gathered around the fires.

'Vagrants, perhaps?' murmured Sinclair. 'Do such people still exist?'

Signalling his friend to silence, Begg pointed to a collapsing house sheltering the bulky shapes of horses. Rough laughter and uncultured voices told Begg they had found another tramwayman gang. 'Guildless outcasts, Taffy, by the cut of their coats. Rejected by every mobsmen's association from here to York.'

Keeping well down, the detectives crept closer. Unlike Tom Anchovy's men, guildless tram thieves were known for their cruel savagery.

'It's been years since such a gang was seen this close to London,' whispered Sinclair. 'They risk life imprisonment if caught!'

Begg was unsurprised. 'I knew Captain Zenith was outside Beaconsfield and suspected of several tram robberies in that region. Quickly, Taffy, drop down.' He flung himself behind a broken wall. 'That's the rogue himself!'

A tall, white-haired man in a black greatcoat sauntered towards one of the fires, eyes burning like rubies in the reflected light. A handsome albino with skin the colour of ivory, Zenith was an old enemy of Begg's. The two were said to be cousins who had often crossed swords.

As they watched, Zenith approached a thin individual, as tall as himself, on the far side of the fire. It was Sinclair's turn to draw in a sharp breath. Henry Marriage, one of the missing passengers, seemed to be on friendly terms with the most notorious tram thief in Europe!

It grew darker until all the inhabitants of the ruins were mere silhouettes.

'We can't take 'em single-handed,' murmured Begg. 'We'd best return to the depot and telegraph to Scotland Yard.'

Picking their way carefully down the hill, they had scarcely gone twenty yards before dark shadows suddenly surrounded them. They heard a horrible, muffled noise.

Moving towards them across the unnaturally damp ground, big pistols threatening, came an unsavoury circle of leering tram robbers.

'Good evening, gentlemen!' The leader doffed his cocked hat in a mocking bow. 'Always pleased to welcome a few more guests to our holiday harum-scarum!' He removed the shutter from his night lamp, showing the face of their unfortunate tram driver. The leverman's hands were tied before him, and a gag had been forced into his mouth. He had been trying to warn his passengers of his own capture.

Chapter Four

THE MOBSMEN HAD not reckoned with the two detectives being armed. In a flash Begg and Sinclair produced the latest repeating Webleys! 'Stand, you scum,' levelly declared the investigator. 'You no doubt recognise this revolver which I intend to use to advantage.'

Triumph draining from their decadent features, the mobsmen fell back, knowing full well the power and efficiency of the Webleys over their own antique barkers. Then a voice cut through the misty air. Sharp as a diamond, it bore the tone of a man used to obedience.

'Fire one chamber, Sir Seaton, and count yourself responsible for the death of an innocent woman.'

Turning their heads, the investigators saw Captain Zenith, a bright lantern in one hand, pressing his barker against the head of a dishevelled coster-girl grinning stupidly from under her raised veil, her hat at an unseemly angle.

Sinclair stifled a cry of outrage. 'You fiend!' He did not let his Webley fall, nor did he disengage the safety catch. 'What have you done to that poor young creature?'

'I, sir?' An almost melancholy smile played across the mobsman's pale lips. 'What d'ye think I've done? Murdered her?' The light from the lantern gave his red eyes a savage sparkle.

'Drugged her!' Sinclair muttered in disgust. 'You're cowards as well as kidnappers.'

Captain Zenith's face clouded for a moment before resuming its habitual mask. 'She's unhurt, sir. However, aggressive action on your part might alter her circumstances.'

'No doubt one of the missing passengers, but where are the children?' demanded Sir Seaton.

'Safe and sound with their mother and full of mince pies,' Zenith assured him.

'Then show them to me.'

'I'd remind you, Sir Seaton, that you are at a disadvantage.'

'And I'd remind you, Captain Zenith, that I am a servant of the Crown. Harm me or those under my protection and you'll answer to Her Majesty's justice.'

'I have been escaping that justice, sir, for longer than you and I have travelled the moonbeam roads. Put that fancy barker aside and be my welcome guest.' He stepped away from the giggling young woman as Begg and Sinclair reluctantly reholstered their weapons. Then, tucking the woman's somewhat limp arm into his, Captain Zenith led them back to the central fire, built just outside the ruined chapel where more of his gang and their captives could clearly be seen.

All but the wide-eyed children were in artificially good humour. Another pair of young women wore their hats on the backs of their heads. Sinclair guessed they had been well supplied with alcohol, but Begg shook his head, saying softly, 'Not beer or spirits, I think, Taffy, old man. I suspect another hand in this, don't you?'

Sinclair nodded gravely. 'Do we share the suspicion of who it was put Zenith up to this crime?'

'I think we do, Taffy.'

Standing among the other prisoners they noticed that only the young mother showed signs of concern. Even the reverend gentleman cheerfully led the leverman, the conductor, and a youth wearing the cadet uniform of the Farringdon Watch in a rather jolly hymn.

'See how our guests enjoy their Boxing Day?' Captain Zenith offered Begg and Sinclair a somewhat cynical grin. 'And all with their pocket books in place.'

'Drugged with laudanum.' Sinclair picked up an empty black bottle and was sniffing it, just as tall, lugubrious Henry Marriage stepped into the firelight and extended his hand. Sinclair ignored the gesture, but Begg, ever the diplomat, bowed. 'Good evening, sir. Are these villains holding you to ransom?'

Marriage's hearty manner thinly disguised an evasive expression. 'Not at all, sir.' He stared around him somewhat helplessly.

'Or is Captain Zenith in your employ?' demanded Sinclair. 'Why do you only bind our driver?'

'He'll be released at once.' Captain Zenith signed for the leverman to be freed. 'He offered my men violence. Whereas these other good fellows accepted our hospitality –'

'And were drugged into doltishness.'

'Please, sir, are you here to help us?' The young mother clutched imploringly at Sir Seaton's sleeve.

With his usual gentle courtesy towards the fair sex, Sir Seaton smiled reassurance. 'I am indeed, madam. What charming children! Is their father here?'

'I am a widow, sir.'

'My dear lady!'

'We have not been mistreated, sir.'

'I should hope you have not!' interjected Henry Marriage. 'I doubt if your children have ever eaten so well!'

'You have been feeding them, Mr Marriage?' Dr Sinclair offered the thin man an intense glare of inquisition.

'I returned from visiting a generous relative who gave me the hamper. It was meant for my family at home.'

'Indeed, sir,' said Sir Seaton. With the toe of his shoe he touched a large, open basket. Stencilled on its side were the words MARRIAGE'S OPIATES, MARRIAGE'S WHARF, LONDON E. 'This is the Christmas Box, eh?'

'The same, sir.'

'You were sharing it on the tram before Captain Zenith appeared?'

'He was very generous, sir.' The conductor looked up from where he sat beside the fire. 'I know it's against regulations, but the company generally turns a blind eye at Christmas. Of course, we didn't take any alcoholic beverage.'

'Quite so. What did you enjoy from Mr Marriage's hamper?'

'Just a piece of game pie, sir. Some ginger beer. And a couple of sandwiches.'

'Whereupon you reached the old Hampstead Model Village stop, broke down and, at Mr Marriage's suggestion, continued up here, eh, conductor?'

'Such merry yule fires, sir. Who could resist 'em? It was commonly agreed, sir, even by that reverend gent, there could be no happier way of celebrating Boxing Day until rescue came.' A stupid, sentimental grin crossed the conductor's long face.

'Except by you, madam, I take it?' Again Sir Seaton turned to the mother.

'I've been pained by a bit of a dicky tummy since we had the goose at my husband's brother's house. I'd rather hoped the children and me'd be home by now. But it was either come here or stay on the tram.' She was close to tears. Again Begg laid a gentlemanly hand on her arm. 'And Mr Marriage promised you his protection.'

'He did, sir. The tramwaymen have offered us no harm. But they're a bad example, sir, and –'

'Captain Zenith and his men make no threats. They keep the traditional tramwaymen's Christmas truce.' Marriage was insistent. 'I offered them a handsome fee to act for our safety when the tram broke down. They helped us guide it up the old line to this spot where we could find some sort of shelter.'

'How on earth did the tram find its own way back to the terminus?' Dr Sinclair was clearly not entirely convinced by this story.

'She slipped backwards, sir, once the horses were untethered,' offered the conductor. 'Somehow she must have reconnected to the overhead power line and continued her journey. It has been known, sir, for such things to happen.'

'So I understand.'

'Stranding us here, of course,' explained Henry Marriage. 'Well, it seems you've brought another vehicle to take everyone home, and no harm done. We are all grateful to you, Sir Seaton and Doctor Sinclair. I am prepared to stand guarantee for Captain Zenith. My honour depends upon promising safe conduct to all parties. I shall elect to stay as evidence of good faith and come morning shall board a fresh tram on the regular morning route. This will give Captain Zenith and his men time to make themselves scarce. A fair bargain, eh, Sir Seaton?'

'Very fair. And very noble of you, Mr Marriage.' Speaking with a certain irony, Sir Seaton was careful not to challenge anything. They were seriously outnumbered and had many innocents to consider. Since Zenith the Albino was mixed up in this affair Begg was convinced not everything could be above board. He had several reasons to suspect Marriage's tale. Nevertheless he did not object when the tramwaymen lit the way with their lanterns to lead the happy party back down the hill. At last the passengers were safely aboard and the leverman reinstalled at his controls.

The passengers cheered as the overhead power rail sparked in the darkness. The magnificent Special hummed, lurched and began to move forward. 'A generous soul, that Mr Marriage,' declared the conductor. 'We'd be mighty hungry by now had he not been so free with his pies.' He reacted with a muttered explanation as Dr Sinclair's eyes stared sternly into his own. 'I speak only the honest truth, sir. I've done nothing against Company tradition.'

'Of course you haven't, conductor,' interrupted Sir Seaton, his hand on his friend's shoulder. 'You must now ensure your charges arrive safely at the terminus.'

'My duty, sir.' The conductor saluted, shaking off his euphoria.

The two detectives returned swiftly to the tram's boarding plate. 'We have to go back, of course,' said Begg.

'Absolutely, old man!'

As soon as the tram took a bend, they dropped quietly from the platform. Ankle-deep in marshy ground, they moved rapidly back to the village.

'You noticed their eyes, I take it, Taffy?'

'Drugged! All but the mother and children. Something in those meat pies, eh?'

'Opium or Indian hemp. That preposterous story of a generous relative!'

'And at least two of the party were not returned to the tram.'

'Two young women? Exactly!'

'No doubt they imbibed more freely from the hamper's contents than any of the others.'

'Hurry, old man! Knowing Marriage's obsessions, you can guess as readily as I what the fiend intends.'

The detectives rapidly regained the camp, creeping carefully up to the ruined chapel where Zenith's gang continued to make merry. Yet of the leader or Henry Marriage there was no sign.

Drawing his Webley, Begg motioned towards the ruined Anglican church. Sinclair had already noticed lights shining through the broken stained glass. They heard voices, what might have been laughter, a stifled cry and then a piercing scream. Caution abandoned, they rushed the building, kicking open the rotting doors.

'Oh, for the love of God!' Sinclair was almost forced backward by the horrible smell. The scene's bestial reality was unfit to be seen by anyone save the curator of Scotland Yard's Black Museum. Two young women hung in ropes above the remains of the church altar. One was bleeding from deep wounds in her lower extremities. Her blood dripped into two large copper basins placed there for the purpose. She had fainted, but her companion shrieked in terror, through her gag. Henry Marriage, long razor in hand, prepared to perform the same operation upon the friend as the gloating albino placed bowls in readiness.

Marriage seemed completely deranged, but Zenith was fully alert, his face a mask of hatred as he saw Begg and Sinclair. His long white hair hanging loose to his shoulders, he snarled defiantly, lifting a copper bowl to his lips.

Levelling his pistol, Begg snapped off a single shot spinning the bowl from Zenith's hands. Sinclair darted forward and with an expert uppercut knocked Marriage to the floor. The razor fell with a clatter from the opiate merchant's hands.

Growling like a wild animal, Zenith produced his own pistol, but Begg's revolver sounded again, and Zenith's weapon went flying. Sinclair jumped up to the altar and, using Marriage's razor, severed the cords, lowering the two young women gently down as he kicked the bowls of blood clear.

Next Begg leapt forward to press the barrel of his Webley against Zenith's heart. The albino raised his hands, his ruby eyes glaring.

Knowing that his shot had probably alerted Zenith's men, Sinclair turned to face the door.

Motioning with his revolver, Begg forced Zenith to stand between them and the entrance. Henry Marriage groaned and came to his senses as the first outlaws appeared in the doorway.

'Stand back there!' The metatemporal investigator held his Webley against the albino's head. But Zenith's gang was already circling the altar.

His lips rimmed with blood, mumbling curses, Marriage climbed to his feet, his eyes staring into space.

'As you guessed, Taffy, he believes he possesses supernatural powers.' Begg motioned with his pistol.

'Let's hope we are not alone, old man. We decidedly need help from those who promised it...'

'Without them we're dead men, I agree. Have you any spare ammunition?'

'None.'

Grimly Begg and Sinclair prepared for the worst. Aware of their dilemma, Zenith grinned even as Sir Seaton's pistol pressed against his head.

The investigator knew his captive too well to demand he call his men off. Whatever dark evil Zenith practised, he was no coward and would die before allowing the two detectives to escape.

Ironically Henry Marriage came to their aid. Drugged eyes rolling in his head, he lifted up his arms and ran for the door. 'I am free!' he cried. 'Free! Invisible, I shall climb like an eagle into the sky.' His long arms flapping at his sides, he stumbled towards the entrance and, before the astonished outlaws, ran wildly into the night. Zenith laughed grimly. 'He believes the spell has worked. He forgets our ritual was interrupted.'

'Silence, you monster!' Sinclair covered as many outlaws as he could. Savouring their anticipated triumph they tightened the circle.

From outside came a fusillade of shots and sounds of Marriage screaming in frustrated rage. 'No! No! I am invisible. I fly. You cannot –' There descended a sudden silence.

Taking advantage of this unexpected turn, Zenith broke free to join the mass of his own men. Grabbing a pistol from one of them, his red eyes blazing, he curved his pale lips in a snarling grin. 'You're lost, Begg! Arming the leverman and a drugged vicar won't save you!'

Then a figure appeared in the smashed doorway. A gold-trimmed tricorn on his bewigged head, a black domino hiding his upper face, he had pushed back his huge three-caped coaching coat, two massive barkers in either beringed hand. Captain Tom Anchovy laughed as the guildless tramwaymen fell back in fear. Behind him, in the fancy coats and three-cornered hats of their trade, pressed his men, contemptuous of the guildless outlaws bringing their trade into disrepute.

'Drop your arms, lads, or we'll blow you all to the hell you thoroughly deserve!' rapped Anchovy.

But Captain Zenith, using the cover of his men, disappeared through the far door.

'After him, quickly!' ordered Tom. Some mobsmen followed the albino into the night.

Realising how outnumbered they were, the remaining outlaws gave up their pistols with little resistance, leaving Sir Seaton Begg, Doctor Sinclair and Tom Anchovy to bind the young women's wounds and get them decently covered.

'Their hats will be waiting for them at the terminus, no doubt,' said Dr Sinclair. 'They owe their lives to that lost headgear.'

'Indeed they do, Taffy. It was our clue that two young women were still held by Marriage and Zenith. All the others we saw still had their hats, even if worn at a rather unladylike angle!' He warmly shook hands with the tobyman. 'You turned up in the nick of time, Captain Tom. Thanks for keeping your word to help us. We remain on opposite sides of the law, but I think we share a moral purpose!'

'Probably true, sir.' Captain Anchovy prepared to leave. 'We'll truss those rogues thoroughly. Should we catch Zenith, he'll also be left for the peelers to pick up. Boxing Day's almost over, and we must return to our regular trade if we're to eat. Marriage's hamper out there was sadly empty of all its vitalls.'

'Just as well. You'd best warn your men that those pies and sausages were poisoned with hern meat and opium. They won't die, but they'll be unable to ride for a day or two should they try any.'

'I'll tell 'em at once. Good luck to ye, gentlemen!' The daring tramwayman disappeared into the night.

'That's what I saw at the Red Mill,' said Sinclair. 'The tiny tracks of the crested hern. I've studied the little creatures a fair bit and was surprised to find some still around London. Brought too early out of hibernation by the unseasonal weather and easily caught by Marriage while staying at the Inn. Some opiates, and his food was ready for those unsuspecting passengers.'

'From what I know of his debased brand of alchemy, Taffy, hern meat is only thought efficacious if fed to female virgins first. Partaking of the flesh, or preferably your victim's freshly drawn blood, imparts great supernatural powers, including those of invisibility and flight. Luckily he proved himself a liar with that tale of his hamper being a relative's gift. It clearly came from his own warehouse.'

The doctor shuddered. 'Thank God we were able to stop him in time.'

The two men strolled from the ruined church to see that Anchovy's band had already bound Zenith's followers. Anchovy, astride his magnificent black Arab, saluted them as they appeared. 'If I know Zenith, he'll be long gone in the direction of London, to lose himself in the twittens of Whitechapel. No doubt our paths will cross again! As for Henry Marriage, I could have sworn my men filled him with enough lead to sink the HMS *Victory*, yet he, too, has disappeared. Perhaps his beliefs had substance, eh?' With that the gallant tramwayman doffed his tricorn in a deep bow, then turned for distant Waymering where Begg knew he lived a double life as Septimus Grouse, a Methodist parson.

Though weak from their experience, the two young victims had recovered somewhat by the time another Special arrived towing a hospital car and a prison van full of peelers. Attended by expert doctors, the women were made comfortable in the hospital car while Zenith's gang were manacled to hard benches, destined for Wormwood Flats.

Thus the tale garbled by the yellow press as 'The Affair of the Hampstead Cannibals' was brought to a successful conclusion and all innocent lives saved. Enjoying their pipes the detectives relaxed in the first-class section of the tram's top deck.

'I think I'll be returning to the Red Mill as soon as possible,' murmured Sinclair thoughtfully.

'You're curious to retrace the stages of the case, Taffy?'

'What's more interesting, old man, was finding those London hern tracks when all naturalists are agreed the species became extinct during the latter part of the last century. I'd like to find another specimen.'

'And vivisect it?' enquired Sir Seaton in some disapproval.

'Oh, not at all. I want to see it in the wild for myself and confirm that Henry Marriage, God rest his soul wherever he may be now, did not destroy the entire species. After all, it isn't every day one discovers that part of the past can yet be recovered, however small that part might be.'

With a sudden rattle the tram began to move forward. Its buzzing electric engine could not quite disguise the sound of Sir Seaton Begg's approving grunt.

Behold the Man

He has no material power as the god-emperors had; he has only a
following of desert people and fishermen. They tell him he is a god;
he believes them. The followers of Alexander said: 'He is uncon-
querable, therefore he is a god.' The followers of this man do not
think at all; he was their act of spontaneous creation. Now he
leads them, this madman called Jesus of Nazareth.

And he spoke, saying unto them: Yeah verily I was Karl
Glogauer and now I am Jesus the Messiah, the Christ.

And it was so.

Chapter One

THE TIME MACHINE was a sphere full of milky fluid in which
the traveller floated, enclosed in a rubber suit, breathing
through a mask attached to a hose leading to the wall of the
machine. The sphere cracked as it landed and the fluid spilled into
the dust and was soaked up. Instinctively, Glogauer curled himself
into a ball as the level of the liquid fell and he sank to the yielding
plastic of the sphere's inner lining. The instruments, crypto-
graphic, unconventional, were still and silent. The sphere shifted
and rolled as the last of the liquid dripped from the great gash in
its side.

Momentarily, Glogauer's eyes opened and closed, then his
mouth stretched in a kind of yawn and his tongue fluttered and he
uttered a groan that turned into an ululation.

He heard himself. *The Voice of Tongues*, he thought. The language of the unconscious. But he could not guess what he was saying.

His body became numb and he shivered. His passage through time had not been easy and even the thick fluid had not wholly protected him, though it had doubtless saved his life. Some ribs were certainly broken. Painfully, he straightened his arms and legs and began to crawl over the slippery plastic towards the crack in the machine. He could see harsh sunlight, a sky like shimmering steel. He pulled himself halfway through the crack, closing his eyes as the full strength of the sunlight struck them. He lost consciousness.

Christmas term, 1949. He was nine years old, born two years after his father had reached England from Austria.

The other children were screaming with laughter in the gravel of the playground. The game had begun earnestly enough and somewhat nervously Karl had joined in in the same spirit. Now he was crying.

'Let me *down*! Please, Mervyn, stop it!'

They had tied him with his arms spreadeagled against the wire netting of the playground fence. It bulged outwards under his weight and one of the posts threatened to come loose. Mervyn Williams, the boy who had proposed the game, began to shake the post so that Karl was swung heavily back and forth on the netting.

'Stop it!'

He saw that his cries only encouraged them and he clenched his teeth, becoming silent.

He slumped, pretending unconsciousness; the school ties they had used as bonds cut into his wrists. He heard the children's voices drop.

'Is he all right?' Molly Turner was whispering.

'He's only kidding.' Williams replied uncertainly.

He felt them untying him, their fingers fumbling with the

knots. Deliberately, he sagged, then fell to his knees, grazing them on the gravel, and dropped face down to the ground.

Distantly, for he was half-convinced by his own deception, he heard their worried voices.

Williams shook him. 'Wake up, Karl. Stop mucking about.'

He stayed where he was, losing his sense of time until he heard Mr Matson's voice over the general babble.

'What on earth were you doing, Williams?'

'It was a play, sir, about Jesus. Karl was being Jesus. We tied him to the fence. It was his idea, sir. It was only a game, sir.'

Karl's body was stiff, but he managed to stay still, breathing shallowly.

'He's not a strong boy like you, Williams. You should have known better.'

'I'm sorry, sir. I'm really sorry.' Williams sounded as if he were crying.

Karl felt himself lifted; felt the triumph...

He was being carried along. His head and side were so painful that he felt sick. He had had no chance to discover where exactly the time machine had brought him, but, turning his head now, he could see by the way the man on his right was dressed that he was at least in the Middle East.

He had meant to land in the year AD 29 in the wilderness beyond Jerusalem, near Bethlehem. Were they taking him to Jerusalem now?

He was on a stretcher that was apparently made of animal skins; this indicated that he was probably in the past, at any rate. Two men were carrying the stretcher on their shoulders. Others walked on both sides. There was a smell of sweat and animal fat and a musty smell he could not identify. They were walking towards a line of hills in the distance.

He winced as the stretcher lurched and the pain in his side increased. For the second time he passed out.

He woke up briefly, hearing voices. They were speaking what

was evidently some form of Aramaic. It was night, perhaps, for it seemed very dark. They were no longer moving. There was straw beneath him. He was relieved. He slept.

> *In those days came John the Baptist preaching in the wilderness of Judaea, And saying, Repent ye: for the kingdom of heaven is at hand. For this is he that was spoken of by the prophet Esaias, saying, The voice of one crying in the wilderness, Prepare ye the way of the Lord, make his paths straight. And the same John had his raiment of camel's hair, and a leathern girdle about his loins; and his meat was locusts and wild honey. Then went out to him Jerusalem, and all Judaea, and all the region round about Jordan, And were baptised of him in Jordan, confessing their sins.*
>
> (Matthew 3: 1–6)

They were washing him. He felt the cold water running over his naked body. They had managed to strip off his protective suit. There were now thick layers of cloth against his ribs on the right, and bands of leather bound them to him.

He felt very weak now, and hot, but there was less pain.

He was in a building – or perhaps a cave; it was too gloomy to tell – lying on a heap of straw that was saturated by the water. Above him, two men continued to sluice water down on him from their earthenware pots. They were stern-faced, heavily bearded men, in cotton robes.

He wondered if he could form a sentence they might understand. His knowledge of written Aramaic was good, but he was not sure of certain pronunciations.

He cleared his throat. 'Where – be – this – place?'

They frowned, shaking their heads and lowering their water jars.

'I – seek – a – Nazarene – Jesus…'

'Nazarene. Jesus.' One of the men repeated the words, but they did not seem to mean anything to him. He shrugged.

The other, however, only repeated the word Nazarene, speaking it slowly as if it had some special significance for him. He muttered a few words to the other man and went towards the entrance of the room.

Karl Glogauer continued to try to say something the remaining man would understand.

'What – year – doth – the Roman Emperor – sit – in Rome?'

It was a confusing question to ask, he realised. He knew Christ had been crucified in the fifteenth year of Tiberius's reign, and that was why he had asked the question. He tried to phrase it better.

'How many – year – doth Tiberius rule?'

'Tiberius?' The man frowned.

Glogauer's ear was adjusting to the accent now and he tried to simulate it better. 'Tiberius. The emperor of the Romans. How many years has he ruled?'

'How many?' The man shook his head. 'I know not.'

At least Glogauer had managed to make himself understood.

'Where is this place?' he asked.

'It is the wilderness beyond Machaerus,' the man replied. 'Know you not that?'

Machaerus lay to the south-east of Jerusalem, on the other side of the Dead Sea. There was no doubt that he was in the past and that the period was sometime in the reign of Tiberius, for the man had recognised the name easily enough.

His companion was now returning, bringing with him a huge fellow with heavily muscled hairy arms and a great barrel chest. He carried a big staff in one hand. He was dressed in animal skins and was well over six feet tall. His black, curly hair was long and he had a black, bushy beard that covered the upper half of his chest. He moved like an animal and his large, piercing brown eyes looked reflectively at Glogauer.

When he spoke, it was in a deep voice, but too rapidly for Glogauer to follow. It was Glogauer's turn to shake his head.

The big man squatted down beside him. 'Who art thou?'

Glogauer paused. He had not planned to be found in this way. He had intended to disguise himself as a traveller from Syria, hoping that the local accents would be different enough to explain his own unfamiliarity with the language. He decided that it was best to stick to this story and hope for the best.

'I am from the north,' he said.

'Not from Egypt?' the big man asked. It was as if he had expected Glogauer to be from there. Glogauer decided that if this was what the big man thought, he might just as well agree to it.

'I came out of Egypt two years since,' he said.

The big man nodded, apparently satisfied. 'So you are a magus from Egypt. That is what we thought. And your name is Jesus, and you are the Nazarene.'

'I *seek* Jesus, the Nazarene,' Glogauer said.

'Then what is your name?' The man seemed disappointed.

Glogauer could not give his own name. It would sound too strange to them. On impulse, he gave his father's first name. 'Emmanuel,' he said.

The man nodded, again satisfied. 'Emmanuel.'

Glogauer realised belatedly that the choice of name had been an unfortunate one in the circumstances, for Emmanuel meant in Hebrew 'God with us' and doubtless had a mystic significance for his questioner.

'And what is your name?' he asked.

The man straightened up, looking broodingly down on Glogauer. 'You do not know me? You have not heard of John, called the Baptist?'

Glogauer tried to hide his surprise, but evidently John the Baptist saw that his name was familiar. He nodded his shaggy head. 'You do know of me, I see. Well, magus, now I must decide, eh?'

'What must you decide?' Glogauer asked nervously.

'If you be the friend of the prophecies or the false one we have been warned against by Adonai. The Romans would deliver me into the hands of mine enemies, the children of Herod.'

'Why is that?'

'You must know why, for I speak against the Romans who enslave Judaea, and I speak against the unlawful things that Herod does, and I prophesy the time when all those who are not

270

righteous shall be destroyed and Adonai's kingdom will be restored on Earth as the old prophets said it would be. I say to the people "Be ready for that day when ye shall take up the sword to do Adonai's will". The unrighteous know that they will perish on this day, and they would destroy me.'

Despite the intensity of his words, John's tone was matter-of-fact. There was no hint of insanity or fanaticism in his face or bearing. He sounded most of all like an Anglican vicar reading a sermon whose meaning for him had lost its edge.

The essence of what he said, Karl Glogauer realised, was that he was arousing the people to throw out the Romans and their puppet Herod and establish a more 'righteous' régime. The attributing of this plan to 'Adonai' (one of the spoken names of Jahweh and meaning The Lord) seemed, as many scholars had guessed in the twentieth century, a means of giving the plan extra weight. In a world where politics and religion, even in the West, were inextricably bound together, it was necessary to ascribe a supernatural origin to the plan.

Indeed, Glogauer thought, it was more than likely that John believed his idea had been inspired by God, for the Greeks on the other side of the Mediterranean had not yet stopped arguing about the origins of inspiration – whether it originated in a man's head or was placed there by the gods. That John accepted him as an Egyptian magician of some kind did not surprise Glogauer particularly, either. The circumstances of his arrival must have seemed extraordinarily miraculous and at the same time acceptable, particularly to a sect like the Essenes who practised self-mortification and starvation and must be quite used to seeing visions in this hot wilderness. There was no doubt now that these people were the neurotic Essenes, whose ritual washing – baptism – and self-deprivation, coupled with the almost paranoiac mysticism that led them to invent secret languages and the like, was a sure indication of their mentally unbalanced condition. All this occurred to Glogauer the psychiatrist manqué, but Glogauer the man was torn between the poles of extreme rationalism and the desire to be convinced by the mysticism itself.

'I must meditate,' John said, turning towards the cave entrance. 'I must pray. You will remain here until guidance is sent to me.'

He left the cave, striding rapidly away.

Glogauer sank back on the wet straw. He was without doubt in a limestone cave, and the atmosphere in the cave was surprisingly humid. It must be very hot outside. He felt drowsy.

Chapter Two

FIVE YEARS IN the past. Nearly two thousand in the future. Lying in the hot, sweaty bed with Monica. Once again, another attempt to make normal love had metamorphosed into the performance of minor aberrations which seemed to satisfy her better than anything else.

Their real courtship and fulfilment was yet to come. As usual, it would be verbal. As usual, it would find its climax in argumentative anger.

'I suppose you're going to tell me you're not satisfied again.' She accepted the lighted cigarette he handed to her in the darkness.

'I'm all right,' he said.

There was silence for a while as they smoked.

Eventually, and in spite of knowing what the result would be if he did so, he found himself talking.

'It's ironic, isn't it?' he began.

He waited for her reply. She would delay for a little while yet.

'What is?' she said at last.

'All this. You spend all day trying to help sexual neurotics to become normal. You spend your nights doing what they do.'

'Not to the same extent. You know it's all a matter of degree.'

'So you say.'

He turned his head and looked at her face in the starlight from the window. She was a gaunt-featured redhead, with the calm, professional seducer's voice of the psychiatric social worker that she was. It was a voice that was soft, reasonable and insincere. Only occasionally, when she became particularly agitated, did her voice begin to indicate her real character. Her features never seemed to be in repose, even when she slept. Her eyes were forever wary, her movements rarely spontaneous. Every inch of her was protected, which was probably why she got so little pleasure from ordinary love-making.

'You just can't let yourself go, can you?' he said.

'Oh, shut up, Karl. Have a look at yourself if you're looking for a neurotic mess.'

Both were amateur psychiatrists – she a psychiatric social worker, he merely a reader, a dabbler, though he had done a year's study some time ago when he had planned to become a psychiatrist. They used the terminology of psychiatry freely. They felt happier if they could name something.

He rolled away from her, groping for the ashtray on the bedside table, catching a glance of himself in the dressing-table mirror. He was a sallow, intense, moody Jewish bookseller, with a head full of images and unresolved obsessions, a body full of emotions. He always lost these arguments with Monica. Verbally, she was the dominant one. This kind of exchange often seemed to him more perverse than their love-making, where usually at least his rôle was masculine. Essentially, he realised, he was passive, masochistic, indecisive. Even his anger, which came frequently, was impotent. Monica was ten years older than he was, ten years more bitter. As an individual, of course, she had far more dynamism than he had; but as a psychiatric social worker she had had just as many failures. She plugged on, becoming increasingly cynical on the surface but still, perhaps, hoping for a few spectacular successes with patients. They tried to do too much, that was the trouble, he thought. The priests in the confessional supplied a panacea; the psychiatrists tried to cure, and most of the time they failed. But at least they tried, he thought, and then wondered if that was, after all, a virtue.

'I did look at myself,' he said.

Was she sleeping? He turned. Her wary eyes were still open, looking out of the window.

'I did look at myself,' he repeated. 'The way Jung did. "How can I help those persons if I am myself a fugitive and perhaps also suffer from the *morbus sacer* of a neurosis?" That's what Jung asked himself...'

'That old sensationalist. That old rationaliser of his own mysticism. No wonder you never became a psychiatrist.'

'I wouldn't have been any good. It was nothing to do with Jung...'

'Don't take it out on me...'

'You've told me yourself that you feel the same – you think it's useless...'

'After a hard week's work, I might say that. Give me another fag.'

He opened the packet on the bedside table and put two cigarettes in his mouth, lighting them and handing one to her.

Almost abstractedly, he noticed that the tension was increasing. The argument was, as ever, pointless. But it was not the argument that was the important thing; it was simply the expression of the essential relationship. He wondered if that was in any way important, either.

'You're not telling the truth.' He realised that there was no stopping now that the ritual was in full swing.

'I'm telling the practical truth. I've no compulsion to give up my work. I've no wish to be a failure...'

'Failure? You're more melodramatic than I am.'

'You're too earnest, Karl. You want to get out of yourself a bit.'

He sneered. 'If I were you, I'd give up my work, Monica. You're no more suited for it than I was.'

She shrugged. 'You're a petty bastard.'

'I'm not jealous of you, if that's what you think. You'll never understand what I'm looking for.'

Her laugh was artificial, brittle. 'Modern man in search of a soul, eh? Modern man in search of a crutch, I'd say. And you can take that any way you like.'

'We're destroying the myths that make the world go round.'

'Now you say "And what are we putting in their place?" You're stale and stupid, Karl. You've never looked rationally at anything – including yourself.'

'What of it? You say the myth is unimportant.'

'The reality that creates it is important.'

'Jung knew that the myth can also create the reality.'

'Which shows what a muddled old fool he was.'

He stretched his legs. In doing so, he touched hers and he recoiled. He scratched his head. She still lay there smoking, but she was smiling now.

'Come on,' she said. 'Let's have some stuff about Christ.'

He said nothing. She handed him the stub of her cigarette and he put it in the ashtray. He looked at his watch. It was two o'clock in the morning.

'Why do we do it?' he said.

'Because we must.' She put her hand to the back of his head and pulled it towards her breast. 'What else can we do?'

We Protestants must sooner or later face this question: Are we to understand the 'imitation of Christ' in the sense that we should copy his life and, if I may use the expression, ape his stigmata; or in the deeper sense that we are to live our own proper lives as truly as he lived his in all its implications? It is no easy matter to live a life that is modelled on Christ's, but it is unspeakably harder to live one's own life as truly as Christ lived his. Anyone who did this would ... be mis-judged, derided, tortured and crucified ... A neurosis is a dissociation of personality.

(Jung: *Modern Man in Search of a Soul*)

For a month, John the Baptist was away and Glogauer lived with the Essenes, finding it surprisingly easy, as his ribs mended, to join in their daily life. The Essenes' township consisted of a mixture of single-storey houses, built of limestone and clay brick, and the caves that were to be found on both sides of the shallow valley. The Essenes shared their goods in common and this particular sect had wives, though many Essenes led completely monastic lives. The Essenes were also pacifists, refusing to own or to make weapons – yet this sect plainly tolerated the warlike Baptist. Per-haps their hatred of the Romans overcame their principles. Perhaps they were not sure of John's entire intention. Whatever the reason for their toleration, there was little doubt that John the Baptist was virtually their leader.

The life of the Essenes consisted of ritual bathing three times a day, of prayer and of work. The work was not difficult. Sometimes Glogauer guided a plough pulled by two other members of the sect; sometimes he looked after the goats that were allowed to graze on the hillsides. It was a peaceful, ordered life, and even the unhealthy aspects were so much a matter of routine that Glogauer hardly noticed them for anything else after a while.

Tending the goats, he would lie on a hilltop, looking out over the wilderness which was not a desert, but rocky scrubland sufficient to feed animals like goats or sheep. The scrubland was broken by low-lying bushes and a few small trees growing along the banks of the river that doubtless ran into the Dead Sea. It was uneven ground. In outline, it had the appearance of a stormy lake, frozen and turned yellow and brown. Beyond the Dead Sea lay Jerusalem. Obviously Christ had not entered the city for the last time yet. John the Baptist would have to die before that happened.

The Essenes' way of life was comfortable enough, for all its simplicity. They had given him a goatskin loincloth and a staff and, except for the fact that he was watched by day and night, he appeared to be accepted as a kind of lay member of the sect.

Sometimes they questioned him casually about his chariot – the time machine they intended soon to bring in from the desert – and he told them that it had borne him from Egypt to Syria and then to here. They accepted the miracle calmly. As he had suspected, they were used to miracles.

The Essenes had seen stranger things than his time machine. They had seen men walk on water and angels descend to and from heaven; they had heard the voice of God and his archangels as well as the tempting voice of Satan and his minions. They wrote all these things down in their vellum scrolls. They were merely a record of the supernatural as their other scrolls were records of their daily lives and of the news that travelling members of their sect brought to them.

They lived constantly in the presence of God and spoke to God and were answered by God when they had sufficiently mortified their flesh and starved themselves and chanted their prayers beneath the blazing sun of Judaea.

Karl Glogauer grew his hair long and let his beard come unchecked. He mortified his flesh and starved himself and chanted his prayers beneath the sun, as they did. But he rarely heard God and only once thought he saw an archangel with wings of fire.

In spite of his willingness to experience the Essenes' hallucinations, Glogauer was disappointed, but he was surprised that he felt so well considering all the self-inflicted hardships he had to undergo, and he also felt relaxed in the company of these men and women who were undoubtedly insane. Perhaps it was because their insanity was not so very different from his own that after a while he stopped wondering about it.

John the Baptist returned one evening, striding over the hills followed by twenty or so of his closest disciples. Glogauer saw him as he prepared to drive the goats into their cave for the night. He waited for John to get closer.

The Baptist's face was grim, but his expression softened as he saw Glogauer. He smiled and grasped him by the upper arm in the Roman fashion.

'Well, Emmanuel, you are our friend, as I thought you were. Sent by Adonai to help us accomplish his will. You shall baptise me on the morrow, to show all the people that He is with us.'

Glogauer was tired. He had eaten very little and had spent most of the day in the sun, tending the goats. He yawned, finding it hard to reply. However, he was relieved. John had plainly been in Jerusalem trying to discover if the Romans had sent him as a spy. John now seemed reassured and trusted him.

He was worried, however, by the Baptist's faith in his powers.

'John,' he began. 'I'm no seer...'

The Baptist's face clouded for a moment, then he laughed awkwardly. 'Say nothing. Eat with me tonight. I have wild honey and locusts.'

Glogauer had not yet eaten this food, which was the staple of travellers who did not carry provisions but lived off the food they could find on the journey. Some regarded it as a delicacy.

He tried it later, as he sat in John's house. There were only two rooms in the house. One was for eating in, the other for sleeping in. The honey-and-locusts was too sweet for his taste, but it was a welcome change from barley or goat-meat.

He sat cross-legged, opposite John the Baptist, who ate with relish. Night had fallen. From outside came low murmurs and the moans and cries of those at prayer.

Glogauer dipped another locust into the bowl of honey that rested between them. 'Do you plan to lead the people of Judaea in revolt against the Romans?' he asked.

The Baptist seemed disturbed by the direct question. It was the first of its nature that Glogauer had put to him.

'If it be Adonai's will,' he said, not looking up as he leaned towards the bowl of honey.

'The Romans know this?'

'I do not know, Emmanuel, but Herod the incestuous has doubtless told them I speak against the unrighteous.'

'Yet the Romans do not arrest you.'

'Pilate dare not – not since the petition was sent to the Emperor Tiberius.'

'Petition?'

'Aye, the one that Herod and the Pharisees signed when Pilate the procurator did place votive shields in the palace at Jerusalem and seek to violate the Temple. Tiberius rebuked Pilate and since then, though he still hates the Jews, the procurator is more careful in his treatment of us.'

'Tell me, John, do you know how long Tiberius has ruled in Rome?' He had not had the chance to ask that question again until now.

'Fourteen years.'

It was AD 28; something less than a year before the crucifixion would take place, and his time machine was smashed.

Now John the Baptist planned armed rebellion against the occupying Romans, but, if the Gospels were to be believed, would soon be decapitated by Herod. Certainly no large-scale rebellion had taken place at this time. Even those who claimed that the entry of Jesus and his disciples into Jerusalem and the invasion of the Temple were plainly the actions of armed rebels had found no records to suggest that John had led a similar revolt.

Glogauer had come to like the Baptist very much. The man was plainly a hardened revolutionary who had been planning revolt against the Romans for years and had slowly been building up enough followers to make the attempt successful. He reminded Glogauer strongly of the resistance leaders of the Second World War. He had a similar toughness and understanding of the realities of his position. He knew that he would only have one chance to smash the cohorts garrisoned in the country. If the revolt became protracted, Rome would have ample time to send more troops to Jerusalem.

'When do you think Adonai intends to destroy the unrighteous through your agency?' Glogauer said tactfully.

John glanced at him with some amusement. He smiled. 'The Passover is a time when the people are restless and resent the strangers most,' he said.

'When is the next Passover?'

'Not for many months.'

'How can I help you?'

'You are a magus.'

'I can work no miracles.'

John wiped the honey from his beard. 'I cannot believe that, Emmanuel. The manner of your coming was miraculous. The Essenes did not know if you were a devil or a messenger from Adonai.'

'I am neither.'

'Why do you confuse me, Emmanuel? I know that you are Adonai's messenger. You are the sign that the Essenes sought. The time is almost ready. The kingdom of heaven shall soon be established on earth. Come with me. Tell the people that you speak with Adonai's voice. Work mighty miracles.'

'Your power is waning, is that it?' Glogauer looked sharply at John. 'You need me to renew your rebels' hopes?'

'You speak like a Roman, with such lack of subtlety.' John got up angrily. Evidently, like the Essenes he lived with, he preferred less direct conversation. There was a practical reason for this, Glogauer realised, in that John and his men feared betrayal all the time. Even the Essenes' records were partially written in cipher, with one innocent-seeming word or phrase meaning something else entirely.

'I am sorry, John. But tell me if I am right.' Glogauer spoke softly.

'Are you not a magus, coming in that chariot from nowhere?' The Baptist waved his hands and shrugged his shoulders. 'My men saw you! They saw the shining thing take shape in air, crack and let you enter out of it. Is that not magical? The clothing you wore – was that earthly raiment? The talismans within the chariot – did they not speak of powerful magic? The prophet said that a magus would come from Egypt and be called Emmanuel. So it is written in the Book of Micah! Is none of these things true?'

'Most of them. But there are explanations –' He broke off, unable to think of the nearest word to 'rational'. 'I am an ordinary man, like you. I have no power to work miracles! I am just a man!'

John glowered. 'You mean you refuse to help us?'

'I'm grateful to you and the Essenes. You saved my life almost certainly. If I can repay that...'

John nodded his head deliberately. 'You can repay it, Emmanuel.'

'How?'

'Be the great magus I need. Let me present you to all those who become impatient and would turn away from Adonai's will. Let me tell them the manner of your coming to us. Then you can say that all is Adonai's will and that they must prepare to accomplish it.'

John stared at him intensely. 'Will you, Emmanuel?'

'For your sake, John. And in turn, will you send men to bring my chariot here as soon as possible? I wish to see if it may be mended.'

'I will.'

Glogauer felt exhilarated. He began to laugh. The Baptist looked at him with slight bewilderment. Then he began to join in.

Glogauer laughed on. History would not mention it, but he, with John the Baptist, would prepare the way for Christ.

Christ was not born yet. Perhaps Glogauer knew it, one year before the crucifixion.

> And the Word was made flesh, and dwelt among us (and we beheld his glory, the glory as of the only begotten of the Father) full of grace and truth. John bare witness of him, and cried, saying, This was he of whom I spake, He that cometh after me is preferred before me; for he was before me.
>
> (John 1: 14–15)

Even when he had first met Monica they had had long arguments. His father had not then died and left him the money to buy the Occult Bookshop in Great Russell Street, opposite the British Museum. He was doing all sorts of temporary work and his spirits were very low. At that time Monica had seemed a great help, a great guide through the mental darkness engulfing him. They had both lived close to Holland Park and went there for walks almost every Sunday of the summer of 1962. At twenty-two, he was already obsessed with Jung's strange brand of Christian mysticism. She, who despised Jung, had soon begun to denigrate all his ideas. She never really convinced him. But, after a while, she had succeeded in confusing him. It would be another six months before they went to bed together.

It was uncomfortably hot.

They sat in the shade of the cafeteria, watching a distant cricket match. Nearer to them, two girls and a boy sat on the grass, drinking orange squash from plastic cups. One of the girls had a guitar across her lap and she set the cup down and began to play, singing a folk song in a high, gentle voice. Glogauer tried to listen to the words. As a student, he had always liked traditional folk music.

'Christianity is dead.' Monica sipped her tea. 'Religion is dying. God was killed in 1945.'

'There may yet be a resurrection,' he said.

'Let us hope not. Religion was the creation of fear. Knowledge destroys fear. Without fear, religion can't survive.'

'You think there's no fear about, these days?'

'Not the same kind, Karl.'

'Haven't you ever considered the *idea* of Christ?' he asked her, changing his tack. 'What that means to Christians?'

'The idea of the tractor means as much to a Marxist,' she replied.

'But what came first? The idea or the actuality of Christ?'

She shrugged. 'The actuality, if it matters. Jesus was a Jewish troublemaker organising a revolt against the Romans. He was crucified for his pains. That's all we know and all we need to know.'

'A great religion couldn't have begun so simply.'

'When people need one, they'll make a great religion out of the most unlikely beginnings.'

'That's my point, Monica.' He gesticulated at her and she drew away slightly. 'The *idea* preceded the *actuality* of Christ.'

'Oh, Karl, don't go on. The actuality of *Jesus* preceded the idea of *Christ.*'

A couple walked past, glancing at them as they argued.

Monica noticed them and fell silent. She got up and he rose as well, but she shook her head. 'I'm going home, Karl. You stay here. I'll see you in a few days.'

He watched her walk down the wide path towards the park gates.

The next day, when he got home from work, he found a letter. She must have written it after she had left him and posted it the same day.

Dear Karl,

Conversation doesn't seem to have much effect on you, you know. It's as if you listen to the tone of the voice, the rhythm of the words, without ever hearing what is trying to be communicated. You're a bit like a sensitive animal who can't understand what's being said to it, but can tell if the person talking is pleased or angry and so on. That's why I'm writing to you – to try to get my idea across. You respond too emotionally when we're together.

You make the mistake of considering Christianity as something that developed over the course of a few years, from the death of Jesus to the time the Gospels were written. But Christianity wasn't new. Only the name was new. Christianity was merely a stage in the meeting, cross-fertilisation, metamorphosis of Western logic and Eastern mysticism. Look how the religion itself changed over the centuries, re-interpreting itself to meet changing times. Christianity is just a new name for a conglomeration of old myths and philosophies. All the Gospels do is retell the sun myth and garble some of the ideas from the Greeks and Romans. Even in the second century, Jewish scholars were showing it up for the mish-mash it was! They pointed out the strong similarities between the various sun myths and the Christ myth. The miracles didn't happen – they were invented later, borrowed from here and there.

Remember the old Victorians who used to say that Plato was really a Christian because he anticipated Christian thought? Christian thought! Christianity was a vehicle for ideas in circulation for centuries before Christ. Was Marcus Aurelius a Christian? He was writing in the direct tradition of Western philosophy. That's why Christianity caught on in Europe and not in the East! You should have been a theologian with your bias, not a psychiatrist. The same goes for your friend Jung.

Try to clear your head of all this morbid nonsense and you'll be a lot better at your job.

Yours,
Monica.

He screwed the letter up and threw it away. Later that evening he was tempted to look at it again, but he resisted the temptation.

Chapter Three

JOHN STOOD UP to his waist in the river. Most of the Essenes stood on the banks watching him. Glogauer looked down at him.

'I cannot, John. It is not for me to do it.'

The Baptist muttered, 'You must.'

Glogauer shivered as he lowered himself into the river beside the Baptist. He felt light-headed. He stood there trembling, unable to move.

His foot slipped on the rocks of the river and John reached out and gripped his arm, steadying him.

In the clear sky, the sun was at zenith, beating down on his unprotected head.

'Emmanuel!' John cried suddenly. 'The spirit of Adonai is within you!'

Glogauer still found it hard to speak. He shook his head slightly. It was aching and he could hardly see. Today he was having his first migraine attack since he had come here. He wanted to vomit. John's voice sounded distant.

He swayed in the water.

As he began to fall toward the Baptist, the whole scene around him shimmered. He felt John catch him and heard himself say desperately: 'John, baptise *me!*' And then there was water in his mouth and throat and he was coughing.

John's voice was crying something. Whatever the words were, they drew a response from the people on both banks. The roaring in his ears increased, its quality changing. He thrashed in the water, then felt himself lifted to his feet.

The Essenes were swaying in unison, every face lifted upward towards the glaring sun.

Glogauer began to vomit into the water, stumbling as John's hands gripped his arms painfully and guided him up the bank.

A peculiar, rhythmic humming came from the mouths of the Essenes as they swayed; it rose as they swayed to one side, fell as they swayed to the other.

Glogauer covered his ears as John released him. He was still retching, but it was dry now, and worse than before.

He began to stagger away, barely keeping his balance, running, with his ears still covered; running over the rocky scrubland; running as the sun throbbed in the sky and its heat pounded at his head; running away.

But John forbade him, saying, I have need to be baptised of thee, and comest thou to me? And Jesus answering said unto him, Suffer it to be so now: for thus it becometh us to fulfil all righteousness. Then he suffered him. And Jesus, when he was baptised, went up straightway out of the water: and, lo, the heavens were opened unto him, and he saw the Spirit of God descending like a dove, and lighting upon him: And lo a voice from heaven, saying, This is my beloved Son, in whom I am well pleased.

(Matthew 3: 14–17)

He had been fifteen, doing well at the grammar school. He had read in the newspapers about the Teddy Boy gangs that roamed South London, but the odd youth he had seen in pseudo-Edwardian clothes had seemed harmless and stupid enough.

He had gone to the pictures in Brixton Hill and decided to walk home to Streatham because he had spent most of the bus money on an ice-cream. They came out of the cinema at the same time. He hardly noticed them as they followed him down the hill.

Then, quite suddenly, they had surrounded him. Pale, mean-faced boys, most of them a year or two older than he was. He realised that he knew two of them vaguely. They were at the big council school in the same street as the grammar school. They used the same football ground.

'Hello,' he said weakly.

'Hello, son,' said the oldest Teddy Boy. He was chewing gum, standing with one knee bent, grinning at him. 'Where you going, then?'

'Home.'

'Heouwm,' said the biggest one, imitating his accent. 'What are you going to do when you get there?'

'Go to bed.' Karl tried to get through the ring, but they wouldn't let him. They pressed him back into a shop doorway. Beyond them, cars droned by on the main road. The street was brightly lit, with streetlamps and neon from the shops. Several people passed, but none of them stopped. Karl began to feel panic.

'Got no homework to do, son?' said the boy next to the leader. He was red-headed and freckled and his eyes were a hard grey.

'Want to fight one of us?' another boy asked. It was one of the boys he knew.

'No. I don't fight. Let me go.'

'You scared, son?' said the leader, grinning. Ostentatiously, he pulled a streamer of gum from his mouth and then replaced it. He began chewing again.

'No. Why should I want to fight you?'

'You reckon you're better than us, is that it, son?'

'No.' He was beginning to tremble. Tears were coming into his eyes. ''Course not.'

''Course not, son.'

He moved forward again, but they pushed him back into the doorway.

'You're the bloke with the kraut name, ain't you?' said the other boy he knew. 'Glow-worm or somethink.'

'Glogauer. Let me go.'

'Won't your mummy like it if you're back late?'

'More a yid name than a kraut name.'

'You a yid, son?'

'He looks like a yid.'

'You a yid, son?'

'You a Jewish boy, son?'

'You a yid, son?'

'Shut up!' Karl screamed. He pushed into them. One of them punched him in the stomach. He grunted with pain. Another pushed him and he staggered.

People were still hurrying by on the pavement. They glanced at the group as they went past. One man stopped, but his wife pulled him on. 'Just some kids larking about,' she said.

'Get his trousers down,' one of the boys suggested with a laugh. 'That'll prove it.'

Karl pushed through them and this time they didn't resist. He began to run down the hill.

'Give him a start,' he heard one of the boys say.

He ran on.

They began to follow him, laughing.

They did not catch up with him by the time he turned into the avenue where he lived. He reached the house and ran along the dark passage beside it. He opened the back door. His step-mother was in the kitchen.

'What's the matter with you?' she said.

She was a tall, thin woman, nervous and hysterical. Her dark hair was untidy.

He went past her into the breakfast-room.

'What's the matter, Karl?' she called. Her voice was high-pitched.

'Nothing,' he said.

He didn't want a scene.

It was cold when he woke up. The false dawn was grey and he could see nothing but barren country in all directions. He could not remember a great deal about the previous day, except that he had run a long way.

Dew had gathered on his loincloth. He wet his lips and rubbed the skin over his face. As he always did after a migraine attack he felt weak and completely drained. Looking down at his naked body, he noticed how skinny he had become. Life with the Essenes had caused that, of course.

He wondered why he had panicked so much when John had

asked him to baptise him. Was it simply honesty – something in him which resisted deceiving the Essenes into thinking he was a prophet of some kind? It was hard to know.

He wrapped the goatskin about his hips and tied it tightly just above his left thigh. He supposed he had better try to get back to the camp and find John and apologise, see if he could make amends.

The time machine was there now, too. They had dragged it there, using only rawhide ropes.

If a good blacksmith could be found, or some other metal-worker, there was just a chance that it could be repaired. The journey back would be dangerous.

He wondered if he ought to go back right away, or try to shift to a time nearer to the actual crucifixion. He had not gone back specifically to witness the crucifixion, but to get the mood of Jerusalem during the Feast of the Passover, when Jesus was supposed to have entered the city. Monica had thought Jesus had stormed the city with an armed band. She had said that all the evidence pointed to that. All the evidence of one sort did point to it, but he could not accept the evidence. There was more to it, he was sure. If only he could meet Jesus. John had apparently never heard of him, though he had told Glogauer that there was a prophecy that the messiah would be a Nazarene. There were many prophecies, and many of them conflicted.

He began to walk back in the general direction of the Essene camp. He could not have come so far. He would soon recognise the hills where they had their caves.

Soon it was very hot and the ground more barren. The air wavered before his eyes. The feeling of exhaustion with which he had awakened increased. His mouth was dry and his legs were weak. He was hungry and there was nothing to eat. There was no sign of the range of hills where the Essenes had their camp.

There was one hill, about two miles away to the south. He decided to make for it. From there he would probably be able to get his bearings, perhaps even see a township where they would give him food.

The sandy soil turned to floating dust around him as his feet disturbed it. A few primitive shrubs clung to the ground, and jutting rocks tripped him.

He was bleeding and bruised by the time he began, painfully, to clamber up the hillside.

The journey to the summit (which was much further away than he had originally judged) was difficult. He would slide on the loose stones of the hillside, falling on his face, bracing his torn hands and feet to stop himself from sliding down to the bottom, clinging to tufts of grass and lichen that grew here and there, embracing larger projections of rock when he could, resting frequently, his mind and body both numb with pain and weariness.

He sweated beneath the sun. The dust stuck to the moisture on his half-naked body, caking him from head to foot. The goatskin was in shreds.

The barren world reeled around him, sky somehow merging with land, yellow rock with white clouds. Nothing seemed still.

He reached the summit and lay there gasping. Everything had become unreal.

He heard Monica's voice, thought he glanced her for a moment from the corner of his eye.

Don't be melodramatic, Karl...

She had said that many times. His own voice replied now.

I'm born out of my time, Monica. This age of reason has no place for me. It will kill me in the end.

Her voice replied.

Guilt and fear and your own masochism. You could be a brilliant psychiatrist, but you've given in to all your own neuroses so completely...

'Shut up!'

He rolled over on his back. The sun blazed down on his tattered body.

'Shut up!'

The whole Christian syndrome, Karl. You'll become a Catholic convert next, I shouldn't doubt. Where's your strength of mind?

'Shut up! Go away, Monica.'

Fear shapes your thoughts. You're not searching for a soul or even a meaning for life. You're searching for comforts.

'Leave me alone, Monica!'

His grimy hands covered his ears. His hair and beard were matted with dust. Blood had congealed on the minor wounds that were now on every part of his body. Above, the sun seemed to pound in unison with his heartbeats.

You're going downhill, Karl, don't you realise that? Downhill. Pull yourself together. You're not entirely incapable of rational thought...

'Oh, Monica! Shut up!'

His voice was harsh and cracked. A few ravens circled the sky above him now. He heard them calling back at him in a voice not unlike his own.

God died in 1945...

'It isn't 1945 – it's 28 AD. God is alive!'

How you can bother to wonder about an obvious syncretistic religion like Christianity – Rabbinic Judaism, Stoic ethics, Greek mystery cults. Oriental ritual...

'It doesn't matter!'

Not to you in your present state of mind.

'I need God!'

That's what it boils down to, doesn't it? Okay, Karl, carve your own crutches. Just think what you could have been if you'd have come to terms with yourself...

Glogauer pulled his ruined body to its feet and stood on the summit of the hill and screamed.

The ravens were startled. They wheeled in the sky and flew away.

The sky was darkening now.

Then was Jesus led up of the Spirit into the wilderness to be tempted of the devil. And when he had fasted forty days and forty nights, he was afterward an hungred.

(Matthew 4: 1–2)

Chapter Four

T HE MADMAN CAME stumbling into the town. His feet stirred the dust and made it dance and dogs barked around him as he walked mechanically, his head turned upwards to face the sun, his arms limp at his sides, his lips moving.

To the townspeople, the words they heard were in no familiar language; yet they were uttered with such intensity and conviction that God himself might be using this emaciated, naked creature as his spokesman.

They wondered where the madman had come from.

The white town consisted primarily of double- and single-storeyed houses of stone and clay-brick, built around a market place that was fronted by an ancient, simple synagogue outside which old men sat and talked, dressed in dark robes. The town was prosperous and clean, thriving on Roman commerce. Only one or two beggars were in the streets and these were well-fed. The streets followed the rise and fall of the hillside on which they were built. They were winding streets, shady and peaceful; country streets. There was a smell of newly cut timber everywhere in the air, and the sound of carpentry, for the town was chiefly famous for its skilled carpenters. It lay on the edge of the Plain of Jezreel, close to the trade route between Damascus and Egypt, and wagons were always leaving it, laden with the work of the town's craftsmen. The town was called Nazareth.

The madman had found it by asking every traveller he saw where it was. He had passed through other towns – Philadelphia, Gerasa, Pella and Scythopolis, following the Roman roads – asking the same question in his outlandish accent. 'Where lies Nazareth?'

Some had given him food on the way. Some had asked for his

blessing and he had laid hands on them, speaking in that strange tongue. Some had pelted him with stones and driven him away.

He had crossed the Jordan by the Roman viaduct and continued northwards towards Nazareth.

There had been no difficulty in finding the town, but it had been difficult for him to force himself towards it. He had lost a great deal of blood and had eaten very little on the journey. He would walk until he collapsed and lie there until he could go on, or, as had happened increasingly, until someone found him and had given him a little sour wine or bread to revive him.

Once some Roman legionaries had stopped and with brusque kindness asked him if he had any relatives they could take him to. They had addressed him in pidgin-Aramaic and had been surprised when he replied in a strangely accented Latin that was purer than the language they spoke themselves.

They asked him if he was a rabbi or a scholar. He told them he was neither. The officer of the legionaries had offered him some dried meat and wine. The men were part of a patrol that passed this way once a month. They were stocky, brown-faced men, with hard, clean-shaven faces. They were dressed in stained leather kilts and breastplates and sandals, and had iron helmets on their heads, scabbarded short swords at their hips. Even as they stood around him in the evening sunlight they did not seem relaxed. The officer, softer-voiced than his men but otherwise much like them save that he wore a metal breastplate and a long cloak, asked the madman what his name was.

For a moment the madman had paused, his mouth opening and closing, as if he could not remember what he was called.

'Karl,' he said at length, doubtfully. It was more a suggestion than a statement.

'Sounds almost like a Roman name,' said one of the legionaries.

'Are you a citizen?' the officer asked.

But the madman's mind was wandering, evidently. He looked away from them, muttering to himself.

All at once, he looked back at them and said: 'Nazareth?'

'That way.' The officer pointed down the road that cut between the hills. 'Are you a Jew?'

This seemed to startle the madman. He sprang to his feet and tried to push through the soldiers. They let him through, laughing. He was a harmless madman.

They watched him run down the road.

'One of their prophets, perhaps,' said the officer, walking towards his horse. The country was full of them. Every other man you met claimed to be spreading the message of their god. They didn't make much trouble and religion seemed to keep their minds off rebellion. We should be grateful, thought the officer.

His men were still laughing.

They began to march down the road in the opposite direction to the one the madman had taken.

Now the madman was in Nazareth and the townspeople looked at him with curiosity and more than a little suspicion as he staggered into the market square. He could be a wandering prophet or he could be possessed by devils. It was often hard to tell. The rabbis would know.

As he passed the knots of people standing by the merchants' stalls, they fell silent until he had gone by. Women pulled their heavy woollen shawls about their well-fed bodies and men tucked in their cotton robes so that he would not touch them. Normally their instinct would have been to have taxed him with his business in the town, but there was an intensity about his gaze, a quickness and vitality about his face, in spite of his emaciated appearance, that made them treat him with some respect and they kept their distance.

When he reached the centre of the market place, he stopped and looked around him. He seemed slow to notice the people. He blinked and licked his lips.

A woman passed, eyeing him warily. He spoke to her, his voice soft, the words carefully formed. 'Is this Nazareth?'

'It is.' She nodded and increased her pace.

A man was crossing the square. He was dressed in a woollen

robe of red and brown stripes. There was a red skull-cap on his curly, black hair. His face was plump and cheerful. The madman walked across the man's path and stopped him. 'I seek a carpenter.'

'There are many carpenters in Nazareth. The town is famous for its carpenters. I am a carpenter myself. Can I help you?' The man's voice was good-humoured, patronising.

'Do you know a carpenter called Joseph? A descendant of David. He has a wife called Mary and several children. One is named Jesus.'

The cheerful man screwed his face into a mock frown and scratched the back of his neck. 'I know more than one Joseph. There is one poor fellow in yonder street.' He pointed. 'He has a wife called Mary. Try there. You should soon find him. Look for a man who never laughs.'

The madman looked in the direction in which the man pointed. As soon as he saw the street, he seemed to forget everything else and strode towards it.

In the narrow street he entered, the smell of cut timber was even stronger. He walked ankle-deep in wood-shavings. From every building came the thud of hammers, the scrape of saws. There were planks of all sizes resting against the pale, shaded walls of the houses and there was hardly room to pass between them. Many of the carpenters had their benches just outside their doors. They were carving bowls, operating simple lathes, shaping wood into everything imaginable. They looked up as the madman entered the street and approached one old carpenter in a leather apron who sat at his bench carving a figurine. The man had grey hair and seemed short-sighted. He peered up at the madman.

'What do you want?'

'I seek a carpenter called Joseph. He has a wife – Mary.'

The old man gestured with his hand that held the half-completed figurine. 'Two houses along on the other side of the street.'

*

The house the madman came to had very few planks leaning against it, and the quality of the timber seemed poorer than the other wood he had seen. The bench near the entrance was warped on one side and the man who sat hunched over it repairing a stool seemed misshapen also. He straightened up as the mad-man touched his shoulder. His face was lined and pouched with misery. His eyes were tired and his thin beard had premature streaks of grey. He coughed slightly, perhaps in surprise at being disturbed.

'Are you Joseph?' asked the madman.

'I've no money.'

'I want nothing – just to ask a few questions.'

'I'm Joseph. Why do you want to know?'

'Have you a son?'

'Several, and daughters, too.'

'Your wife is called Mary? You are of David's line.'

The man waved his hand impatiently. 'Yes, for what good either has done me...'

'I wish to meet one of your sons. Jesus. Can you tell me where he is?'

'That good-for-nothing. What has he done now?'

'Where is he?'

Joseph's eyes became more calculating as he stared at the madman. 'Are you a seer of some kind? Have you come to cure my son?'

'I am a prophet of sorts. I can foretell the future.'

Joseph got up with a sigh. 'You can see him. Come.' He led the madman through the gateway into the cramped courtyard of the house. It was crowded with pieces of wood, broken furniture and implements, rotting sacks of shavings. They entered the darkened house. In the first room – evidently a kitchen – a woman stood by a large clay stove. She was tall and bulging with fat. Her long, black hair was unbound and greasy, falling over large, lustrous eyes that still had the heat of sensuality. She looked the madman over.

'There's no food for beggars,' she grunted. 'He eats enough as it is.' She gestured with a wooden spoon at a small figure sitting in the shadow of a corner. The figure shifted as she spoke.

'He seeks our Jesus,' said Joseph to the woman. 'Perhaps he comes to ease our burden.'

The woman gave the madman a sidelong look and shrugged. She licked her red lips with a fat tongue. 'Jesus!'

The figure in the corner stood up.

'That's him,' said the woman with a certain satisfaction.

The madman frowned, shaking his head rapidly. 'No.'

The figure was misshapen. It had a pronounced hunched back and a cast in its left eye. The face was vacant and foolish. There was a little spittle on the lips. It giggled as its name was repeated. It took a crooked step forward. 'Jesus,' it said. The word was slurred and thick. 'Jesus.'

'That's all he can say.' The woman sneered. 'He's always been like that.'

'God's judgement,' said Joseph bitterly.

'What is wrong with him?' There was a pathetic, desperate note in the madman's voice.

'He's always been like that.' The woman turned back to the stove. 'You can have him if you want him. Addled inside and outside. I was carrying him when my parents married me off to that half-man...'

'You shameless –' Joseph stopped as his wife glared at him. He turned to the madman. 'What's your business with our son?'

'I wished to talk to him. I...'

'He's no oracle – no seer – we used to think he might be. There are still people in Nazareth who come to him to cure them or tell their fortunes, but he only giggles at them and speaks his name over and over again...'

'Are – you sure – there is not – something about him – you have not noticed?'

'Sure!' Mary snorted sardonically. 'We need money badly enough. If he had any magical powers, we'd know.'

Jesus giggled again and limped away into another room.

'It is impossible,' the madman murmured. Could history itself have changed? Could he be in some other dimension of time where Christ had never been?

Joseph appeared to notice the look of agony in the madman's eyes.

'What is it?' he said. 'What do you see? You said you foretold the future. Tell us how we will fare?'

'Not *now*,' said the prophet, turning away. 'Not *now*.'

He ran from the house and down the street with its smell of planed oak, cedar and cypress. He ran back to the market place and stopped, looking wildly about him. He saw the synagogue directly ahead of him. He began to walk towards it.

The man he had spoken to earlier was still in the market place, buying cooking pots to give to his daughter as a wedding gift. He nodded towards the strange man as he entered the synagogue. 'He's a relative of Joseph the carpenter,' he told the man beside him. 'A prophet, I shouldn't wonder.'

The madman, the prophet, Karl Glogauer, the time-traveller, the neurotic psychiatrist manqué, the searcher for meaning, the masochist, the man with a death-wish and the messiah-complex, the anachronism, made his way into the synagogue gasping for breath. He had seen the man he had sought. He had seen Jesus, the son of Joseph and Mary. He had seen a man he recognised without any doubt as a congenital imbecile.

'All men have a messiah-complex, Karl,' Monica had said.

The memories were less complete now. His sense of time and identity was becoming confused.

'There were dozens of messiahs in Galilee at the time. That Jesus should have been the one to carry the myth and the philosophy was a coincidence of history…'

'There must have been more to it than that, Monica.'

Every Tuesday in the room above the Occult Bookshop, the Jungian discussion group would meet for purposes of group analysis and therapy. Glogauer had not organised the group, but he had willingly lent his premises to it and had joined it eagerly. It was a great relief to talk with like-minded people once a week. One of his reasons for buying the Occult Bookshop was so that he would meet interesting people like those who attended the Jungian discussion group.

An obsession with Jung brought them together, but everyone had special obsessions of their own. Mrs Rita Blenn charted the courses of flying saucers, though it was not clear if she believed in them or not. Hugh Joyce believed that all Jungian archetypes derived from the original race of Atlanteans who had perished millennia before. Alan Cheddar, the youngest of the group, was interested in Indian mysticism, and Sandra Peterson, the organiser, was a great witchcraft specialist. James Headington was interested in time. He was the group's pride; he was Sir James Headington, wartime inventor, very rich and with all sorts of decorations for his contribution to the Allied victory. He had had the reputation of being a great improviser during the war, but after it he had become something of an embarrassment to the War Office. He was a crank, they thought, and what was worse, he aired his crankiness in public.

Every so often, Sir James would tell the other members of the group about his time machine. They humoured him. Most of them were liable to exaggerate their own experiences connected with their different interests.

One Tuesday evening, after everyone else had left, Headington told Glogauer that his machine was ready.

'I can't believe it,' Glogauer said truthfully.

'You're the first person I've told.'

'Why me?'

'I don't know. I like you – and the shop.'

'You haven't told the government.'

Headington had chuckled. 'Why should I? Not until I've tested it fully, anyway. Serves them right for putting me out to pasture.'

'You don't know it works?'

'I'm sure it does. Would you like to see it?'

'A time machine.' Glogauer smiled weakly.

'Come and see it.'

'Why me?'

'I thought you might be interested. I know you don't hold with the orthodox view of science...'

Glogauer felt sorry for him.

'Come and see,' said Headington.

He went out to Banbury the next day. The same day he left 1976 and arrived in AD 28.

The synagogue was cool and quiet with a subtle scent of incense. The rabbis guided him into the courtyard. They, like the towns-people, did not know what to make of him, but they were sure it was not a devil that possessed him. It was their custom to give shelter to the roaming prophets who were now everywhere in Galilee, though this one was stranger than the rest. His face was immobile and his body was stiff, and there were tears running down his dirty cheeks. They had never seen such agony in a man's eyes before.

'Science can say how, but it never asks why,' he had told Monica. 'It can't answer.'

'Who wants to know?' she'd replied.

'I do.'

'Well, you'll never find out, will you?'

'Sit down, my son,' said the rabbi. 'What do you wish to ask of us?'

'Where is Christ?' he said. 'Where is Christ?'

They did not understand the language.

'Is it Greek?' asked one, but another shook his head.

Kyrios: The Lord.

Adonai: The Lord.

Where was the Lord?

He frowned, looking vaguely about him.

'I must rest,' he said in their language.

'Where are you from?'

He could not think what to answer.

'Where are you from?' a rabbi repeated.

'*Ha-Olam Hab-Bah...*' he murmured at length.

They looked at one another. '*Ha-Olam Hab-Bah*,' they said. *Ha-Olam Hab-Bah; Ha-Olam Haz-Zeh*: The world to come and the world that is.

'Do you bring us a message?' said one of the rabbis. They were used to prophets, certainly, but none like this one. 'A message?'

'I do not know,' said the prophet hoarsely. 'I must rest. I am hungry.'

'Come. We will give you food and a place to sleep.'

He could only eat a little of the rich food and the bed with its straw-stuffed mattress was too soft for him. He was not used to it.

He slept badly, shouting as he dreamed, and, outside the room, the rabbis listened, but could understand little of what he said.

Karl Glogauer stayed in the synagogue for several weeks. He would spend most of his time reading in the library, searching through the long scrolls for some answer to his dilemma. The words of the Testaments, in many cases capable of a dozen interpretations, only confused him further. There was nothing to grasp, nothing to tell him what had gone wrong.

The rabbis kept their distance for the most part. They had accepted him as a holy man. They were proud to have him in their synagogue. They were sure that he was one of the special chosen of God and they waited patiently for him to speak to them.

But the prophet said little, muttering only to himself in snatches of their own language and snatches of the incomprehensible language he often used, even when he addressed them directly.

In Nazareth, the townsfolk talked of little else but the mysterious prophet in the synagogue, but the rabbis would not answer their questions. They would tell the people to go about their business, that there were things they were not yet meant to know. In this way, as priests had always done, they avoided questions they could not answer while at the same time appearing to have much more knowledge than they actually possessed.

Then, one sabbath, he appeared in the public part of the

synagogue and took his place with the others who had come to worship.

The man who was reading from the scroll on his left stumbled over the words, glancing at the prophet from the corner of his eye.

The prophet sat and listened, his expression remote.

The Chief Rabbi looked uncertainly at him, then signed that the scroll should be passed to the prophet. This was done hesitantly by a boy who placed the scroll into the prophet's hands.

The prophet looked at the words for a long time and then began to read. The prophet read without comprehending at first what he read. It was the book of Esaias.

The Spirit of the Lord is upon me, because he hath anointed me to preach the gospel to the poor; he hath sent me to heal the broken-hearted, to preach deliverance to the captives, and recovering of sight to the blind, to set at liberty them that are bruised, to preach the acceptable year of the Lord. And he closed the book, and gave it again to the minister, and sat down. And the eyes of all of them that were in the synagogue were fastened on him.

(Luke 4: 18–20)

Chapter Five

T HEY FOLLOWED HIM now, as he walked away from Nazareth towards the Lake of Galilee. He was dressed in the white linen robe they had given him and though they thought he led them, they, in fact, drove him before them.

'He is our messiah,' they said to those that enquired. And there were already rumours of miracles.

When he saw the sick, he pitied them and tried to do what he could because they expected something of him. Many he could do nothing for, but others, obviously in psychosomatic conditions, he could help. They believed in his power more strongly than they believed in their sickness. So he cured them.

When he came to Capernaum, some fifty people followed him into the streets of the city. It was already known that he was in some way associated with John the Baptist, who enjoyed huge prestige in Galilee and had been declared a true prophet by many Pharisees. Yet this man had a power greater, in some ways, than John's. He was not the orator that the Baptist was, but he had worked miracles.

Capernaum was a sprawling town beside the crystal lake of Galilee, its houses separated by large market gardens. Fishing boats were moored at the white quayside, as well as trading ships that plied the lakeside towns. Though the green hills came down from all sides to the lake, Capernaum itself was built on flat ground, sheltered by the hills. It was a quiet town and, like most others in Galilee, had a large population of gentiles. Greek, Roman and Egyptian traders walked its streets and many had made permanent homes there. There was a prosperous middle class of merchants, artisans and ship-owners, as well as doctors, lawyers and scholars, for Capernaum was on the borders of the provinces of Galilee, Trachonitis and Syria, and though a comparatively small town was a useful junction for trade and travel.

The strange, mad prophet in his swirling linen robes, followed by the heterogeneous crowd that was primarily composed of poor folk but also could be seen to contain men of some distinction, swept into Capernaum. The news spread that this man really could foretell the future, that he had already predicted the arrest of John by Herod Antipas and soon after Herod had imprisoned the Baptist at Peraea. He did not make the predictions in general terms, using vague words the way other prophets did. He spoke of things that were to happen in the near future and he spoke of them in detail.

None knew his name. He was simply the prophet from Nazareth, or the Nazarene. Some said he was a relative, perhaps the son, of a carpenter in Nazareth, but this could be because the written words for 'son of a carpenter' and 'magus' were almost the same and the confusion had come about in that way. There was even a very faint rumour that his name was Jesus. The name had been used once or twice, but when they asked him if that was, indeed, his name, he denied it or else, in his abstracted way, refused to answer at all.

His actual preaching tended to lack the fire of John's. This man spoke gently, rather vaguely, and smiled often. He spoke of God in a strange way, too, and he appeared to be connected, as John was, with the Essenes, for he preached against the accumulation of personal wealth and spoke of mankind as a brotherhood, as they did.

But it was the miracles that they watched for as he was guided to the graceful synagogue of Capernaum. No prophet before him had healed the sick and seemed to understand the troubles that people rarely spoke of. It was his sympathy that they responded to, rather than the words he spoke.

For the first time in his life, Karl Glogauer had forgotten about Karl Glogauer. For the first time in his life he was doing what he had always sought to do as a psychiatrist.

But it was not his life. He was bringing a myth to life – a generation before that myth would be born. He was completing a certain kind of psychic circuit. He was not changing history, but he was giving history more substance.

He could not bear to think that Jesus had been nothing more than a myth. It was in his power to make Jesus a physical reality rather than the creation of a process of mythogenesis.

So he spoke in the synagogues and he spoke of a gentler God than most of them had heard of, and where he could remember them, he told them parables.

And gradually the need to justify what he was doing faded and his sense of identity grew increasingly more tenuous and was replaced by a different sense of identity, where he gave greater and greater substance to the rôle he had chosen. It was an archetypal rôle. It was a rôle to appeal to a disciple of Jung. It was a rôle that went beyond a mere imitation. It was a rôle that he must now play out to the very last grand detail. Karl Glogauer had discovered the reality he had been seeking.

> And in the synagogue there was a man, which had a spirit of an
> unclean devil, and cried out with a loud voice, saying, Let us alone;
> what have we to do with thee, thou Jesus of Nazareth? art thou come
> to destroy us? I know thee who thou art; the Holy One of God. And
> Jesus rebuked him, saying, Hold thy peace, and come out of him. And
> when the devil had thrown him in the midst, he came out of him,
> and hurt him not. And they were all amazed, and spake among them-
> selves, saying, What a word is this! for with authority and power he
> commandeth the unclean spirits, and they come out. And the fame of
> him went out into every place of the country round about.
>
> (Luke 4: 33–37)

'Mass hallucination. Miracles, flying saucers, ghosts, it's all the same,' Monica had said.

'Very likely,' he had replied. 'But why did they see them?'

'Because they wanted to.'

'Why did they want to?'
'Because they were afraid.'
'You think that's all there is to it?'
'Isn't it enough?'

When he left Capernaum for the first time, many more people accompanied him. It had become impractical to stay in the town, for the business of the town had been brought almost to a standstill by the crowds that sought to see him work his simple miracles.

He spoke to them in the spaces beyond the towns. He talked with intelligent, literate men who appeared to have something in common with him. Some of them were the owners of fishing fleets – Simon, James and John among them. Another was a doctor, another a civil servant who had first heard him speak in Capernaum.

'There must be twelve,' he said to them one day. 'There must be a zodiac.'

He was not careful in what he said. Many of his ideas were strange. Many of the things he talked about were unfamiliar to them. Some Pharisees thought he blasphemed.

One day he met a man he recognised as an Essene from the colony near Machaerus.

'John would speak with you,' said the Essene.

'Is John not dead yet?' he asked the man.

'He is confined at Peraea. I would think Herod is too frightened to kill him. He lets John walk about within the walls and gardens of the palace, lets him speak with his men, but John fears that Herod will find the courage soon to have him stoned or decapitated. He needs your help.'

'How can I help him? He is to die. There is no hope for him.'

The Essene looked uncomprehendingly into the mad eyes of the prophet.

'But, master, there is no-one else who can help him.'

'I have done all that he wished me to do,' said the prophet. 'I have healed the sick and preached to the poor.'

'I did not know he wished this. Now he needs help, master. You could save his life.'

The prophet had drawn the Essene away from the crowd.

'His life cannot be saved.'

'But if it is not, the unrighteous will prosper and the kingdom of heaven will not be restored.'

'His life cannot be saved.'

'Is it God's will?'

'If I am God, then it is God's will.'

Hopelessly, the Essene turned and began to walk away from the crowd.

John the Baptist would have to die. Glogauer had no wish to change history, only to strengthen it.

He moved on, with his following, through Galilee. He had selected his twelve educated men, and the rest who followed him were still primarily poor people. To them he offered their only hope of fortune. Many were those who had been ready to follow John against the Romans, but now John was imprisoned. Perhaps this man would lead them in revolt, to loot the riches of Jerusalem and Jericho and Caesarea. Tired and hungry, their eyes glazed by the burning sun, they followed the man in the white robe. They needed to hope and they found reasons for their hope. They saw him work greater miracles.

Once he preached to them from a boat, as was often his custom, and as he walked back to the shore through the shallows, it seemed to them that he walked over the water.

All through Galilee in the autumn they wandered, hearing from everyone the news of John's beheading. Despair at the Baptist's death turned to renewed hope in this new prophet who had known him.

In Caesarea they were driven from the city by Roman guards used to the wild men with their prophecies who roamed the country.

They were banned from other cities as the prophet's fame

grew. Not only the Roman authorities, but the Jewish ones as well seemed unwilling to tolerate the new prophet as they had tolerated John. The political climate was changing.

It became hard to find food. They lived on what they could find, hungering like starved animals.

He taught them how to pretend to eat and take their minds off their hunger.

Karl Glogauer, witch-doctor, psychiatrist, hypnotist, messiah.

Sometimes his conviction in his chosen rôle wavered and those that followed him would be disturbed when he contradicted himself. Often, now, they called him the name they had heard, Jesus the Nazarene. Most of the time he did not stop them from using the name, but at others he became angry and cried a peculiar, guttural name.

'Karl Glogauer! Karl Glogauer!'

And they said, Behold, he speaks with the voice of Adonai.

'Call me not by that name!' he would shout, and they would become disturbed and leave him by himself until his anger had subsided.

When the weather changed and the winter came, they went back to Capernaum, which had become a stronghold of his followers.

In Capernaum he waited the winter through, making prophecies.

Many of these prophecies concerned himself and the fate of those that followed him.

> Then charged he his disciples that they should tell no man that he was Jesus the Christ. From that time forth began Jesus to shew unto his disciples, how that he must go unto Jerusalem, and suffer many things of the elders and chief priests and scribes, and be killed, and be raised again the third day.
>
> (Matthew 16: 20–21)

They were watching television at her flat. Monica was eating an apple. It was between six and seven on a warm Sunday evening. Monica gestured at the screen with her half-eaten apple.

'Look at that nonsense,' she said. 'You can't honestly tell me it means anything to you.'

The programme was a religious one, about a pop-opera in a Hampstead Church. The opera told the story of the crucifixion.

'Pop-groups in the pulpit,' she said. 'What a comedown.'

He didn't reply. The programme seemed obscene to him, in an obscure way. He couldn't argue with her.

'God's corpse is really beginning to rot now,' she jeered. 'Whew! The stink!'

'Turn it off, then,' he said quietly.

'What's the pop-group called? The Maggots?'

'Very funny. I'll turn it off, shall I?'

'No, I want to watch. It's funny.'

'Oh, turn it off!'

'Imitation of Christ!' she snorted. 'It's a bloody caricature.'

A negro singer, who was playing Christ and singing flat to a banal accompaniment, began to drone out lifeless lyrics about the brotherhood of man.

'If he sounded like that, no wonder they nailed him up,' said Monica.

He reached forward and switched the picture off.

'I was enjoying it.' She spoke with mock disappointment. 'It was a lovely swan-song.'

Later, she said with a trace of affection that worried him, 'You old fogey. What a pity. You could have been John Wesley or Calvin or someone. You can't be a messiah these days, not in your terms. There's nobody to listen.'

Chapter Six

THE PROPHET WAS living in the house of a man called Simon, though the prophet preferred to call him Peter. Simon was grateful to the prophet because he had cured his wife of a complaint which she had suffered from for some time. It had been a mysterious complaint, but the prophet had cured her almost effortlessly.

There were a great many strangers in Capernaum at that time, many of them coming to see the prophet. Simon warned the prophet that some were known agents of the Romans or the Pharisees. The Pharisees had not, on the whole, been antipathetic towards the prophet, though they distrusted the talk of miracles that they heard. However, the whole political atmosphere was disturbed and the Roman occupation force, from Pilate, through his officers, down to the troops themselves, were tense, expecting an outbreak but unable to see any tangible signs that one was coming.

Pilate himself hoped for trouble on a large scale. It would prove to Tiberius that the emperor had been too lenient with the Jews over the matter of the votive shields. Pilate would be vindicated and his power over the Jews increased. At present he was on bad terms with all the Tetrarchs of the provinces – particularly the unstable Herod Antipas who had seemed at one time his only supporter. Aside from the political situation, his own domestic situation was upset in that his neurotic wife was having her nightmares again and was demanding far more attention from him than he could afford to give her.

There might be a possibility, he thought, of provoking an incident, but he would have to be careful that Tiberius never learned of it. This new prophet might provide a focus, but so far the man had done nothing against the laws of either the Jews or the Romans. There was no law that forbade a man to claim he was a messiah, as some said this one had done, and he was hardly inciting the people to revolt – rather the contrary.

Looking through the window of his chamber, with a view of the minarets and spires of Jerusalem, Pilate considered the information his spies had brought him.

Soon after the festival that the Romans called Saturnalia, the prophet and his followers left Capernaum again and began to travel through the country.

There were fewer miracles now that the hot weather had passed, but his prophecies were eagerly asked. He warned them of all the mistakes that would be made in the future, and of all the crimes that would be committed in his name.

Through Galilee he wandered, and through Samaria, following the good Roman roads towards Jerusalem.

The time of the Passover was coming close now.

In Jerusalem, the Roman officials discussed the coming festival. It was always a time of the worst disturbances. There had been riots before during the Feast of the Passover, and doubtless there would be trouble of some kind this year, too.

Pilate spoke to the Pharisees, asking for their co-operation. The Pharisees said they would do what they could, but they could not help it if the people acted foolishly.

Scowling, Pilate dismissed them.

His agents brought him reports from all over the territory. Some of the reports mentioned the new prophet, but said that he was harmless.

Pilate thought privately that he might be harmless now, but if he reached Jerusalem during the Passover, he might not be so harmless.

Two weeks before the Feast of the Passover, the prophet reached the town of Bethany near Jerusalem. Some of his Galilean followers had friends in Bethany and these friends were more than willing to shelter the man they had heard of from other pilgrims on their way to Jerusalem and the Great Temple.

The reason they had come to Bethany was that the prophet had become disturbed at the number of the people following him.

'There are too many,' he had said to Simon. 'Too many, Peter.'

Glogauer's face was haggard now. His eyes were set deeper into their sockets and he said little.

Sometimes he would look around him vaguely, as if unsure where he was.

News came to the house in Bethany that Roman agents had been making enquiries about him. It did not seem to disturb him. On the contrary, he nodded thoughtfully, as if satisfied.

Once he walked with two of his followers across country to look at Jerusalem. The bright yellow walls of the city looked splendid in the afternoon light. The towers and tall buildings, many of them decorated in mosaic reds, blues and yellows, could be seen from several miles away.

The prophet turned back towards Bethany.

'When shall we go into Jerusalem?' one of his followers asked him.

'Not yet,' said Glogauer. His shoulders were hunched and he grasped his chest with his arms and hands as if cold.

Two days before the Feast of the Passover in Jerusalem, the prophet took his men towards the Mount of Olives and a suburb of Jerusalem that was built on its side and called Bethphage.

'Get me a donkey,' he told them. 'A colt. I must fulfil the prophecy now.'

'Then all will know you are the messiah,' said Andrew.

'Yes.'

Glogauer sighed. He felt afraid again, but this time it was not physical fear. It was the fear of an actor who was about to make his final, most dramatic scene and who was not sure he could do it well.

There was cold sweat on Glogauer's upper lip. He wiped it off.

In the poor light he peered at the men around him. He was still uncertain of some of their names. He was not interested in their names, particularly, only in their number. There were ten here. The other two were looking for the donkey.

They stood on the grassy slope of the Mount of Olives, look-ing towards Jerusalem and the Great Temple which lay below. There was a light, warm breeze blowing.

'Judas?' said Glogauer enquiringly.

There was one called Judas.

'Yes, master,' he said. He was tall and good-looking, with curly red hair and neurotic intelligent eyes. Glogauer believed he was an epileptic.

Glogauer looked thoughtfully at Judas Iscariot. 'I will want you to help me later,' he said, 'when we have entered Jerusalem.'

'How, master?'

'You must take a message to the Romans.'

'The Romans?' Iscariot looked troubled. 'Why?'

'It must be the Romans. It can't be the Jews – they would use a stake or an axe. I'll tell you more when the time comes.'

The sky was dark now, and the stars were out over the Mount of Olives. It had become cold. Glogauer shivered.

> *Rejoice greatly O daughter of Zion,*
> *Shout, O daughter of Jerusalem:*
> *Behold, thy King cometh unto thee!*
> *He is just and having salvation;*
> *Lowly and riding upon an ass,*
> *And upon a colt, the foal of an ass.*
> (Zechariah 9: 9)

'*Osha'na! Osha'na! Osha'na!*'

As Glogauer rode the donkey into the city, his followers ran ahead, throwing down palm branches. On both sides of the street were crowds, forewarned by the followers of his coming. Now the new prophet could be seen to be fulfilling the prophecies of the ancient prophets and many believed that he had come to lead them against the Romans. Even now, possibly, he was on his way to Pilate's house to confront the procurator.

'*Osha'na! Osha'na!*'

Glogauer looked around distractedly. The back of the donkey, though softened by the coats of his followers, was uncomfortable. He swayed and clung to the beast's mane. He heard the words, but could not make them out clearly.

'Osha'na! Osha'na!'

It sounded like 'Hosanna' at first, before he realised that they were shouting the Aramaic for 'Free us'.

'Free us! Free us!'

John had planned to rise in arms against the Romans this Passover. Many had expected to take part in the rebellion.

They believed that he was taking John's place as a rebel leader.

'No,' he muttered at them as he looked around at their expectant faces. 'No, I am the messiah. I cannot free you. I can't…'

They did not hear him above their own shouts.

Karl Glogauer entered Christ. Christ entered Jerusalem. The story was approaching its climax.

'Osha'na!'

It was not in the story. He could not help them.

Verily, verily, I say unto you, that one of you shall betray me. Then the disciples looked one on another, doubting of whom he spake. Now there was leaning on Jesus' bosom one of his disciples, whom Jesus loved. Simon Peter therefore beckoned to him, that he should ask who it should be of whom he spake. He then lying on Jesus' breast saith unto him, Lord, who is it? Jesus answered, He it is, to whom I shall give a sop, when I have dipped it. And when he had dipped the sop, he gave it to Judas Iscariot, the son of Simon. And after the sop Satan entered into him. Then said Jesus unto him, That thou doest, do quickly.

(John 13: 21–27)

Judas Iscariot frowned with some uncertainty as he left the room and went out into the crowded street, making his way towards the governor's palace. Doubtless he was to perform a part in a plan to deceive the Romans and have the people rise up in Jesus' defence, but he thought the scheme foolhardy. The mood amongst the jostling men, women and children in the streets was tense. Many more Roman soldiers than usual patrolled the city.

Pilate was a stout man. His face was self-indulgent and his eyes were hard and shallow. He looked disdainfully at the Jew.

'We do not pay informers whose information is proved to be false,' he warned.

'I do not seek money, lord,' said Judas, feigning the ingratiating manner that the Romans seemed to expect of the Jews. 'I am a loyal subject of the emperor.'

'Who is this rebel?'

'Jesus of Nazareth, lord. He entered the city today...'

'I know. I saw him. But I heard he preached of peace and obeying the law.'

'To deceive you, lord.'

Pilate frowned. It was likely. It smacked of the kind of deceit he had grown to anticipate in these soft-spoken people.

'Have you proof?'

'I am one of his lieutenants, lord. I will testify to his guilt.'

Pilate pursed his heavy lips. He could not afford to offend the Pharisees at this moment. They had given him enough trouble. Caiaphas, in particular, would be quick to cry 'injustice' if he arrested the man.

'He claims to be the rightful king of the Jews, the descendant of David,' said Judas, repeating what his master had told him to say.

'Does he?' Pilate looked thoughtfully out of the window.

'As for the Pharisees, lord...'

'What of them?'

'The Pharisees distrust him. They would see him dead. He speaks against them.'

Pilate nodded. His eyes were hooded as he considered this information. The Pharisees might hate the madman, but they would be quick to make political capital out of his arrest.

'The Pharisees want him arrested,' Judas continued. 'The

people flock to listen to the prophet and today many of them rioted in the Temple in his name.'

'Is this true?'

'It is true, lord.' It was true. Some half a dozen people had attacked the money-changers in the Temple and tried to rob them. When they had been arrested, they had said they had been carrying out the will of the Nazarene.

'I cannot make the arrest,' Pilate said musingly. The situation in Jerusalem was already dangerous, but if they were to arrest this 'king', they might find that they precipitated a revolt. Tiberius would blame him, not the Jews. The Pharisees must be won over. They must make the arrest. 'Wait here,' he said to Judas. 'I will send a message to Caiaphas.'

> *And they came to a place which was named Gethsemane: and he saith to his disciples. Sit ye here, while I shall pray. And he taketh with him Peter and James and John, and began to be sore amazed, and to be very heavy; And saith unto them, My soul is exceeding sorrowful unto death: tarry ye here, and watch.*
>
> (Mark 14: 32–34)

Glogauer could see the mob approaching now. For the first time since Nazareth he felt physically weak and exhausted. They were going to kill him. He had to die; he accepted that, but he was afraid of the pain that was to come. He sat down on the ground of the hillside, watching the torches as they came closer.

'The ideal of martyrdom only ever existed in the minds of a few ascetics,' Monica had said. *'Otherwise it was morbid masochism, an easy way to forgo ordinary responsibility, a method of keeping repressed people under control...'*

'It isn't as simple as that...'

'It is, Karl.'

He could show Monica now. His regret was that she was unlikely ever to know. He had meant to write everything down and put it into the time machine and hope that it would be recovered. It was strange. He was not a religious man in the usual sense. He was an agnostic. It was not conviction that had led him to defend religion against Monica's cynical contempt for it; it was rather *lack* of conviction in the ideal in which she had set her own faith, the ideal of science as a solver of all problems. He could not share her faith and there was nothing else but religion, though he could not believe in the kind of God of Christianity. The God seen as a mystical force of the mysteries of Christianity and other great religions had not been personal enough for him. His rational mind had told him that God did not exist in any personal form. His unconscious had told him that faith in science was not enough.

'*Science is basically opposed to religion,*' Monica had once said harshly. '*No matter how many Jesuits get together and rationalise their views of science, the fact remains that religion cannot accept the fundamental attitudes of science and it is implicit to science to attack the fundamental principles of religion. The only area in which there is no difference and need be no war is in the ultimate assumption. One may or may not assume there is a supernatural being called God. But as soon as one begins to defend one's assumption, there must be strife.*'

'*You're talking about organised religion...*'

'*I'm talking about religion as opposed to a belief. Who needs the ritual of religion when we have the far superior ritual of science to replace it? Religion is a reasonable substitute for knowledge. But there is no longer any need for substitutes, Karl. Science offers a sounder basis on which to formulate systems of thought and ethics. We don't need the carrot of heaven and the big stick of hell any more when science can show the consequences of actions and men can judge easily for themselves whether those actions are right or wrong.*'

'*I can't accept it.*'

'*That's because you're sick. I'm sick, too, but at least I can see the promise of health.*'

'*I can only see the threat of death...*'

★

As they had agreed, Judas kissed him on the cheek and the mixed force of Temple guards and Roman soldiers surrounded him.

To the Romans he said, with some difficulty, 'I am the King of the Jews.' To the Pharisees' servants he said: 'I am the messiah who has come to destroy your masters.' Now he was committed and the final ritual was to begin.

Chapter Seven

IT WAS AN untidy trial, an arbitrary mixture of Roman and Jewish law which did not altogether satisfy anyone. The object was accomplished after several conferences between Pontius Pilate and Caiaphas and three attempts to bend and merge their separate legal systems in order to fit the expediencies of the situation. Both needed a scapegoat for their different purposes and so at last the result was achieved and the madman convicted, on the one hand of rebellion against Rome and on the other of heresy.

A peculiar feature of the trial was that the witnesses were all followers of the man and yet had seemed eager to see him convicted.

The Pharisees agreed that the Roman method of execution would fit the time and the situation best in this case and it was decided to crucify him. The man had prestige, however, so that it would be necessary to use some of the tried Roman methods of humiliation in order to make him into a pathetic and ludicrous figure in the eyes of the pilgrims. Pilate assured the Pharisees that he would see to it, but he made sure that they signed documents that gave their approval to his actions.

> *And the soldiers led him away into the hall, called Praetorium; and they called together the whole band. And they clothed him with purple, and platted a crown of thorns, and put it about his head, And began to salute him, Hail, King of the Jews! And they smote him on the head with a reed, and did spit upon him, and bowing their knees worshipped him. And when they had mocked him, they took off the purple from him, and put his own clothes on him, and led him out to crucify him.*
>
> (Mark 15: 16–20)

His brain was clouded now, by pain and by the ritual of humiliation; by his having completely given himself up to his rôle.

He was too weak to bear the heavy wooden cross and he walked behind it as it was dragged towards Golgotha by a Cyrenian whom the Romans had press-ganged for the purpose.

As he staggered through the crowded, silent streets, watched by those who had thought he would lead them against the Roman overlords, his eyes filled with tears so that his sight was blurred and he occasionally staggered off the road and was nudged back onto it by one of the Roman guards.

'You are too emotional, Karl. Why don't you use that brain of yours and pull yourself together…'

He remembered the words, but it was difficult to remember who had said them or who Karl was.

The road that led up the side of the hill was stony and he slipped sometimes, remembering another hill he had climbed long ago. It seemed to him that he had been a child, but the memory merged with others and it was impossible to tell.

He was breathing heavily and with some difficulty. The pain of the thorns in his head was barely felt, but his whole body seemed to throb in unison with his heartbeats. It was like a drum.

It was evening. The sun was setting. He fell on his face, cutting his head on a sharp stone, just as he reached the top of the hill. He fainted.

And they bring him unto the place Golgotha, which is, being interpreted, The place of a skull. And they gave him to drink wine mingled with myrrh: but he received it not.

(Mark 15: 22–23)

He knocked the cup aside. The soldier shrugged and reached out for one of his arms. Another soldier already held the other arm.

As he recovered consciousness Glogauer began to tremble violently. He felt the pain intensely as the ropes bit into the flesh of his wrists and ankles. He struggled.

He felt something cold placed against his palm. Although it only covered a small area in the centre of his hand it seemed very heavy. He heard a sound that also was in rhythm with his heartbeats. He turned his head to look at the hand.

The large iron peg was being driven into his hand by a soldier swinging a mallet, as he lay on the cross which was at this moment horizontal on the ground. He watched, wondering why there was no pain. The soldier swung the mallet higher as the peg met the resistance of the wood. Twice he missed the peg and struck Glogauer's fingers.

Glogauer looked to the other side and saw that the second soldier was also hammering in a peg. Evidently he missed the peg a great many times because the fingers of the hand were bloody and crushed.

The first soldier finished hammering in his peg and turned his attention to the feet. Glogauer felt the iron slide through his flesh, heard it hammered home.

Using a pulley, they began to haul the cross into a vertical position. Glogauer noticed that he was alone. There were no others being crucified that day.

He got a clear view of the lights of Jerusalem below him. There was still a little light in the sky but not much. Soon it would be completely dark. There was a small crowd looking on. One of the women reminded him of Monica. He called to her.

'Monica?'

But his voice was cracked and the word was a whisper. The woman did not look up.

He felt his body dragging at the nails which supported it. He thought he felt a twinge of pain in his left hand. He seemed to be bleeding very heavily.

It was odd, he reflected, that it should be him hanging here. He supposed that it was the event he had originally come to witness. There was little doubt, really. Everything had gone perfectly.

The pain in his left hand increased.

He glanced down at the Roman guards who were playing dice

at the foot of his cross. They seemed absorbed in their game. He could not see the markings of the dice from this distance.

He sighed. The movement of his chest seemed to throw extra strain on his hands. The pain was quite bad now. He winced and tried somehow to ease himself back against the wood.

The pain began to spread through his body. He gritted his teeth. It was dreadful. He gasped and shouted. He writhed.

There was no longer any light in the sky. Heavy clouds obscured stars and moon.

From below came whispered voices.

'Let me down,' he called. 'Oh, please let me down!'

The pain filled him. He slumped forward, but nobody released him.

A little while later he raised his head. The movement caused a return of the agony and again he began to writhe on the cross.

'Let me down. Please. Please stop it!'

Every part of his flesh, every muscle and tendon and bone of him, was filled with an almost impossible degree of pain.

He knew he would not survive until the next day as he had thought he might. He had not realised the extent of his pain.

And at the ninth hour Jesus cried with a loud voice, saying, 'Eloi, Eloi, lama sabachthani?' which is, being interpreted, My God, my God, why hast thou forsaken me?

(Mark 15: 34)

Glogauer coughed. It was a dry, barely heard sound. The soldiers below the cross heard it because the night was now so quiet.

'It's funny,' one said. 'Yesterday they were worshipping him. Today they seemed to want us to kill him – even the ones who were closest to him.'

'I'll be glad when we get out of this country,' said another.

He heard Monica's voice again. 'It's weakness and fear, Karl, that's driven you to this. Martyrdom is a conceit. Can't you see that?'

Weakness and fear.

He coughed once more and the pain returned, but it was duller now.

Just before he died he began to talk again, muttering the words until his breath was gone. 'It's a lie. It's a lie. It's a lie.'

Later, after his body was stolen by the servants of some doctors who believed it to have special properties, there were rumours that he had not died. But the corpse was already rotting in the doctors' dissecting rooms and would soon be destroyed.

Acknowledgements

Breakfast in the Ruins was first published by New English Library, 1972.

'The Time Dweller' first appeared in NEW WORLDS No. 139, edited by John Carnell, February 1964.

'Escape from Evening' first appeared in NEW WORLDS No. 148, edited by Michael Moorcock, March 1965.

'A Dead Singer' first appeared in *Factions*, edited by Giles Gordon & Alex Hamilton, Michael Joseph, 1974.

'London Flesh' first appeared in *London: City of Disappearances*, edited by Iain Sinclair, Hamish Hamilton, 2006.

'Behold the Man' first appeared in NEW WORLDS No. 166, ed. Moorcock, September 1966.

MICHAEL MOORCOCK (1939–) is one of the most important figures in British SF and Fantasy literature. The author of many literary novels and stories in practically every genre, he has won and been shortlisted for numerous awards including the Hugo, Nebula, World Fantasy, Whitbread and Guardian Fiction Prize. He is also a musician who performed in the seventies with his own band, the Deep Fix; and, as a member of the space-rock band, Hawkwind, won a platinum disc. His tenure as editor of NEW WORLDS magazine in the sixties and seventies is seen as the high watermark of SF editorship in the UK, and was crucial in the development of the SF New Wave. Michael Moorcock's literary creations include Hawkmoon, Corum, Von Bek, Jerry Cornelius and, of course, his most famous character, Elric. He has been compared to, among others, Balzac, Dumas, Dickens, James Joyce, Ian Fleming, J.R.R. Tolkien and Robert E. Howard. Although born in London, he now splits his time between homes in Texas and Paris.

For a more detailed biography, please see Michael Moorcock's entry in *The Encyclopedia of Science Fiction* at: http://www.sf-encyclopedia.com/

For further information about Michael Moorcock and his work, please visit www.multiverse.org, or send S.A.E. to The Nomads Of The Time Streams, Mo Dhachaidh, Loch Awe, Dalmally, Argyll, PA33 1AQ, Scotland, or P.O. Box 385716, Waikoloa, HI 96738, USA.